THE  PROJECT

A new story with an old friend

BEN DESANTIS

ISBN (Print) 978-1-48359-811-6 (Ebook) 978-1-48359-812-3

For Laura, and the road before us.

Contents

"Life biggest tragedy is that we get old too soon and wise too late"

— Benjamin Franklin

Chapter One

Philadelphia, July 1776

On a street called Market in the port of Philadelphia, stood a print shop. Composed of wood, brick, iron, ink, and parchment paper, the institution featured enlightening influences for the many residents of his majesty's colonies along the Atlantic coast. The *Pennsylvania Gazette* and *Poor Richards Almanac* were microcosms of the oil-pressed publications that helped shape the hearts and minds in the notion of always "doing good." At times, its former proprietor was the chief engineer of submissions published by the *Gazette* that addressed social issues. Their positions were celebrated by some, antagonized by others, but through it all, the Socratic writer of Philadelphia was never hesitant to provoke his fellow countrymen. At a time of great peril the once printer composed a persuasive argument and associated the article with one of the most illuminating illustrations, which revealed the predominant division amongst the King's colonies when unity was in desperate need. His work was well received and redistributed with the highest regard, as were many other publications during his tenure. Without an equal, it was the most esteemed print shop in North America.

By fortune's design fifty-three years prior, at seventeen years of age, the destined printer ran away from Boston to arrive at a city trying to mature and be recognized. While its colony, Pennsylvania, remained the middle child between the older and imposing New York and Virginia. The young man was quickly embraced as one of their own and became their leading representative as he went on to form a volunteer fire company, a university, the first hospital, and the first lending library. He redefined the postal system and contributed immensely to the world of science, philosophy, and medicine. He was an avid inventor and his research noted in the manuscript *Experiments and Observations on Electricity,* led to the lightning rod, which was now protecting homes and saving lives throughout the globe. With so many accomplishments it seemed only fitting that the son of a soap maker, with roughly two years of school as a child, would receive honorary degrees from Harvard and Yale, and an honorary doctorate from the University of St. Andrews, all before the age of forty-seven. From that day on, he would be addressed as "Doctor."

Possessing such an immense portfolio of accomplishments this once-was printer merited the right to retire from the everyday obligations and live out his days in peace and quiet in the home he built near the cherished print shop on Market Street. Only, retirement was not a viable option for the good Doctor. He was a social being, and on this night of the second day in July, this Doctor, this scientist, this philosopher, this politician, and this forever-proud printer was not walking in the city he betrothed. He was five hundred feet away sitting in the assembly chamber at the Pennsylvania State House. The Doctor was an elected delegate, representing his home colony of Pennsylvania for the Second Continental Congress. Having reached twice the age of half of the delegates, he was the most senior representative chosen by any of the thirteen colonies.

The State House was the largest structure in the province. The Supreme Court and the Pennsylvania Assembly resided in two chambers separated by a twenty-five-foot hallway. To some, it was a haunting place. Where the echoes of Parliamentary procedure resonated in the belfry, and the English-style of political resolutions saturated the walls. Its remnants lurked in the corners and resided within the shadows like an apparition. But unlike a spirit of the past, faded and dreary, the State House was alive this evening with the passion of liberty spawned from discontented Englishmen.

Since the Congress started in May 1775, the elected delegates deliberated on a range of issues that affected the lives of their fellow countrymen under the control of the British Empire. Before this evening, multiple attempts were made in an earnest effort to seek an accord with their adversaries in any division of England's government, all the way up to King George himself.

When the first Congress was held two years earlier, some delegates concluded that Parliament was unwilling to reason and the constituents residing on the land between New Hampshire and Georgia were not considered equal to those living across the Atlantic. After years of failure, combined with the latest engagement outside of Boston between the Massachusetts militia and British Army, it was apparent that a new course of action was of paramount importance if any change in sovereignty was going to be made in their lifetime.

As dusk approached outside of the State House, the representatives were seated at their designated table within the chamber. Congressional Secretary Charles Thomson stood to read the motion once more.

> *Resolved! That these United Colonies are, and of right ought to be, free and independent States, that they are absolved from all allegiance to the British Crown, and that all political connection between them and the State of Great Britain is, and ought to be, totally dissolved. That it is expedient forthwith to take the most effectual measures for forming foreign Alliances. That a plan of confederation be prepared and transmitted to the respective colonies for their consideration and approbation.*

A low cheer, complemented with knocks on the tabletops, rumbled through the assembly from those who were in great favor of the resolution offered by Virginia. The proposal was born in Williamsburg, on May 15, and traveled the long route to Philadelphia, where Richard Henry Lee had the honor of presenting it as the first colony to formally call for Independence. The proud brother of Richard, Francis Lightfoot, along with many of his fellow patriots, had waited long enough to cast their vote after the resolution was first read aloud on June 7, it was a Friday.

After *Lee's Resolution* was motioned for a vote there were three days of referrals before the delegates could agree on a postponement of twenty days to hold the final call on July 1. Should the proposal have come from any other colony, it would not have carried the weight to reach the floor. Due to the motion coming from the largest colony, the congressional body felt compelled to give it a full up and down vote.

The postponement was not to avoid the question of breaking ties with England. Rather, it was to afford some delegates an appropriate amount of time to correspond with their respective legislatures for instructions on how to proceed with the vote for Independence. Some delegates were confident their decisions were objective and sound enough to not require instructions. Dr. Lyman Hall, age fifty-two, a Connecticut-born man who migrated to southern establishments in Georgia to be a physician and a clergyman, was one such representative, along with most of the men from New England. New York Delegates William Floyd, Philip Livingston, both over the age of sixty, and Francis Lewis were primarily merchants and not as secure with casting their vote based solely on their interpretations. Edward Rutledge, a well-schooled lawyer at the age of twenty-seven, was not going to vote without instructions. The same went for his twenty-seven-year-old associate Thomas Lynch, and the other youthful plantation-owning, London-schooled delegates from South Carolina, who also required the deferment.

When the postponement was called, the request of an accompanying declaration had also been ordered. It was to outline and affirm all delegates in the room were fully cognizant for the reason behind the call for Independence and the engagement of war with their mother country.

Selected to author the declaration was a young, quiet, and tall redhead named Thomas Jefferson. Thomas was already a respected lawyer by thirty-three, and had come a long way since his graduation from William and Mary, a short thirteen years earlier. Always the enthusiastic student, Thomas was renowned for possessing a desire to absorb as much as possible and loved to understand topics from all perspectives before forming his own opinion. As a gifted craftsman of the English language, Thomas could form a rational summation of an argument and take monumental political positions with assuredness. His reputation achieved national attention while representing Samuel Howell, who was a grandson of a black man and a white woman. In that case, Thomas, who owned slaves, became the first public official to defend a person on the grounds of "Natural Law", stating that "all men are born free and come into the world possessing personal liberty which is bestowed upon him by the author of nature."

Thomas' enlightening command of the written word, outlined in what he titled *A Declaration by the Representatives of the United States of America, in General Congress Assembled,* was firmly adjoined to Virginia's resolution and, from what he concluded, placed common sense sentiments on the subject of Independence written in language so plainly to command the assent of not just the men the room, but of all people everywhere.

After a few long days of deliberation on its composition, Secretary Thomson stood next to the table of the residing president of the Congress, John Hancock, and began the call. For this resolution to pass, all colonies agreed that unanimous acceptance was required, and a single rejection would dismiss the call for Independence. It was July 2, a Tuesday, and it was time to decide who they were: Englishmen or Americans.

"New Hampshire?" asked Secretary Thomson.

Josiah Bartlett, age forty-seven, stood from his chair, "New Hampshire votes, *yay.*"

The representatives of Massachusetts were by far the most enthusiastic members of Congress, even more so than on June 7, 1776, when their now-dear friends had called for secession from the British Empire. After years of atrocities felt mostly within the New England region, Massachusetts representatives Samuel Adams, Robert Pain, Elbridge Gerry, John Hancock, and Samuel's cousin, a fiery short-statured lawyer named John Adams, were finally receiving the much-required support from their colonial brethren. The Boston Massacre, the Boston Tea Party, and the marches on Lexington and Concord were the national highlights for the people of Massachusetts. The colony's stance on Independence was never in doubt. They just had to wait for other colonies to recognize there were no other diplomatic paths to explore.

When the words of the Declaration were read aloud, Samuel, at the age of fifty-three, was relieved that the demand for Independence was coming from someone other than a Massachusetts man. That a Virginian constructed an argument that epitomized the emotions he shared within his *Committee of Correspondence* pamphlets, vindicated all the hard work he put into the call for liberty over the past decade.

From the start of the first Congress, the representatives from Massachusetts were calling for proportional action to the civil unrest, violence, and reprehensible discrimination that their parent country incessantly bestowed on them. Massachusetts plead for action was dismissed for acts of petitions to be transcribed and shipped to the King in a desperate attempt to resolve the hostilities without violence. Thomas Jefferson, during the first Congress, listed the grievances against England and the King, which he titled *A Summary View of the Rights of British America.* In it, he made harsh criticisms and declared that since the colonies were founded, they were independent of each other, and therefore were independent from Great Britain, and British rule. The dispute was warranted and the composition of the argument was most agreeable; however, many delegates were not prepared to allow a document of that tone to represent themselves or their colony. Most, including forty-four-year-old John Dickinson of Pennsylvania, were looking for a moderate approach that offered a compromise and a sensible response to their objections. The summary was dismissed, without Thomas being present for the vote, and as a result, the committees requested a second Congress to reconvene and find an absolute conclusion on the matter. Two years later, the cries from New England were now represented in the Declaration being voted on.

"Massachusetts?" asked Secretary Thomson.

Samuel Adams, one hand trembling on the knob of his walking stick, pressed down to raise himself from his chair. His heart was beating heavy and his breathing was short but that did not prevent him from looking around the room with a smile of admiration for his fellow delegates and the brave leap they were taking as one. Gazing toward the front of the assembly where his longtime friend John Hancock was sitting, he lifted his chin, inhaled deeply, and boldly proclaimed, "Mr. President, the 'state' of Massachusetts says, *yay!*" Those who were always sympathetic toward the people of Massachusetts were showing gratitude by knocking on the table, some even stood, to show their admiration of Samuel's courage and endurance, fathering the call for liberty and freedom all these years.

"Rhode Island?"

Stephen Hopkins, the second oldest man in the chamber at the age of sixty-nine, was a home-schooled student who arose to the seat of chief justice and governor of his proud home. He slowly straightened up from his chair and said, "Mr. Thomson, Rhode Island's vote is, *yay.*"

"Connecticut?"

"Connecticut says, *yay,*" replied Roger Sherman, a vibrant fifty-five-year-old home-schooled lawyer.

The four pages of Thomas' edited declaration was resting in a clean stack in front of Secretary Thomson as he continued to call on each colony.

After the original draft was presented on June 28, there was a great debate over its wording. One order was to remove the phrase "sacred and undeniable" from a passage on rights endowed by a higher order. Another was to remove the section regarding the King's "cruel war against human nature itself", and the principal argument was over the call for the abolishment of slavery.

Some delegates considered the indictments on slavery were not just marks against the King but also against the men in the room. For the language to be adopted by some colonies and to fortify their affirmation to the call of Independence from the British Empire through this Declaration, the four members of the declaration committee complied and eliminated any references to the slave trade. After all the posturing and postponements, discussions, and negotiations, and with a total of eighty-six amendments, the members of Congress concluded the now retitled *Declaration of Independence* represented the universal view of all colonies in America.

"New York?"

Francis Lewis, a successful merchant at the age of sixty-three, voted to abstain, as New York instructed its delegates to not obstruct its passing, should all colonies vote in its favor. Being the leading merchant port on the Atlantic, New York was always cautious when it came to enacting rulings that could provoke the government, which was in possession of the largest military on Earth. On this particular night, this abstention was even more reasonable given New York's recent situation. Two days prior, the Minutemen of the Continental Army captured Staten Island and were now stretched along the southern tip of Manhattan. They, along with their forty-four-year-old commander-in-chief, General George Washington, a Virginian, were awaiting the arrival of the British Navy into New York harbor.

"New Jersey?"

The fifty-three-year-old clergyman and president of the distinguished College of New Jersey in Princeton, John Witherspoon stood and said, "*yay.*"

As each vote was recorded, a sentiment of alliance was growing in the room. Although a disproportioned scale of disputes existed within each colony, a strong youthful unified movement of liberty was still spreading, which was eroding any remaining allegiance to the royal government. This move for liberty was the by-product of an abuse of authority, which in turn empowered individuals to feel they possessed rights that did not require an ordinance from a King. The young men began to sense that liberty was given to them by nature, by God. Following the absence of empathy for their grievances, support in favor of liberation from that government spawned. As each colony pledged their devotion, they could hear a new nation was being declared.

Secretary Thomson paused in his role call, "Pennsylvania is not ready to cast a vote and has requested to be the last called upon," he said. "Delaware?"

The tough forty-eight-year-old former sheriff and respected veteran of the Delaware militia during the French and Indian war, Captain Caesar Rodney, who returned to Philadelphia in time to split the quarrel between the divided delegates, George Read and Thomas McKean, stood over his antagonist, Read, and said, "Mr. President, Delaware affirms a vote as *yay.*"

When the committee was assembled to compose the Declaration three weeks earlier, Thomas Jefferson's previous body of work made him the obvious choice to act as the primary engineer to design the dissertation. The committee also included the young thirty-year-old, Robert Livingston of New York, Roger Sherman of Connecticut, and John Adams of Massachusetts. It was important from John Adams's perspective, that a Virginian took the lead since the resolution originated from that colony and because more delegates would approve the composition should someone author it other than the hot-tempered man from Massachusetts.

Half-way through the call the count stood at six yay votes, with no opposed, New York abstaining, and Pennsylvania requesting to be called last. Five southern colonies remained, including South Carolina. Who, since the debate was forced upon the Congress a month ago, argued more for the sovereignty of the Empire than the unity of the Colonies. Some of South Carolina's objections were adhered to and some were dismissed. As Secretary Thomson was close to calling upon that colony, the tension in the hearts and minds of the some of the delegates was reaching their apex. Without being aware on how Rutledge was instructed to vote, South Carolina still posed to be the firewall for Independence.

"Maryland?" shouted Secretary Thomson.

Thomas Stone, a lawyer who personally favored compromise but was acting on instructions, arose from his seat, "The people of Maryland," he said, "proudly vote, *yay.*"

Of all the lawyers in the chamber, arguably no one was more nationally recognized than the gentleman sitting with the Massachusetts Delegation, Boston's resilient John Adams, who had been a respected lawyer of the English court since he passed the bar at age nineteen in 1754. He firmly believed in the rule of law and that, from those laws, all citizens were protected and all citizens were required to oblige them—only from that unspoken agreement was prosperity even possible. Although his cousin Sam, as John and most people addressed him, was the more outspoken political figure and arguably the more favored and famous Adams. John complemented his cousin's passion with his own unapologetic zeal for liberty.

Being only forty-two, John's unsought fame was achieved for having the courage to represent the British soldiers involved in the infamous Boston Massacre proceedings six years prior. Although his allegiance to the crown had grown weary over the years, John was proud of his actions on that day. He successfully defended the argument that the unruly protesters provoked and antagonized the young men wearing the red coats of the British military to fire on them, which left five dead and six injured on March 5, 1770. John defended the eight soldiers after many anti-British lawyers refused and some Loyalist lawyers passed on taking the case out of fear of reprisal. John rationally argued on the facts of the case and deflected the emotions of the citizens of Boston. Based on these facts, which John labeled as "stubborn things," he said that due to the actions of the mob, the men of the British Army were in the right to fight back and could not be convicted as murderers. In the end, six soldiers were acquitted and two were charged with manslaughter, and John Adams became a national figure.

"Virginia?"

Francis Lightfoot placed his hand on the table and was about to spring out of his chair to cast Virginia's vote, but he paused to look at Thomas Jefferson who equally deserved the moment to cast the colony's vote, as it was his masterpiece being used to weigh Lee's resolution. Thomas gestured with his right hand that it was appropriate for Francis to take the lead. Francis stood up, tugged the base of his coat to straighten out any wrinkles, and with his head held high said, "On behalf of my brother, Mr. Jefferson, General Washington, Patrick Henry, and all Virginians the vote is, *yay*."

"North Carolina?"

"Yay," stated the forty-six-year-old Quaker, Joseph Hewes.

As much as he was a man about the law, John Adams knew in his heart that the statutes and actions from England were crimes against humanity. John felt America was a new country, inspiring new ideas, and cultivating a new nationality that spawned from modern European decent, which became rugged when they conquered the new world and self-reliant after the Wampanoag's helped the initial New England settlers survive the first winter.

During the first Congress, John was part of a small fraction of delegates that included the esteemed patriot Patrick Henry, who called for others to rise to their level of commitment. When addressing the House of Burgesses in Richmond on March 20, 1775, Patrick was noted as saying, "Give me liberty, or give me death!" Although Patrick's leadership was no longer associated with the Virginia delegation in Philadelphia as he tended to matters away from the Congress, his spirit for liberty remained present but his influence on the southern delegates was greatly missed.

"South Carolina?"

The chamber went silent, nobody breathed, and any movement came to an abrupt halt. All eyes now focused on the young steadfast Edward Rutledge. He looked around and gave each person a moment of acknowledgement before he rose to his feet. He looked towards the ceiling and took one last deep breath before he said, "Mr. President, Mr. Secretary, and esteemed colleagues. It is with tremendous pride, that the good people of South Carolina happily votes, *yay.*"

Heavy cheers burst from all corners towards Edward and the South Carolina Delegation. Some, who were too excited to wait until the roll call finished, walked over, and shook the hands of the young men. Some patted Edward on his back, to affirm he made the right decision. Others, like the members of the Massachusetts Delegation, refused to show any sign of jubilation since two votes were still yet to be counted. John Hancock gave a few smacks with his gavel to regain order and asked that everyone remain seated until all votes were cast.

As the men returned to the chairs and softly whispered to each other, John Adams remained still, reflecting on those who bravely took the lead on the path all delegates now found themselves on. John adored Patrick Henry's passion and missed his counsel during the recent events. A few months into the second Congress, the Virginia legislature voted to place Patrick as the commander of the Virginia regiment right after the Royal governor ordered the British troops to raid and seize all the ammunition from the magazine holding in Williamsburg. This did not stop John from corresponding with the patriarch of the great cause, for with the many cries of liberation, it was the necessity to foresee the aftermath from declaring

Independence, which was the establishment of the next government. Not only outlining the structure of the national government but local as well.

To his credit, John was truly committed to the call of this Congress, and he devoted his entire being to its purpose. John was a marvelous manager of his time and was involved in a multitude of committees, and even though he may have had adversaries in the Congress, many respected his devotion and sought his counsel. This included the design of new state governments emerging from the new constitutions the current legislatures were ambitiously drafting. To ease the demand for his valued time, John published a pamphlet called *Thoughts on Government*, defining a representative republic composed of three branches, including a legislative branch with two bodies. The driving force behind the design was to instill a system of checks and balances, while, at the same time, removing the possibility of corruption by not having a single body of government. This outline was inspired by a proposed national government for the colonies offered twenty years ago, during the first national congress held at a major trading post on the Hudson River, in upstate New York.

"Georgia?"

Dr. Lyman Hall arose from his seat and said, "Mr. President, the good people of Georgia vote *yay*."

After reaching the bottom of the call sheet, Secretary Thomson returned to the colony yet to cast their vote.

"Second call, Pennsylvania," asked Secretary Thomson.

Several days earlier, John Adams wrote to Patrick Henry about the subject of the new government design while Thomas Jefferson was locked in his writing room two blocks from the Statehouse. John was pontificating to his ally regarding the misconceptions about the reveal of the Declaration. John noted that the Declaration would encourage the creation of new governments and that these new governments in their infancy would serve the greater purpose of supporting our war with ammunition, clothes, food, and "everything necessary for the support of life."

Another fear among some representatives was that this *Declaration of Independence* would alienate the Americans from the world, and they would be isolated in the war against Great Britain. John told Patrick that fortification of the American cause, represented in the Declaration, would send a signal that this rising nation had a new governing body and enemies of the British monarch would support that body monetarily and militarily. John also noted that after the passing of this Declaration, another committee was completing the *Confederation of the Colonies*, which was going to outline the national government and was to be presented to the Congress in a few days. But for tonight, John relished in his triumph and spent the evening reflecting on years of dedication and hard work. He was by all accounts, happy, and was unselfishly looking forward to the dawn of a new nation.

"Nay"

As John was poised in deep reflective thought, he was startled when Robert Paine grabbed his arm. "Dear God," Robert said. John leaned in, "What?" Robert was stoned face. John asked again, "For God sakes, Robert, what?" On John's right side, Sam Adams jumped out of his chair and shouted, "Traitor!" His head snapped right to Sam, then back again to Robert. "Robert, what the hell just happened?" John asked.

A grumbling began to grow within the chamber as more men stood and were shouting. The incoherent outbursts engulfed John Adams. Remaining in his seat, John tried to look around the room to sense where and to whom the streams of accusations were being fired upon.

"How can you do that to us?" one voice shouted.

"Traitor," cried another.

John Hancock was trying to restore order to the room by hammering his gavel, but it was to no avail.

"I thought you were with us!" Sam Adams shouted.

Sam was standing beside John and yelling something incoherent while he continued to sit and look around the room. He pulled on Sam's arm to bring him down, below the sea of aggression two feet above his head. As Sam was returning to his chair, he cried, "You sir, are no American; God will forever look down upon you with shame, and so too, will the true patriots of this land whom you have turned your back on."

"What, John?" Sam asked of his cousin.

"What just happened, Sam?"

"Weren't you listening, cousin?" Sam sprung to his feet to again resume his participation in the barrage of anger being directed toward someone John was still trying to identify. Reaching up again to grab hold of Sam's sleeve, John heard faintly, "Why, Ben?" "Why now?"

John Adams was troubled; he whispered to himself "Ben?" as he slowly stood and looked toward the location of the Pennsylvania delegates. He finally understood to whom all the epithets and anger were being focused on. As John heard all sorts of names and labels being shouted, sitting, and looking straight toward the front of the room was the senior representative of Pennsylvania, Dr. Benjamin Franklin. Chaos was erupting among the shouts of anger and the banging of the gavel. One could not hear the person beside them. John Hancock was shouting for a call to order, but no order was coming.

John Adams reached behind him to find the arm of his chair; the shock made his legs weak. Sam Adams no longer had the energy to stand as well, his hand brushed back his tricorn cap and he collapsed awkwardly with a look of despair toward John Hancock who himself had ceased the use of his gavel and returned to his seat. Sam looked to John and said, "Pennsylvania killed the resolution. All this time we were worried about South Carolina and those that endorsed slavery."

Thomas Jefferson made his way to the Massachusetts table. Exasperated from the events unfolding he sought out John for his support. With tears in his eyes, he asked, "How could Franklin do this to us?"

Sam Adams looked up towards Jefferson, "One word Thomas; Albany."

All feelings of hope and triumph were now turning to despair for John Adams, Thomas Jefferson, Sam Adams, and many others in the Pennsylvania State House. Despair for there was no adoption of the Declaration, there was no unity, and there was no recognition of a new, prosperous nation called America. It all vanished after the vote was casted by the printer from Market Street.

Chapter Two

Sunrise

The quiet before the dawn is peaceful in any part of the world. In the suburbs surrounding New York City, the commotion of life settles just long enough into the quaint domiciles to present a sense of calmness in the early hours of the morning, before the sun makes its appearance. As the distant light began to peer over the horizon, crack the seal of serenity, and set in motion the customary schedule, one house in Yonkers ensured that the morning sunlight would not breech through the bedroom window with its unwelcoming arrival. The room darkeners were in their positions to permit Ethan Pope to rest beyond daybreak. He wrapped himself in an admiring nightfall atmosphere while the world outside began its routine.

At 9:00 a.m., a slight vibration began to reverberate through the hypoallergenic memory foam pillow under his head. A few seconds into the sequence, the soft sound of Mozart's *Serenade for Winds* began. Although the rising volume was in perfect time with the tempo of the clarinets, the vibrations kept to their own rhythm. When the oboe entered with its signature note, the smartphone reached its peak volume and the alarm was awaiting instructions to snooze or to stop.

The young man reached under his pillow and extracted the phone. With his eyes squinting, he stretched out his finger and hit *Snooze*.

When the time reached 9:15 a.m., the extended hibernation period was coming to its end. The slight vibration began the stirring sequence again, *Snooze*.

The time was now 9:30 a.m., hibernation, once again, was about to end. With its first vibration on the third stanza in the awaking ritual, Ethan grabbed the smartphone and with the swipe of a finger, stopped its shiver. Barely awake, and before anything else was attempted, he made sure to send out a morning message to his wife Lauren. After the first couple of days of being home and putting in eight grueling hours of online *Star Wars Battlefront* and *Halo* battles, Lauren had asked if it would be too much trouble for him to text her while he was home and she was out working. Not wanting to quibble over a simple request and recalling the instructions bestowed upon him by more experienced matrimonial veterans, Ethan obliged to keep the peace.

Ethan: Good morning, Mrs. Pope.

After that peace offering was sent, calmness set in and he placed the phone on the opposite side of the bed. Ethan rested his head on the pillow one last time before starting his day.

Ethan awoke, again, at 10:10 a.m. when the alert from Facebook reminded him of past events that occurred on this day. He sprang upright, and let out a groan with a yawn as he tensed all muscles and stretched his arms to increase the circulation, hoping to come out of the daze he was in. He slid off the side of the bed and his feet touched the cool laminated wood floor. He fixed the pillows, adjusted the sheets, and pulled the covers to a tight corner. As he made his way to the other side, he powered off the air conditioner that kept the room at a crisp, comfortable 68 degrees. When he reached his wife's bedside stand, he turned off the sound machine which played the soothing rush of a waterfall. Ethan favored the device as it drowned out Lauren's motions as she prepared to leave for school. Lauren wanted it to drown out Ethan's snoring. He also preferred the sound machine as it muffled the racket from surrounding neighbors that rudely interrupted the bedroom sanctuary during the late morning. When first used, Ethan feared the noise would prevent him from hearing any unlawful entry during the night, but since they lived on the second floor of a private two-family home, the concern narrowed after each passing week.

Ethan was not accustomed to this domestic type of lifestyle. For the past two weeks, he had been staying up late watching television or playing games on his Xbox One. This bachelor nightlife revival was not by choice. Ethan was unexpectedly laid off from a financial institution where he had been employed for the last five years. As much as becoming unemployed had heightened financial concerns for the newlywed couple, not all was lost. The company had given him a six-month package, which along with his wife's income, unemployment checks, and some leftover wedding money, gave Ethan the opportunity to take some time off.

Wandering in the dark of their bedroom, Ethan felt around with his bare foot for two socks which were tossed to a corner so Lauren would not slip on them. After both crew socks were recovered and returned to their proper place, Ethan was prepared to start the day. With a squint to guard his eyes from the profound sunlight on the other side of the door, Ethan turned the door knob and stepped into the hallway. Upon entering the living room, he reached for the one thing to fill in the silence of the apartment, the cable remote. When his eyes adjusted to the bright light after a few moments, he noticed a reflection on the screen; he walked over to the stand and rotated the television away from the window until the obstruction was no longer visible. As he wandered through his make-shift unemployed routine, his phone alerted him of an incoming text.

Lauren: Good morning.

On most mornings, the television was dedicated to the latest in the world of sports or Ethan's Xbox, but if political hot topics were pressing, Ethan would flip between cable news channels and if not enough information was broadcast, his iPhone 5s and iPad were never too far away. After flipping between the two political channels, Ethan was aware of the morning headlines in politics. President Obama said this or that, and this group or that person was elated or outraged.

In 2008, when Ethan reached his twentieth birthday, he developed an interest in government affairs. As he grew to have a better understanding of how and why things worked in places of government, the world of politics became an intriguing arena to observe. Given its complexities and constant fighting between the two major parties, even as they always report to have "worked together" to get this bill or that resolution passed, captivated Ethan with its irony. It never helped that to gain proper perspective, he would have to watch the news network that favored one side or the other and then gather the remaining tidbits on the Internet, to piece it together. These actions allowed Ethan to attain his own perspective to assure his views were mindful and not emotional.

When the historical election of 2008 approached, Ethan's enjoyment of a politic debate peeked. During the administration of President George W. Bush, he never liked to discuss politics too often, but when the national election began to draw near and it was Senator Barack Obama for the Democrats and Senator John McCain for the Republicans, Ethan no longer avoided political discourse. No longer was he just listening. Instead he was asking a question or two and sharing his view. He had positions that were accompanied with confidence. He even was inspired to take the debate online to a few websites, leaving substantive comments on certain news stories or responding to some posted by others. Yet during this process, Ethan realized then, social networking was not the platform to discuss; it was to argue. He discovered some people could be too aggressive, insulting, and bullying in their approach to political discourse than he cared for, which put a sour note on engaging in social political discussions as the election drew near, and practically every day thereafter.

On Election Day, even though he did not cast his ballot for then Senator Obama, Ethan could never deny the historical effect the election of President Obama was going to have, and the spiritual uplifting that would engulf the nation in that moment. For evident reasons, that uplifting was to be experienced more strongly by those in the African American community. When Ethan watched President Obama's victory speech from Chicago, whether he agreed with the political outfall, he saw tears of pride fall from some of the onlookers, including Oprah's. It caused a sense of national pride to sweep over him that night, several years ago.

In the kitchen, Ethan searched the cabinets for anything quick he could call breakfast. While looking through his snack drawer, his phone vibrated again.

Lauren: Are you going to look for a job today?
Ethan: Yes, I will.

In the month of June not much happens in the world of politics, so there were no major headlines to pull Ethan's attention away from SportsCenter. Being a follower of most professional sports, watching ESPN was the perfect counterpart to Ethan's fanaticism. Growing up in the Bronx, Ethan's father took him to many Yankee games, which turned him into a loyal fan as the years progressed. Along with the Yankees, they also watched the New York Giants, the Knicks, and the Rangers. The triumphs of the 1990's and 2000 Yankees and the historic 2008 Giants win over the New England Patriots, were shared with his father and witnessed from the living room of his parents' home.

Despite the decades spent living in the Bronx, Ethan did not only follow the professional teams that resided in New York. Any major event or unique sport storyline would peak his interests. The FIFA World Cup and the Olympics would always be viewed with a certain enthusiasm not shared by many within his social circles. But the game Ethan had a true passion for, to watch and play, above all, was golf. He was introduced to it by his older cousins at sixteen, but he fell in love with it immediately. During a summer break, he had the opportunity to spend a week in Georgia and play a few rounds with his late Uncle, and although he was told, "let's face it Ethan, you stink," he never stopped playing.

The individual control of achievement or defeat attracted Ethan the very first day he stepped on to a golf course. Unlike other sports, golf presented an opportunity to experience the depths of self-discipline. Ethan approached the game as if he were playing chess, and although he was not a good chess player, the layout of the eighteen holes on a golf course was the chessboard. You either would make a great move, and leave a hole with a positive score. Or you would make an error in judgement and the hole would destroy all hope. And just like chess, golf required a player to remain headstrong and in control, even when the course was not allowing it, because everything could change with one good move.

Since his layoff, Ethan kept himself occupied during the day by going to the driving range, playing the local courses, or selling personal items on eBay. On most days, he took a ride over to the post office and the coffee shop that was next to it. Ethan was having success selling his abundance of no-longer-played Xbox games and self-indulgent purchases of Disney movies, many of which were still sealed. Ethan had pocketed a sizable amount of money when he sold the company laptop the other day. Ethan figured when they didn't ask for it back, it was part of his layoff package.

Standing over the kitchen sink and making a breakfast out of several chocolate chip cookies, Ethan stared out his kitchen window and noticed there was not a cloud in the sky. It was a perfect late spring day to be on the golf course. Ethan stepped quickly into the laundry room, sprayed his balled-up khakis with a dewrinkler mist, and tossed them into the dryer. On the door to the office, next to the laundry room, was a pull-up bar he and Lauren used to dry clothes. Ethan grabbed a hanging polo shirt and popped open the dryer door to pull out a warm, less-wrinkled, pair of pants. In the kitchen, Ethan grabbed a couple of bananas hanging in their hammock and a water bottle from the fridge. He ran down the stairs and out the door. Halfway to the car Ethan realized he left the ready-to-ship laptop on the office sofa. He raced back inside, up the stairs, and rushed back out. All of Ethan's motions were being witnessed by his postman, Henry, who was standing across the street.

"Morning, Ethan," Henry said.

"Oh, morning, Henry," Ethan said with a polite wave of his hand.

Henry was one of the few exterior constants in Ethan's life. As it typically goes in populated areas, like the Tri-State, familiarity with one person providing a service is rare. You grow accustom to adjusting to new people. Occasionally changing doctors or mechanics. Of course, changing neighborhoods always introduces a new bank, a new pharmacy, or a new barber. After Ethan moved he could not adjust to a new barber. He did try a few in the area, but they never could cut it the same way, which made Ethan return regularly to the Bronx for his haircut and to visit his parents. But for Ethan, when he moved, of all that should have changed, his postman remained the same.

Henry, had been in Ethan's life for as long as he could remember. Henry's old route was in the Bronx and he was always outgoing and welcoming. Ethan's mother, who is always a pleasant conversationalist, would always have discreet discussions with Henry about anything that fit their mood. It was this way from the time his parents purchased their home in 1987. When Ethan joined the family a year later, until he moved out, Henry was a regular visitor at the doorway. When Ethan battled for supremacy on his Super Nintendo system, he could hear the discussions between his mother and Henry taking place ten feet away. About the same time, Ethan was preparing to marry Lauren and move out of the Bronx, Henry told the people on his route he was moving to Westchester. When Ethan and his wife moved into their new apartment, he was amused to see Henry delivering mail on that same street. It was slightly uncanny, but at least it was a familiar face in a new neighborhood.

Henry always had a presence about him that was kind and enthusiastic. He never appeared to be in negative spirits and was always supportive of anything Ethan was pursuing. More times than not they held simple talks about regular run-of-the-mill topics. If ever Ethan disclosed a personal situation he was experiencing, such as embarking on a new journey in life, school, job, or relationships, Henry always encouraged him. For this, Ethan grew to have a strong bond with someone with whom he interacted with in small bursts but if added together would amount to years. Henry and Ethan never intentionally socialized outside of the path of Henry's post route, but that was enough for both of them. Ethan was not looking for companionship, and from what he knew, Henry, being thirty years older, never demonstrated a need to yield more of his time. Since the move, every once and a while they would cross paths at The Roasting Plant for a brief back and forth, which fit into their lifestyles perfectly.

As Ethan continued to walk away from Henry, he shouted, "You know if you have postage on that, you can hand it to me. I'll take care of it."

Standing at his car, twenty yards away, Ethan shouted back, "No, I didn't have time last night. I'll stop at the post office before it closes."

"Okay. Going anywhere fun?"

"Bethpage!"

"Ah, good luck then."

"Thanks, Henry, see ya."

It was a Wednesday morning, so Ethan thought he would try his luck at the Tri-State Area's most popular golf course. On a weekend, one could wait for hours if they didn't arrive by sunup. Ethan figured being a single player he should be able to walk right on. As Ethan made his way to the parkway for the thirty-plus-mile trip, he used his GPS system to find the address and have it route him to the hardest and therefore the *best* golf course on the planet, Bethpage Black. It seemed fate was on his side today. The parkway was clear. The Throgs Neck Bridge, which usually involved a half-hour of traffic, was not a deterrent this day, and the Belt Parkway, the stretch of road that makes rush-hour commuters curse the Almighty, moved at a fast pace. Thanks to all of this, Ethan arrived at Bethpage within a half-hour and was on the tee box, paired with a few other golfers, before 11:15.

Waiting to start his round, Ethan reached into his pocket; he wanted to text his wife that he was at the course.

Ethan: Wish me luck, I tee off next.

Ethan then went to his golf GPS app to configure it for the Black Course at Bethpage. As the app's download status bar was slowly progressing, he received Lauren's response.

Lauren: You're playing golf today?
Ethan: Yes.
Lauren: No job search? What happened to looking for a job???

Trying to respond, Ethan could hear the ranger call, "Next group is up. Good Luck gentlemen." Ethan, texting quickly now, had to calm the situation.

Ethan: I am going to job hunt as soon as I get back home.

Ethan sensed a problem and quickly followed up with another olive branch.

Ethan: I did the dishes and the laundry. I have all night to search, the weather was too perfect. Is that okay?

All he got back was a single word response.

Lauren: Fine.

Ethan tried to focus on golf. No reason to engage in a text argument. Especially when he's on the golf course and she was busy at school teaching her students which meant Ethan could wait thirty to forty minutes before getting a reply. Ethan went back to his GPS app. With the course information for Bethpage Black now successfully downloaded, he had a great advantage walking the course, as he would always know the yardage to the green on every hole.

The first tee box of Bethpage posts a warning sign to its would-be victims that the Black Course is a difficult course and should be played only by highly skilled golfers. It was a warning to be heeded. When the USGA hosted the 2002 U.S. Open, the winning score was three under par; in 2009, it was only one better, four under par. The onlookers stood around the first tee box, some not brave enough to play the Black Course, others standing in wait for their moment to be called, and then there were the few who had just finished the eighteen holes having an appearance of a broken, beaten, and humbled golfer, wanting to regain some dignity as they left the course to gaze upon its next victims.

Ethan's group was now on the tee; he was warming up, taking a few swings of his driver to loosen up his shoulders. The first golfer sliced the ball at a forty-five-degree path to the right—he almost put it on the fairway of another hole. The second golfer hit a hard shot, but it drifted left and was in the rough. It was now Ethan's turn. He set his ball on the tee, took a deep breath, started his swing, and made contact. When Ethan looked up, he could see that he had placed the ball right in the center of the fairway. Relieved from the result, Ethan received a smattering of light golf claps from the gallery, and as he walked towards his ball he sensed he was going to have a good round on this day.

Ethan ended the round with a score of 135.

Chapter Three

The Contest and Coffee

The humbling round of golf ended just after 4:00 p.m., which presented Ethan the opportune time to depart and avoid the joy that is Long Island rush-hour traffic. He wasted little time getting to his car, and although there were some unavoidable slowdowns, Ethan arrived at the Bronxville post office in forty minutes. It was structured within a refurbished nineteenth-century brick building. By outward appearance one would believe it was from the colonial era, but the color mismatch of the bricks revealed the coffee shop was an addition and not part of the original construction. The appeal, that made Ethan drive one town over to ship the items he sold, also came from with the small-town setting that surrounded the Georgian-style structure.

As Ethan set the car into park, another pulled into the handicap space closer to the entrance. He glanced over to see the driver, but the reflection of the sun blocked his view. When the driver's door was opened slightly, it revealed the worst thing imaginable: an elderly woman. Given the time, the post office was going to close in fifteen minutes, which meant one thing—only one counter would be open for service. This presented Ethan with a first-in-line post office showdown. If there was one thing Ethan liked less than waiting in traffic, it was waiting in line at the post office behind an elderly person. Waiting at the bank and the queue for Space Mountain in Disney World were neck and neck for third, but a well-lived person at the post office spelled tragedy for those in their wake.

Ethan witnessed this encounter many times before and found that the event occurs in three stages. First was the miscalculated postage totals on the letters and packages. Next came the endless stamp comparison shopping that could rival the amount of time it takes to deliver a next-day package from New York to San Diego. Finally, came the grandchildren or the small talk, either of which had the chance of holding someone in line long enough for a family member to file a missing person's claim. Ethan knew he had to get in first.

He jumped out of the seat, still wearing his golf cleats, and quickly made his way to the tailgate. By the time Ethan put on his sneakers, got to his box, and locked his car, precious seconds were lost and the woman was already out with packages in hand. Then Ethan had an idea, one that works ninety-nine times out of a hundred, for a young man. If he held the door open for her, in kind she would let him go ahead in line. He could see she was walking with both hands full. He quick stepped his way passed her, reached for the door to hold it open, and said, "After you ma'am."

"Why thank you, kind sir," said the old woman.

Stepping inside the post office, Ethan saw there were no customers waiting in queue, and as expected there was one counter open. As both walked toward the line, the old woman turned to Ethan and said, "Why don't you go ahead of me, young man?"

"Thank you. That's nice of you." Ethan said with a grin.

"Hi, Ethan," the woman behind the counter said.

"Heeey, how's it going today?" Ethan stammered. As per usual with social encounters, he could never remember names, and being a female he could not just look down at her name tag at that moment. Ethan feared she would ascertain that he could not recall her name or that he was being rude.

"My day is great, it's almost time to go home," she replied, "Is this all you're shipping today?"

"Yes, economy shipping, no tracking or insurance." When her head went down to input the information, Ethan took a quick glance at the name tag. "Tracy," he said to himself. After the total cost of shipping was determined, Tracy asked, "Cash, debit, or charge?"

Ethan reached into his pocket but all he felt was his phone. Ethan let out a sigh and realized in his rush to be first on line, he had left his wallet in his golf bag. With one hand in his pocket he began to let out a small laugh. To bring Tracy into his present predicament, he held his phone up and said, "This is all I got."

With a laugh of her own, Tracy noted, "We don't take that."

Red faced, Ethan said, "You know, I left my wallet in the car. Why don't you take care of this nice lady behind me and I'll be right back?" As he walked toward the door he glanced up at the ceiling as if he was looking up to God and thought "well played."

Having returned with his wallet, Ethan was alone in the queue. From where he was stood, he could hear the old woman and Tracy talking about anything but postal services. From the faint sounds reaching his location he could make out, "Did I tell you my grandson graduated head of his class?" Ethan was digging his teeth into his bottom lip, while his inner voice shouted, "Are you serious!" He knew it was going to be a while, so he figured he'd take this time to reach out to Lauren. After the issue he created for himself by playing golf and not job-hunting, and given the fact that neither one had sent a text since the round started, he knew she would be amused by his current situation, which could thaw any annoyance she may have had towards him, before they both reached home.

After he hit the send button, Ethan focused back on the inter-action between Tracy and the old woman. Picking up the exchange in mid-sentence; he heard Tracy say, "Remember I told you I was going to visit my grandmother last month?"

"Oh yes!" replied the old woman. At the same time his smartphone began to vibrate, he unlocked it to read Lauren's response.

Lauren: LOL

As he lowered the phone to his side it vibrated again.

Lauren: SUCKER!

Ethan was becoming annoyed. More than five minutes passed and the elderly woman was holding conference with both packages, wrapped in both arms. Ethan began to look around the lobby to kill time and the six-foot standing advertisement that had been in the same position for the past couple of months caught his eye. The ad was for the national contest the USPS was currently holding. The title was "Priority for Life," and it displayed a female surrounded by dozens of boxes with her arms over her head in celebration. At the base of the ad there were three words, "Flat. Free. Forever." The rules were just as simple to read as the ad itself: "1. Ship Priority, 2. Win Priority." To get an entry one would only needed to ship an item via the priority services; your entry number was on the receipt. The best disclaimer of the rules was that you could have as many entries as you wanted, but of course, only one entry per day. The contest was scheduled to end on July 26 but Ethan already had several entries thanks to all the items he was selling on eBay.

"Ethan?" Tracy shouted from behind her kiosk. When Ethan looked in her direction, the woman was still standing there with those two packages embraced in her arms, but Tracy was waving him over. Not about to wait a second longer, Ethan sprinted those three yards as if where he was standing was on fire.

"Yes," said Ethan.

"Let me take care of you so you can get out of here. Brianna and I are having too much fun, and you look like you want to get home."

"Ah, sure, thank you. Thank you. . . Brianna," Ethan muttered.

Brianna nodded as she said, "You remind me a lot of my grandson."

Oh my god! She's talking to me now, Ethan thought. He was politely nodding as she spoke in the typical lovely, disarming, and grandmotherly, style, but was not paying attention to Brianna, and when she finished speaking he said, "Thank you."

"What?" said Brianna.

"I'm sorry?" Ethan replied.

Brianna smiled, "I asked if you worked in the city."

"Oh," said Ethan. He was instantly embarrassed because he knew how rude he was behaving and now both Tracy and Brianna were aware of this hidden quality. To save himself, he softened his antagonist position and said, "I'm sorry. My mind was someplace else. Yes, I used to work in the city, but I was laid off a few weeks back. Now I am taking it easy, while I sell some things on the Internet and catch up on my golf game."

"Well don't take it easy too long. You're a young man," Brianna said, "You have a lot ahead of you."

"I won't. I promise," Ethan said as he was finished the transaction. When Tracy handed him the receipt, Ethan looked up and said, "Thank you." Then he looked back at Brianna, who in the end was a sweet old woman who no longer was living at Ethan's pace. She was now in her twilight years, and all she wanted was to talk to someone. This trip to the post office was probably the second or the only item on her to-do list for the day. Realizing this, Ethan looked at her in a different light and said, "Thank you, Brianna for letting me go ahead of you. Have a good afternoon."

"You're welcome," she answered.

Once outside, Ethan took in a deep breath of fresh air and could not ignore the inviting scent of freshly ground and brewed coffee. He planned to grab a cup to go, but it was therapeutic to the senses to inhale the aroma while he walked towards the entrance. Ethan remembered the first time he entered *The Roasting Plant*, he knew immediately that it was a unique coffee shop and would quickly become his favorite place. What stood out to anyone who walked in was the system of clear pipes and tubes that connected the coffee beans to the brewers. Along the wall were a dozen or so cylinders. Inside each tube were either raw or roasted beans. They carried all types of exotic coffees, from Jamaica Blue Mountain and Ethiopian to Hawaii Ka'u and, Ethan's favorite, Kona.

The pipes would move the raw beans from their individual tube to the roaster, and then after the roast completed, the system would send them into another tube where the beans waited to be brewed. At the counter, the preparer inputted the bean selection and size of the cup ordered, then the system would do the rest. For just a couple of seconds, all one would hear is the sound of the air transferring the beans through the pipes above and down to the station. When the beans reached the brewer, they made a sound as each one hit the metal funnel. It was impressive from a technological aspect, and it was impressive from a coffee connoisseur perspective, which Ethan considered himself, or at least aspired to be. Maybe he did not know every bean, but he knew enough to know the difference between Kona and Jamaica Blue. Jamaican Blue made him shake more with the caffeine rush.

The Roasting Plant was a hangout for some postal employees. Since parts of Yonkers and Bronxville overlapped, one of the regulars included Henry, who normally stayed in the corner by the window reading the newspaper. The rest of the seats in the coffee shop were taken by the typical patrons with their laptops or notebooks with an add-on keyboard case, always engaged to what was on their screen.

"Hi, welcome to The Roasting Plant. May I take your order?" the barista asked.

"I'd like a small Kona please," Ethan replied. With that, the preparer entered the order on the panel and the beans traveled on air through the plastic pipes above, making a *Ssshhhhhh* sound before the *clank-clank-clank-clank* when each bean reached its destination. After the grinder completed its task, Ethan knew he was moments away from receiving his drink, but while waiting he heard someone approach him from behind.

"How did it go today?" a voice said.

Ethan turned around to see Henry standing there. "Oh, hey," said Ethan, "not bad. I shot a ninety-something I think. I don't know. I wasn't keeping score."

"Hey, shooting in the nineties on Bethpage Black is something to be proud of," said Henry.

"Yes, it would be if that's what I shot," admitted Ethan. "Actually, the course handed me my ass, and I shot in the one-thirties."

"Oh, well, you'll do better next time," said Henry.

"Thanks."

"I saw you arrive here before. What happened? Did Tracy talk your ear off in there?" Henry asked.

"Ah, no," Ethan said. "A nice old woman was," Ethan gave a short pause as he searched for the right words, "doing her thing."

"That's always a show," said Henry. As Ethan put cream and sugar in his freshly brewed cup of Kona, Henry continued, "But the oldest women also have more 'knowledge of the world, and their minds are better stored with observations; their conversation is more improving, and more lastingly agreeable.' What do you think about that?"

"That was nice. Did you just think of it?"

"No," said Henry.

"Who said it? Shakespeare?" Ethan asked as he brought the coffee to his mouth and flinched when the heat coming from the spout on the lid hit his upper lip.

"Benjamin Franklin said that."

"Really? Nice," Ethan said as he raised his cup to compliment Henry's demonstration of reiterating historical verse. "You know I don't know that much about Benjamin Franklin. I mean, I know what everyone else knows: lightening, key, Founding Father of the country. But, I know he accomplished and wrote so much more than that. Maybe someday I'll read his work, get to know him a little better, quote a clever line now and then."

"You should. Hey, speaking of Franklin," said Henry. "Are you shipping priority? We have that contest going on, and it seems like you are making a trip here every other day. This may be your chance to save some money."

"Yes, I'm using Priority," said Ethan. "What does that have to do with Franklin?"

"Oh, the contest ends on July 26," said Henry.

"So?"

"That was the date in 1775 when the post office was created by the Second Continental Congress and named Benjamin Franklin our first Postmaster General," said Henry.

"Interesting, I'll try to remember that." Ethan again lifted his cup as a salute, "Well, I'm off. Have a good night Henry."

"Goodnight, Ethan," Henry said with a smile.

Chapter Four

BFMS7475

When July 26 arrived, it was a day like any other. The morning arrived like any other, and was going to be lived like any other. The morning alarm ritual continued to reprise itself as Ethan was still unable to find new employment. Lauren, now on summer break, was out for the day. During her time-off from teaching she liked to stay very active, with either daily trips to the beach or the county pool in the morning, followed-up with tutoring, a kick-boxing class, or shopping.

Alone in their apartment, with no items to ship, and rain in the afternoon forecast, solidified that Ethan had no chance to insert a round of golf into his daily impromptu schedule, and he was stuck indoors. By midmorning he was reclined on the loveseat, watching his favorite episode "17 People" from *The West Wing* on Netflix. Thumbing through the news of the world posted on Twitter, as he ate the nutritious kick-start breakfast of Oreo's and coffee, Ethan's conscience started to question his sixty-day milestone of unemployment and how the lack of mobility brought with it an expanding waistline.

Without a moment to let procrastination disrupt his thoughts, Ethan sprang up, walked into the kitchen, and disposed of the rest of his coffee. He grabbed a bottle of water from the fridge, went to the bedroom to change his shirt, and put on his three-year-old, yet still nearly pristine, running shoes. He walked into his office, arranged the folded-up treadmill to point toward the television, grabbed the remote, and started to jog.

As he reached the three-quarter-mile mark, Ethan's breathing was becoming heavier. He knew he was out of shape, but he was surprised how quickly his endurance dropped. As a child, he was never the quickest runner, and if he ever turned the burners on to maximum throttle, they would never last long. When he played sports with his friends, he experienced a few moments of glory, but they tended to have more over on him. It did discourage him at the time, but they would not have been much of a friend had they patronized him by letting him win. Playing hard and winning outright was the only way, and as Ethan got older, he was better for it. It prepared him for handling competition. It trained him to balance his emotions between the unfair and the fortunate situations life threw at him, such as being laid off.

Ethan lowered the speed to where he could continue to walk at a quick pace. "Three times more around the track," he told himself. The display on the treadmill had an image of a quarter-mile track outlined by small red bulbs. Ethan was determined to reach that mile, so he could move on to lifting weights. In the home office, Ethan had all the equipment one would find at the local gym. A few years ago, he had taken part of a weight-loss contest at his office in which the winner was set to win more than a grand. Not to be denied, Ethan invested a couple of hundred in a home gym, which turned out to be a wise purchase as he was triumphant in the end. After the success, Ethan purchased a stationary bike and elliptical. When he moved to the new apartment, his father let him take the treadmill, but not all pieces could fit in one room. The treadmill and gym were in the office, but the bike was put into the dining room, which blended in naturally, and the elliptical was squeezed into the bedroom, much to Lauren's delight.

Ethan raised the speed lever above the jogging levels. The tread beneath his feet picked up, and for the first time in a month, Ethan was running. Now on the third lap, with one remaining to finish a mile, the iPhone started playing *The Imperial March* from *The Empire Strikes Back*, which Ethan set as his ringtone. When he reached for it, he noticed the caller ID read "unknown." "*Unknown,* you are not important to me right now," Ethan said aloud. He then placed the phone back on the treadmills' dashboard, letting the call go to voicemail.

Approaching his final lap, Ethan was out of breath and energy. His legs continued pumping while he told himself "you can do this." Staring at the display panel, annoyance set in when it seemed the red bulb at turn two was not going to make its way to the start of turn three. Suddenly, *The Imperial March* started playing again. The caller id displayed "unknown" once more. Now curious to find out who was being so persistent, he slowed down the treadmill to a simple walk speed and muted the television to accept the call.

"Hello," said Ethan. To be polite, Ethan flipped the microphone end of the phone up to the ceiling, away from his mouth, this way the caller would not hear him panting so loudly from the cardio and have any misconceptions of Ethan's present state.

"Is this Ethan Pope?" the woman on the line asked.

Not recognizing the person's voice Ethan brought the mic end back to his mouth. "Yes, it is," he said. He then flipped the phone to the ceiling again to take another deep breath and brought it back to ask, "Who is this?" Ethan figured it was a sales call, and whoever was on the other line was going to speak for a good twenty seconds, which would give him time to catch his breath.

"My name is Keely, and I am calling on behalf of the United States Postal Service. I would like to congratulate you on being selected as the grand-prize winner of our *Priority for Life* contest."

Stunned, Ethan shut off the treadmill and jumped off. His breathing was already heavy, now with the added excitement, it was becoming harder to slow it down. Taking a deep inhale, Ethan was able to pace his breathing just enough to ask, "I'm sorry, can you repeat that?"

"Of course, sir. I said my name is Keely, and I am calling you on behalf of the United States Postal Service. I would like to congratulate you on being selected as the grand-prize winner of our *Priority for Life* contest. How does that sound?"

Ethan was ecstatic. Sure, it was the post office, but winning a national contest in which he no longer had to worry about the shipping cost of the items he sold was, as Ethan saw it, like winning free money.

"How does that sound?" Ethan said. "I can't believe I won. It sounds amazing!"

"Well, that is good to hear," said Keely. "To claim your prize, please go to the office you frequently ship from in Bronxville. Give them your name, and they will help you out. Congratulations sir and have a good day."

"Thank you. You, too," said Ethan.

Being full of joy, Ethan texted his wife the good news as fast as his could. He then called his parents, sent out a text blast to every contact on his phone, and posted it on Facebook. After sharing his excitement with the world, Ethan ran down the hallway to shower. While the water ran, he could hear the faint sound of alerts from his smartphone notifying him of incoming texts and Facebook updates of congratulations from friends and family.

When Ethan arrived, a few cars were parked in the front, but when he went inside the lobby was empty. He went right up to the counter and shouted, "Hello Tracy!"

"Well don't you look happy? What are you shipping today?" Tracy asked.

"Nothing."

"Nothing? So, what do you want? Stamps?"

Ethan shook his head, "No. I'm here because I won the contest! I got the call a little while ago."

"What contest, sweetie?"

"The contest!" Ethan exclaimed. "Your contest! The post office's contest?"

"Oh," Tracey said as she continued to ponder what Ethan was referring to. When her eyes locked on to the contest ad still standing in the lobby, it finally made sense, and she said with a smile, "Ohhhh! That contest."

"Yes! Free flat rate for life, baby!" Ethan said with glee. "Where do I sign?"

"Well, congratulations, honey, I'm happy for you. Wait right here, and let me get my manager." Tracy left Ethan at the counter and disappeared into the backroom. When she emerged, there was another, taller, postal worker with her.

"Hello Ethan. My name is Robert. I'm the postmaster of this district, and I hear you were called today for being the winner of our contest. First, let me shake your hand and offer my congratulations." As they both locked hands, Robert continued, "Second, I'll just need to see your ID, and we'll get everything you need."

"Sure." While he retrieved his driver's license, Ethan felt compelled to say something to assure Robert that he was not being dishonest. As he handed Robert the card, Ethan said, "A woman named Keely called me and instructed me to come here to claim it."

"Very good," Robert said. "Kelly informed me yesterday the winner was selected in our district, so we could have everything prepared for your arrival. Let me just verify your name, and I'll be right back."

Several minutes passed as Ethan waited patiently while Tracy tended to customers who entered the building. Then the door to his right, which was for postal employees only, opened and Ethan was shocked to see a large box was being wheeled out on a handcart. On top of it rested a medium-size Express box and envelope.

"Alright sir," said Robert. "You can say we have here a few 'bonus' prizes for you as well." The size of this item fascinated Ethan, never being one to properly eye measurements, he figured the box was roughly three feet tall and stuck out about two feet. It was a regular brown cardboard box with writing on the side going lengthwise. Ethan tilted his head to get a better view. The label read *Property of the Postmaster*, and underneath that, it had a catalog reference *Item: BFMS7475.*

Robert grabbed a clipboard from behind the counter, turned back to Ethan and asked, "Would you like me to wheel this out to your car?"

"Yes, please," said Ethan. "Thank you."

Robert handed Ethan the envelope and both walked out of the lobby. As they crossed the lot, the rain started to come down on them in a light drizzle. Ethan was concerned, given the size of the box, that he was not going to be able to move it on his own without it becoming damaged. He asked Robert, "What's in that thing?"

"Don't know, son," said Robert. "This was shipped here this morning, and I was authorized by the Postmaster General of the United States himself to personally wait for your arrival and oversee the transfer of these packages to your person."

"Really?"

"Yes, and as I have worked in the postal service for thirty years, I can tell you that I have never taken a sick day, I have never stayed home on a snow day, I have never received a complaint against me, and I never have spoken personally any of the sitting Postmasters General," Robert said with a grin. "You can bet I was shocked yesterday afternoon when my phone rang and he said who he was and that I had to be here for the arrival of these packages to ensure they were safely transferred to you. That is all I know."

Noticing the cardboard box was becoming polka-dotted as drops of rain landed on it, Ethan unlocked the car doors on his SUV and opened the passenger door to place the Express box and envelope inside. After the tailgate was lifted, Ethan had to move his golf clubs and empty plastic bottles scattered about the back to make room for his large prize. Once he made enough space, Ethan turned to Robert to assist with placing the box in the car. As they lifted it, Ethan sensed it had to be no more than fifty pounds, so getting it into his home on his own was not going to be as daunting as he envisioned.

Ethan grabbed the tailgate handle and was about to pull it down when Robert said, "And thanks to the signature you are about to give me, I can tell the Postmaster that the items were indeed transferred to the correct party, safely, unharmed, and undamaged, and only got a few drops." Ethan was standing underneath the rear door and was protected; as for Robert, small droplets of rain started to fall as he held out the clipboard. On it was a single sheet of paper; Robert handed Ethan the clipboard with a pen and said, "Please confirm all information, then print, sign, and date it on the bottom. After that you will be all set, Mr. Pope."

Ethan laughed politely, "Very good sir, and thank you for your help," he said as he applied his signature. Before handing the items back, Ethan asked, "What does 'BFMS7475' mean?"

"It's an internal code for shipment between offices," Robert said. "This package came from Philadelphia. I know that because the *BF* means it was the Ben Franklin office on Market Street, which is what the *MS* represents. The *7475* is a reference number. But what is inside, I have no idea." Robert turned to run back indoors to get out of the oncoming rain. As he left he shouted. "You have a good day now."

Ethan pulled down the rear door and shouted back to Robert, "Thanks!" He then made his way into the driver's seat and eagerly texted Lauren.

Ethan: At the post office. There were two "bonus" prizes!

After he hit *send*, he went for the envelope, pulled the tab to rip it open, and reached inside to grab the paper. It was an official letter, with a seal on the top center of the page, dated July 2, and was addressed "*To the winner of the national contest.*" It read:

> *On behalf of myself and all the employees of the United States Postal Service, I would like to congratulate you on being selected as the winner of our national contest PRIORITY FOR LIFE. This is the first national contest held by this department, and in that regard, we would like to also present to you these two additional gifts that have been in our possession for quite some time.*

> *The U.S.P.S. has been mistaken as only a transporter of letters and packages. There is more to the post office that is unknown and unnoticed. From Benjamin Franklin to present day, the United States Postal Service has played an essential part in communication between and within each state, and throughout the entire world. Thanks to participants like yourself, the U.S.P.S. exists and will continue to exist for generations to come. We thank you for being a great American and again for choosing the U.S. Post Office.*

> *May God, bless you and follow you wherever life may take you.*

It concluded with the words *Thank you* and was followed by a signature that Ethan could not make out, but underneath the title was typed *Postmaster General of the United States of America.*

After reading it, Ethan could not figure out that last line "May God bless you." That didn't sound very governmental, but there was something else that stood out in the letter which captured his imagination. The postmaster wrote "gifts that have been in possession . . . for quite some time."

Ethan was thinking to himself how long is "some time," and more important, what could it be?

Chapter Five

A Nice Antique

Sitting quietly and hearing the rains drops hit the roof of his car, Ethan reflected on the events of the afternoon. He put the key into the ignition but did not turn the engine. Looking in the mirror, he was unable to take his eyes off the huge box in the rear. The suspense of discovering its contents swelled inside of him. He contemplated jumping to the middle row and breaking the seam so that he could get a quick peek. It was as if he was back at his parent's house at Christmas, being too excited to wait before opening the presents. He opened the door and moved to the middle row as quickly as he could, to avoid getting wet. With his knees on the seat, Ethan examined the box, trying to imagine what kind of item from the United States Postal Service would be so large to qualify as a gift. Also, would this item be worth holding on to or reselling? These were the questions that Ethan needed to have answered immediately.

He shook the box, but it did not make a sound. Whatever was inside was either solid or packaged extremely well. Beside a vintage countertop mailbox, Ethan was not picturing any items of interest from the post office inventory that would be of this size. When the rain began to come down harder, Ethan knew opening the box now would only create more work later when he needed to seal it up again or make use of a blanket to avoid exposing it to the elements when he returned home. He decided it would be best to leave it alone for now. He turned and faced forward, hearing only the sound of raindrops impacting the shell of the car.

Ethan then leaned forward and looked for the smaller box he tossed on the passenger seat. He reached over, grabbed it, and took the key out of the ignition as well. He popped open the door and made a dash to The Roasting Plant. Ethan tried pulling his shirt over the box to shield it from the rain, but it was too large, so he hunched over and pressed it against his waist. Instead of a walk, Ethan was making a waddle to the entrance. Once he was a few paces away from the door, he sprang upright so no patron inside could have noticed his awkward walk.

Inside the Roasting Plant, he saw a few regular faces; it was not that crowded so there were plenty of seats. Ethan walked up to the counter and ordered his Kona coffee. As it brewed, Ethan looked around the room and was thinking of yelling so all could hear, *"Hey everyone, I'm the big winner today!"* which made him smirk a little. After being laid off, Ethan carried with him a lack of motivation. He enjoyed his job and the people he worked with, but it wasn't until today that he felt energized, confident, and genuinely happy. As he glanced around the room, the sound of the outside weather intensified behind him when the door was pulled open.

"Hey, Ethan," a familiar voice said. Ethan turned and standing at the entranceway, dripping wet, was Henry.

"Hey, Henry," Ethan said. "Nice weather we're having."

"Thankfully, it started after I finished my route," said Henry as he was catching his breath. "I only ran from the office to here, and I got this wet! But, when I got back, I noticed our district PM, Robert, was visiting. He said we had the grand prize winner, and the person just picked up some items. When I saw your name on the paper and your car parked outside, I figured you were in here so I ran over. Congratulations!"

"Yes, I got the call this morning," said Ethan. "Not only did I get the free shipping thing for life, I also got this." Ethan raised the box up to show Henry.

"Do you know what's in it?" asked Henry.

"I have no idea. If it wasn't raining I would have opened it already but I decided to wait until I got it inside."

Seeing Ethan pay for his drink Henry said, "Let me get that for you, Ethan."

Ethan turned his head back and said, "No, that's okay. I can get this."

"No, no. It's a big day for you. I'll take care of it. Put it on my tab," Henry instructed the worker behind the counter.

"Thank you."

"No problem, Ethan. Congrats."

Ethan grabbed his cup of coffee and walked over to the creamer station. He had to place the box on the floor as he added some raw sugar and half and half to his Kona. With the coffee in one hand and the prize in the other, Ethan head for the corner table by the window. Seeing the table had some sugar and crumbs on it, he headed back to the station to get a handful of napkins. After wiping it down and inspecting it from all angles to make sure whatever he took out of this box was not going to become damaged, Ethan rested the item on the table. He tried to take a sip of Kona, but as always, he could feel the hot steam come through the cover, so he placed it back down to cool off and grabbed the box to satisfy his growing curiosity.

With great excitement, Ethan ripped the seal to reveal the top of a plastic object. He tipped the box to let it slide out to his right hand. Ethan could see it was a clear container with what appeared to be a letter inside a clear plastic sleeve, which was inserted into a piece of styrofoam at the base to prevent it from moving around. "*Another letter?*" Ethan said to himself. Thinking this was turning out to be a bust after already receiving a typed letter from the postmaster, Ethan reluctantly gave the piece a quick look over but instantly changed his mood when he noticed the year on top of the paper read *1790*. Eager to learn its subject, he popped the top off the container, carefully retracted the hard-plastic sleeve, and held it gently in his palms. Ethan tried to determine if the letter was authentic or not. Having watched pawn and antique shows, he thought he could try to replicate a few tactics the graders noted when they examined letters like this.

First, it appeared that the paper was old fashioned, like the parchment paper the Declaration of Independence and the Constitution were written on. But Ethan recalled after he saw both documents in Washington, the gift shop had various replicas to purchase, and they looked similar in construction to the letter he was now holding. Second, he was trying to determine the type of writing material, was it genuine ink or toner from a modern printer? Ethan held the sleeve perpendicular to his eyes, to see if the ink strokes had any bubbles or blots. However, this proved to be too difficult as the overhead lights caused multiple reflections on the plastic. Ethan was getting frustrated and decided to end his novice effort in eighteenth-century letter authentication.

Holding the letter in proper view now, he started to read its contents. There appeared a symbol of an eagle stamp at the top. It reminded him of the eagle used on the Presidential seal. As for the letter, there was not much to it. There must have been only twenty lines in total. The cursive was picture perfect in being transcribed in a straight line across the page, and each letter was clearly written. Ethan made out the first line that read, "*To my late father-in-law's companion and my friend.*" Before he could continue, he heard his name being called.

"Ethan! What did you get?" Henry shouted from across the room.

Ethan looked over to Henry, sitting a few tables to his right, and tilted the letter toward his direction. When Henry noticed the antique letter, like a magnet, he got up from his chair and walked over. Standing above Ethan's right shoulder, Henry got a better look at the writing and mumbled, "Richard Henry Bache."

"What?" Ethan asked.

"Richard Henry Bache," replied Henry, as he pointed to the bottom the letter. "The signature is signed *Richard H. Bache*. The *H* stands for Henry."

"Do you know who he was?"

"I do," said Henry. "He was a member of the original post office during the Revolution."

"Really?"

"You see, in July of 1775, the Continental Congress created their own postal service so they could parcel letters from Boston to Philadelphia, and all places thereabouts. Its primary purpose at inception was to keep certain correspondence out of the hands of the British. In September of '75, Richard Bache was appointed the secretary and comptroller for the newly established postal service. A year later, during the Revolution, he became the second Postmaster General in our nation's history. Lucky for him, he was the in-law of our first PMG, which could have been the main reason for his appointment to the post."

"Franklin?"

"Yes," Henry said. "Do you know why Franklin was the first PMG?" he asked.

"No, I don't." said Ethan.

"Franklin, running a well-respected and well-operated print shop in Philadelphia, was selected to serve the British government as the postmaster of Philadelphia in 1737. Sixteen years later, he was the deputy postmaster of North America. Thanks to him, the routes improved and for the first time, the postal service was turning a profit for Parliament," said Henry. "As a result, he served for decades but was removed from the position in 1774. Of course, that was when the American Revolution was starting. When Congress desired the implementation of a postal system, Franklin was the obvious choice to create the Continental Postal Service." Henry looked up and out the window as he contemplated. While still looking out the window, he said, "Not to sound outdated, but when you look at that accomplishment, he designed our nation's first network for communication in the eighteenth century."

"Yes, you can say that," said Ethan. "Did they also have tracking numbers? Signature confirmation?" Now smirking with his clever questions, Ethan posed another, "How about two-day mail?"

"Alright, son," said Henry. "Delivery time did increase thanks to Franklin, for what it's worth."

Ethan felt the mood in the coffee shop had changed a little, since he entered. It was not Henry's fault, but he wanted to drink his coffee and look over his prize in solitude. After seeing the smaller prize was a simple letter and now having finished his coffee, Ethan felt he could head home and read this antique letter in the quiet of his office. Also, the suspense of not knowing the contents of the larger box was growing. Ethan put the sleeve back into the hard-plastic container and returned the container to its cardboard box. Looking up toward Henry, who was still standing beside him, Ethan said, "I'm going to head out. I have a few house chores to do before Lauren gets home. I can't make it look like I sat around all day."

"Okay. Hey, next time we see each other, you have to let me know what was in the other box," Henry said.

As Ethan was getting up from his chair, he groaned as his back stretched, "Sure, will do. Have a good one, Henry," Ethan said. "And, thank you again for the coffee."

"Not a problem. Congratulations again. I'm jealous. It must be great having a piece of our nation's history like that."

As Ethan made his way out the door, with his back to Henry, he shouted, "Thanks!"

As the door was closing, Henry yelled, "Hold on to that letter Ethan," he said, "Don't sell it online!"

Twenty minutes later, Ethan arrived home. Fortunately, he found a spot right in front, which was not common. To avoid fumbling with his keys while attempting to transport the box in his arms, Ethan first opened the front door that led to the parlor. He then unlocked his main door to expose the steps up to the apartment, giving himself a cleared entrance. After some clever maneuvers, Ethan made it to the second floor, then walked the familiar steps to the sofa in his office. The side of the box was placed on the cushion for a moment, then he gently rolled it over to the floor. Ethan could no longer wait, he dashed to the kitchen to grab the scissors. After sliding the blade through the box's edges held together by thick packing tape, he was ready to view his bonus prize.

When the cardboard flaps were opened, all Ethan could see was a wooden top. "What the hell?" he said to himself. The wooden top had less than an inch of space on either end. Ethan slid his hand down the right side to see if he could lift the item out, but his fingers hit a piece of wood that was roughly six inches long and attached in the center. The same piece was connected on the left side. Caring more about knowing what was inside the cardboard box than the box itself, Ethan put his hands on both sides of the item and pushed out to tear the cardboard. Thanks to the sturdy design, and Ethan's lack of upper body strength, he was unsuccessful in his attempt. He had to resign himself to use the scissors to slowly cut down the corners to loosen the cardboard. Cutting down half way, Ethan was now able to yank and pull the corners apart so he could fold down the sides. He could clearly see the six-inch wood pieces his fingers were touching. They were handles connected to a wooden crate.

Like Indiana Jones lifting the Arc of the Covenant in *Raiders*, Ethan stood up over the item and using both hands on the wooden handles, he resurrected the crate out of its recycled harden pulp prison. With his feet, Ethan kicked the paper box to his left, so that he could gently set the crate on the floor.

The mahogany crate was completely sealed. The top and two ends were solid cuts of wood, and the long sides were made from two solid pieces with no air between them. The aged brown sheen gave off a slight reflection from the light. The handles were not the same color as the crate itself. It appeared as if they were added at a later time. Ethan knelt on the floor to continue inspecting the crate, he grabbed the right handle, and pulled it toward him to check the other side. As the hundred-and-eighty-degree turn was nearly complete, some writing came into view. There were three lines that read:

Property of the Postmaster

Market Street

Philadelphia, PA 1789

Ethan thought that if this date was authentic, this could have great value. He attempted to remove the top portion by pulling on each corner, but the cover did not budge. Examining where the cover touched the sides of the crate, Ethan noticed a thin black substance along the edge that created a tight seal. He knew he could not remove the top without potentially damaging the wood. A bit frustrated, Ethan stood up and grabbed both sides of the crate and gave it a shake to see if anything rattled inside. After a few rough jolts left and right Ethan could not hear anything moving within the crate and figured it was empty. It seemed that his second prize was just the crate itself dated from 1789 Philadelphia.

Disappointed, Ethan made his way to the kitchen to prepare a cup of coffee. While the unit warmed up the water, Ethan grabbed the letter he tried to read earlier at the coffee shop before he had been interrupted. Thanks to Henry, however, he now knew who wrote the letter. Ethan placed his coffee cup under the dispenser and inserted a half-calf pod in the holder. As the machine brewed, Ethan read the letter.

To my late father-in-law's companion and my friend,

As I write you this letter I tremble with an emotion of immense joy knowing the journey it will go on to reach your person. It is amusing to me as well, to consider you are but a stone's throw from my quarter and that I could almost reach out and hand this to you myself. However, its true purpose would not be served should I not follow the instructions designated to me by my late father-in-law and continue the work he and you started in that tavern seventeen years prior.

By your part, you gave him a life after death of sorts that I dare presume he was unable to fully comprehend while he was alive. The establishment of this country with your assistance is an accomplishment I estimate no single God-fearing being ever achieved with such modesty. The magnitude of your influence and foresight was revered and admired deeply by my father-in-law, which I presume is why he took such a liking to you from the first time the two of you crossed paths. He always spoke highly of you when not in your company and I believe, with humble appreciation, your presence in the latter part of his life filled him with a second wind, which expanded it beyond the good Lords' planning. I also personally thank you for the services you rendered to my father-in-law in his time of need. Being at his bedside and singing that kite song he loved so much, brings a tear to my eye just reminiscing about it.

I will conclude by informing you all requests have been put in motion, and there should be someone who will assist you from here on out. It is all in God's hands now. I thank you again for your services, and I pray for you and the loved ones you had to sacrifice a lifetime away from to achieve the creation of the finest nation ever conceived. May God bless you on your travels.

Richard H. Bache

The signature of Richard Bache was neatly written. It did not have the John Hancock flow, but it closed out the letter well. Although the letter did not indicate the original recipient, from the recent history lesson Ethan received at the coffee shop, it was evident that Benjamin Franklin's son-in-law was thanking a close colleague of Franklin's after his death. Still being the clever online auctioneer, Ethan speculated that since the letter was not directly written to a figure like Washington, Jefferson, or an Adams, its potential value may have been substantially diminished. It was still an impressive homage to someone very important. Not wanting to spend the whole night contemplating the possibilities, Ethan returned the letter into its protective clear container to prepare his cup of coffee. He stood in his kitchen reflecting on the day's events. Along with winning the national contest for free shipping for life, he now possessed a nice antique from the eighteenth century.

"Better than nothing," Ethan thought.

Chapter Six

The Journal

Since winning the contest a week ago, Ethan became more active and health conscious. He engaged in daily exercise and stayed on a more healthier diet. Along with running on the treadmill and lifting weights on the home gym, Ethan was attempting, for the third time, to get through the sixty-day intense cardio DVD program he purchased a few years back. All of this was not for vanity, Ethan was ready to be more aggressive in his job-hunting, but his suits, collecting dust in the closet, were a little snug around the midsection, and he knew appearance was a huge factor in making a first impression with a potential employer.

After a cool down and shower, Ethan made himself a recovery shake with bananas, strawberries, blueberries, peanut butter, low-fat milk, and a scoop of protein mix. A few seconds in the *Nutribullet* and Ethan downed it, standing over the sink. Once all items were cleaned, put away, or thrown away, he proceeded to leave the kitchen, but before breeching the door-frame, he reached out and grabbed one Oreo out of the box. Ethan then grabbed the first three boxes that were going to be shipped for free.

When he arrived at the post office, he approached the counter and could not help but have a smile on his face. "All priority, please," he said to Tracy.

Always in a pleasant mood, Tracy made small talk with Ethan as she entered the zip code, printed the tags, and scanned the bar codes on each box. "Debit or credit?" she asked.

Still holding his grin, Ethan said, "No thanks, I'll use my *get-out-of-postal-fees* card."

"Okay, where is it?" Tracy asked.

"Well, I don't actually have a card," replied Ethan. "I am making use of the *free shipping for life* service that I won." Seeing the look on Tracy's face, Ethan could tell she was confused. "Remember, Tracy? The Post Office contest I won?"

Tracy pondered for a moment, then suddenly realized what Ethan was referring to, "Oh, that's right!" she said. "Well, did you get anything, like a code I can enter or a card I can swipe?"

"No, I just filled out a couple of forms. I did not receive anything else, I figured you would know me here, so all I had to do was show up," said Ethan.

Tracy let out a laugh. She asked Ethan, "How would the service be available to you if you went to a different office? Or if I wasn't here?"

"Ah, I didn't think of that. So, what do you suggest?"

"Let me make a quick call," she said. As the phone on the other end continued to ring, Tracy looked at Ethan with a little smile while she waited for someone to answer. "Robert!" she said. "It's Tracy from office 8505." There was a brief pause and then she said, "Yes, that's right. How are you, sir?" It then felt like a minute passed without a word said, then she started to make small laughing noises and yelled, "Oooh, you're bad." Ethan than gave a little wave, to remind her why the made the call. She noticed his hand and nodded to convey that she did not forget.

As Ethan stared at Tracy, all he heard was her side of the conversation.

"Robert, I have a quick question if you don't mind. Remember that man who won the free shipping contest? Yes, him."

"Well he's here, and he doesn't have anything for me to swipe or enter and I don't know how to apply the . . ."

"Uh huh, okay. Got it."

"Thank you. Okay."

"Oooh, you are fresh."

"I'll speak to you soon sweetie, bye."

Tracy hung up the phone and glanced at Ethan with a look that did not exude delight for his current situation. "Robert said that they sent your card to his office, and he's sending it out to your address now, which means you'll have to pay today."

"Seriously?!" Ethan shouted.

"Yes, I'm sorry, honey," Tracy said.

"Can I pay for it and submit the receipt for a payback?" asked Ethan.

"I can't tell you if that will work, but I'm sure you'll have a number you can call," Tracy responded.

"Fine," Ethan said while reaching for his wallet. "But this is the last time!" he said with a smile to show Tracy he was not annoyed but found it amusing to know the post office was unable to send their own mail to the correct destination at times.

"Here you go, Ethan," Tracy said, handing over the receipt. "Have a good day."

"You too, thank you."

At his first attempt, he was unable to reap the monetary reward from the contest. Feeling disheartened, Ethan felt a cup of Jamaican Blue Mountain was needed to ease his spirits. As he walked toward the entrance he texted Lauren the events that just transpired.

Ethan: So, I go to the Post Office, and of course my first "free shipment" I had to pay for because I do not have the official card yet. LOL

Lauren planned to go out with her girlfriends that evening. Ethan promised he would update his resume and post it to head hunting sites. However, because she was out, he also had some extra time to kill and was in no rush to return home. When the doors opened, the smell of the brewing coffee and the sound of the beans rustling their way through the pipes provided a therapeutic atmosphere making Ethan's mind carefree once again. After placing his order, Ethan stood by the pickup counter. Suddenly, a cramp began to make its presence in his right calf. He bent over to massage the area and as he released the tension, his phone received an incoming text.

Lauren: LOL

While bent at the waist, Ethan heard his name called out. "Ethan?" he looked at the preparer, but they were still preparing his order. "Hey, Ethan!" the voice called out again, only this time he recognized the voice. Still rubbing the backside of his leg Ethan contorted his upper body to locate the source. Seated a few tables away, was Henry, waving.

Ethan straightened up and acknowledged the wave with a single hand raise of his own and replied, "Hey, Henry, nice day." When the barista put the finished cup on the counter, Ethan cautiously walked over to add the cream and sugar. His calf still cramping, he slowly made his way over to Henry. "Mind if I sit?" Ethan asked.

"Oh, please do," said Henry, "You look to be in some pain."

"Yes, I started exercising again. Not drinking enough muscle shakes I guess."

"That must be it."

"Shut it!"

Before Ethan was seated, Henry eagerly asked, "So? What was the letter about?"

Ethan took a small sip of his coffee and winced. "*Every time,*" he thought to himself. Ethan pressed his tongue over the burned lip. Then he used his bottom lip to cover the upper lip to relieve the pain, but to no avail. Ethan then pushed out his lower lip and with a hard exhale forced excess air rushing across his hot coffee induced flesh wound. When the pain was gone, Ethan looked across the table at Henry and said, "I'm sorry, what did you say?"

"I can't believe your threshold, or lack thereof, toward hot liquid," Henry said. "But my question was about the letter."

"What about it?" asked Ethan.

"I am curious to know what Richard Bache wrote in that letter you had in here the other day before I came over uninvited, bothered you, and made you leave," Henry said.

To cover up his embarrassment, Ethan replied, "You didn't bother me, I had to leave. That's all. I realized the time and wanted to get home." Henry nodded politely to accept the fib, but it truly did not matter to him. Henry was having a little fun at Ethan's expense. "Anyway, there was nothing much to the letter itself," said Ethan. "Richard was writing to someone who was an acquaintance of Benjamin Franklin's and appeared to have a close relationship with him near the end of this life."

"Wow, that's amazing!" Henry said. "Did Richard indicate who this person was?"

"No," said Ethan. "It was addressed to no one in particular, and Richard never mentioned them by name in the letter. Hence my suspicion why that letter was given to me as a quote-unquote *prize*."

Henry leaned in to interject, "I wouldn't worry so much about the value aspect of it. Focus on the longevity of the letter and the source. Richard was the postmaster during the Revolutionary War. He overlooked the network that transferred top secret correspondence across enemy lines from General Washington to Congress and all places in between." Henry leaned back in to his seat and concluded, "He was a very important man. He just had the misfortune in the annals of history to follow and be related to Franklin."

"Yes," moaned Ethan as he drank his coffee, which now reached a tolerable temperature. "But still, if I said I had a letter by Benjamin Franklin *that* would be worth something to almost anyone. If I say, I have a letter from Richard Bache, the first question I will get is *who*. Still, I don't want to sound ungrateful. It was a nice letter."

"What did it say?" Henry asked.

Ethan looked up at the ceiling trying to recall what was written in the letter. "Something about being there for his father-in-law at his time of need and giving him a new purpose by helping establish the new country. I really don't remember that much of it."

"Wait, help him establish the new country?" said Henry. "Richard is thanking a person who evidently helped Benjamin Franklin during the founding of America and that doesn't hold any value to you?"

"No, it does," said Ethan, "but I mean, *who* is Richard writing to and *what* did this person help with, are two huge questions that someone would ask in gauging its value." Ethan lifted his cup to drink, the temperature was now perfect. "Come to think of it, there was one thing that was curious to me."

"What was that?" asked Henry.

"Richard noted that the person he was writing to was close by, but then he remarked on he couldn't give the letter to that person because his father-in-law had plans for it. Then something about things being in motion. It was all very strange," Ethan said.

"Speaking of strange," said Henry, "what was in the other box?"

"It was a wooden crate," said Ethan. "Nice one too. It was a brown, Mahogany I believe. I had to look up images on Google to compare, and it looks to be a Mahogany-ish-type wood."

"Did it say anything?" asked Henry.

"There wasn't a note with it if that's what you mean?" said Ethan.

"No, I mean, was there any writing on the box? Or anything in the box?"

"Oh!" Ethan said. "Yes, there was an address. Market Street, Philadelphia, seventeen-ninety-eighty something. Wait, I took a picture." Ethan reached for his iPhone to search for the photos.

Henry snickered, "You can't remember the date?"

Ethan held up his hand, "Hold on, just wait," he said. "Ah, here it is. Let me zoom in." Ethan stretched the photo on the screen. Squinting, Ethan said, "seventeen eighty-nine."

"Ah, so close," said Henry with a smile, "Seventeen eighty-nine, seventeen-ninety-eight. You weren't off by that much. What was in it?"

"I didn't open it."

Henry looked perplexed. "You didn't?"

"No, the box is perfect, and the only way to open it would be to crack the seal at the top, and that could ruin it." Ethan paused as he took another sip of coffee. "Besides, I shook the whole crate, and there was nothing in there."

"How do you know?"

"It didn't make a sound when I picked it up," said Ethan, "I'm pretty sure it's hollow. Also, in its condition, it should carry a very good value. I've watched enough antique and pawn shop shows to know this is a unique piece. It's still in excellent condition and worth a lot of money to the right person."

"You're willing to sell the crate without knowing what's inside?"

"I don't believe there is anything inside," replied Ethan. "And, if I take a screwdriver and a hammer to it, and end up damaging the wood, I will lose a good amount of money that could be of great use to me right now."

"I see. If it were me," Henry then paused for a few seconds and said, "Remember there was a man who found an original copy of the Declaration of Independence behind an oil painting he purchased at a flea market for four dollars, because all he wanted was the frame?"

"No."

"Well, what happened was when he got his $4 purchase home and ripped the backing off, he found an envelope. What he discovered inside sold for more than $2 million."

Sarcastically, Ethan retorted, "Are you saying I'm going to find the Declaration of Independence?"

"No," Henry said. "But I would rather determine with my eyes and not my ears whether the crate contained anything."

"I agree," said Ethan, "Still, I'm playing with percentages when it comes to breaking this antique. I am looking at the crate as a means of earning thousands." Ethan became more energized as he started to talk with his hands while he continued, "It's as if I am playing chess. I can only sacrifice a piece, if I have another piece. If I crack this thing open and damage it in the process to find nothing inside, it would be as if I sacrificed the king to save the queen! I'd be at a loss."

As the minutes passed, Ethan finished his cup and prepared himself to make an exit. Henry looked up as Ethan patted his pockets to account all his possessions. "Ethan," Henry said as he stood up. "I have a little insight on what was given to you, and I was forcing myself not to say anything because I wanted you to discover it on your own. But, I fear after our conversation just now, that you have no intention of cracking the tar seal around the top of the crate. Let me assure you, if you do open it, what you will find inside will eclipse the value of that box."

Ethan gave Henry a puzzled look and thought about what he could have been alluding to, but as his curious side became eager to discover what possible historic treasure awaited him, he began to smile. With a grin, Ethan said, "Well, I better get home then." Before exiting the coffee shop, Ethan turned to Henry and shouted, "Thanks!" Henry, relieved, acknowledged with a single wave.

Once he arrived back home, Ethan ran up the stairs to the laundry room where he kept his toolbox. He found a flathead screwdriver and a hammer, entered the office and knelt next to the crate. Starting in one corner, Ethan carefully placed the edge of the screwdriver on the black sealant and gave it a light tap to the handle with the hammer. With a small indent visible, he continued this process all around the crate's top, hoping to loosen the cover without damaging it. After twenty minutes of hammering, Ethan was losing his patience and started to put more force on the screwdriver head. Finally, there was hope and the top piece began to move and rise off the base. Ethan ran to get a second screwdriver for more leverage. With the two screwdrivers wedged in place on opposite ends, Ethan pushed down on both handles and, with a pop, the cover shot off the crate and he fell forward with the sudden give.

Moving the cover aside, Ethan saw what appeared to be discolored hay, tightly rolled up, which explained why nothing was heard when he shook it. Ethan took his fingers and pried it from the middle, creating a hole. He pulled strands apart by the handful and tossed it on to the floor. With more insulation removed, he could see brown leather through the straggling stems. As he pulled more packaging apart, Ethan was able to retract the treasure from within the crate. It was made from hard leather, which gave it weight. He tried to unfold the tucked-in edges when a strip of leather fell from the fold and swung. Ethan reached for the strip and extended the whole piece to reveal a satchel. It was simple in its appearance, no pockets on the front or on the side. It had one long flap that could be secured with a buckle toward the bag's base. Lettering appeared on the flap side. The black ink was difficult to see against the almost equally dark leather, but Ethan could make out the label "Post 001."

"Wait, is this it?" Ethan thought at first, but when he grabbed the makeshift buckle and opened the flap, he saw a suede bound book. He reached in and took it out from the case. It was tied with a single suede string. For fear the pages could come loose and spill all over the floor, Ethan walked into the dining room and cautiously rested the items on the table. After untying the restraint, he opened the covers to expose the papers inside. It was a decent stack, maybe two inches high, and the pages were not bound to a strong spine as Ethan suspected. They had two holes on the left margin, and each hole had a single string holding them together. Ethan could plainly see this item was not recently manufactured.

The first page was blank. Ethan then bent over from the waist and delicately lifted the bottom corner to flip through the pages to determine if any pages had writing on them. They all appeared blank at first glance.

"Why would Henry encourage me to open up the crate for this?" Ethan thought to himself.

Given the time of day, the natural light in the dining room was dim. Ethan turned on the standing lights around the room to help examine this antique, which was not meeting the expectation he built up in his mind on the car ride home. Neither was it coming close to the value Ethan placed on the once sealed crate that was now in pieces. Frustrated Ethan reached out and turned the first page over to the left side to discard it from the pile. To his surprise, there were a few lines of writing in the center. It was in block print and looked to be a title page of a manuscript, which read:

The Franklin Project:

My Conversations with Dr. Benjamin Franklin

May 1775 to October 1776

"Why is everything about Franklin lately?" Ethan said aloud.

The date range indicated the author was with Benjamin Franklin during the events leading up to and a few months after July 4, 1776, Independence Day.

"Who wrote this?" Ethan thought.

Ethan's joy at finding such an antique was coupled with disappointment. It appeared this journal was never used to record conversations with Benjamin Franklin. They were clean but as Ethan stared at the paper he saw a faint scribble at the bottom. The ink was faded a bit, so he bent down to get closer, and noticed it was a scripted name. He leaned his head left and right and once the light in the room illuminated the strokes on the page just right, he immediately became queasy. The penmanship of the title was block print which gave no cause for apprehension but the stroke, the pattern, and the flow of the name were all too familiar, because it was his own and it was dated 1775.

Chapter Seven

History as We Know It

Sitting alone in the silence of the apartment, Ethan's mind was a meld of questions and assumptions. His inner dialogue was going in circles which created greater frustration. Ethan took a deep breath and closed his eyes for three seconds. Thinking aloud, he said, "Okay, what's going on here? This journal has my name written in it, but it's dated from the eighteenth century."

Ethan attempted to examine the print along the surface of the page. As he did with the letter from Richard Bache earlier, he wanted to conclude for himself whether the ink was real or whether he was looking at another simulated document. He could see that the words were not perfectly straight. Moving his eyes to view the surface of the sheet, Ethan could make out ink spots at the intersections of some letters. Analyzing the structure, unlike the finely written letters of the time, the person who penned this page possessed poor penmanship.

"This is real," Ethan said. "This is my handwriting."

"Now, this was a gift from the post office. Franklin and the postal service have a connection," Ethan thought. "But why is my name here?" Suddenly it occurred to Ethan, "Wait a minute!" he shouted. "They have my signature." Ethan stood up and paced across the room, as he started to piece the facts together. "I've signed numerous documents, I've even signed on the electronic pad, so they must have used what they had on record to duplicate my signature to this page. They wrapped it up, put it in this crate, and that is why Henry was so adamant for me to open it." Ethan's mind was now at ease. "Makes perfect sense," he said.

Ethan continued to ponder, but he couldn't imagine what motivated Henry to go out of his way to ensure that he opened the crate. "Maybe it was the satchel that Henry wanted me to find?" Ethan thought. Still, the scenario fashioned was puzzling to him. "How could they have done this in twenty-four hours," he thought, "if I was just randomly selected in a contest?" What was discomforting to Ethan was the journal, with his signature, was placed in an antique crate to give the impression that it was a genuine 18th century item. Also, the tar-like substance would not be something any modern person would use as a sealant for a quickly assembled bonus gift.

Frustrated all over again, Ethan tied up the journal, placed it back in the satchel, and took it with him to get some answers from Henry. On his way to the car, he started to text Lauren what happened but given that he had no idea what was going on, he didn't want to confuse her as well. He decided to send a quick text to let her know he was leaving the house.

> **Ethan: Hi babe, I am running to the coffee shop for a minute, I need to get something.**

> **Ethan: BTW I made a mess of the office, I'll take care of it when I get back.**

> **Lauren: Okay, babe. Don't forget about your resume.**

> **Ethan: I won't.**

When Ethan arrived at The Roasting Plant, he looked around for Henry, but was unable to spot him. He walked up to one of the workers behind the counter to ask where he was. She responded with a shrugged of her shoulders. Ethan again looked around the dining room of the café trying to spot a familiar face. He thought that if maybe he could find another postal employee, they could assist him. Ethan ran out of the coffee shop to the entrance of the post office, but the doors were locked. He pounded on the glass and tried to look inside but was unable to see anyone. Ethan ran around the side of the building to the loading dock. Although there was no one standing outside, the door behind the dock was open. Ethan shouted, "Excuse me, I'm looking for Henry. Has anyone seen him?"

"Henry?" a voice replied, "Henry who?"

"What?" Ethan yelled.

"Henry who?" the voice said again.

This time Ethan could see a man around his age walking toward the docks' edge. Ethan said, "You know I don't know his last name but I'm looking for Henry, the Postman. He does my route, and I need to speak to him. It's extremely important that this happens now."

"Oh, well if you need to report a carrier, you can call the customer service number," the young man said.

"No, it's not that," said Ethan.

"Oh, okay. Is there anything I can help you with?" he asked.

"No thank you, sir," said Ethan. "It's something I need to address with Henry, and it's urgent."

"Well, Henry is not here," he said, "Now, if he made an error on a delivery or damaged a package, like I said you can call our customer service line. Other than that, it's not customary for us to call postal carriers out of hours because someone on their route wishes to speak to them."

"Look, I'm sure you can contact Henry in some way," said Ethan, "Cellphone or text him, I don't care. You must contact him and say Ethan is looking for him, and it concerns the crate he spoke about earlier."

The man standing above Ethan on the loading dock platform looked down and with a puzzled expression said, "Ethan you say?"

"Yes, Ethan."

"Ethan, I'm John. We'll try to get a hold of him for you." John then turned away toward the cargo pass through. "Hey, Mike," John shouted.

Faintly from within the building, a voice shouted back, "What?"

"Can you call Henry and tell him Ethan is asking for him?" John said.

A man from behind the plastic slates appeared. "Ethan?" asked Mike.

"Yes," said John, "He'll know what it means." Mike reached into his pocket and took out his cell phone to make a call. As Mike was trying to reach Henry, John looked at Ethan and asked, "You're the Ethan that won the contest?"

"Yes, how do you know?"

"Tracy said something about it."

"Ah, I see."

"Okay," Mike said, "Henry said to wait in the coffee shop. He'll be there in about ten minutes."

Ethan reached for his phone so he could see the time. It was ten past six. "Great. Sorry to bother you two," said Ethan. "Thank you."

"No problem, Ethan," said John, "Good luck."

Knowing he was going to be a little longer than anticipated, Ethan wanted to notify Lauren.

Ethan: Hey babe, I'm meeting someone at the coffee shop regarding the prize I won. I don't know when I'll be home. Have fun with your friends tonight.

When Ethan returned to The Roasting Plant, he did not have a taste for coffee. He grabbed a bottle of water from the cool shelves beneath the registers and made his way to the windows at the far end of the café. He placed the satchel on the table while he waited. Ethan looked around the seating area and now saw one postal worker, who was not in the café earlier, reading the paper. In the back of the room sat a classic coffee house patron with his laptop out. He was a young man, possibly a college student, wearing cargo pants, a tee shirt, and giant headphones that made his head look smaller in size.

Ethan felt the vibration of his phone. It was a text from Lauren.

Lauren: Is he bringing you a JOB? LOL

Lauren: BTW, I'm back home and had to get on the treadmill so I put all your stuff on the sofa. I'm not going out tonight with my friends, so I brought home some buffalo pizza. I had a craving. Now I'm walking it off. Don't judge me! Loooove you.

Ethan: Haha, Love you too.

The sound of the door opening caught Ethan's ear. He turned to see whether Henry had arrived, but to his disappointment, it was not. However, a young woman was making her way into the shop. She was very appealing. Her long curly brown hair rested perfectly between her shoulders and fell to the middle of her back. She wore a white tank top with pink tennis shorts and white sneakers. What struck Ethan's appeal was she looked just like his wife Lauren from years past when they first started dating. The woman's back was to Ethan as she spoke to the person at the counter. Ethan lifted himself off the seat a bit to get an unrestricted view. Only seconds passed until Ethan noticed the barista was making eye contact with him. He dropped like a rock, back into his seat, and looked down on his phone. He knew he had been caught.

Sitting embarrassed and wanting to do something to get out of chair, Ethan had a great idea. He would go over to the counter and place an order for a coffee. That way, the person behind the counter would think he was observing the menu. The only flaw with his plan was that tables and chairs did not obstruct the menu board. Nor was the menu in his line of sight when the barista caught him, it was hanging above the registers. In either event, Ethan did not want to be recognized as the "creepy guy" by the workers at his regular shop, even if his looking was innocent and out of curiosity to learn who was this person, who held the resemblance of a younger Lauren. He got out of his seat, grabbed the satchel, and walked slowly while he finished the bottle of water. The young woman was still at the counter conversing with the worker as Ethan tossed his plastic bottle in the recycling bin. Then he turned to walk to the bakery case where the normal make-shift line began. As he stepped forward, the door behind him opened.

"Ethan?" a familiar voice said.

Ethan closed his eyes for a second and could not believe the timing of all of this. He turned to see Henry standing there. "Hey," said Ethan.

"Let's have a seat," Henry said as he extended his arm towards to seating area. Ethan cautiously walked to a round four-seat table, large enough to give them proper personal space. Ethan reached out to one chair, then Henry grabbed the back of the chair next to it. Ethan, who was not a close talker, moved to the chair on the opposite side of the table so that he could sit across from Henry.

Ethan held the satchel on his lap as both adjusted themselves in their seats. Over Henry's shoulder, Ethan could still see the young woman, and it caused him to pause long enough for Henry to notice something was capturing Ethan's attention, that he turned his head in the same direction. "Oh," Henry said, he then turned back to Ethan, their eyes connected, and he continued, "So tell me why I was called."

"Shouldn't you know?"

"Why?" asked Henry. "I don't know."

"I think you do. You must. You asked me. In fact, you told me to open the crate, and that's what I did."

"Oh good."

"No, no. Not good," Ethan said. He then placed the satchel on the table. "There was this leather bag with a suede bound journal of some sorts wrapped inside of it."

"What's the problem with that? That looks like a nice antique."

"That's not the problem. The problem is in this journal, where all the pages were blank, except one. Where I found my name, written in my handwriting, with the year 1775 underneath it. That's what has me worried!"

"Amazing," Henry said, "An authentic colonial post office portmanteau and an eighteenth-century journal inside of it too. Those are great prizes to win Ethan. You should be happy. Not worried."

"What's a portman-tea?"

"A portmanteau," replied Henry. "It's a travel bag. The portmanteau of the post office was a satchel with multiple compartments. The satchel usually was made of hard leather to protect the contents from the rain, if the carrier was so kind to care in those days. It would have a lock for the post rider and the local post office clerk to open. On long postal routes, the mail would be taken out and sorted so many times that plenty of letters were damaged and sometimes lost along the way. It wasn't a perfect system, but it was profoundly efficient for what we had."

Henry opened the bag to examine the interior. "Thankfully, Franklin corrected things when Britain made him a postmaster." Henry reached in and pulled out the journal. "Now, this book," Henry said. "This journal, you say has your signature in it." Henry paused for a moment. "What's the big deal?"

"Henry!" Ethan shouted. "Why would I win a prize from the post office, dated from 1775, containing my signature?"

"Well, let's see," said Henry. "How many times have you used the electronic signature at the counter when you pay with your credit card? Could it be someone is having a little fun with you?"

"At first I thought it was a fake as well," said Ethan. "You know, a reprint of my name. But when I noticed the ink was real, that made me suspicious. Then, I considered the age of that wooden box and the condition it was in, and I figured it was impossible in twenty-four hours for anyone to assemble something like this for a measly contest prize."

"What are you saying?"

"What I'm saying is something weird is going on. Something is odd about this whole thing. For instance, why was this stuff given to me in the first place? It was a postal service contest I won. But now I have that strange letter from Richard, written to "a friend" of Benjamin Franklin's and a journal that is personalized with my name. It doesn't make any sense to me."

"Okay," said Henry.

"Now add that you knew something was inside the crate, which would also mean you knew about the journal. A journal with one page, titled *The Franklin Project*, and it has my name on it!" said Ethan. "Oh, and why of all years, does it say 1775?"

"That's the year you wrote it," said Henry.

Ethan then took a long pause and stared at Henry, "What do you mean *that's the year I wrote it*?" he said.

"Hold on one second," Henry said. He then turned his head slightly to the direction of the counter and shouted, "We're going to need the room."

After Henry said those words, one worker, asked one patron to leave, walked them to the door, and locked it. The postman reading the paper, the college student on his laptop, the other barista behind the counter, even the young woman, who caught Ethan's eye, all left through the back door. The only noise that could be heard was the music being played.

Ethan sat panic stricken after the mass exodus leaving him alone with his postman. A variety of scenarios were racing through his mind. It was alarming, his chest began to weigh him down, his heart was pounding, and his breathing was shortened. Ethan tried to remain calm to show Henry that he was not intimidated by the charade that was just put on display from his *instruction*.

With a little grin, Ethan nodded his head, attempting to give the impression of confidence. Ethan began to say, "that was," but lost his nerve between the words *that* and *was*. He was now holding his facial expression and holding the last syllable of *was* with his voice as he tried to search for the right word. Ethan knew he had to be clever, but not "James Bond" clever. This man was not his arch nemesis or at least had not revealed himself to be. Ethan released the hold of the last consonant from his voice, looked back at Henry and said, "unexpected."

Henry gave a slight head shrug and said, "I know." After a few moments of silence, he continued, "This has been a long time coming for me, Ethan. I was getting impatient with my superiors and I'm relieved that they decided to begin the final stages of this project. My entire life has been dedicated to this very moment, and I am excited that it has arrived as much as I am excited for you."

"So, what are you saying?" Ethan asked. "You're not really a postman?"

"No, I'm a postman," Henry replied. "I mean, I did have real letters and packages in my hand and I did deliver them, and I did it for over twenty-five years. I've been with the Post Office for much longer but I only handled the routes that gave me the opportunity to monitor you from your birth, to your marriage, to this moment." Henry slowly arose from his chair, which caused Ethan to straighten his back and clench the arms. Henry's eyes were no longer locked on Ethan when he started to stand, so when he looked back and saw Ethan's body language, it troubled him. Henry gave Ethan a puzzled look and shook his head in disappointment. Peering out the windows behind him, Henry said, "Ethan, I am someone you have seen throughout your life, and although I cannot say for sure the emotions you're going through right now, I want to assure you, you are in no danger. In fact, your life and your safety is my primary concern."

Henry continued, "If anything, you are in the safest location for your self-interest. The people you saw walk out of this place a few minutes ago, the people you have noticed day in and day out as regulars, are all here to protect you. Just as I am here to protect you from this point forward, as I always have. Now, given the time if you want to leave and come back tomorrow to hear what I have to tell you, that is fine with me. However, if you think you will be able to walk out of here, let tomorrow pass, and the day after, and the day after. Let weeks turn into months and months turn into years without fulfilling your requirements, well, that we will not allow."

"*We* will not allow?" Ethan said, "We? I thought you said I wasn't in any danger and already you are trying to intimidate me."

"Oh stop it," said Henry, "I'm telling you, I swear, you are in no physical danger. I am also telling you that it is imperative that you become aware of a few things. Such as the meaning of the journal's existence and why it was given to you. This knowledge needs to be passed to you as soon as possible for things to go in motion. But, as a gesture of good faith, I am saying you can go now and regain your faculties since you look as if you are going to pass out. Or, you can stay and we can begin. It's up to you."

Ethan looked long at Henry. He had no idea what was going on or what Henry was alluding to but was compelled to understand what he meant by "this knowledge." Also, Ethan wanted to demonstrate that he was not intimidated by his antics. "I'll stay," he said.

Henry smiled. "Glad to hear it," he said. "Okay, take a deep breath and relax, because what I am about to tell you—will change your perception of our world forever. Before we begin let me make you a drink. What do you want?"

Still overcome with anxiety, there was a tremble in Ethan's voice when he said, "Ah, I guess I'll take water."

74

"Water?" Henry said sarcastically. "Okay, I'll get you a bottled water but what coffee drink would you like to have?"

Ethan sighed, threw his hands up, and said, "Any coffee will be fine."

"Come on Ethan, you're still being paranoid. You still believe you are in danger?" Henry asked. When he returned, Henry held a bottle out. "Here's your water," he said. As Ethan nervously took the bottle, Henry said, "I know you like Pumpkin Spice Latte's, with a pump of mocha. Right?"

"Ah, yes," said Ethan "but it's August; there's no pumpkin spice flavor to use."

Henry placed his hand on Ethan's shoulder to help him regain his composure. "All right. What can I make you?"

"I'll take a Kona coffee."

When Henry lifted his hand to give Ethan a pat on the shoulder, Ethan flinched and nearly fell out of his seat. Henry gave him a couple of gentle pats and left for the coffee bar. "Coming right up," he said. Behind the counter, Henry reached for a large paper cup from the stack and flipped it up in the air and did a complete turn of his body as a bartender flips bottles when he is showing off to make a mixed drink. Only when the paper cup made its return, Henry juggled it and dropped the cup. He gave a glance to see Ethan not paying attention. Without hesitation, he grabbed another cup from the stack and placed it under the dispenser. He pressed a few buttons, while the sound of the beans traveled through the pipes, Henry looked at the bakery display and reached in to grab a slice of pound cake. Once the process completed, the cup and the piece of cake were handed to Ethan. "There you go," said Henry

"Thanks."

"Ethan, I'm about to tell you a story that you will most likely find impossible to believe," Henry said while he returned to his seat. "Some of the events and the people I mention, you will recollect from history. Then, you'll note several historical truths that have never been revealed to the public to protect the facts." Henry gave Ethan a few seconds to ponder before he continued, "I am asking you to release the governor in your subconscious to allow the *historical facts* intertwine with these *historical truths*. This will give you the freedom to accept all information. That way, you will feel more at ease when we come to our conclusion. I think after you hear all the facts, all the details, all the events that have preceded your existence and are responsible for the reality in which we operate within today, you will gain a higher appreciation for the sacrifices that have been made by those before you. At the end, you will understand why we tried to ease you into this whole thing with our contest, the prize, and, well, everything else."

Sitting dumbfounded, Ethan felt the need to stand up. "Is it all right if I go prep this coffee first?" he asked.

"Sure," said Henry.

As Ethan made his way to the creamers, Henry saw the look of confusion on his face and felt he had better start talking immediately or he'd risk losing Ethan's attention. "Ethan, the America that you know is a fabrication from its true destiny when it was conceived over two hundred years ago." Henry tried to read Ethan's reaction but his head was down as he poured half and half into his cup. Henry continued, "To know what I mean by *true destiny*, let's revisit what we know to be our country's 'founding.'"

Ethan returned to his seat and tried to sip the coffee. As always it was too hot and he placed it on the table. He looked toward Henry who was patiently waiting. Ethan sat back in his chair and gestured to Henry for him to proceed.

Henry began, "America was born on July 4, 1776, and we celebrate it as the 'birth' of this nation because that was the day we say the Declaration of Independence was ratified. When, by all accounts, it was the day the final revisions of the Declaration were completed. The actual voting, the part of the process that unified the hearts of fifty plus men to which their very lives were being hurled into the realm of sedition should they have failed and ever been captured, well, that vote commenced on July 2, 1776. Also, some have a misconception that it was on July 4 when we, the collective *we,* declared war on England. That's half true, because on July 4, 1776, George Washington and the Continental Army were already engaged in battle with the British Army for a year. Yet even though we were engaged in a physical fight, all thirteen colonies were not in the fight together. It was in early July 1776 when all thirteen colonies in the Second Continental Congress voted as one group and declared that we were a sovereign nation, and that one nation was going to revolt against the rule of a British monarch."

Henry paused for a breath and asked, "How did this come about?"

"I don't know," Ethan nervously stated.

"No, I'm telling you. Just let me finish. I've rehearsed this story several times."

"Oh, I'm sorry. I thought you were asking me a question. Okay I'll listen."

"No problem. Now where was I?"

"You were talking about revolting against the rule of the British monarch and asked how did this come about," said Ethan.

Henry continued, "Yes, how did this come about? Well, the motion of Independence from Britain was passed by two colonies, first by the committee in North Carolina with the 'Halifax Resolves' and then by Virginia. In Virginia, the local assembly approved the resolution in Williamsburg during May 1776, which allowed the largest colony in America to bring that motion to Philadelphia so that the Congress could vote on it. North Carolina was the very first colony to instruct its delegates to vote on Independence but did not instruct them to propose it."

"Interesting, right?" asked Henry.

"Yes, I never knew that."

Henry explained, "Richard Henry Lee of Virginia proposed the resolution for complete separation on June 7, 1776, in Philadelphia. Now, even though the resolution came from Virginia, many felt and argued that it was the loud and defiant lawyer from Boston, John Adams, persuading this order for Independence. It was he who politically orchestrated the tides for Richard to propose the call for Revolution. So of course, not everyone embraced the resolution when it was read.

"John Adams was not well received by a lot of members. He was brash, he was irksome, and he was considered egotistical. This doesn't help one maneuver well through the political process. To help himself, John had to find an association with some of the members of Congress who did not view him as a political antagonist. John could find a trust with the respected representative from Pennsylvania, a local Philadelphian, and someone you keep hearing about: Benjamin Franklin.

"Before Franklin, John's true ally in Congress was Patrick Henry, a prominent Virginian. They both formed a tight allegiance over their shared desire for liberty during the First Continental Congress, in 1774. When Patrick had to leave the Second Continental Congress in August of 1775, John needed to find a new partner. Franklin, who had just returned from London in May 1775, was a renowned statesman the day he entered the chamber. Franklin carried a grand reputation throughout the colonies. It was only their mutual respect which allowed a partnership between John and Benjamin to form. It was cordial at the beginning but it only magnified John's appeal to more moderate representatives. Adams, with Franklin in his corner, was now more influential to the delegates. Many of the congressional associates had an admiration for Franklin's aptitude and his diplomatic proficiencies, and it was this respect held by many, if not all, that helped John form allegiances with members of other colonies, including Virginia.

"Now, back on the day when 'Lee's Resolution' was brought to the floor in June 1776, some delegates did not know how to vote for Independence. It's important to state that not everyone was ready for this type of drastic tactic as a means of resolving their differences with England. To postpone the vote, Congress agreed to give those members 30 days and it was suggested that a formal argument be prepared to make it clear why Congress was voting on complete separation from the Crown. It was agreed that a committee be formed to prepare a document outlining the grievances. John Adams, Thomas Jefferson, Roger Sherman, Robert Livingston, and Benjamin Franklin made up the so-called *Committee of Five.*

"Now no meetings minutes exist to recount how the committee functioned, but what we do know is that Adams asked Thomas Jefferson to write the Declaration, and he agreed. After Jefferson penned the document, the committee read the first draft, and Franklin was the one who suggested that the words 'sacred and undeniable' be replaced with 'self-evident.' After that, the committee agreed on its composition, and Thomas Jefferson, standing with the four other members, presented to the Congress on June 28, 1776, our Declaration of Independence.

"The wording and sentence structure were debated, modified, enhanced, and rejected in some key areas. After a total of eighty-six amendments, it was voted and unanimously approved on July 2, 1776. Then, the Declaration was rewritten in the great penmanship of Timothy Matlack with the approved revisions. On July 4, it appeared as the famous document we all cherish and was read aloud in Philadelphia on the steps of the State House. From that moment on, we were one nation, engaged in a revolution."

"With me so far?" Henry asked.

"Yes, I am," said Ethan.

Seeing that glazed look in Ethan's eye, Henry asked, "Are you sure? Would you like to take a quick break? Get some water?"

Ethan tilted his cup toward him. "No, I still have plenty of coffee here," he said. With a sigh, Ethan explained, "I guess I'm curious where all of this is going."

"We're getting there," said Henry, "it's important that you understand how things occurred. That way, when I tell you why you have the journal, you'll be able to fill in the blanks."

"I see," said Ethan.

Henry gave Ethan a little smirk and said, "Okay, here we go."

Henry resumed the story, "Benjamin Franklin played an indispensable role in setting the foundation for this country. Following his return to Pennsylvania on May 5, 1775, he was selected as a delegate to the Second Continental Congress, which was starting on May 10. He was then put on a committee to establish the continental postal system, and, as we have talked about before, he was made our first postmaster general in late July in 1775. Before he was a member of the Declaration committee in 1776, he sat on the Olive Branch committee with Thomas Jefferson, also in July of 1775. Then, a year later, he and Thomas found themselves on the Declaration committee writing the antithesis to the Olive Branch.

"After the Declaration was passed, and signed in August, Franklin was sent to France in October of 1776 to help acquire naval, as well as financial, support from England's biggest foe. When the war ended, he signed the Treaty of Paris in 1783, which was the principal document that ended the war with Great Britain and recognized the United States of America as a sovereign nation. Franklin stayed in Europe and was one of the first to go to London as a diplomat of the newly formed United States. Franklin then returned in 1785 to a new country, which was in complete legislative mayhem with the Articles of the Confederation in operation. He, along with a multitude of state representatives, including General George Washington, participated in the Philadelphia Convention in 1787, which we have named the 'Constitutional Convention.' Once again, Franklin's presence, his diplomacy, his boundless insight, and his exceptional worldwide reputation helped many members within that chamber, who were at great odds with one and other, come together as a central unit to outline our Constitution of the United States.

"The ratification of the Constitution almost failed when the debate of abolishing slavery consumed the divide between northern and southern states. Franklin was one of the chief arbiters that bridged that divide that helped all states reach a compromise. This of course became the three-fifths compromise that the north provisioned to prevent southern states from overwhelming the national vote with enslaved people casting votes on behalf of their slave-holder. An interesting note is that before dying in 1790, Benjamin Franklin submitted a petition to the United States Congress to abolish slavery in 1789. He was president of a group called the *Society for Promoting the Abolition of Slavery,* which he joined after he returned from Europe in 1785. Of the several essays he wrote, one popular piece was called *An Address to the Public* that boldly stated, 'Slavery is such an atrocious debasement of human nature.' These essays, along with the petition to Congress, would make anyone conclude that these were the acts of a man seeing the error of his ways at the end of his life because he was guilty for not abolishing slavery when the Declaration or Constitution was passed. Once we were a unified country with a solid form of government in place, Franklin knew abolishing slavery could now be accomplished with a national movement.

"And that is why he became a voice in favor of abolition at the end of his life. He knew humanity would remember that America failed when its first step was on the backs of others. This made us an imperfect nation from the start, which is something modern-day scholars use to deny admiration for the achievements of the founders. Franklin knew more than he ever let on and is known as one of the greatest patriots this country ever had. All those who made great contributions to the formation of our country are called 'Founding Fathers,' but Franklin, for all of his contributions, could very well be considered *the* Founding Father of our country."

"Impressed?" asked Henry.

"Very," replied Ethan, "I knew Franklin played an important part in the American Revolution. But the way you explain it, it sounds like much might not have happened if he was not there."

"Well, you have a point," said Henry. "It's important to know, Franklin was not for absolute separation until he returned from London in 1775. Franklin was seeking a compromise between both parties. He wanted his fellow Americans, as many started to identify themselves, and Englishmen to have a diplomatic relationship. He was never timid to point out the discretions on either side, which is what led him to appear in front of the Privy Council in 1774 after it was discovered that Franklin, from his own confession published on Christmas Day in December 1773, disclosed private letters from the governor of Massachusetts, Thomas Hutchinson, to the Massachusetts Assembly. The letters from the governor commented that no colonist would ever have the full rights of an Englishmen under Parliament's rule. When the patriots of the assembly saw those letters, they ignored Franklin's request to keep them private. Of course, they were published and, in the end, Franklin was publicly reprimanded for his actions.

"Timing is everything, and events took much longer to play out in that era, so consider this. Had Franklin been for Independence when sending the letters to the assembly in 1773, wouldn't he have just left London after they were published and avoid the lecture from the Privy Council? Yet, he publishes a letter that reveals he is responsible for the 'Hutchinson Affair,' stays in London, and is embarrassed in the court. A year later he returns to America.

"To prove my point even further, Thomas Jefferson told us in the last section of his own autobiography that he was given papers by Franklin when he was on his death bed in 1790. Jefferson thought those papers, which were letters, were not for him to keep, but Franklin insisted. After the death of Benjamin Franklin, Thomas reached out to William Temple Franklin, his grandson, who received all his grandfather's written works upon his passing. William quickly found Thomas and retrieved the papers, stating he was not sure whether they were copies or original.

"What makes this interesting is that Thomas Jefferson was reminiscing about this exchange thirty years later while writing his personal accounts, but what makes it profound is that with everything this man experienced, he was able to remember the context of the letters Benjamin

Franklin handed to him at his bedside in Philadelphia as if he still possessed them. The letters contained correspondences between Franklin, Lord Howe, and the British Ministry. The letters were negotiations to end the confrontation, which dated before the Declaration was passed. Thomas Jefferson stated in 1821 that after William took the papers from him, he never saw them published . . . and they never were.

"Now, consider Franklin's actions from his time in London to his return to Philadelphia. Franklin was all for compromise, but within a couple of months, on a particular day, he has a revelation and is for Independence. How does someone pivot like that on such an important question? Like I said, timing is everything, and it's amazing how it worked out for us."

"Yes, amazing," said Ethan. "And, that's great how all of it worked out for us, and this country. I still don't understand what any of that has to do with me, and I really don't get what that story has to do with the journal that has my signature at the bottom!"

Henry put his hand up, "Relax," he said. "I am giving you the bread crumbs. If you don't understand the cause, you will never understand the effect." Henry moved from the chair across from Ethan to the one on his right. "You are asking why that journal has your handwriting in it. Now I'm going to tell you why."

Ethan started to lean forward in his seat to come closer to Henry. His senses became heightened by his curiosity. His leg was trembling with excitement, or it could have been a reaction to the caffeine from the Kona. In either case, Ethan was poised to receive the answer.

"Remember I said Franklin changed his point of view upon returning to Philadelphia on a particular day?" Henry asked.

"Yes, I heard you say that."

"Franklin was influenced," said Henry. "Someone convinced him that Independence was the necessary route to undertake and that he should abandon trying to mend ties between the colonies and the Crown. He was told that not seeking Independence for the colonies would lead to more tyranny and devastation for the people of America as time went on. This person had the foresight to influence Franklin to be for total dissolve of the alliance to the British Empire. Do you have any questions?"

"Who convinced Franklin?" asked Ethan.

"Let me explain the *why* this happened." Henry said. "But before we do that, let's take a break. Get some air, use the rest room, and then we'll finish for today. I promise you, what I have to say next will change your life."

Chapter Eight

Franklin and the Vote

Taking a break from Henry's history lesson, Ethan stood outside to get some air. The time was approaching 7:00 p.m. and the sun was beginning to set in the distance. His frustration grew as time passed. He was seeking answers but so far all he received was history lessons. He wanted to be home, not locked in a coffee shop with his postman who just revealed the United States Post Office has been "monitoring" him since birth. Although he was caught off guard earlier, and he felt compelled to call the authorities, Ethan did not sense anything Henry said or did to this point posed a threat. As he slowly walked in the parking lot to stretch his muscles, Ethan contemplated the last thing Henry said, that *someone convinced Franklin*. "What does that mean?" he thought. What was more troubling was that when asked who that "someone" was, Henry stalled and put off answering the question. "Why would he do that," he whispered. Just then his phone buzzed.

Lauren: YOU OK? WHERE ARE YOU?

Ethan began feeling anxious. He lost track of time and didn't want to say exactly what was preventing him from being home. At the same time, he didn't want to lie to Lauren over something he was still not fully comprehending. After a couple of minutes passed, Ethan figured he'd tell a half-truth.

> **Ethan: Still at the coffee shop. I'm talking to Henry about something incredibly important. We're almost done. If you are hungry, start without me.**

> **Lauren: The postman?**

> **Ethan: Yes, the postman.**

> **Lauren: You're missing dinner with me so you can talk to our postman?**

> **Ethan: It's not what you think. It has to do with that prize I won. Something's not right, and I have questions. Henry seems to know about it and is helping me understand.**

> **Lauren: LOL Okay.**

Ethan walked back inside and shouted the moment he entered, "How much longer is this going to take? I'd like to get home to my wife."

"Shouldn't be much longer," said Henry, "I'll try to speed through this next part so you can go home."

Ethan went to the fridge to get water from the case. He looked up at Henry, held up the bottle, and asked, "Is it all right if I grab this?"

"No problem."

Ethan sat back down as Henry remained standing, and said "Now buckle up, this will blow your mind. I am going to tell you how the vote played out—the first time around."

"The first time around?" asked Ethan.

"Yes," said Henry, "the first-time Franklin, and the Second Continental Congress voted for the Declaration of Independence."

Henry began again, "When Franklin returned to America in 1775, he did not believe America Independence was the solution. He was not looking to engage the British Empire in an all-out war. Being a gifted chess player and having exercised the muscle of foresight, Franklin had a strong inclination of the various consequences that would befall his fellow countrymen if they took up arms in a revolution against the entire British fleet and failed. Franklin feared it would bring nothing but death to the countrymen he held dear to his heart and of whom he had been proud to represent as a national figure in Great Britain. Retaliation from England for a failed rebellion would most undoubtedly destroy the unique identities and the evolving nationalities that were becoming indigenous to the colonies that raised them. Some provinces had populations consisting of families in their fifth or sixth generation, and some had immigrants starting their first. A full engagement with the powers of Britain would forever sever ties between friends and families throughout the colonies and across the sea.

"Franklin feared that moving the fight out of Massachusetts, which to this point represented a microcosmic demonstration of our grievances with the Parliament, and expanding it to a rebellion stretching across the east coast risked an economic decline for the entire continent. This would entail unprecedented sacrifices from its citizens and private funding from fellow patriots during the conflict and after the fighting was over. Should America lose, the British monarch would most certainly reclaim any land not owned by a loyal subject to the King. Followed by new orders which would naturally be met with massive rejection from the citizenry, leading to more extreme acts of desperation from the secessionists against the men of the Royal Army. All of which would lead to anarchy.

"Franklin envisioned complete annihilation of the American colonies win or lose. During a confrontation of this magnitude could expose the land of America and the Empire as a fragile institution. Uncertain whether Britain's foreign adversaries would seek an alliance with the Americans to defeat a common foe or claim the land under their own banner only complicated the matter. Should the protection of the British Empire be removed, would Spain and France see it as an opportunity to fight their war on American soil to reclaim the land they lost during the Seven Years' War? Franklin could not say for sure and because he believed that a defeat of the British Empire or a defeat of the rebellion would make all colonies vulnerable, he sought reconciliation as the proper move.

"Now I know I'm going a little quick here, but do you understand what I'm trying to say?" Henry asked.

"I think so," said Ethan, "Benjamin Franklin returned to Pennsylvania in May of 75 and he was not for Independence even though many thought he was? That's where you are confusing me. So, then what was Franklin really doing if he wasn't for Independence when Congress convened?"

Henry pulled out the chair on Ethan's left, flipped it around so the back was against the table, and sat with his chest pressed against it. "Have you ever heard of the *Albany Plan of Union*?" he asked.

"No," said Ethan. "Should I have?"

Henry let out a grunt, "I guess its contribution was not profound enough to make it into our American History text books," he said. "But to my associates, it's an incredibly important moment in time."

"You see, when Franklin entered the Second Continental Congress, he was trying to complete the adoption of a twenty-year-old proposal that outlined a central governing body of representatives for all colonies which put a single representative in Parliament. Franklin was the chief architect of this proposal when it was drafted during the Albany Congress of 1754. Almost twenty years after it was dead on arrival in nearly every colony, Franklin saw an opportunity to reintroduce the idea, convince the delegates to vote in favor of it, then use it as a bargaining tool, with the assistance of some of his closest friends in London, to end hostilities and bring a peace between the British–American colonies and their King."

"Wait," Ethan shouted. "Franklin drafted an outline of government for the colonies in 1754?"

"That's correct," said Henry.

"And they called it *The Albany Plan*?"

Henry smiled, finding the question amusing, "Yes, because it was written during the Congress that met in Albany, New York, and they were too lazy to call it anything else," he said with a slight snicker. "No, I'm teasing. Franklin gave it that name, but it wasn't in 1754 when it was originally drafted. It was in 1766 when he prepared to testify against *The Stamp Act* before a committee in London. Should they have asked for his suggestion on a means of calming the rising discontent from the colonists, Franklin would have offered this outline of a national government. In his notes, he titled it, *Albany Plan*."

"Why did they meet?" asked Ethan.

"Well, we don't have time to cover everything about it tonight," Henry said. "Also, I'm not the expert on the Congress of 1754. But as Franklin stated in his autobiography, had Parliament agreed to the terms of the plan it, quote, *'would have avoided the bloody contest it occasioned.'* Meaning, we would not have had an American Revolution. Many historians and public figures of the time, including John Adams and Thomas Jefferson, have agreed with that sentiment."

Ethan nodded his head, "Now that's interesting. America might not have existed had Benjamin Franklin succeeded in passing his Albany Plan."

"Correct." Henry then reached out and placed his hand on Ethan's shoulder. "Now listen very carefully to what I am about to say next. You have never heard this story before."

Henry continued, "As much as Franklin worked at finding the right people to back his reimagined Albany Plan, he wasn't getting enough support to bring the proposal to Congress. Such a commitment required instructions from the local legislatures. In the spring of 1775, the cries of liberty and freedom from many citizens was acting as the North Star for some of the delegates and their colonies. Also, some believed that enacting the Albany Plan would overthrow their powers, which had been their chief concern twenty years earlier. The wealthiest colony, Virginia, felt that any new government should no longer be beholden to Parliament. They preferred to fight for the freedom to create their own government rather than beg for one.

"Before the winter break, Franklin could only get a commitment from Pennsylvania, New York, Delaware, and Maryland, but decided to wait and give the other delegates more time to realize his solution was the best means to peace.

"By the end of spring of 1776, Franklin's proposal had yet to become popular enough to bring to the floor, and little traction was being made with the more stubborn delegates. Now, Franklin was not acting as a Loyalist within the Congress. He did not prevent or vote against necessary resolutions that helped his countrymen. He was just not as empathetic to the call for Independence at this juncture. He and Adams formed their union but Franklin never encouraged, nor discouraged, any sentiments Adams shared on separation. Franklin's true gift in discourse, as you will inevitably discover, was based on Socratic methods. Meaning, he would ask questions, never speak in absolutes, and would lead a person to the conclusion he wanted them to go to. This method worked most of the time. But for John Adams, his heart and mind were unyielding, he wanted Independence.

"Now, remember how I said with support from Franklin, John Adams was able to maneuver through the Congress and influence the call for Independence? Well, in this scenario, since Franklin was not for Independence, John Adams depended more on his former congressional ally Patrick Henry, and both were still able to achieve the approval for Independence, from the Williamsburg legislature, which arrived in Philadelphia by Richard Henry Lee in June of 1776. Franklin excused himself from any participation in the creation of the Declaration, given that its composition alone would be considered an act of treason. As he saw it, how could the members of Parliament have trust in him as an ally seeking peace if he was associated with a slanderous document?

"On July 2, the voting on the Declaration started. With everything that Franklin had done up to that moment, it led no one to believe that he would vote against it if all the other colonies were for it. When Pennsylvania was called to vote, Franklin stood up and said, 'Nay.'"

Ethan's hand jumped off the table, "Wait?" he shouted. Seconds of silence passed as he closed his eyes to replay in his mind what he thought he just heard. While holding his hand out, towards Henry, Ethan asked, "What?"

"Yes," said Henry, "Benjamin Franklin gave a no vote for the motion on American Independence."

"But that's not possible," Ethan said. "Everyone knows he voted for Independence. His signature is on the Declaration!"

"Relax, hold on a second. Let me finish the story."

Henry continued, "The chamber erupted in anger. A few were relieved and voiced their honest opposition to Independence. Others were relieved in secret. As it turned out, after Pennsylvania voted no, Georgia, South Carolina, Maryland, Delaware, and New York changed their vote to be against the Declaration of Independence on July 2, 1776."

Ethan was staring at Henry in disbelief. His mouth dropped. "I don't understand," he said. "You want me to believe that *originally* the Declaration was voted down? Then, how is there a Fourth of July celebrating the *passing* of the Declaration?"

"You'll see in a few minutes," explained Henry. "Now, we don't know . . .."

"Hold on a sec," Ethan said. He looked down at the table as his phone was buzzing with an incoming text.

Lauren: Good night, I'm going to bed. BTW I saw the doctor. I need to figure out why I've been breaking out so much since the wedding. I will get results tomorrow.

Ethan: Goodnight. Okay. Sorry, I'm still here. This went a little long. I'll explain everything tomorrow.

Lauren: Whatever, it's fine.

Ethan: I love you.

"Is everything okay?" asked Henry.

"Sure," said Ethan. "My wife is going to bed a little early it seems. Okay, I'm sorry for interrupting you before. Go ahead."

Henry started again, "Now, we don't know everything, but after the vote, there was so much confusion and hostilities among the delegates that a duel was attempted between Samuel Adams of Massachusetts and John Dickinson of Pennsylvania outside of the State House. That altercation brought too much attention for the local military to ignore. They confiscated the Declaration of Independence, and some delegates were incarcerated. A couple of days later, Governor John Penn recommended that the men be charged with treason, a decision which could have been considered as an act of desperation to remain in good standing with the King and Parliament. In the past, the members of the local assembly, as well as the governor, were accused of being too mild to these rebellious constituents. British Loyalists were outraged for allowing these traitors to assemble in Philadelphia all these years, and because of this uprising, they demanded for the governor to carry out harsh punishment. After the detainment of the delegates and the language in the Declaration became public knowledge outside of the city, Governor Penn sent dispatches to New York to have General William Howe come to Philadelphia to help with the arraignment of these traitors.

"General Charles Cornwallis was on his way to New York to join Howe after failing to capture Charleston. When word was received that Howe was coming to Philadelphia, he too made his way to the city. Howe and Cornwallis saw their opportunity to break the spirit of all rebels. The punishment was swift as they sentenced all the congressional delegates from Massachusetts to be hung for starting the insurgency, which was provoking the rest of the colonies to breakaway from Great Britain. After the political voices were silenced, the next target was General George Washington. Howe organized the whole British Army to corner and capture George Washington off Long Island. Somehow, they succeeded, and a public hanging was held in New York City where Washington was put to death for leading the militia that killed *innocent* British men. They also executed Thomas Jefferson, Roger Sherman, and Robert Livingston in the capital of their home colony for composing the treasonous Declaration. These hangings were done for their symbolism. The cries for revolution retreated immediately. The remaining men who participated in the illegal assembly lost their lands. They were cast out by Loyalists and their closest allies prior to July, now avoided them out of necessity."

"This is crazy," said Ethan. "What is this, Henry? What's with this gruesome depiction of what could have happened if Franklin voted down Independence?"

"But this is what happened," said Henry.

"No, it's not what happened," Ethan shouted. "It's not! Franklin did not, *not* vote for Independence. Washington, Adams, and Jefferson were *not* hung. They each went on to be Presidents of the United States. And, and," Ethan stuttered as his emotions were getting the best of him. He paused to collect his thoughts. As he gazed around the room he said, "and, you're wrong. This did not happen."

Henry lifted his hand again as a signal for Ethan to relax. "What I'm trying to tell you Ethan is that this is what *originally* happened. When humanity had its first go at it, this was the sequence of events that transpired in Philadelphia in the summer of July 1776. This was our true and natural destiny."

"Henry!"

"Ethan!" Henry replied by raising his voice over Ethan's. "This. Did. Happen," he said as his drove his finger onto the tabletop.

The room was silent as both Ethan and Henry glared across the table at each other. Henry was frustrated because he knew there was more Ethan had to know. If Ethan was unwilling to listen and absorb the information without having an open mind, Henry knew he would not be able to give the proper background to explain the journal, still placed in the middle of the table.

"I'm sorry. I wasn't yelling at you," Henry said, as got out of the chair to stretch. He lifted his arms over his head and twisted his neck to crack it a little to ease the tension. "You know, your reaction just now reminded me of my initial response when I heard the story decades ago. It was difficult for me too but, I can't go back and forth with you on every detail. I still haven't answered your pending question about the journal, and if you would permit me, I will tell you what happened after Franklin's rejection of Independence and the chain of events that caused destiny to change to what you and everyone alive today knows as the *Birth of America*."

Ethan raised his finger and was about to speak, but Henry cut him off and said, "and, yes, why you have the journal."

"Okay, I will listen and let you finish."

"All right," Henry said, "Here it is."

He began again, "After the hangings, Benjamin Franklin was praised locally by those loyal to the Crown and at the same time, ostracized by the purists in London for not turning down the delegation post from

Pennsylvania when it was presented to him. And because he had participated in this *Congress*, this unlawful assembly, and was on record as not objecting to every motion that carried the potential harm towards the Royal Army, he was found guilty for confiding with the enemy and committing crimes detrimental to the sovereignty of his majesty's colonies. However, since he possessed such a high level of notoriety among the members of Parliament, they reduced his sentence to what was pretty much house arrest, town arrest, till death. The local assembly would not allow him to leave the colony under any circumstances. He was shunned by many who used to be his closest acquaintances and he was not able to associate with the various social groups he was a part of, even those he started. Franklin was never the same again.

"Now Franklin did write his autobiography, but since he had so much more time on his hands, he expanded on it. In this version, he wrote how his sole regret in life was '*being the single person responsible for the lifestyle all Americans were living today.*' Franklin regretted seeing the strength of the British monarch twisting harder on all colonies and removing many personal freedoms. He wrote, '*If I could do it all over again, I would have voted for the Declaration and fought for the greater cause I was too naive and arrogant to see. Now those who held the torch of liberty are dead and I have been spared to witness the retribution.*'

"Toward the end of his life, he did try one more time to create some sort of reconciliation with the Parliament. He wrote a letter to the King, begging, not for forgiveness for himself, but for the country. Franklin wrote something to the effect of '*Embrace us as loyal subjects, not as foreign kin. Release the shackles of the heavy burden weighing on our shoulders, preventing us to excel and expand the wealth for his majesty. America could be the strongest component of the Empire so its peaceful reign can bless this world until the return of the Almighty himself. This I beg of you.*'

"That plea was published every year on the anniversary of Franklin's death. It was a reminder to anyone contemplating a revolution against their

King and country. For those who wanted Independence always saw it as the final plea from the *traitor of 76* who recognized the error of his ways only when his life served no purpose to anyone, not even himself."

As Henry concluded his thought, he paused and asked, "Hold up, what time is it?"

Ethan reached for his phone, "It's 8:05," he said.

"Okay, how about we order some Chinese food? You said your wife was going to sleep, so another hour shouldn't be a problem, right?"

"No," Ethan sighed, "no problem."

Henry clapped his hands and said, "Excellent! Give me your phone. I'll call it in. It's on me. What do you want?"

"General Tso's chicken, with pork fried rice."

Henry's eyebrows lifted. "Hey, that sounds good. I'm ordering two of those."

Ethan excused himself to use the restroom. When he returned, the coffee shop workers were back and so was the attractive woman from earlier, only now she was wearing dark blue jeans and a casual black button-down shirt. She and Henry were conversing when her eye caught Ethan. Henry swung around and waved Ethan over. Henry then held his arm out as to welcome him into the circle. "Ethan I'd like for you to meet Audrey."

"Hello, nice to meet you." Ethan then looked at Henry, "What's going on?" he asked.

"Oh, well, we're going to let these guys clean up the store for the night," Henry said. "The food should be here in a few minutes. We'll let everyone go home, so you and I can eat in peace and finish what we need to. But I wanted you to meet Audrey. She's going to help us out as we go along."

"Go along?"

"It's nice to meet you Ethan," Audrey said, "Henry has told me so much about you, and from the other things I know, I feel like I've known you forever." Ethan's defenses were weakened immediately as Audrey reached her hand out to shake his. "I look forward to seeing you soon," she said.

Ethan was tongue-tied. Awkwardly he muttered, "Nice, so do I."

"Okay," Audrey said. "Well, I'm going to go, and Henry, everything is set for this weekend."

"Great, thank you," said Henry. After Audrey left and the door closed, Henry turned to Ethan with a grin. "Smooth, Ethan," he said.

"Shut up," said Ethan. "It's nothing like that," he said. "It's just she remains me of Lauren when I first courted her. Or as she would put it, 'stalked' her."

"Ah, I see."

As the night crew finished with the cleanup, Henry pointed to the back of the room and said, "Let's set up in the corner. That way we can quickly clean up and leave out the side door when we're done."

"How much more of this is there, Henry?" Ethan asked.

"This?" Henry asked.

"This story," said Ethan. "How much more of this story is there?"

"Oh, it's about to come together. I promise."

Chapter Nine

The First Trip

The Roasting Plant staff left for the evening, leaving Ethan and Henry alone in the single lit corner of the café. Not a word was spoken between them as they both arranged the takeout containers of General Tso chicken and pork fried rice. Henry reached deep into the large brown paper bag to grab a few packets of soy sauce. "Can you get me a mustard?" Ethan asked. After two failed attempts to extract the condiment of his choice, Henry became impatient and turned it over to let all the contents drop to the table. He picked up his two packets and tossed them to Ethan. Henry was just about to eat, but paused to observe Ethan while he continued to prepare his meal. Ethan mixed the pork fried rice with mustard and then spread it across the plate, creating a bed. He then placed the chicken on top and lightly sprinkled drops of soy sauce over the whole dish. It was a work of art, and Henry was amazed with the attention Ethan gave to his dinner presentation.

"Looks beautiful," Henry said sarcastically.

"Thanks!"

"Do you mind if we try to talk while we eat?"

With a mouth full of food, Ethan nodded.

"Okay. We've discussed the original events that unfolded in July 1776 and the effects of Benjamin Franklin voting down the resolution for American Independence."

"Yes," said Ethan. "I didn't forget. It was thirty minutes ago."

"Well, it's important that you understand both sides of the story," said Henry. "Before I could tell you that version, I had to remind you of our history as we know it today. Remember, I told you Franklin originally voted against the motion for Independence." Henry could see Ethan was listening, but was unsure if he was processing the information as he attended to his plate. Henry felt the need to repeat himself, "Originally, do you understand?"

Ethan dropped his fork. "Oh my god, Henry. Yes, I understand." He then used air quotes to mock Henry, "'Originally,'" he said, "Benjamin Franklin did not vote for Independence but everyone today knows he voted for it, and the Declaration was passed on July 2."

"Very good."

"There was a cover-up," said Ethan, "a conspiracy."

"Yes," Henry said, then paused with a perplexed look. "Wait, what? No. There was no cover-up or a conspiracy. The events you and everyone else know did in fact happen. What I'm trying to tell you is that without someone assisting Franklin, the vote for independence and the birth of this nation would have not come to fruition."

"Ahhh," Ethan said with a smile, "I was testing you. I know you said before that someone helped Franklin, but you still haven't connected all the dots for me." Henry gave Ethan a look of relief but before he spoke, Ethan held up his finger to conclude, "nor have you fully explained why I've spent the last three hours here tonight sitting through a history lesson!"

"Yes, understood," said Henry. "Let me bring everything together for you. Let your mind wonder for a moment. You may have a lot of questions but I want to let you know now, this story has been passed on and retold. I'm sharing with you all the information I have and will most likely be unable to fill in the blanks. It's best that you accept it and move on, try not to dwell on the particulars."

With a shrug of his shoulders, and mouth full of food, Ethan said, "Whatever you say, Henry."

"After Franklin's nay vote, I mentioned how the British Empire came down on the colonies. Before the turn of the 18th century, all thirteen colonies were now defined as individual countries with royally appointed ministers, whose unwavering obedience was solidified with huge plots of land and a salary no man would ever risk losing. They had one simple rule; no country could ever seek an alliance with another, and all laws for each legislature were to be ministered by Parliament. Individual treaties were created which explicitly stated that any attempt of a confederation in any degree would be treated as a revolt against the King and an act of war against the other members in British America, which meant they could be forced to fight if so ordered. You can imagine how that kept not only the government, but the citizens, in line.

"Now, Franklin's nay vote did not just prevent the Revolutionary War and bring down the full might of the British Empire to suppress the American spirit. The absence of the Revolutionary War in the course of human events, also prevented some of history's most memorable and significant moments that transpired after.

"For you see, our Revolution was a small pebble in a still pond, that started a ripple, and sparked a reaction throughout the world. The first and biggest reaction was the offspring of the American Revolution; the French Revolution. In 1775, there was already friction within France but the catalyst was the debt incurred from our war. Much like how Britain flamed liberty in Americans with the Stamp Act and those acts that succeeded the Seven Years War, France followed similar overreach to provoke the people. Only, their debt was compounded with the Seven Years' War and the

American Revolution. After the Revolution was completed and America was a new nation, it inspired droves of French men and women to unite under the cause of liberty for themselves. If our Revolution was prevented, the spirit of liberty would have been abated, and as a result, we can determine that the French Revolution would not have happened."

Ethan lifted his hand to stop Henry. "Excuse me, Henry. I'm sorry but if you are going to tell me a fable, it would be better if it made sense. I mean, 'we can determine.'"

Henry closed his eyes and took a deep breath. "Well, I'm glad to see you are paying attention," he said. "The French Revolution was the by-product of the American Revolution for two reasons. One, was their error in handling the debt after the war. Second, which is more significant, the American Revolution proved the idea that liberty can be achieved by the people and it was not something granted by a monarchy. The war was fought and won by men and women from all levels of society, including farmers, blacksmiths, shop-owners, and carpenters, to name a few. The victory, and the establishment of America by the men and women with these *simple* lives, inspired others to turn their revolutionary ideas from talk, to action."

Ethan, reclined in his seat, reflected for a moment. "I see," he said.

Henry continued, "Third, and perhaps more relevant to our discussion, when our Declaration of Independence was signed, Benjamin Franklin was dispatched to France to request financial support and establish a military alliance. Franklin was the best person to adhere to the style of French politics, which ran at a slower pace and were influenced more by social encounters. Franklin, being the most popular person in the world, drew a lot of attention and very large crowds. His libertarian views, combined with the movement he was representing, indirectly influenced many people. He was not over there trying to divide the country. He was trying to align with it. So now remove the American Revolution, the Declaration, and Franklin's influences from the French Revolution equation and you're left with the simplest answer. If you're a student of history what you must do is play it back and remove a moment along the timeline of events. Then you look at what would have come next, and if what you removed is essential for that event to take place, meaning there could not have been an influence greater or equal to it, you can conclude what would have proceeded next did not happen. Action and reaction, cause and effect. This is how we know."

"I understand," said Ethan. "That all makes sense. I'm just having a hard time, you know, accepting this version of history you are telling me."

"Which is why I said earlier, it would pay not to question too much. Just let me tell you the story, and then we can talk about it another time."

"Very well," said Ethan.

Henry continued, "So with the failed attempt at a revolution in America, the British tightened their control on the citizens of the colonies. It made people in other countries glad to *not* be under the British rule and it made them relieved to be wherever they were. The call for individual freedom was diminished around the world for the time being.

"How did the world progress over time? That we do not know. Was there a World War during the 1900's? Did Churchill defeat the Nazi's? And for that matter, without debt from World War I, did Germany end up with Hitler? The formation of these countries and those in the Middle East, is completely unknown. What we do know for sure is that by the year 2020, Great Britain was still the proprietor of much of the land in North America, including British Canada. We know there was a Spanish providence where Mexico is currently located, but everything north belonged to the United Republic of Great Britain."

"2020?" challenged Ethan. "We went from Benjamin Franklin, to no American Revolution, to stronger British rule in the colonies, to no French Revolution, and now we move ahead to the year 2020?"

"Yes," said Henry. "Like I said earlier, I don't have many of the answers."

"I see," said Ethan. "Okay, I apologize. I just wanted to make sure I understood what you were saying and that I didn't miss anything. You went from 1775 to 2020. I thought I might have tuned you out."

Henry laughed, "Don't worry. I'll make sure you don't miss anything. This is going to sound like something out of a science fiction movie, but with the journal as my evidence, you will believe what I tell you occurred in some capacity."

"In 2020, the United Republic of Great Britain was well advanced in many technologies. I don't know how the lifestyle differed from how we live today, but in that year, they were advanced enough to begin the early stages of a project for the exploration of Mars, which included using the Moon as a launching platform. A Moon-base was viewed as a cost-saving venture because of the lower gravity, which would allow the 'EMDrive' propulsion system to thrust a spacecraft out of Earth's orbit. They used 3-D printers on the Moon's surface to build huge facilities, environmental systems, and most of the spacecraft parts. However, the transportation of raw materials to the Moon was still only viable through small and slow cargo ships. The program called for research into the possibility of a faster, more efficient way to transport material, so a department was started to research teleportation.

"In Pennsylvania, outside of Philadelphia, a group of scientists and engineers began research on a system that would teleport objects from the Earth to the Moon. A few years into their test phase, they succeeded in sending an object across two buildings with electromagnetic energy or lightening. Of course, word got out to the financiers about the one successful test, and as a result, the government pushed hard to establish the receiver on the Moon and start transfers immediately. Toward the end of 2025, that lab in Pennsylvania had become a fully operating government military base with a huge system in place to transmit or send objects to the Moon.

"Here is where our tale turns. Going back to the days and years after Franklin's death, an underground group was formed called *The Franklin Fighters* of all things. Much like other social groups of the time, Freemasons, and so on, these Franklin Fighters were a living movement in homage to Benjamin Franklin's dying regret: voting against Independence. But unlike the Freemasons, this group was more aggressive in their demonstrations. After Franklin's death, the Second of July became an anniversary for this group. To celebrate they caused havoc in colonies that joined Pennsylvania in turning down Independence and sometimes it got very violent. There were arrests, there were convictions, and there was death as well.

"The movement had to go more underground and become a secret society. They became more agitating than violent on their anniversaries as decades passed. In 1876, the group tried to overtake the Governor's mansion in Williamsburg, Virginia. In 1976, they caused a week-long riot in Jamestown, New York City, and Philadelphia. Even though you can say they failed, it seemed to light a spark with a considerable number of people and the organization began to grow stronger. The advent of the Internet only helped spread the cause of the group, and by the year 2025, there were millions of members throughout the nations."

"Fascinating," Ethan remarked, "Were the Franklin Fighters a political group as well? Couldn't they have just infiltrated the government with elected officials and get change that way?"

"I don't know," said Henry. "I don't know what type of government they had, but that doesn't matter because you'll be more interested to know who was a member."

"Oh yeah?" Ethan replied, "A member of Parliament?"

"No, no," said Henry. "Here let me finish this last part. You'll love this, because back in the teleportation lab in Pennsylvania, there were two lead scientists, and it just so happens that one of them was a member of the Franklin Fighters."

Ethan started laughing, "Of course! Of course, one was," he said, "and a *teleportation* device to boot! Okay, this is getting out of hand, but interesting. Please go ahead."

"Hold on," Henry said, "it gets better."

Henry continued, "Now again, one was a Franklin Fighter named Louis or Lou. He was near the age of fifty when this started. About thirty days before the first lunar teleportation test Lou was working very late and alone in the lab. When suddenly a flash of lighting appeared outside near the platform. It was a clear evening so he was concerned that something just broke around the transporter. He checked it out and didn't see anything wrong with the machine, but as he made his way around the area he stumbled on a tile near the transporter. Lou recognized the tile from the stockpile they used to absorb the electromagnetic pulses. There was a little heat emanating from the tile and Lou noticed there was writing on it that read 'Ad Astra.' It's Latin for 'To the stars.' Lou concluded that the someone must have left a couple of tiles around and it caused an electromagnetic event that created a spark. With nothing appearing to be wrong with the multi-billion-dollar expenditure, a small tile with writing on it was of no interest to Lou and he tossed it away.

"A month later they were ready to test the transporter. A lot of investors and high-ranking military personnel were present. Lou's superior always intended to send the flag of the Republic as the first object to be transported. When the Major General, who did not have much faith in the machine, saw the flag being used like this, he put a stop to the scientist's action immediately. 'If you are going to destroy something, destroy something of yours,' the General ordered. The scientist, in a panic, grabbed one of the magnetic tiles from his workstation and wrote 'Ad Astra' on it. When Lou saw this, he recognized the quick scribble was on the exact same tile he saw weeks prior.

"The tile was secured in a container, which was then placed in the center of the transporter platform 500 yards from the main lab. The platform was fifty feet in diameter and was above a silo. From beneath the platform, a small but concentrated blast of energy was to be emitted to send the object toward the Moon to be captured by the receiver. The order was given and a bright flash of blue and white light shot through the silo and into the sky. The object cleared off the platform; however, those at the receiver station reported a split-second flash, but nothing arrived. In the end, the test was considered a failure. Lou and his superior had a moment to discuss the event. When Lou asked whether he was the one who left the tile by the transporter thirty days prior, the agitated doctor dismissed him.

"Fast-forward to around January of 2026, on another clear evening, Lou saw another lightning strike by the transporter and found another tile. Only this time the tile read 'Feb 20, 2026, partial eclipse, it's the darkness' signed in Lou's handwriting. Just as you were a little concerned when you saw your signature in the journal, he was freaked out too seeing his signature on this tile. He was still unable to reason on how this object appeared with a date from the future. If by chance this arrived from a future point in time, Lou was smart enough to know that such an outlandish hypothesis would have him mocked and removed from the project.

"Lou went about his business for the next thirty days, then on the night of the February 20, he scheduled a test with a couple of low-level techs. He waited for the partial eclipse on the left side of the Moon to reach its apex and he fired the machine. If he was right, the object would be gone without a trace and sure enough the tile never reached the Moon's base. Lou outwardly shared the feeling of disappointment with the rest of his staff, but internally he was ecstatic for he had just stumbled on the one thing man has pondered about for all time: the ability to travel through it."

"Time out!" shouted Ethan, "Really? This is where we've been going with this whole story, time travel?"

"Pretty cool," said Henry.

"Wow, Henry. I mean, wow! This is going into a realm of delusion I can't even begin to comprehend." Ethan looked across the table and saw how quickly he was upsetting Henry by his teasing. "I'm sorry," Ethan said. "You're a great story teller, but to understand what it is you want me take out of it, I just do not know. I've been here for three and a half hours waiting for the punch line, and I guess you just hit it—time travel."

"It's important to know these things," Henry said. "Because if you don't know this story, nothing after will ever carry weight. You will never truly appreciate the task, or risk, before us. The risk is great—if we fail to succeed in meeting the mandate, life as we know it, your loved ones, your friends, would be gone. As fast as if someone flipped a light switch, everything would go dark." Henry gave Ethan a chance to respond but Ethan remained silent. "Let me bring this all together for you," he said.

"Lou spent night after night alone trying to determine the exact properties that caused the event. He finally concluded that the darkest part of the lunar eclipse, the umbra, created a wormhole for the electromagnetic stream to travel through. It was looping around the outskirt of the Moon and returning to its place of origin on Earth. The wormhole effect was based on the attraction of tiny molecules, called dark-matter. Now, dark-matter makes up over 25 percent of our universe. It's in bunches and no light emanates from within it. When Earth's shadow is cast during the eclipse, and blocks the radiation from the Sun, those dark-matter particles appear in their smallest form. Lou's research led him to determine that the greater the umbra's magnitude, the more dark-matter appears. And the stronger the electromagnetic pulse, the more dark-matter particles are pulled in to create the wormhole. The size of the wormhole would dictate how far back in time an object could travel.

"Now pay attention, this is all I know about this next part, so please do not dwell on the particulars, I beg you. The year 2026 marked the two hundred and fiftieth anniversary of Franklin's nay vote. Because the Franklin Fighters felt their members were greater in size than ever before, they were not going to risk waiting another fifty years to launch their scheme of overthrowing the government. On May 15, 2026, a public protest started in

Williamsburg, Virginia. This protest alerted the national defense to be on guard for similar organized mobs throughout the coming months leading up to July.

"These protests started getting worldwide attention, and its leaders were becoming popular on the news and web. Many were calling for a new revolution and many others, who were just as unhappy as the rebels, began protesting. On July 1, mass riots occurred in the cities of Philadelphia, Boston, New York, and elsewhere. It reached a boiling point too fast for anyone to control. There was gunfire and homemade bombs, which forced the military to respond with deadly force to end the conflict.

"From his lab, Lou saw the events unfold on television. During the live broadcast, Lou had an insane idea: he was going to prevent all of this from ever happening. He knew the protesters were going to lose any fight with the military, and the causalities would be great. However, he knew of a time when the common man had a chance and figured he could save the lives, remove the hate, and change the world for the better. He saw a full eclipse was set to take place in two weeks. He calculated how much energy he would have to produce to open a wormhole great enough to travel back approximately 251 years.

"Being thirty miles east of Philadelphia, Lou was now feeling a sense of a higher purpose to his life. He used the riots in town as an excuse to stay near the lab. It was a military base, so no one found it odd. As the days drew near, Lou knew he'd have only one chance at this. He couldn't test it; he figured the energy used was going to blackout the entire east coast. If he attempted to test this before July 18, it would definitely bring attention.

"When the faithful evening arrived, Lou inputted his calculations into the computer, started up the machine, and set out to the transport platform. As the system was in countdown, an intern noticed where Lou was headed, and raced out to stop him. Lou tried to calm him down and say it was all right, but the intern started screaming for help. Two officers on night watch began running over. Lou punched the young intern to knock him down and made a mad dash for the platform. The officers were a greater distance away and still did not understand what was going on. The young intern got back up and screamed for the officers to stop him. They warned Lou they would fire on him if he continued. Lou did not stop. One officer took a shot and caught his left hip. Lou stumbled on to the platform. He then reached into his pocket, pulled out a remote trigger, and activated the mechanism."

Henry stopped talking and just stared at Ethan. Several second of silence passed, until Ethan shouted "And?"

"The rest is the history as we know it today."

Ethan was shocked. "Wait, that's it?" he said. "That's it? A scientist from the future went back in time and changed our past to what we know it to be today? He, Lou, convinced Franklin to vote for the Declaration of Independence, which started the Revolutionary War?"

"Hey!" said Henry, "I must have told it right because when the story was relayed to me the first time, it took me days to understand what it all meant."

"And he gets shot, too!" shouted Ethan. "Let's not forget that and let's still not forget you failed, after hours of lessons and stories, you have failed to explain to me why I have this book!" Henry stood up out of his chair, walked over to Ethan and put his hand on his shoulder.

"When that scientist, Lou went back in time, we call that the 'first trip,' and he recorded what he was able to do. Lou's writings focused on revealing to Franklin how time travel was achieved. He worked with Franklin to ensure that the facts would be revealed only to those involved when the time came. Lou was smart enough to conclude that his interaction with Franklin was changing the history of the world. With that change came a few possibilities. One, the change from British control might turn out to be more horrific and would have to be undone. Two, the change in history would be positive and the world would be a better place for it. And three . . . this is where you are involved. The event having changed the true destiny of our existence would create a paradox; one that would have to be replayed to remain permanent in the altered timeline."

"Replay it? To be permanent?" asked Ethan. "Why would you have to replay a moment in time? That doesn't make any sense to me. Of all the time travel theories I have ever heard, nowhere have I read if you saved President Lincoln, you must go back and save him over and over again."

"Well, this is no longer being explained as theoretical physics or played out in a science fiction story," said Henry. "This is now proven from what we have learned. The entity responsible for the time alteration will forever be connected to it in a *causality loop*. Thanks to assistance from Einstein I can mathematically explain it like this: A, which is Lou, goes back in time and confronts Franklin, Subject B, which then creates this reality: C. A acts with B and creates C. If we remove A from the equation, what does C become? That's not something we even want to find out. It is essential that the subject A meets B to ensure that C endures. Ethan, you are involved in the greatest moment in the history of the world. I don't think you have realized that yet."

"You're trying to tell me that the reason I received the letters and the journal and the reason I have been here all night was for you to say that I was involved in the birth of our nation?" asked Ethan.

"In a word, yes," said Henry.

"That I was the scientist who went back in time?"

"Well, yes and no," said Henry. "No, you will not become a scientist because your life has gone down a completely different path in this *altered* timeline. But yes, you are the person who helped Benjamin Franklin change his opinion and vote for Independence. The only thing is, *you*, the person sitting here in this cafe has not yet achieved this."

"What do you mean, *yet*?" asked Ethan, "Hold on, back up. You said the event may have to be replayed? What does that mean?"

Henry pulled a chair closer to Ethan and placed his left hand on top of Ethan's. Henry took a deep breath and said, "For Franklin to vote for Independence, for this world to exist, and for your loved ones to exist, Benjamin Franklin will have to meet you and you will have to meet him."

Ethan let out a laugh, "Henry, you are out of your damn mind. Do you know that?"

"Ethan, we have been involved in your entire life for this connection to occur," Henry said. "You will befriend Benjamin Franklin and assist him in a very volatile time in our history. From your friendship, Franklin will go on to become one of, if not the greatest, founders in our country's history. And in nineteen months, we are going to have to send you back to fulfill this remarkable duty."

"Sure, whatever you say.".

"I'm quite serious, Ethan. Myself, Audrey, and some others are members of a division of the post office that's been devoted to this one event." Henry picked the journal up from the table. "This journal is yours. This journal was yours and you used it to record your interactions with Benjamin Franklin from his return to Philadelphia in 1775 to his departure for France in 1776. You did it for this country, and you must do it again."

"That journal is blank, Henry," said Ethan. "Look, it's late. I'm tired and want to go home. Can I have my blank journal back?"

Henry reached out to hand Ethan the journal, but as he was about to grab it, Henry pulled it back, "Do you believe anything I just told you?"

"About Franklin voting down the Declaration, causing a world without an America, which leads a scientist in 2026 to discover time travel, only to use it to come back in time to convince Franklin to vote for the Declaration, creating this world we live in?"

"Yes?"

"Ah, no," said Ethan. "Sorry, it's a great story. One I hope to retell someday, but I don't buy a word of it. Again, it's late. Can I please go now?"

Henry handed Ethan the journal back. "Okay, I'm going to give you a couple of days to think this over, but I'm confident you'll be back here soon to discuss your part in American history."

"Sounds great," Ethan said with a smirk. "You, me, and hey, let's invite Lou and Franklin as well. Oh, and Audrey can join us too, okay?" Ethan turned and headed for the door, "Have a good night, Henry."

"Good night, Ethan."

Chapter Ten

March 23, 1775: Arrival

The next morning when Ethan awoke, he found a note on the kitchen counter.

Hello babe, I have been very patient with you wanting to take some weeks for yourself and enjoy some time off from working. But today you are doing nothing but job hunting. That is your job today. Fill out the resumes on the search sites and print them out. I don't care that you were out all night, I care that you had the time to be out all night, and have nowhere to go today.

Ethan stopped reading the note and tossed it back on the counter. After what Henry told him he got very little sleep. Although he told Henry he did not believe a word of it, on the drive home, Ethan started to contemplate on the possibility of there being a chance of legitimacy. The fact that Henry revealed this side of him, after all of these years, mixed with the depths and details he went into, worried Ethan. He was in no mood to be passive aggressively chastised for his perceived lack of commitment to finding new employment. He snatched his phone and started texting Lauren.

Ethan: Good morning.

Waiting for a response, he started to make his morning coffee. As the water brewed Ethan peered into the dining room where he tossed the satchel and journal. His mind was pondering a thousand questions that only brought on a thousand more. "I can't do this to myself," Ethan thought. He rubbed the sides of his head to release the tension. He started to think about the last thing Henry was telling him, that this journal was something he did write. "But, the pages are blank," Ethan asserted to himself. While the hot water was dispensing, Ethan took a step toward the dining room to reexamine the pages of the journal again when his phone vibrated back on the counter.

Lauren: Good morning. Late night? I saw you sleeping in the office. What time did you finally get in?

Ethan: A little after ten. I didn't want to wake you, so I slept on the sofa.

Aggressively touching each letter, Ethan started typing the response he envisioned: *BTW I don't need to be reminded that I should start updating my resume. I had every intention but last night Henry was telling me this story about . . ..* While typing, the phone vibrated again.

Lauren: Did you get my note?

In a sarcastic tone, Ethan said aloud, "Did I get your *noooote*? Yeah, I got your note!" Ethan then let out a sigh and with better judgment, he deleted the text he drafted. To keep the peace between them, he simply responded.

Ethan: Yes, I got it. I'm going to take care of it today.
Lauren: No coffee shop. JOB! JOB! JOB!
Ethan: No don't worry, I'm not going there today. I just got up.

I'm going to focus on re-drafting the resume. Tomorrow I'll start
uploading it and searching the job sites.
Lauren: Okay.
Lauren: I love you.
Ethan: I love you too.

Ethan took a deep breath to release the tension. He did not need to get into a texting argument with Lauren, especially when she was right. He needed to find employment. He was becoming more uncomfortable with the reality that Lauren's income, along with what she earned as a tutor, was their own stream of financial security, while he was playing golf and binge-watching *The West Wing* on Netflix. Ethan put the phone in his pocket and grabbed his Mickey Mouse coffee mug. As he passed the doorway to the dining room, he took another look at the satchel.

Ethan fell into his office chair and powered on his computer. Before it finished booting, he jumped to his feet and made his way to the dining room. Ethan opened the satchel to retrieve the journal, dropped it on the table, and untied the knot. The title page was still creepy, but examining it again, Ethan traced his fingers over the signature to touch the ink. Feeling the separation between ink and paper with every letter, Ethan noticed something. With help from the morning light coming through the windows, Ethan could make out very faint ink strokes all over the page.

Ethan was sure every page, after the title page, was blank. With the light's reflection, Ethan thought it was ink that must have bled through from a sheet of paper that was placed on top. He leaned in to get a closer look and squinted to see if he could make out any words. Ethan then realized the ink strokes were not leaked, they were coming from the page beneath it.

With a slightly trembling hand, Ethan held his breath as he lifted the cover sheet to reveal a full entry in his handwriting. Ethan gasped, his breathing immediately became heavier. Becoming light headed he leaned against the wall and rested his head back. He took slow deep breaths to calm himself. "There was nothing there yesterday," he said aloud, "There was nothing on that page yesterday. There's nothing there now!"

After everything Henry had said, as implausible it sounded, Ethan was starting to believe something beyond his grasp was now in motion. He was growing petrified by the idea that what Henry explained last night could be the truth. Ethan was letting his mind wander so he could ignore what his eyes were seeing. It baffled him. How could a page that was empty yesterday have writing on it today? Ethan knew that he had not taken a pen to the journal and the only other person in the apartment was Lauren.

"Wait," he thought. "Lauren? Did she fill this out to look like my horrid penmanship? Is she having fun at my expense?" Ethan read the first few words on this *new* page, which stated, "It has been a week since I arrived . . .." Ethan knew instantly that Lauren did not transcribe this. With minor trepidation, Ethan took a seat and read on:

> It has been a week since I arrived and have finally regained the strength in my hands and upper body so that I can begin to properly record the effects the passage had on me. I have had to force myself to relive the events that unfolded over the past several days. I thought it would greatly benefit my psyche to record the experience with no more words than are required to properly convey exactly what happened to me the instant the event took place.

> The last few moments in the tube went as follows: After the injection, the signal was given to energize KITE. Then a thick liquid rushed in from the sides and started to fill up the cylinder. A bright haunting light began to form beneath me and reflected through the clear liquid at my feet. Once the liquid reached my head, I held my breath and closed my eyes. I heard a buzzer faintly through the compartment, and then the base gave way. I knew my feet were no longer touching the floor. I didn't drop

because at that exact moment a thunderous, booming sound ruptured my ears, and this massive ball of light and energy surrounded me, forcing my eyes to close even harder. I felt myself being pushed upward and suddenly I was weightless. My skin was tingling and my hair had the feeling as if it was being pulled out of its roots.

The light surrounding me was penetrating through my eyelids, and I could tell the color changed from a pure white, then to complete darkness, then to a slight red, and back to white. If I had to assume, I would say the sequence of colors was from the surrounding environment the light was traveling through. The white was from the electromagnetic light itself when it escaped the atmosphere and collided with the dark matter, which turned the rich white into blackness. That could also explain the split-second feeling of a great force pushing down on the crown of my head. Also, the darkness would make sense as I would have been within the umbra. The red hue on reentry was just a flash before the white light returned and without any warning, I felt my body hit something hard. I fell into an unconscious state.

When I came to, I was face down on the ground. I was paralyzed. I tried to squeeze my hand or lift my leg, but I couldn't. I experienced blindness, as my eyesight was reduced to a white film, as if I just stared into the sun. My hearing was impaired and drowned out by a high pitch tone. I tried to speak but was unable to open my mouth.

My body was in tremendous pain. My skin was tingling, my muscles were randomly contracting as if they were being poked with an electrical rod, and the voltage was channeling down into my bones. The faint scent of burning electricity corroded my nasal passages and gave off a metallic taste. It was excruciating and terrifying.

I could tell my body was on grass. As the minutes passed, the movement in my fingertips returned, and I was digging into the ground. The dirt and the blades were sinking into my fingertips. My lack of faculties made it impossible for me to know where I presently was. I had no true means of knowing whether the event was a success or a failure. And if I had traveled to the past, was I at the right point in time?

I was vulnerable with no ability to move myself, to see, to hear, or even speak. All I felt was the cold wind blowing over my sensitive skin.

I then felt someone grip my right hand and then another on my left. I let out a loud moan for the fear and the pain. Of course, I anticipated Philip or Mary to assist me when I arrived, but when I felt my arms being held down and stretched over my head, somebody was ripping and pulling the clothing off my body, I started to panic even more. I wanted to struggle, but all I could move was my fingertips. My body was wrestled back and forth as they stripped every bit of clothing off me. I was then wrapped in blankets and rotated on to a stretcher.

I couldn't hear myself when I was trying to speak. I desperately wanted to plead for them not to hurt me, but my jaw was locked shut. I was scared beyond anything I ever experienced in my life.

As they continued to move me, I could sense from the impact of vibrations through the stretcher, we entered a building and were no longer walking on dirt. I was promptly rolled onto a bed and attended to. When I hit the mattress, it was the first suggestion to me that I was not taken to a modern laboratory but most likely in a rustic bedroom. The height at which they lifted me was no more than two feet. When they moved me from the stretcher to the bed, I sunk into the middle and felt a beam under my back. It wasn't the most comfortable feeling, but it was better than resting in the dirt.

They washed me and dressed me, and there was nothing I could do about it. A cotton strip was wrapped around my head to cover my eyes. I felt hot towels rubbing my hands and feet. A lotion with menthol was rubbed on my chest that immediately helped me breathe more easily. Then a hand was pressed on my forehead, and I felt a sudden calm wash over me. I began to trust that I was in the care of my colleagues, Philip and Mary.

At that same moment when I sensed I was under the protection of my cohorts, my wrists and ankles were wrapped with a cloth and tied to the bed posts. The touch of the cotton felt like sandpaper against my skin. I could not understand why they would strap down my extremities when I was unable to move any of them. Suddenly something poked my arm, hard! Right in the crease! It was a huge needle! I cringed immediately and the hand on my head, which I thought was placed out of compassion, was there to press my head down. I moaned and screamed in anguish and desperation. Each tear that streamed down the sides of my face stung with every run.

After the shot, my muscles started to relax and I could feel myself drifting to sleep. I tried to fight the effects, but I had no energy within me. The ringing in my head began dropping to a low tone and I could tell I was going under, against my will. Before I closed my eyes, I said a prayer asking God to please help me and see me through. I feared the worst and did not want to die like this.

When I awoke, I was still immobile but there was little improvement in my condition. I could sense the paralysis was beginning to wear off as my neck had some movement, and I could bend my fingers more. My arms and legs, thank God, were no longer tied down, and were responding. But with intense muscle ache and joint pain, it felt like I was trying to pick up a thousand pounds. As for the other senses, my eyesight started to show dull shadows appearing along the peripheral, but much of my vision was obscured by a bright light. The high-pitch ringing in my ears faded to low-toned muffled sounds. Nothing was coherent. Thankfully, my jaw was no longer locked, and I could open my mouth slightly to let some cool air in, but my mouth was so dry I couldn't create any saliva to wet my lips, all the muscle strain in my cheeks prevented me from attempting to speak.

While I laid there, helpless, I was still uncertain of my current location. My vulnerability made me impatient, I wanted to regain my functionality at that moment. With every failed attempt, I tried even harder, which made my breathing heavier. Then that hand returned to my forehand with a cool wet cloth. It was wiped over my face and my lips, and washed away my frustration. My head was lifted and the edge of a cup was placed on my mouth. I took a sip but choked immediately. My head was lifted again, and the cup was placed once more to provide me with much needed sustenance. After several sips, my head was gently lowered back, and I was at ease until I felt the piercing of the needle again, which made me fall into another deep sleep.

During that second sleep, I had such a vivid dream that it has remained in the forefront of my thoughts. I feel it necessary to record it now.

I was in a room primarily made of wood in a cottage along the Swamp Creek. Sitting at a writing desk, I was penning a letter, I can't recall what was on the page. The only sound I heard was the running of the water from the creek and the passing of the wind by my window. But then I realized the sound was not the wind, it was the faint moan of a woman in grief, gently echoing on the night air. I ran to the window to locate this person and see if my help was needed. From my view, I couldn't see anything, all that was before me was natural darkness. No shadows, no moonlight, just a void. But, although my eyes saw nothing, my ears continued to hear the sound, and the moaning was becoming louder.

Someone was calling my name. "Ethan!" "Ethan!"

I jumped through the window and my feet touched the ground. I ran toward where the sound was originating. Once outside, the moonlight appeared, the home I left disappeared, and I found myself in a forest. Dodging the trees, I began shouting, "Hello, I'm here. I'm here."

The voice shouted, "Ethan it's me! Where are you?" Immediately I recognized the voice. It was Lauren, and she was calling for me. My heart was full of joy and at the same time a great panic came over me. Why was she here? Did someone violate the agreement and risk her health by sending her back here?

I kept moving about, but there were so many trees to dodge, I lost my sense of direction. I called for my wife again, "Lauren! Lauren!"

"Ethan, why did you leave me!" Her voice was becoming louder. I continued, hoping the next tree dodged would reveal Lauren.

I felt I was getting close but then, suddenly, the voice changed its location and was now behind me. I spun in my shoes and fell to the ground. I got right up and headed in the new direction. As I moved, the number of tress began to grow with every step, every dodge; they were surrounding me and closing me in. I yelled, "Lauren, where are you?"

She shouted back, "I don't know where I am. I'm scared, please find me and don't leave me again!"

I stopped moving, "Leave you?" I cried, "I'm trying to find you." Her voice was now further away, it seemed no matter how hard I tried, I was not getting any closer and was not going to be able to help her in her time of need.

I stood still and waited to hear her voice. "You left me!" she said. The accusation struck my heart and hit me deep in my soul.

I had to refocus on the sounds' orientation and figured it was coming from my right side. I ran as hard and as fast as I could. Lauren cried out, "you left me when I needed you the most." I broke through the tree line and found myself in an enormous grassland. In the distance was a hillcrest and there was a figure, standing alone in the cold dark night.

"Lauren!" I shouted. There was no response but the figure turned to me. I knew it was her, so I ran with great speed, but as much I ran, she was not getting any closer.

Above her was the Moon, and I saw a lunar eclipse commencing over her. "No Lauren!" I screamed, "don't, do this!" I was losing my breath and I could not speak anymore, I just ran with all my might. My heart rate was so high I thought it was going to erupt. As the eclipse reached halfway to full coverage, I stumbled and fell to the ground. "Lauren, come to me," I cried as tears started to fall.

"Yes, Ethan, I'm coming to you, I will be with you soon." I jumped up and continued to run, but made no progress, no matter how much I tried.

As the Moon was about to be covered in darkness, I heard a man whisper my name, "Ethan." I turned around and next to me stood a dark figure. It wasn't hard to conclude by seeing the moonlight reflect off his spectacles that the man was Benjamin Franklin.

He just stood there, with no expression. "Ben?" I asked. He didn't respond, but then he smiled at me and his eyes looked up at the eclipse. When I turned back, a giant lightning bolt came from the heavens and struck Lauren. She screamed with agony. I dropped to my knees and cried like a child. Then a hand was put on my shoulder and rocked me. I thought it was Dr. Franklin consoling me. I heard him say something, but it was muffled. Suddenly I awoke from my nightmare and heard my name called, "Ethan? Ethan?" It was a female voice, different from Lauren's.

As I started to regain my faculties, I moved my jaw ever so slightly and could mumble out a response. "What?" I said.

"It's Mary, you were dreaming. I wanted to make sure you're okay."

"Where's Lauren?" I asked.

"There is no Lauren here, Ethan. Your trip was a success. You arrived safely in the year 1775 and today is March 23. I am sure wherever Lauren is, she is okay, thanks to you being here."

After knowing Lauren was safe, and I was where I should be, I drifted off back to sleep. It was March and I had arrived, but I only had a short amount of time to recover and prepare with Philip and Mary before meeting Benjamin Franklin.

The walls in the dining room were closing in on Ethan when he reached the last line. With cold hands still trembling with anxiety he lifted the page to see whether the next contained any writing. It was blank, as were all the pages that followed. He sat in the lonely silence of his dining room. He slowly closed over the journal pages with the leather binder, tied it, and with a tremble in his hand, gently placed it back into the satchel.

"This isn't real. This can't be real," he said to himself.

Ethan knew he had to seek out Henry for more answers, and he had to do it now. After reading this story, he could not put it off a single day. Ethan grabbed his phone to text Lauren. He knew there was going to be hell to pay, but he had no choice. He thought for a moment on what he could say to explain why he was leaving the house and not seeking employment.

> **Ethan: Babe, I have a thought. Before I go all in updating my resume everywhere I want to check the post office and see if there are any jobs available. A couple of the people know me there, so I thought I'd try it first.**

After a quick change of clothes, Ethan grabbed the satchel and his phone. A text message arrived while he was getting ready. The response was not good. It confirmed that Lauren read the text and understood he was once again leaving the apartment, but its short composition clearly indicated she was not happy.

> **Lauren: K**

Chapter Eleven

Kronos

Ethan needed answers. He ran into the coffee shop expecting to find Henry sitting at a table with an antagonizing stare. Panning the room Ethan could not see tell if he was sitting anywhere in dining area. Ethan turned to the young girl behind the counter, and shouted "Where is he?"

She shrugged her shoulders and mouthed the word, "who?"

"Henry! Where is he?"

She pointed to a table in the corner. From where Ethan stood, all he saw someone holding up a newspaper. On the table in front of him rested a cup of coffee and a chessboard with some of the pieces scattered around. In a quick pace, Ethan made his way over. He was a few steps away when the person behind the counter shouted, "Henry, Ethan is here!" Henry bent one side of the paper down and gave a smile.

"Well, I should say this is unexpected," said Henry. "We figured you wouldn't be back for another day or two. You just cost me ten bucks." Ethan dropped the satchel on the table, which caused the coffee to shake and spill over. Henry raised it arms up, "Thanks," he said.

Ethan was a ball of emotions. His fear and anger made him breath heavy through his nose. Henry showed no concern for Ethan's annoyance as he dabbed the liquid off the table and the few chess pieces. When he finished cleaning up the spilled coffee, Henry looked back at Ethan, "Something wrong? Did you not sleep well?"

Ethan pointed toward the satchel. "You have to tell me the truth? Why are you doing this to me?"

"I don't understand?"

"You don't understand?" Ethan replied. "I don't understand! I don't understand any of this! I don't understand how a journal page that was blank yesterday, has a complete story in it now. In my handwriting."

"Really!" said Henry. "The journal has a new story?"

"Yes, and I am certain it was not there the day before. So, what happened? Did you put that page in there last night, when I was outside or went to men's room?"

"No."

"What is going on here, Henry?" asked Ethan. "I feel like I'm losing my mind."

Henry folded his newspaper and tossed it on the chair next to him. He gestured for Ethan to sit as he turned to the counter and held up two fingers, asking for two cups of coffee. The barista behind the counter gave a wave of acknowledgment. When Henry turned back he saw Ethan had yet to take a seat and was rocking back and forth. "Ethan, you must let your anger go. Take my advice, breathe easy and relax. Grasp the excitement to this new reality of which you are a part of," said Henry. He then extended his hand and slowly lowered it, to gesture to Ethan to sit down. "Have a seat and let's talk this out. I can see you are a little worried."

"A little worried?" Ethan shouted. He pointed to the journal, "It updated, Henry!"

"Okay," said Henry. "I heard you. Please have a seat and let me try to explain this to you." Ethan slowly placed himself in the chair across from Henry.

Staring at the satchel, Henry leaned back in his chair and placed his chin between his thumb and forefinger to collect his thoughts. Rubbing his fingers over his lips, Henry was stalling as he searched for the right words. With a deep breath, Henry lifted his eyes to meet Ethan's gaze. He sat upright, leaned forward, and folded both hands on the table. In a soft tone, not wanting to antagonize, Henry said, "Ethan—"

"Yes?" said Ethan.

Henry paused again and looked around the room for a second to carefully construct his next sentence. "Ethan," he said, "I swear I cannot for the life of me imagine the conflict you must be going through. What's not clear to me is why you are so angry now?"

"I have every right to be angry," said Ethan. "I was told the most obscure version of history last night."

Henry lifted his hand to stop Ethan in mid-sentence, "Hold on, not so loud," he said. "Not everyone in here is one of our guys, so please just lower your voice a little."

Ethan turned his head to see who else was in the room. A few people were in line, and a few single patrons were scattered about the dining room, including the nice old lady from the other day, Brianna. Ethan got up from the chair across from Henry and moved to the one on his right. Holding his scowl, he leaned in, and said, "Then you talk about time travel and how you're sending me back. I didn't believe any of it, mind you, but then this morning I awoke to read, in my handwriting, the physical effects I experienced after what is described as *the event*. So yes, I'm angry. I'm uneasy with the notion that there could be an ounce of validity to what you said because I'm telling you right now, I'm not partaking*u* in whatever it is you alluded to yesterday."

Henry leaned back in his seat, "Okay Ethan," he said, "now I under-stand, but you abruptly walked out of here last night. I still had a few details to cover but, for future reference, should you ever have any questions, any at all, I will tell you whatever I know, because there is nothing I can hide from you." Henry leaned in and touched Ethan's forearm, "But!" he said. "It is essential that you begin to absorb that what I am telling you is fact. Otherwise we'll get nowhere and put our very existence at risk."

The heated discussion subsided as the two coffees arrived. "Here, Henry," she said, "and Ethan, I brought you a Kona, light and sweet, is that okay?"

Ethan did not lift his head to make eye contact with the girl but to ensure that he displayed some form of gratitude, he softly said, "That's fine, thank you."

Henry waved his hand and then pointed at himself, to tell the young girl not to take Ethan's present demeanor as a reflection on her; it was his fault. She nodded and left the table, "Thank you, Jean," Henry said as she walked away.

Ethan let out a deep sigh, and said, "Okay, here's my first question. The journal?"

"What about it?"

As Ethan spoke he pointed to the satchel on each syllable. "It up-da-ted."

"I know," said Henry.

"On its own!" Ethan shouted, but remembering what Henry said, he crouched in his seat and looked around to see if anyone reacted to his outburst, then whispered, "How did it get there?"

"Here is the simplest way to understand what happened. The jour-nal is a record of the events you experience from the day of arrival, which would be in March 1775." Henry placed his hand on the satchel, "This is, was, or will be, a book written by you. However, you, the *you* who is sitting here, have yet to become aware of what will or what is expected to happen. This journal could be viewed as your looking glass into future endeavors. The reason the page updated this morning is connected to information you received yesterday."

"So, I have a book from the past that is telling me what I am going to experience in my future?" asked Ethan.

With a smile, Henry threw his arms up and said, "Hey, I couldn't have said it better myself. I'll explain further, but for you to understand this whole story you need to know something about *time* and how that pertains to your situation. So, for a minute, let's explore the concept of *time*"

"Now I'm not a physics expert, but from what we discovered about time, and have not shared with the theoretical world, is that it *is* constant. Time is always moving. It is flowing in one direction, and we are all existing and participating within it. When and where time is being observed, it can never slow down and can never be sped up. It always *is* and is always present in relation to your location. Meaning, even though we created seconds, minutes, hours, days, months, and years to help us track and measure time, the relation between *tracking time* on Earth and say on the Moon are not in perfect sync. Therefore, the five minutes you live on Earth will take longer on the Moon.

"Thanks to this whole endeavor, we know only one timeline exists in our universe. What is happening now will be viewed as the past as we continue to move forward to the future. What we do next is a consequence of what has occurred along the timeline. Meaning if someone went back in time and changed the past, we would have no idea because we would be living in the outcome of that alteration. No one would say, 'Hey wait a minute, this isn't right.' Everything would just be accepted as being as it should.

"In that respect, your actions have reactions as you channel through time and space. And not space, as in outer space. I am referring to the space that surrounds you and the place you are in. That is called your *world line*. A map shows latitude and longitude and where those two lines meet is your location. In geometry, it's known as your vector. Well, the same principle applies to your world line. Only we can conclude that your world line is relative not only to your location, sitting in that chair, but also to time—as in *this date* and *this time*. When world lines cross, there is an effect, sometimes positive and sometimes negative. This happens all the time. It never stops.

"Here's an example: you are walking through your neighborhood. You come to a blind corner, and you cause someone to brake on their bike because your physical 'space,' your body, crossed that person's path. At that same time, in the direction you were walking, a car is coming to the intersection, but they continue to drive on down the road. Now, let's say, before that moment when your world line crossed the biker which made them to brake, you did one thing different in your day that caused you not to not arrive at that intersection, at that exact time. That would mean you were not there to walk in front of the biker, they did not hit their brakes, and the car driving to the intersection did not see them, which causes an accident.

"Your momentum through life, through time, has cause and effect. That is the most complicated compound equation in our true existence. It's not just about the *big* recorded events in our time. It's the little ones that no one ever gives a second thought to. Those little events are what trigger the chain reaction, which leads to whatever event you want to conclude as being monumental and a shift in our existence."

"Isn't that the 'Butterfly Effect'?" asked Ethan.

"Correct," said Henry, "the only thing is, no one ever knows what that starting point is. Everyone can determine what it *was*. But, no one lives in the moment and says *this* will be the start of something."

"Big?" Ethan said with enthusiasm.

Giving no expression, and shaking his head, Henry said, "No." He then reached for the arm strap of the satchel and lifted it over the chessboard to place it in front of him. Grabbing the journal, Henry was untying the leather-bound band and said, "Let me look at this thing, I've never actually seen the entries in your handwriting. I only read the transcripts Richard Bache provided us. But just like this journal, all those copies and electronic backups, went blank on the day of your birth." Henry pushed away the chessboard to rest the journal on the table and carefully opened the binder. Henry said, "Let me see what you wrote here."

"I did not write it."

Henry let out a laugh, "No I mean, what you will write." While reading, he commented aloud, "Hmmm." At one point Henry's eyes widened, "Damn!" he said. Before reaching half way through, he looked up at Ethan across the table, "Ouch. This is painfully graphic, Ethan. I mean paralysis, blindness, hearing loss, the inability to speak for Christ sake! Almost makes you want to consider not going through with it?"

Ethan still simmering, replied, "You find this amusing?"

"No, not at all," said Henry, "I'm just saying, 'damn'! The account in here is from someone going through excruciating pain and remorse, but because I know the source, I can say you're stronger than me."

"It also mentioned someone named Mary. Who is Mary?"

"Ah, Mary," replied Henry. "Boy, have I missed her."

"You knew her?".

"Yes, I knew her. Mary Smith is her name, was her name, but when I joined the group, I called her Mrs. Smith. She was a brilliant technician, a student of Franklin and American history, and someone who embraced her participation and contribution to the project."

"Participation in what?"

"Well, we needed to have insurances of survival," said Henry, "If we just sent you back on your own, not only would we have to equip you with the information concerning Franklin and the birth of the country, we also would have to train you to be self-reliant in colonial America, which is a whole other task that could take years to complete. Somewhere along the line, it was decided to send back two people, a man, and a woman, who will help you through it all. Mary will be your source of all accounts of American history, so that you don't do anything drastic and risk our existence. And then we have Philip, who has agricultural, medical, and military training. He's also a great carpenter. An interesting point is that he was sent back to 1765, ten years earlier than your arrival. His objective is, was, to create a timber mill operation as cover. This will give you a place of residence, provide ample resources, and added security. As you go along, you will find more references to them in your writings. Philip was sent back on September 28, 2003, and Mary was sent back November 9, 1965 which caused a couple of large blackouts."

"When did Mary arrive?" Ethan asked.

"She arrived in 1774," Henry said. "And there is a reason for that, because Philip was sent back when he was twenty-two and Mary was sent when she was twenty-five. But when she arrived in 1774, Philip would have been thirty-one, while she was still be twenty-five. I find that fascinating. When you arrive, it will appear as if they are a married couple and they will go by the last name Montgomery."

"Okay, this still doesn't make sense to me," Ethan said. "How can a book mysteriously update like that?"

"It's not that easy to explain. The simplest explanation is that until yesterday you were unaware of your true destiny. If I just handed you the journal with no explanation, it's very likely it would have stayed blank. The letter from Richard Bache was vague on purpose, but it kick-started your insight into a world you never knew existed, which explains the cover page updating. But then last night, I told you about Benjamin Franklin, his project, and time travel. Those subjects enlightened you to what experiences lay ahead for you personally. Because that was more of an intimate education, the journal updated."

"The experiences that lay ahead," said Ethan, "have already taken place in the past."

"It has to do with the fact that our existence, America's existence, is caught in a *causality loop*, and you are the person caught in what is called a *predestination paradox*."

"What am I?" Ethan asked. "I'm a paradox?"

Henry laughed, "No, no, you're not a paradox. You are *in* a paradox. Your life achievement predestines your date of birth, that why it's called a *predestination paradox*. Now the *causality loop* is the result of your actions and what this operation is meant to preserve."

"Okay," said Ethan, "So the more I learn about it, the more I become aware, the more pages will update?"

"Exactly," said Henry, "So let's fill in some of the blanks from our discussion yesterday, and maybe it will help clarify what you are a part of. Yesterday we left off with the story of Lou. Now going forward, you will always want to remember the story of Lou and it will be useful to you when you arrive but know that we are living in the reality of *your* interactions with Benjamin Franklin, not Lou's.

"When Independence was voted for on July 2, 1776, that set-in motion a chain of events that triggered throughout the world, and were played out over time. When Lou went back the first time, he considered the possibility that his life would cease to exist after the vote. Why? Because the alteration could set forth actions that inevitably would have prevented his parents from ever meeting. Of course, that was an extreme concept, but it was relevant.

"As noted yesterday, Lou revealed to Franklin all the elements to achieve time travel. To conceal this, Lou and Franklin constructed an incredibly intelligent plan. It's almost the way many high-profile companies go about doing things to have anonymity. Dummy corporations are established that concentrate on one piece of the project, but together they serve one goal. Well, Franklin and Lou did just that during the latter half of 1775. The goal was to accelerate human discoveries that eventually would lead to all the essential properties of time travel. But instead of designing a plan that would attempt to do this whole thing as a secret operation, Franklin decided to have the public research and discover the required elements. Then all we would have to do is cherry pick them all to achieve the objective, which is time travel.

"Think of how a person who owns a pizzeria makes a pizza. They don't have the wheat field to make the flour, or the cattle ranch to make the milk for the mozzarella, or a farm to grow the tomatoes. For the flour, the milk, and the tomatoes to be made, demands constant attention, tending to the crop, feeding the animals, and then processing. A man who owns a pizza shop can't do all of that, so he purchases those ingredients to make his pizza, which is the basic approach Franklin decided on. Lou was more a military and secretive type of person, while Franklin was much more liberal about sharing his ideas. Ben said, *'An investment in knowledge pays the best interest.'* Well he believed that the piecemeal approach would not only further their needs, but also could open the door to other discoveries beneficial to everyone.

"Franklin outlined a simple plan. Establish a commission to overlook the progress, research, and development of components necessary for time travel. This committee would have the highest clearance and for anonymity, Franklin conveniently hid it into the Continental Post Office. *Why the post office?* Well, think about it this way. Franklin established the postal routes, by hiding this group within his post office, it gave Franklin the needed control of monitoring information and concealing it.

"Also, looking at it from today's perspective, we are absolutely fortunate to be covered behind the shield of the USPS. Think about it? Any enemy we currently have would never consider the Postal Regulatory Commission as an organization with a secret division, which has researched and devised the means of time travel to achieve the establishment of the nation. Go outside and tell anyone on the street that the Post Office has a secret division that has discovered time travel, and then call me when you are picked up by the local police for suspicion of public intoxication.

"So, you wonder, *how did all of this go down to get us to where we are today?* Lou explained the mechanism to Franklin. He outlined every method of it down to the elements needed. So even though it could not be comprehended what a computer was, to someone in the eighteenth century, Franklin could understand it in principle. But Franklin wanted to analyze this information with an 18th century mind he could trust, he reached out to his old friend Ebenezer Kinnersley, who was a collaborator during Franklin's research on electricity. By 1775 Ebenezer was the leader in the field of electrical research and Franklin reviewed some of the properties Lou spoke about to see if any of it was familiar to him. Once Ebenezer dismissed Franklin's "theory" as complete bunk, Franklin and Lou were assured that no one on the planet would understand any of the science, engineering, and mechanisms. All of this needed to be discovered, but it would take generations.

"Now even though Franklin knew many of the world's premiere mathematicians and scientists, he had to be careful regarding the information he was now holding. He couldn't just tell them what he knew in hopes that they would stumble on the discovery. Anyone of the highest academic prestige would be humiliated by artificially achieving monumental discoveries in the world of mathematics and science, even if Benjamin Franklin outlined them. Meaning, you wouldn't tell Dr. Franklin to write to Dr. Joseph-Louis Lagrange and tell him to research what will be called *partial differential equations,* which will help the world understand things like sound, heat, electrodynamics, and quantum mechanics. Or you wouldn't tell Dr. Franklin to notify Dr. Johann Pfaff that he must instruct Carl Gauss to become the brilliant mathematician, so that he can instruct Julius Plücker who will then advance the usage of cathode rays, that will lead to the discovery of the electron.

"After Franklin received what he could understand from Lou, being the clever mind that he was, he knew he could plant the seeds in the minds of only some of the academia doctors in Europe. He did this to let the path of discovery grow through the years in a natural way. Its conclusions would be pure, the usage would be organic, and its founder would be the sole owner of the enlightenment. You know why? So, it would help that doctor score with the physics groupies.

"What?" said Ethan.

Henry smiled, "I'm just kidding. I wanted to make sure you were paying attention."

Henry continued, "Okay, so Franklin was advancing the conversation of math and science a couple of decades. He accelerated and encouraged some discoveries, which led to advancements in research, which ultimately led to advancements in electricity, hydropower, and atomic energy. From those early years of nudging, it helped inspire quantum physics. Today is not the day to confuse you with a history of physics and mathematics. I will go into broader detail of Franklin's meddling some other day because it will play a pivotal role in how he traveled through Europe after he secured a treaty with France and England. For today, I think you will find it intriguing to learn how we got to this point, where you and I are discussing this operation that was started in Benjamin Franklin's dining room all those years ago."

"Wait!" shouted Ethan. "I can't sit here for another lecture. I promised my wife today I would find a job. She thinks I came down here to see if there were any employment opportunities at the post office." Ethan reached for the journal and said, "I came here to ask you about this thing, and although I'm not thrilled with your explanation, I'll take it. But now, I need to go home and give the appearance I'm looking for a job so my wife doesn't kill me."

Henry reached out with both arms, "Ethan!" he said. "Why didn't you say something sooner? I mean, I can save you from getting in trouble with your significant other." Henry put his right hand on Ethan's shoulder. "We are going to put you on our payroll. You will have full benefits for the remainder of your tenure in our time. Best of all, we will make sure Lauren is financially and medically secure for the rest of her life."

"Are you serious?" asked Ethan. "What am I going to be doing?"

Henry let out a deep sigh of frustration. He dropped his head and scratched his forehead. "We are going to prep you, Ethan. We are going to prepare you for the next nineteen months."

"Henry, this is all nonsense to me. You tell great detailed stories but, even if what you were saying was true, it wouldn't matter. I am not meeting Benjamin Franklin."

"What else do you need, Ethan?" asked Henry. "I mean last night I described how your life influenced one of the finest figures in our nation's history to vote for a resolution that changed the world. I defined the two versions of the world's path from that one event. One that was in turmoil and was pulling itself apart—and this one, the one where you and Lauren are living in today. And let's not forget the letters you received from Bache and Franklin along with this journal."

Ethan interrupted, "Letter from Franklin? I never received a letter from Franklin."

"No?" said Henry.

"No!" said Ethan.

"Oh, well, I'm sure something might come up."

"A letter from Franklin *might* come up?" said Ethan. "You see how you lead me to conclude that this whole thing is a bunch of bull! Something 'might come up' and I *might* believe your nonsense story! Let's look at things from my point of view. You are trying to have me believe that the U.S. Post Office has had a secret operation in which it has influenced and monitored the advancement of science and technology in the world? So they can send someone through time to ensure Benjamin Franklin votes for the Declaration of Independence? Do you want me to point out where you lose me?"

"It's back in time," said Henry.

"What?"

"You said through time, when it's actually *back* in time. You can't send someone through time. I mean you are going through time right now. I can't send you *more* through time."

"Whatever!" said Ethan. "Whatever! The point is nothing will convince me that this operation you keep talking about is 100 percent real. That's what I'm saying. You said the Post Office's secret division was involved in other moments of our history. So then tell me. I'll hang around for a few more minutes. I'm curious now."

"Well, I don't want to bore you with the little things," said Henry. "But, if you would like to know, I can share a few interesting factoids to help you grasp the magnitude of our operation." Before Henry began, he waved two fingers Jean, standing behind the counter. When she saw him, Henry mouthed the word "two more." He then noticed Ethan was thumbing through his phone. "Why don't you text your wife and tell her you found a job?" Henry said. "That will save you from getting in trouble with Lauren and give you more time to understand what it is you are involved with."

"I'm not signing on to anything, Henry. I'm not agreeing to anything."

Henry sighed, placed both hands on the table and began knocking his thumbs in a sporadic rhythm as he collected his thoughts. "Ethan, your wife wants you to get a job. I don't want you to get a job. I need this to be your job. There's a reason you became unemployed. It was so you can commit yourself to be ready, and getting ready means you will go through a crash course in Colonial-Era American history. So, by the time we are done with you, you will have a doctorate in Benjamin Franklin and Early American History."

Ethan stared astonished at Henry. "You got me fired?" he said.

"We had to free up your time, Ethan." Across the table, Henry saw Ethan's eyes widen in anger. "Stop looking at me like a bull," Henry said. "You're not going to charge me."

"I liked that job Henry," Ethan shouted. "I worked hard to show those in my department that I deserved to be there. I'd like to think I achieved that before I forced out the door! Now I'm without a job, I'm without income, and I'm selling my stuff online to bring in extra money."

Hanging on the right side of Henry's chair was his single-strap messenger bag. Henry turned slightly, grabbed the strap, and placed the bag on his lap. As he opened the flap he said, "I have been holding on to something for a while now that will settle your furnace." He retrieved a brown legal-size envelope from the bag. "We are going to pay you and provide for Lauren $250,000 a year, forever. Now, all you're going to have to do is commit, but I know you don't want to right now. So, I'll give you a day or two to think it over. However, and this is critical, you can't tell your wife what you are doing, what you are learning, and why you are learning it."

"Why?"

"Because it's not her place to know right now," said Henry. "She could become emotional, angry, just like you became. She may reject the notion to such a point that she could put herself in a bad state of mind, and if she is under duress, there's a chance she could jeopardize the whole thing. We will not take that chance, Ethan, under any circumstances. If she knows anything before the appropriate time, we will have to hold her."

"Hold her? You mean arrest her?"

"Something like that," said Henry. "This is as real as I can get with you. Just go about the next year having your wife believe you are an employee of the USPS as a technician. Your so-called job will involve travel along the northeast district of the United States. You will say that you are responsible for the deployment of new self-post stations. That way, we can send you to Virginia, Washington, Philly, and Boston, and we can keep you in New York City without her having any suspicions. You will get paid and both of you will be covered with health insurance, on par with the President."

Henry stared at Ethan and saw no expression on his face. "Ethan?" he said.

"Yes."

"How does that sound?"

Ethan said, "It sound's okay but." He then abruptly stopped talking as Jean stepped to the table with their coffee refills. When she placed the new cup on the table, Ethan looked up, smiled, and said, "Thank you, Jean." She smiled back, rubbed Ethan's shoulder as she left. Ethan picked up the hot cup of coffee and started blowing on it to cool it off.

"I know you still don't believe me," Henry said.

"No, I don't."

"Before you wanted to know more about our operation. Like I said, I don't want to bore you with the particulars, because you don't need to know them now. That's what Philip and Mary are for. But I will let you in on a few events in the history of Kronos. I will share the moments in our past in which we were influential, and the moments that almost exposed our secret to the world."

"What's Kronos?" asked Ethan.

"Kronos, is the name of our group," said Henry. "It's named after the Greek God of time."

"Oh," Ethan said.

"You don't know who Kronos is?"

"No, I do," replied Ethan. "I just wasn't sure if you meant *that* Kronos."

Seeing that he was covering, Henry smirked and said, "Well, I did mean *that* Kronos. Franklin thought it would be clever to reference a deity. Even though Franklin had his own questions about God, he figured that a venture of this magnitude may require a little divine intervention."

"Okay, I see," said Ethan.

"This was not the first-time Franklin used a deity in his works," said Henry. "When his brother James named him the publisher of his newspaper,

The Courant, on February 11, 1723, Franklin printed the 'Master of the paper will be the Roman God Janus.'"

"Why Janus?" asked Ethan.

"Because Janus has two faces and can look in either direction," said Henry. "Franklin was telling his readers, and the authorities in Boston, that his paper would always look at both sides of the issue. So, just like the clever use of Janus for his paper, Franklin used Kronos for his time travel project."

Ethan took a sip of his coffee, leaned back in his chair, and looked toward the ceiling. "Okay, so, the group is called Kronos. Now what?"

Chapter Twelve

Franklin to Lincoln

By eleven the August sunshine brought a warm light into the dining area of The Roasting Plant. The rays that were shielded by the trees and nearby buildings now breached the windows and surrounded Ethan. Most of the morning patrons had already exited the café, leaving Henry and Ethan alone in the corner. With all being thrown at Ethan, his frustrations were already high. Now, with the heat coming down on him, he started to nervously shake his leg under the table with each passing minute. The vibrations were enough to form small ripples in the two cups of coffee. When the tremor caused a small pawn from Henry's chess set to roll near the edge of the table and fall to the floor, Ethan jumped out of his seat. He looked around to find which tables were out of the sunlight. "Can we sit over there?" he asked.

"Sure," replied Henry.

Once resettled, Ethan asked, "So you were going to say something about Kronus?"

"Kronos," Henry said. "Kronos, with an *os*, not an *us*."

"Okay," said Ethan. "When did they come into play?"

"Kronos was first thought of on July 4, 1775," Henry said. "It was exactly one year before the Declaration was voted for."

"Of course it was," Ethan said. "Of all dates, it had to be July 4." Ethan then closed his eyes and let out a deep breath as he shook his head in disbelief.

"What?"

"Really?" Ethan responded. "You don't see the irony of saying exactly one year before the Declaration of Independence was signed, Franklin miraculously had this change of heart?"

Henry reached for his bag and pulled out an eight-by-ten photo and handed it to Ethan. "Read that."

Ethan examined the glossy sheet; it was an image of an old letter. The ink on the captured note appeared faded and the penmanship was such that Ethan needed to squint and hold the letter closer to his face to make out the words. In the upper right corner the date read, "July 5, 1775." Ethan glanced over the top edge of the print to see Henry rocking in his seat, anticipating his reaction. Ethan's attention returned to the photo.

Mr. Strahan,

You are a Member of Parliament, and one of that Majority which has doomed my country to destruction. You have begun to burn our towns and murder our people. Look upon your hands! They are stained with the blood of your relations! You and I were long Friends. You are now my Enemy, and I am yours.

B. Franklin

Ethan placed the sheet back on the table and pushed it across. "Did you see who wrote that?" Henry asked as he returned the photo to his bag.

"Yes, I saw," said Ethan. "B. Franklin."

"That letter was drafted by Franklin on July 5, 1775," retorted Henry. "That passage was transcribed for William Strahan, a fellow printer who resided in London, and printed many works, including proclamations for the King. He also attended sessions in Parliament and composed reports that were circulated in Franklin's paper *The Pennsylvania Gazette*. William Strahan and Benjamin Franklin were close associates and good friends. He developed a stronger likeness for William after his objection to the Stamp Act when it was enacted in 1765, but as the years went on, William developed a dislike for the colonies, and by 1774, it had soured their relationship. Once Franklin was convinced to be for Independence, he drafted this letter addressed to William on the next day, July 5, 1775. The letter, however, was never sent directly to William, instead it was printed in many newspapers in every colony. It was also printed in London and throughout some places in Europe for all to see."

By Ethan's expression, Henry could tell the Strahan letter was making little to no impression. He also knew he had to help Ethan read between the lines. "What makes the publication of this letter monumental," Henry said, "is by characterizing William as *his enemy*, Benjamin Franklin was really calling England his enemy and with that deliberate act, he affirmed his commitment to American Independence. This is why this date is critical to our mission."

"Really?" replied Ethan, "How so?"

Henry answered, "After Franklin devoted his life to American liberty and Independence, he entered the chamber of Congress with a new perspective. He was no longer attempting to resurrect the Albany Plan as a compromise. Franklin was now focused on liberation.

"Now, Franklin wrote that letter the evening of July 5, 1775. Earlier that afternoon the Second Continental Congress started their consideration on a rewrite of a potential petition to the King. This first draft, originally composed by Franklin, was abruptly rejected several days earlier on

June 24, much to his embarrassment. John Dickinson, also of Pennsylvania, stepped in to assist in its composition after Franklin's was dismissed.

"The purpose of the petition was to list the transgressions and request a compromise, such as reduction in taxes and removal of the trade regulations that had crippled commerce and the respective businesses of the delegates. This petition is known as the 'Olive Branch.'

"John Dickinson made the language of the petition much softer, less accusatory, more reconciling than the original draft, which was deemed 'too strong' and had 'too much fault finding.' Much of that strong language came from someone Franklin used to help transcribe the first draft, Thomas Jefferson. It was Jefferson, during the First Continental Congress, who drafted a petition called *A Summary View of the Right of British America*. In that essay, Jefferson was already of a mind that the King was not justified in his absolute rule over the colonies, and he argued that the colonies were afforded the right, based on their founding, to be self-governing. Similar language and sentiments were used when Thomas Jefferson wrote the Olive Branch based on Franklin's notes.

"John Dickinson had a strong voice in the Congress and, at that time, was the leading representative of 'reason' and sought absolute reconciliation. Jefferson was never comfortable speaking aloud, but he was a gifted author. Jefferson's strong language in the Olive Branch draft almost appeared to be an ultimatum. Franklin was going to use Thomas' words to capture the attention of some sympathetic representatives of Parliament to ignite discussions of a national government. Although many members in Congress shared Jefferson's opinions, at the same time, they were not ready to risk all they had. So, for their protection, they sided with Dickinson, and the committee rejected the draft. It never made it to floor for a vote, but a few people appreciated the tenor the Virginian was willing to use, most notably John Adams.

"That brings us to July 5, 1775, at which point you have John Dickinson petitioning the King for peace. On the other side is John Adams, who has been the loudest in the chamber calling for liberty, second to Patrick Henry. You also have Thomas Jefferson, who articulates the message better than anyone on paper, and now sitting in the chamber, unbeknownst to all in the room, is the newest member in favor of total liberation, Benjamin Franklin. When the new draft is presented by Dickinson, Franklin does not oppose the alterations, but he firmly acknowledges the letter will fail to achieve its purpose. Later that day, Franklin writes this letter and in fifty words made his position plainer in comparison to the thirteen hundred words transcribed to make a plea to King George III.

"On Saturday July 8, when the vote on the Olive Branch was called. John Adams voiced his frustrations, but it was to no avail. The problem with Adams's objection was that it was expected. He wrote to his wife Abigail and other associates about his disgust with Congress and its perpetual dis-inclination to engage the enemy. Adams feared the they lacked the nerve to do what was necessary and only acted to protect their self-interests, namely their land. After the Olive Branch petition passed, it was dispatched to King George and Lord Dartmouth. Lord Dartmouth was the King's Secretary of State for the colonies. Upon receiving it, the King refused to read it and, in turn, responded to this assembly in Philadelphia by issuing *A Proclamation for Suppressing Rebellion and Sedition* in late August. It called for officials and citizens to suppress this ill-conceived rebellion. Otherwise, those who continued to engage in the treasonous acts—would be hung.

"Now, even though the King rejected the 'Olive Branch' petition, what arose from that chamber over those four days, culminating on July 8, 1775, was the unexpected unity of three men: Franklin, Jefferson, and Adams. That is why it is imperative that Benjamin Franklin concedes to the vision of a free and independent country by July 4, 1775."

Ethan nodded his head. "That's incredible," he said. "I never knew it was a failed plea for peace that united them. It seems incomprehensible. The timing of it all."

"Well, if you like that, I have another one that's incomprehensible," said Henry. "On July 6, the day after the Olive Branch Petition was tabled, Congress approved the *Declaration of the Causes and Necessity of Taking Up Arms*, which also was drafted by Thomas Jefferson and modified by John Dickinson. So, on Wednesday they started to debate on a draft for reconciliation, on Thursday they approved a declaration to engage in battle with whom they were trying to reconcile with, and on Saturday they approved their Olive Branch. Go figure."

"What happened on Friday?" asked Ethan.

Henry let out a loud laugh. "I don't know," he said. "What I'm trying to demonstrate is that it is amazing how the existence of this nation happened in relation to laws of causality. It is mind boggling to know when something took place and what was required for the event to take place. When you are associated with our group, the notion of *time and place* can terrify the psyche if you dwell on it long enough, especially when we know it can be altered."

"What do you do?" asked Ethan. "To not let it get to you."

Henry was pleased to hear the absence of any antagonizing tone in Ethan's voice with his last question. Not wanting to resurrect any of Ethan's negative emotions, Henry quickly answered, "Focus on the task at hand. It does require a great degree of trust on your part. Each passing day, you trust that the part you are playing is as it is meant to be. When Franklin started Kronos, he said if your actions are organic, the results will be as you envision."

"What does that mean?" asked Ethan.

"It means if I force you to take part in this operation, your reluctance to participate will create a negative emotion. From there will stem hostility and aggression, which will affect your state of mind. It might have a negative impact on your personality, which in turn could affect your interactions with Benjamin Franklin, which in turn will harm our very existence. Unless you do this under your own free will, we remain compromised."

Just then, Ethan's phone vibrated. He reached down into his pants pocket to retrieve it. "Sorry," he said to Henry.

> **Lauren: Any jobs at the post office?? I haven't heard from you for two hours now, so I figure you're either at the post office or you lied to me and are wasting time in the coffee shop.**

Ethan looked up to Henry, "She's asking if I found a job at the post office?"

"Did you?" asked Henry.

> **Ethan: I found a regional technician position and I am talking to a supervisor. I'll have to fill you in later.**

Ethan looked back up at Henry, "Hell no," he said. Ethan than placed the phone face down on the table with his hand still firmly holding the edges. When it vibrated again, Ethan flipped the face over to view the text.

> **Lauren: Great! I'll be home later. Good Luck.**
> **Ethan: Okay, thanks babe**

Ethan sat back to reflect. With his elbows on the arms of the chair, he interlocked his fingers to rest his chin. He was contemplating the complexities of his present situation. Ethan wanted to reject what Henry was saying to be truth, but the more Henry spoke, the more Ethan found himself believing it. Should this be true, however, the thought of leaving Lauren and never seeing her again, or other members of his family, terrified him. On the other hand, Henry's offer for an occupation with such a substantial salary was too much for anyone to unequivocally refuse. "Tell me about Kronos," he said.

Ethan's increased curiosity brought a smile to Henry's face. "All right, let's get something to eat while I fill you in," said Henry as he waved to the workers behind the counter. "We need some lunch," he told them. "You like Five Guys, right?"

"Yes, that's fine."

Henry shouted to the baristas, "Let's get some Five Guys bacon cheeseburgers with fries and let's get this man a mocha something or other."

"Thanks," said Ethan.

"Don't mention it, this is fun for me. And, it's nice being indoors." Henry then adjusted his chair to bring his body closer to the table's edge. He straightened up his back and lifted his arms over his head to stretch. "Okay, no more distractions. Let's get into this."

"All right," said Ethan.

Henry resumed, "On July 26, 1775, the Continental Congress voted on a proposal and established the postal service for the colonies. For those in Kronos, we recognize the start of the USPS on July 4, 1775, when it was conceived that an agency shall be designated to the advancement and formation of technologies for achieving the capability of preserving the historic alteration, or otherwise noted as Franklin's Great Project or as we have come to call it, *The Franklin Project*.

"Kronos, with some Freemason influences along the way, served as the facilitator for its primary objective and as an antagonist to any civilization if the risk of the ultimate discovery, time travel, was ever perceived."

"Wait," said Ethan. "What does that mean?"

"What?" replied Henry.

"Being an antagonist to any civilization?" Ethan asked. "I mean does the post office have like a Seal Team Six that goes in and takes down scientists?"

Henry burst out laughing. "You are funny Ethan, I'll give you that," he said. "No, we don't have a S.W.A.T. team or anything like that. But we make use of highly sensitive intelligence and at moments create confusion to throw governments off. We don't do it ourselves, we communicate with just a few high-ranking government officials, who carry things out for us. As an example, something needed to be researched, but it required the public to be *aware* of it in some capacity. And that was the exploration around and on the lunar surface. After Sputnik was orbiting the Earth, we took advantage of the moment, and, with no traces back to the United States, influenced the Soviet's to announce a plan to build a lunar base. That kicked off the Moon race, and we were the beneficiaries. With every mission, we'd ask NASA to measure this, or check for that, and that's how it went. Now during the race, somehow the Soviet's got the notion that if a spacecraft looped around the Moon it would travel back in time. We knew they didn't possess the means of time travel but how they made this conclusion was of some concern for us. But after their first manned lunar orbit appeared to be a *failure* to them, they stopped sending cosmonauts on moon missions which assured us of what they didn't know."

The room was quiet, Ethan starred at Henry with no expression. Henry leaned in, "Does that answer your question?"

Staring at Henry wide-eyed, Ethan mumbled, "I guess it does."

"Okay," replied Henry. "Let me get back to Franklin because I want to tell you a story that *no one* knows about. It's a story about Benjamin Franklin and Abraham Lincoln. This will give you clarity into what has come before and bridge what started in 1775 to you and me sitting here today. Ready?"

"Sure," Ethan said with a shrug.

Henry continued, "Many revolutionaries distrusted the royal postal service before the First Continental Congress. When the second congress convened, one of the first acts was to have a committee establish a patriot friendly postal system. It would handle all sensitive dispatches and it would be a means of revenue. Benjamin Franklin was selected to chair the group. Samuel Adams of Massachusetts, Richard Henry Lee of Virginia, Philip Livingston of New York, Thomas Lynch of South Carolina, and Thomas Willing of Pennsylvania were also part of this committee.

"Franklin was so eager to form *Kronos* that he pushed the Congressional Postal Committee to reach an agreement. Franklin knew none of the other members possessed the experience or desire to over-look the implementation of this new system, especially one that had to be concealed within the King's country. Congress agreed to their proposed Continental Postal System on July 26, 1775, and by unanimous decision, named Benjamin Franklin postmaster general.

"A few days into running his new post, Franklin made a recommendation that he knew not one member of the committee or congress would object. The stipulation was this: the postmaster general shall hold his office in Philadelphia.

"This was a brilliant step on Franklin's part. It solidified his selection as postmaster general, which made him responsible for all offices from Maine to Florida. He had the authority to hire as many postmasters as necessary, and could select his own secretary and comptroller. With the façade in place Franklin was now able to create his own underground network of communication throughout the colonies under the guise of serving the colonies. With the addition of the first law enforcement agency of the national government, the Postal Inspection Service, who worked with the Congressional Committee of Safety, and being appointed to intelligence gathering groups such as the Committee of Secret Correspondence and Committee on Spies, Benjamin Franklin had complete power of authority and communication throughout the entire country. More power than General George Washington."

"Wait," said Ethan. "How did he have more power than George Washington? He was General of the Continental Army?"

"True, but they were not a law enforcement unit. The Postal Inspection Service could fine and arrest civilians. So, at this moment in time, Franklin was the most powerful, popular, and influential American in the thirteen colonies."

"I see."

Henry continued, "Now, remember when you won Richard Bache's letter? I told you Franklin selected him to be secretary and comptroller.

Franklin needed someone he could trust and his son-in-law was handpicked to help implement not only the postal system, but the new Kronos agency.

"With everything in place, we move to September of 1776. The Declaration is signed, and we are engaged in war, Franklin is then selected to form an alliance with France. As he prepared to resign his post as postmaster, he strongly urged Congress to vote in Richard Bache. It was an easy vote, and Bache served as Postmaster General from late 1776 until 1782 when the war was all but officially over. Richard needed to step down and begin working on concealing documentation for Kronos.

"With Franklin's approval, Ebenezer Hazard was selected to succeed Richard. He was the first surveyor and postmaster out of New York. Being the major hub of communication and trade, Hazard helped Franklin and Bache immensely while New York was under siege by the British Army during the war and he served as Postmaster General until the Constitution was ratified. However, one of the first action from President Washington was that he forced Hazard out for his handling of newspaper distribution."

"Sounds like Washington wasn't in support of Franklin's pick," said Ethan.

"Sure he was."

"Washington took out Franklin's guy," said Ethan. "How can that be in support of Franklin and his network?"

"I think you have the wrong idea of Washington's decision to terminate Hazard's post," Henry said.

"The post office was running to the beat of its own drum since 1775 but now we had established a country and the post office appeared to be making its own interpretation of free speech. It started when Hazard stopped giving newspaper publishers the ability to exchange copies by mail during the Constitutional Convention. Hazard knew the postal network operated more freely under the Articles of the Confederation. However, George Washington stated that Hazard was '*inducing a belief that the suppression of intelligence at that critical juncture was a wicked trick of policy contrived by an aristocratic junto.'* Now as President Washington, he could exercise the powers of the office, he removed Ebenezer to ensure that the freedoms he fought during the Revolution were enforced. Washington helped Franklin more than you know.

"At some point, we will discuss how and when Franklin entrusted your origin with such people as George Washington, John Adams, Thomas Jefferson, and other patriots of the era but today, we'll stay on Kronos.

"Until the federal government was established under our Constitution, a member of Kronos operated as postmaster general. After the constitution was ratified in 1789, we were so embedded and hidden within the structure of the national postal system that it was nearly impossible for any congressional leader or presidential-appointed secretary to discover an agency that had an operating budget of one carrier's salary. When President Washington appointed Samuel Osgood to be the 'first' Postmaster General of the United States, he decided the *time travel* part of Kronos was no longer to be revealed to any incoming postmaster, since the position was a revolving door of appointees and there was very little a postmaster could have done in the early stages. The primary operatives would remain small and communicate directly with each sitting president.

"The lifeblood of Kronos was communication, nothing more. Until we had to build the mechanism, we never required an abundance of resources. Those performing tasks for our core group were full-time employees of the U.S. Post Office, the Postal Inspection Service, and the Committee of Safety. Granted at the time of the Revolution, the Committee of Safety was authorized to intercept, open, and detain letters. All intelligence gathering was used for the security of the colonies and then the United States, but Kronos had people within each department of intelligence gathering. Unfortunately, all departments operated within the fiscal and political structure of the federal government.

"From the beginning the U.S. Post Office experienced problems. The network was growing exponentially with new towns, new homes, and demands from Congressional leaders for more post routes. Under the Articles of Confederation, Congress was given too much control over the post office. Article Nine stated that *Congress establishes the post offices in each state, and can charge postage on items handled by the post office to help pay expenses.* For years there was concern the federal postal system would be splintered into congressional districts. Members of Kronos reached out to President Washington for a solution. It took some years but when the *Postal Act of 1792* was signed on February 20, Congress lost their influence and money, for all profits now went to the Treasury. This reduced the state-to-state corruption and ensured that the postal system was to be recognized as one national network.

"Kronos had just a few early mandates from 1792 to 1819, such as monitoring suspicious activity and handling the storage of all reference material created by Franklin and his distinctive colleague."

Ethan held up his hand to stop Henry for a moment. "I'm sorry, who?" he asked.

"His colleague," said Henry, "you." Henry reached out and pointed toward the journal. "See, you have this journal, but it had to be concealed, passed through time, and then revealed."

"Oh, I see," said Ethan. "The journal was hidden within the post office."

"Yes, and anything else you wrote or anything that might have referenced you or events out of place."

"What else did I write?" asked Ethan.

"Just some notes but, I wouldn't give it too much thought," said Henry.

"And what do you mean by 'events out of place'?"

"Well, as we go along, you will learn that you had, or will have, interactions with a variety of people. In some cases, a letter might have been written where you are referenced, and if that happened, we had to retrieve those letters at the appropriate time to conceal them. For example, anyone who owns a copy of Benjamin Franklin's autobiography will notice his memoirs end before returning to Philadelphia in 1775. Thankfully everyone believes he was unable to complete it due to old age and are sadden that his personal accounts of the Continental Congress, the Revolution, and all events thereafter, were never recorded for prosperity." Henry then raised his eyebrows and gave Ethan a grin, "lucky us, huh?"

"You removed chapters from Franklins' Autobiography?"

"His autobiography doesn't have chapters," replied Henry. "They are a collection of self-reflecting letters. Which made it easy to pull everything and spread the perception that it could not be completed due to his mortality."

Before Ethan could speak, a delivery boy walked into the shop. "Who ordered Five Guys?" he shouted.

Henry held up his right arm and stuck out his pointer finger. "Yo! Right here," he shouted. As the young man brought the bag over, Henry touched both pants pockets. "Uh oh," he said. "This is embarrassing." He stood up and patted around the pockets on the rear of his jeans, "I would have sworn it was back there," he mumbled to himself. With his right hand, still in his back pocket, he looked up at Ethan, "You have anything on you?" he asked.

Ethan's mouth opened. He thought to himself that it was Henry who suggested ordering this food, and if he and the staff were a part of a government agency, why not just have someone in the front pay for it? Contemplating all of this, Ethan mouthed, "seriously?"

"Hey, Henry," said the young man.

"Hey AJ. How's it going today?"

"Good, good," said AJ, as he handed the bag to Henry. "Thanks for the generous tip."

"Oh, not a problem, I know I caught you right when you opened. I appreciate you coming out."

"No problem, boss," said AJ. "You have a good day."

"Thanks," said Henry, "you too." As he opened the paper bag he looked at Ethan, "I'm a boss," he said. Henry then leaned over the top of the bag and inhaled deeply. "Ahhhh," he said. "I love that smell. Fresh fried potatoes. They just know how to do it over there."

"You're an ass," said Ethan. "I take it you paid for it already."

"Yes. They used my account when the order was placed." Henry then removed the individual paper bags of burgers and fries. He threw Ethan his two items. "You eat, and I'll wrap this up," he said, "because, I'd like you to know some of the pivotal moments of our history."

"One thing, before you start," said Ethan. "What did you mean about *lucky us* regarding Franklin's autobiography?"

Henry replied, as he reached in and ate the fries from the bottom of the paper bag, "What I meant was that Franklin made a couple of slips." He then had to stop before choking on the few fries he was eating. After a forced swallow, Henry continued, "He slipped in his autobiography. He made references to people and places that he thought were inconsequential, but it would have raised the more dangerous questions of 'How did he know that' or 'Why did he say that.' So, we decided it would be easier if we just ended his autobiography in 1775 before your arrival."

"Get out of here?" replied Ethan. "That's crazy."

"Well again, it worked out for us," said Henry. "I mean it wasn't just the autobiography that contained compromising information. We knew documents, written by some of our founders, existed but none of the proprietors at any time were a risk. None of them could ever read all the letters and documents in their possession. Nor, would any of them be able to form a conclusion that would jeopardize our mission. It wasn't until we moved into the computer age that our group acted to assure all information relevant to your identity was appropriated. In 1950 we worked with President Truman and helped influence the creation of the Federal Records Act. With the help of National Historical Publications Commission, we were then able to retrieve all the founding father's records and pull what we wanted. To this day different entities continue to review and release the massive collection, which is known as the 'Founding Fathers Paper Project'. Yale is still in the process of releasing the massive works of Benjamin Franklin, but some items, you can say, are *missing*."

"Wow," said Ethan. "Impressive."

"Yes, it was," Henry said with a smile. "But let me get back to what I was telling you earlier."

"All right."

Henry continued, "In the country's infancy, there were problems seen in every part of the system. The post office was no different as it expanded over the decades. Just like anything with good intentions, it became too easy to corrupt in regional areas. There wasn't a strong structure from state to state, and appointed postmasters started to add their own rules that created additional revenues for themselves.

"In 1822, under President James Monroe, at a pivotal time when the postal system was falling apart, John McLean was hand selected to save the integrity of the USPS by instituting the spoke-and-wheel concept of delivery, which revolutionized the system and is still in use. Simply put, a central hub takes in the bulk of mail for the region and then it gets distributed locally to the branches.

"Why is that important? Cause and effect. While John McLean was working to save the postal system, the idea of decommissioning the federal unit and turning it over to the states was beginning to softly echo, again, in certain circles. When John Quincy Adams was elected President in 1825, he appointed John McLean Postmaster and felt it was paramount to bring McLean on the inside of Kronos and the Franklin Project. President Quincy Adams knew if McLean was made aware of everything, he would work twice as hard to succeed at his appointment. This was a risk, but it seemed prudent. McLean dedicated more of his facilities to structure and expansion to revitalize the integrity of the postal system to ensure the Kronos network remained hidden within the USPS. Under McLean's leadership, the post office turned around and generated a profit for the first time in decades."

"What effect did that have?" asked Ethan.

"Well," replied Henry, "Because McLean did such a tremendous job, the Post Office Department, as McLean referred to it, was a respected government institution. The reputation of the Post Office Department was structurally sound and gained the public trust again. When President Andrew Jackson arrived, he wanted that strong operating government institution connected with his White House. In 1829, the prized post of Postmaster General became a seat in the presidential cabinet.

"Signs of the nation heading towards a civil engagement began to show in 1833, when President Jackson had to confront the potential secession from South Carolina. Even though we were thirty years away, tensions were quite high. President Jackson was trying to avoid war, but antislavery advocates wanted something done. They used the post office as a means of distributing abolitionists information. Slavery proponents stormed post offices to obtain these documents. Many offices were raided and burned in protest."

"Why is this important?" asked Ethan. "I don't understand the comparison between the establishment of the agency and all these anecdotes about the Post Office Department."

"I'm trying to show you how one effects the other," said Henry. "History, or trying to make history, must be observed or engaged in like a game of chess. Each move dictates a countermove. Each move throughout time dictates an event in time. Those events branch off, which create other events, and other moments, and so on and so on."

"You mean every action has a reaction?" asked Ethan.

"Yes, exactly."

"Why couldn't you just say that?"

Henry mused for a moment. "Well," he said, "I have found when thinking of our mission the phrase 'every action has a reaction' implies chaos, whereas viewing the mission on a chessboard gives it structure and control. Mistakes will be made. We are only human, and painful sacrifices must be endured, but in the end, you want to know what the proper reaction should be."

"I see," said Ethan. "I guess you view the Franklin Project is a single chess piece and the Kronos as one giant board?"

Henry started laughing at the image Ethan was depicting, "Sure that's a good way to vision it," he said. "Just like in a game of chess, every now and then, a player has a surprise move. For us, the surprise move came during the Civil War."

Henry continued, "After the election of President Lincoln in 1860, war appeared to be inevitable. We tried to lure the few associates we had in the South to remain in Washington before war broke out in 1861, many refused. When the Confederacy established their post office, Jefferson Davis selected John Reagan as postmaster. John Reagan was a former congressman in the U.S. House Representatives and Union supporter, but being from the recently seceded state of Texas, he sided with the Confederacy. At the time of his appointment the Confederate postal system was a joke. Reagan's first effort was to recruit nearly every high-level employee of the U.S. Post Office Department in Washington by promising them God knows what. Unfortunately, not enough were able to see through the acts of desperation within the unattainable promises. Reagan power grabbed a lot of post office workers from the Union. This included many workers who performed tasks for Kronos.

"Now imagine you are the President of the United States and your postmaster informs you that a mission, which has been in progress for the past eighty-five years and is still one hundred and fifty years away from reaching completion, is at risk of exposure should John Reagan and Jefferson Davis become informed of some of the unusual undertakings the post office was engaged in. But informed of what exactly? Neither Lincoln nor Postmaster Montgomery Blair could conclude with absolute certainty.

"From the start, the decree from Franklin was to make all discoveries occur as gradual as nature intended. But how do you do that? How do you contain an operation that requires a level of domestic communication monitoring, a level of international intelligence gathering, and a high-level of management to overlook the project? Franklin knew the more people you bring in to an operation, the more complex the management of disclosure would become. If two or three people at a time know what is at stake but make use of whomever to take care of minuscule tasks, then by outward appearance it would look like nothing was happening. The most rational politician would first conclude that the information was being gathered for an agency outside of the post office. Such organizations like the Secrets Committee or the recently created Bureau of Military Information would be the sensible beneficiaries of that material. That would be for any rational politician to think, but if you were the President of the United States, would you take that chance?

"A breach of classified information was not the only threat to the postal system of the Union. There was a lack of able men. Appropriately, the post office looked to women to fill the empty positions. In 1862, Postmaster General Blair became the first high-ranking government official to employ women in the Washington, D.C. headquarters of the Post Office Department. The women who were hired were designated to sort and file in the Dead Letter Office. Blair consistently praised them. For the incredible hard work and dedication, mind you, these women were earning 35 percent less and outnumbered the staff thirty-eight to seven.

"But as the nation was pulling itself apart, everyone was pulling together. In 1862, when word of the post office defection became publicly known in Washington, the former U.S. Senator Robert John Walker requested President Lincoln to hold an audience with his daughter, Mary. No one was present when they spoke, but we do know that when the great-great-great granddaughter of Benjamin Franklin, Mrs. Mary Walker Brewster, sat with President Lincoln she asked him if he still retained the letter her distant grandfather wrote to him. She reminded him that the letter was hand delivered by a kind old man, named Ethan, when he was the postmaster of New Salem, Illinois, thirty years prior.

"In the letter Franklin wrote toward the end of his life, he identified Abraham as the one who could correct what he and his fellow countrymen were unable to achieve when the country was formed. Namely, ensure the context of the two cherished documents of the federal government applied to all inhabitants within it.

"The letter, in part, urged Lincoln to always use *every possible means to ensure the anonymity of his postal network and to be cognizant that although the actions themselves may appear to be unmerciful, the failure to follow this mandate doesn't only risk the failure to win a war, it risks the abortion of the nation while it was being conceived, and the extermination of his life and all lives present.* Lincoln made the deserters of the post office, traitors, and enemies of the state. Some were brought to justice, but Lincoln only sought retribution against the handful of men who held higher knowledge of the inner operations of the Post Office Department.

"President Lincoln did not have time to devote to the restructuring of the Kronos network. That mandate was put on the postmaster general with encouragement from Mary Brewster. She persuaded Blair to work with the women of the Dead Letter annex and brought the first woman he hired, Adeline Evans, inside as an associate to Kronos. It was Adeline's attention to detail and evident dedication to the cause of the Union that Blair trusted her immensely. In a session with President Lincoln, Blair, and Brewster, Adeline was counseled and entrusted with the secrets of our founding. Mary shared with her the great contribution one of her descendants would make. Adeline, in the end, dedicated thirty years of her life to the Post Office and Kronos.

"What was the *great contribution*?" Ethan asked.

"Well, I was going to get to that," said Henry. "Remember Mary? Who was referenced in the journal? Who is *waiting* for you in the past?"

"Yes," replied Ethan.

"Her name is Mary Evans Smith," said Henry. "She is the great, great, ah great." Henry was attempting to picture in his mind the linage but gave up and threw his hands up in the air, "I don't remember. Let's say about five *greats,* from Adeline. I forgot the exact number of great-great's there are, but Mary is a direct descendant. Her involvement with Kronos started at a young age. She knew her destiny while she was a teenager. Her training was slightly more militaristic, more operative, than yours will need to be. You needed to develop an organic personality to engage with Franklin, whereas for Mary, we needed someone who would focus solely on the operations."

"I see," said Ethan. "Was Mary Brewster running Kronos after the Civil War?"

"Oh no," said Henry. "Her contribution was completed in a couple of meetings, but she revitalized the purpose of Franklin's work and helped refine the structure of the operation. It breathed new life into the project, and with the inclusion of women in the system, it helped keep everything in check, while working under the good ole' boy's government."

Ethan started laughing at Henry's jab at old-style politics, just then his phone vibrated.

Lauren: The doctor just called back. I missed the call but he left me voicemail. I called the office, he's seeing a patient and will call me.
Ethan: Ok, what did he say?

163

Lauren: He said the blood work showed something he wanted to talk about. WTF?
Ethan: I'm sure it's nothing. Let me know what he says.
Lauren: Ok.

Ethan put the phone down and looked up at Henry, "Sorry," he said.

"No problem. Did you tell her you got a job?" he asked with a grin.

"No," said Ethan. "So how do we get to here from the Civil War?"

"All right, I will go faster to give you the abridged explanation," said Henry. "After the Civil War, we were rebuilding, not just the Post Office Department but the Nation. We fought for many things, but in the end, after all the blood, we reformed our identity, and the assassination of Lincoln solidified that identity. His death unified the nation more so than General Lee's surrender at Appomattox Court House. Lincoln's industry was used to rectify our sins, and his life was sacrificed to bind our American spirit again.

"As for the workings of the Post Office Department, we went almost a whole century without any inclination that another body of government was aware of anything regarding The Franklin Project. Before the Civil War, we had the U.S. Postal Inspection Service and the Marshals Service as our federal law enforcement, along with the Justice Department. Then came the Civil War. From that point, we developed our first public American Intelligence agency, the Bureau of Military Information. Ironically, the day he was assassinated, President Lincoln signed the legislation that was then used to create the Secret Service. As these new facets of the federal government formed, we sought means to take full advantage of them through the executive office.

"Knowing that technology was about to expand, continuing to have the post office monitor communication outside of the letters that traffic through the postal network would raise suspicion and risked shining a light onto our operations. Kronos needed to step out of intelligence monitoring and collecting and retreat into the shadows. Postmaster General

George von Lengerke Meyer, at the start of 1900s, discussed with President Roosevelt the need to create a bureau to help with intelligence gathering. Roosevelt conceived with Attorney General Charles Bonaparte the Justice Department's Bureau of Investigation, which would be renamed thirty years later to the Federal Bureau of Investigation.

"Now, with that aspect of governance out of our hands, Kronos's focus was directed to the discovery of the elements and establishment of the technologies needed to accomplish our chief assignment: time travel. As stipulated by Franklin, we needed to wait for the world to go to war to accelerate the discoveries. Advancements of electricity, hydroelectricity, atomic energy, and rocket propulsion allowed us to create the mechanism."

"The mechanism?" asked Ethan.

"Correct," replied Henry. "The mechanism we created that triggers the time travel sequence. We call it a Kinetic Inductance Transport Engager, or KITE."

Ethan let a laugh and rolled his eyes, "Oh god," he said. "Really? That's what was written in the journal. It referenced KITE. I didn't know what that meant."

"Yes," said Henry. "And we call you 'The Key.' But if I were you, I wouldn't make fun of it. Many great scientific minds helped create that machine, including Einstein and Tesla."

"Was Kronos ever a part of the military?" asked Ethan.

"No," replied Henry. "We have always been hidden behind the shield of the post office and with the help of President Nixon, we turned the post office into a semi-independent corporation with the Postal Reorganization Act. The postmaster general was no longer a part of the cabinet, and it essentially drew up a curtain to congressional leaders. This was vital to our operation as we were beginning preparation for the arrival of the key, a.k.a. your birth."

"Very funny," Ethan said with a smirk. His phone then vibrated, alerting him to an incoming text.

> **Lauren: I need you home right now. I spoke to the doctor, he saw something wrong with my protein and thinks it's dangerously high. I need you here. Please come home.**
> **Ethan: On my way.**

Ethan jumped out of his chair, "Henry I have to leave right now, I'm sorry."

Henry could see the concern in Ethan's face. "What? Is everything okay?"

"I don't know," Ethan said, "Lauren said she needs me. We'll talk again."

"Understood," said Henry, "Good luck."

Chapter Thirteen

April 19, 1775: It Begins

This is the day the Lord has made. Let us rejoice and be glad!

The quote from Psalms was echoing, in the hallways, in various rooms, and outside in the field throughout the entire day. Before the sun hinted that it was going to rise, that verse was used like a morning alarm as it was shouted in my room. When my faculties focused and I recognized it was Philip; my first thought was he was going out of his mind and the ten years of colonial living has drove him mad to the point he was now quoting scripture. But while he stood quiet in my room for several seconds, candle in hand, I was hoping to hear him say something else. It has been more than three weeks now, and I have had the impression since my arrival that Philip holds some resentment towards me. Our conversations have yet to go beyond my current health status and the salutations one gives at certain parts of the day.

From the reflection of the candlelight, I could make out a slight grin. Was it because he scared me half to death and it brought him amusement? Or was there another reason? Before I could ask, he turned and closed the door. While making his way through the hallway and down the stairs, he continued to make his proclamation. He even poked the ceiling in the room beneath mine and yelled it once more before exiting the house. Although he was outdoors, I could still hear Philip through the windows while he entered Andrew's house to alert him and the few members of his crew who stayed overnight. After that, the sound of the proclamation slowly faded as Philip headed towards his office on the opposite end of the field. With silence returning, and darkness still holding in the sky, I drifted back to sleep.

It felt as if only a few minutes passed since I closed my eyes before Philip was back in my room crying out again, "This is the day the Lord has made. Let us rejoice and be glad!" At least this time when my head jumped off the pillow, the sun was out. "What is it Philip?" I asked him. "Wake up brother, let us celebrate this day. Celebrate and remember those sacrificing themselves for the glorious cause," he said to me before leaving the room, again. Mary then entered with the housemaid Elizabeth. They were bringing me breakfast and fresh linens.

From when I arrived, until last week, I had depended on others to get out of bed, stand upright, and move just about anywhere. Slowly, thanks to their therapy, I've recaptured the strength to do things on my own again. This morning I'm pleased to report that I propped myself up out of bed, rolled to one side, and stood up using the walker Philip designed for me. The walker had a shield in front which provided a little privacy as my night garment was removed, and I received a quick wash and fresh garments.

No more than ten paces from the bed, next to the window, sits my chair, but with the tension in my hip, the popping in my knees, and continuing sensation of my ankles vibrating every few seconds, it was as if the chair was set a few hundred yards away. With every step, I still sense shooting pain from my heel into the hip and lower back. I wince with every motion but I am more embarrassed for my lack of mobility. With so many passing weeks, I assumed I would have overcome these side effects by now. A good sign this morning was that I persevered under my own power. Although it did take several minutes to walk those ten paces to the chair, after that strenuous display of human triumph, I received a polite applause from Elizabeth.

Thankfully this morning was overcast, with a cool breeze that kept me from perspiring. Elizabeth brought in the food trolley and arranged it for my breakfast and then left the room, taking out my night garments and linens. Mary remained to administer my morning shot and then we talked for a bit about my current health status, what symptoms I was experiencing and so forth, as she fixed the bed. When I finished my meal of dry toast with peanut butter, two cups of tea, and bananas with oatmeal, Mary had set up the parallel bars and the massage table on the other side of the room. It was a foldable wooden table with some cotton and straw padding. It was not the most comfortable thing in the world, but it did serve its purpose.

Elizabeth returned with towels, hot water, and the metal bucket of warm stones. She left those items on the massage table and then moved the food trolley to the hallway to make extra space. In hopes to prolong the return of self-mobility, I lifted myself out of the chair and grabbed onto the bars. Mary kept herself right in front of me and Elizabeth was behind me for support. For the most part, today I required little assistance to complete the exercises that consisted of lunges, squats, leg extensions, and triceps dips. Although to anyone watching none of my motions resembled those exercises. For my own defense, I did do them to the best of my current physical abilities. What was more encouraging was that I walked back and forth on the bars twenty times, which was twice as long than I accomplished any previous day. I kept picturing Philips' grin from this morning, and I carried the presumption that he was looking down on me due to my slow recovery. I pushed myself to show Philip and Mary that I was a strong individual and, as foolish as this may sound given that I require assistance moving about my room, the leader of this group.

When I finished the exercises, I grabbed the walker and moved over to the massage table. I lifted myself on to the edge on my own, but I did require assistance from both Mary and Elizabeth to ensure my head would not slam into the table when I attempted to lay down. As both attended to me, they pulled and bent each limb. They massaged, rubbed in aloe, and wrapped them in warm towels. Then when I turned over, they placed the warm stones along my spine and all the tension in my back melted away. When we finished, I got a quick wash over and new clothes. I grabbed the walker again and made my way back to the chair to relax. All equipment was removed and the food trolley was brought back in for lunch.

Sitting alone in the room I heard the echoes from the field. "This is the day the Lord as made. Let us rejoice!" only this time the rest of the verse was now being shouted by the crew. In one massive collected voice, I heard ten men shout, "AND BE GLAD!" When Mary returned, I asked, "Why does Philip keep saying that phrase?" Mary said today was April 19, as she grabbed the walker and took it out of the room. She then returned with a cane, handed it to me, and told me this was going to be what I used from now on. It was a well-made piece—it had a dark cherry color with a brass footing of a couple of inches and the top did not have a handle, instead it was a large knob.

I placed the cane along the windows edge and asked Mary, "Why is Philip saying that phrase again?" With a baffled look, Mary said, "Today is April 19." For some reason, I wasn't catching on and Mary saw this. She said, "You know? The start of the Revolution? The Battles of Lexington and Concord? Which are happening at this very moment? Did Henry not go over this with you? Or better yet, did you not go over this in eighth-grade history?" I laughed at her bewilderment, then I mentioned that Henry and I covered more of the people and events I was going to be involved with, or the events that involved them, and that I was not entirely familiar with the battle.

Mary was shocked and shook her head saying, "Oh Henry." She then said, "Wait, please tell me he at least explained the Covenant Chain and the two decades of turmoil that led to the Revolution?"

"Of course," I told her. "Henry and Audrey explained that to me since it was related to Dr. Franklin. I just meant we did not go into the particulars of the Battles of Lexington and Concord." Mary then sat on the bed and told me to pay attention, which made the little hairs in my ears stand up because that was what Henry always said before he told me something important.

She explained how the townsmen of Lincoln, Menotomy, Cambridge, Lexington, and Concord were warned last night, April 18, by Paul Revere, Samuel Prescott, and William Dawes that the British fleet was sailing into Boston. Revere and Dawes rode on horseback to the small town of Lexington and instructed the townsmen to grab their arms to defend themselves. They then proceeded to warn Samuel Adams and John Hancock to leave under the cover of night to avoid apprehension. Along the route, they met Prescott, who was a godsend because shortly after, Revere was captured and Dawes was hurt and unable to proceed. It's only due to Samuel Prescott the people of Concord were warned. For it's in Concord where a large arms cache is held and per the order from British General Thomas Gage, six companies were dispatched last night to "seize and destroy all military store whatever."

When dawn approached this morning in Massachusetts, as Philip awoken me with verse, seven hundred British men in their red coats arrived in Lexington and found a minuscule road block of militia composed of seventy-seven men, led by Captain John Parker, who fought for Britain during the French and Indian war but much like many of his countrymen, he was tired of the King over-stretching his power and overtaxing to pay for the tremendous debt incurred due to the first world war. As Mary pointed out, little did colonial merchants care to realize that it was London who carried the heavier burden to pay for the King's victory, while many colonies in America were essentially practicing "free trade." However, it was the principle of not allowing the King to erode their liberties one proclamation at a time that rang stronger than the argument of taxation in return for the security by the Empire.

When the red coats approached Lexington, they saw defiant rebels standing in their way. John Parker and his militia saw representatives of the King's tyranny. The British Commander told the townsmen to surrender. The line was held by many locals, who didn't have much to their names, along with some slaveholders. John Parker told his Minutemen to hold and famously said, "Stand your ground. Don't fire unless fired upon, but if they mean to have a war, let it begin here!" And that is when, in Lexington, the crumbling of the British Empire began with a single shot fired from the side of the British Army. That moment will be recorded as "the shot heard round the world," for with that gunshot—started the American Revolution. Shortly after all guns fired, when the first round of shooting came to a stop, nine militia men and one British soldier were killed. Of the nine militiamen, one slave named Prince Estabrook, recorded as "Prince Easterbrooks, A Negro Man" in future archives (and oddly enough, missing the honorific "Mr."), was the first African American to *give* his life for the glorious cause.

The massive red coat army then marched the seven miles to Concord. Along the way, they met more resistance, accompanied by both slave and freed men, including Peter Salem who was recently freed by Major Lawson Buckminster to serve with the militia. When the British Army finally reached Concord, they searched for the armaments cache. What they found was just a few weapons, along with some equipment, and they decided to burn them all. However, the fire grew and it sent out a signal for miles. A group of militiamen saw this fire from outside of Concord and they thought it was going to burn down the whole town, so they ran toward it. A contingent of British soldiers, occupying the North Bridge into Concord, noticed this group of men with arms running toward them. To defend themselves, the soldiers opened fire, but they promptly retreated when the large militia began to return the favor. In the armament, the fire never grew out of control, but the British would remain in Concord, hoping to find the depot.

Hours passed, and by the time the British decided to stop searching, about two thousand Minutemen were now in and around Concord, ready to fight. The British Army had eighteen miles to cover to return to Boston harbor, but now they found themselves surrounded and had to engage. But, on this day a new style of warfare was introduced to the London-based battalion. By applying the tactics some of these former men of the Kings Armed Forces adopted and used during the French and Indian War, the Minutemen were spread out, using trees, houses, and stone walls for cover. The British Army still engaged in their classic warfare—they stood together, shoulder to shoulder, musket to musket, and in the open road.

With numerous points of origin, the shooting would come toward the British Army from various locations. The British Commander had to order the retreat to the naval ships for additional protection. As they withdrew, more local townsmen arrived to fight them off, but being under attack from the uncoordinated militia was the only saving grace for these British soldiers. When a shot was fired, there was a higher probability that it would miss. Once the British made it to Lexington, they were met with reinforcements. The attacks from the militia continued heading into Cambridge as this British Army retreated and at the same time were trying to stop the Colonists from fighting.

At the end of the day, or should I say at the end of today, more than three thousand Americans united. Killing around two hundred and fifty British soldiers and losing ninety of their own. Had this group been trained and more organized, they could have killed all seven hundred. But, it was not meant to be. Mary said that today was not about their inability to organize and execute attack maneuvers. Today was about their ability to organize for the same cause. Today, men of all different backgrounds and all different occupations stood together as one and fought for freedom. Some would go on to serve under George Washington, in the Continental Army. One of the fighters of Lexington and Concord, Peter Salem, the recently freed slave who lived until 1812, ended up serving in the Army for five years.

Mary said, today will be a great day, forever remembered because of what's to follow. She said, I'm sure when Franklin stopped Independence the first time, no one cared to remember the Battles of Lexington and Concord but because history will go down a more favorable path, the lives that were taken from us today will be canonized as long as Americans want liberty and freedom.

I heard the pride in her voice. I never looked at the engagement as anything more than the start of a bloody and hard-fought revolution. I never observed this day with the same appreciation and commemoration Philip and Mary displayed. I know it never dawned on me that the men who came together to fight would begin to outline the definition of being an American. I always, or have recently, looked toward Franklin and Washington as the early definers of what it meant to be an "American." But, after what I was just told, I know I will always remember and appreciate what took place outside of Boston today.

Before Mary left, I complimented her on her attention to detail and said how it reminded me of my conversations with Henry. She then said with a smile, "Where do you think he learned it?"

Overwhelmed with a new sense of pride, I understood why Philip was so joyous. I reached for the cane and stood up without thinking of any pain and only thinking of what those three thousand Americans did for us today, I leaned to the window where I could see Philip and the other men. I shouted as loud as I could:

"THIS IS THE DAY THE LORD HAS MADE! LET US REJOICE . . .."

Chapter Fourteen

Purpose

The heavy mid-afternoon rain clouds provided no seam of autumn sunshine to peak through, and a dull gray cascaded along the world outside. In the office, Ethan looked toward the dreary sky, as he rested on the sofa. The glow from the monitors was the only light illuminating his gloomy sanctuary. Alone with his emotions, his thoughts were putting him on the verge of tears. Exhausted from several sleepless nights, Ethan closed his eyes to recoup his energy. Pandora provided the background distraction to mute his inner dialogue. A gentle calm rushed over, his eyes grew heavy, the tension in his muscles began to relax, his lungs opened a bit more, and he exhaled strongly. Ethan started to descend into much needed sleep.

Minutes into his rest, the doorbell rang. Ethan jumped off the sofa, grabbed his jeans from the chair, and attempted to dress himself as he walked toward the stairs. The left leg went in with no effort, but trying to get the right leg in caused him to lose his balance. Hobbling around the room, Ethan made his way back to the sofa. The doorbell rang again. The front windows in his office were slightly open. Knowing that if he yelled loud enough the person below would hear him, Ethan shouted, "HOLD ON!"

When he reached the bottom of the stairs Ethan quickly unlocked the door to find Henry standing there. He was not in his postal gear. He was dressed casually, holding an envelope, and carrying a plastic bag.

"Hi, Ethan."

Feeling a bit annoyed by the intrusion, Ethan shook his head in disappointment. He knew it was only a matter of time before Henry would approach him again. "What do you want, Henry? I told you a month ago, I am out! You will need find yourself another candidate for your venture."

"I know, Ethan, but we need to talk."

"Henry, I have too much to deal with now, and I cannot be bothered with anymore history lessons."

"May I come in, Ethan, I just want to talk to you." Henry then held up the bag he was holding. "I brought a half a pound of Kona for you. I thought that might cheer you up a little."

"Henry," Ethan said with a sigh.

"I'll be quick. Five minutes."

Ethan stepped back and put his right arm up in a welcoming gesture. As Henry passed, he looked back at Ethan. "Five minutes," Ethan said.

As Henry made it to the top of the stairs, not sure which room to enter, he pointed to both, asking Ethan where he should go.

"Go to the office on the right," said Ethan. "Sorry it's a little messy."

"Not a problem."

Being the polite host, which he learned from his parents, Ethan was compelled to offer his uninvited guest something. "Would you like a drink?" he asked.

Henry reached into the bag. "Do you want to make this?" he said with a smile as he shook the coffee beans.

Ethan knew with the task of brewing a pot of coffee would make Henry stay longer than five minutes. However, within the first few moments of Henry's presence it brought a comfort to the dreary room Ethan tried to sleep in, just a few minutes ago. "All right," said Ethan as he grabbed the coffee. "I'll be right back, have a seat."

Just as Ethan exited the room, he swore he heard Henry ask, "*How's Lauren?*" Ethan quickly turned around and stepped back into the room. "What did you say?" he asked.

"I said where's Lauren," replied Henry.

"She went out with her mother. She needed some time out of the house." Ethan than left the room again and made his way to the kitchen.

While sitting in the office, Henry could hear the music from the computer. The final track from *The Dark Knight Rises* score was playing, and as the volume grew, it drowned out the faint sounds coming from the kitchen where Ethan was preparing the coffee maker. Henry walked over to the desk and was impressed with the three-monitor setup Ethan had for his computer. He observed the different websites that were opened on each one, and noticed the multiple tabs in every Google Chrome browser. Henry could see that Ethan was doing extensive research. In the center screen, he noticed a medical research website was up, and it was on the subject of blood cancers. The other tabs showed more sites on the topic of myeloma. On the right screen, two tabs were linked to support pages from Sloan Kettering and the Leukemia and Lymphoma Society; on the left screen was an Amazon page with a list of books from a search for "spouses with cancer." Henry leaned in to read the list of books, but then jumped in his seat when he heard the coffee grinder start.

Henry made his way to the kitchen entrance, and he saw Ethan standing with his back to him. He was hunched over with both hands pressed on the counter top. With the sound of steam puffs and water drips escaping the coffee maker, Ethan heard the faint footsteps behind him. Holding his position Ethan said, "Henry, this just dawned on me as you arrived." Ethan then turned around and rested against the counter. "Last time we spoke, you told me a couple of times about how Lauren would be taken care of. How she would have the best health coverage, and so on."

"That's right," said Henry. "I wanted to make it clear to you that it wasn't just financial support we were trying to give you. It was an assurance for anything that could occur in your absences."

"Well, I thought that it was just a tactic to play on my emotions to compel me to agree to take part in your project. But now that I recall the number of times you mentioned health care and by coming to my door after I told you I wanted nothing more to do with your *Franklin Project*, you must answer me this. If you want to gain my trust, you must answer me straight. You must do it right here, and right now."

Henry looked across the room at Ethan. He could see the exhaustion from his posture, the paleness in face, and the frustration in his eyes. He knew Ethan was a on the brink of breaking down. Henry walked up to the Ethan and rested his right hand on his shoulder. "What do you want to know."

"Did you know about this? Did you know what was going to happen to my wife?"

Henry began to shake his head. He looked away for a moment as he could not find the words.

"Did you know she was going to be diagnosed with cancer? Multiple Myeloma? A blood cancer? Something that she will *never* be able to rid her body of? Did you know you that?"

Henry took a deep breath and looked back to Ethan. "Yes, I did. We all did."

"When did you know?"

"We've known, well, forever," said Henry.

"How?"

"You told Franklin, and us. So, it has been an objective of our group to, at the right time, intervene with her care."

Ethan closed his eyes and leaned his head back against the counter, "Then tell me, is she going to die?"

Henry squeezed Ethan's shoulder, "No, no, no, Ethan," he said. "Lauren is going to be fine. She is going nowhere. Through the grace of God, she caught this early."

"Right," Ethan said. "But if you knew why didn't you tell me? Why when you were telling me about this Franklin nonsense, didn't you say that Lauren should go see a doctor?"

"Well, had I said that, I doubt you would have been receptive to the suggestion from your postal carrier that your wife should see a doctor to be tested for cancer. The plan was, once our doctors screened her, we would have told her."

"That day I left you in the coffee shop, her general doctor said he 'saw' something wrong with her protein levels and was concerned that it was cancerous. We checked with a hematologist, who confirmed the levels indicated Myeloma. After multiple scans, blood tests, and two spinal fluid tests later, it was confirmed two days ago—she has cancer."

"I'm very sorry, Ethan" said Henry.

"Why didn't you just say something years ago?"

"Ethan, it wouldn't have made a difference. This cancer doesn't form from being exposed to anything, it comes from within, from the bones. No matter what was done, we would have never been able to prevent her from having cancer."

"I haven't slept since. She's stronger than me. She's making the best of it. Not letting it get her down. I mean, she's worried, but earlier she was joking around and went out to do some shopping as we both are waiting to hear when she has to start treatment."

"Well, now it can be treated before there is any danger," said Henry. "What she will go through will be difficult and painful at times. Always remind yourself that you cannot fully comprehend it. All you can really do is be available, and try to make everyday a little easier. Trust me when I tell you Lauren is going to endure much longer than you and I will."

"I hope so," said Ethan. "I'll be honest, I broke down last night, hard. For the past couple of weeks with all the scans and blood marrow tests, I prayed that the results would come back negative and that first doctor who noticed it, made a mistake. When they confirmed she had it, it was a shock. She didn't gasp, she didn't cry, she just listened as everything was explained. I couldn't believe it, I was frozen in my seat, and my legs were like led. When the doctor hugged her, finally I jolted and stood up. It was as if I was watching a play and none of it was really happening."

Henry stepped over to the refrigerator and leaned against it as he and Ethan stood silently in the kitchen while the coffee maker continued to puff and drip. When the unit began beeping, Ethan was relieved and gave a small grin. He took a deep breath and rubbed his face. "Coffee is ready," he said.

"I'll pour, Ethan. Just point to where the cups are." With a head gesture, Ethan directed Henry to the cabinets near the sink. "Okay," he said, "I'll take care of this."

Ethan walked back to his desk and collapsed into his chair. Looking at all the information stretched across the monitors, Ethan minimized all browsers to show his latest wallpaper. It was a white-washed wedding photo of just the two of them. The picture was taken from the shoulders up and it was the photographer's suggestion for them not to smile. It was a nice, quiet, and calm capture of that hectic day.

"Nice photo," Henry said as he handed Ethan his cup.

Reaching out to grab his mug, Ethan looked back at the photo. "Yeah, I like it," he said. "I just don't know what I am going to do now."

Henry took a seat on the couch. He looked around the room for a place to set his mug, but with no surface nearby, he placed it on the floor. "What do you mean?" he asked.

"I mean, paying for this," said Ethan. "I've applied to a dozen jobs a day, hoping to score the best medical coverage to help us through this. I can't imagine what all of this will cost in the end."

Henry reached over to the end of the sofa to grab the brown envelope he brought with him. He then stretched out his arm to pass the envelope to Ethan.

"What's this?" asked Ethan.

"It's an answer," said Henry, "A solution. Or whatever you want it to be."

Ethan ripped the edge of the envelope and pulled out the documents inside. There was a lot of writing on the first page but Ethan did not possess the strength or patience to read it. He lightly tossed the packet on his desk and turned to Henry. "What is it?"

"It's my offer to you," Henry said. "Do you remember from the cafe?"

"Yes, I remember," Ethan said. "But even if I did want to believe you. About Franklin, the founding of this country, and this loop, this paradox that I am in, it would require me to abandon my wife in her time of great need. So even if I bought your tale, I still would not participate in it. I am needed here. I am needed to care for and love my wife."

"I wish you did believe me already," Henry said, "Because this is as real as it gets."

"Oh stop it," shouted Ethan, "this is nonsense. Look, you said Benjamin Franklin returned to Philadelphia in 1775 with one goal but someone changed his mind. Right?"

"Correct."

"So, have someone else change his mind," said Ethan, "It doesn't have to be me. Change the formula of the loop and have someone else, with no attachments, stand in my place."

"It doesn't work that way."

"Why not?"

"I told you, the bond you form with Franklin is something we cannot synthetically reproduce. Who you are, whatever life experiences you've had, and the persons who have influenced you the most, have made you into the individual you are today. This is what connects you to Benjamin Franklin. There's too much at risk if we send someone else back."

"What's the risk?" asked Ethan.

"It's the same risk that would exist if we didn't send you back," Henry said. "The world would switch off. Reality would reset and our existence as we know it today would evaporate in a second and turn into whatever the alternative is. With that, also comes a complete rearrangement and in some cases the acceleration of lineages from the eighteenth century. When I told you the story of Lou, did you notice that he was in his fifties in 2026? You wouldn't reach your fifties until 2040." Henry paused, he saw Ethan's eyes were closed and his head was resting on the chair. Henry shouted, "Ethan!"

Ethan's eyes popped back open. "What?"

"What about the journal?"

"What about it?"

"The journal is your connection to the past, Ethan. Your possession of the journal dictates events that will occur for you."

"Okay," said Ethan, "but the journal keeps updating only with stories at the mill. Nothing about crossing paths with Franklin. I read something about how I embarrassed myself asking too many questions to Andrew about slavery. Other than that awkward moment, nothing in that journal is convincing me that I am the only person who can do this. Just send someone else, consequences be damned. I'm staying here."

"Sending someone to stand in your place and alter history will erase our existence, I have no doubt about that. You must believe me. If there was another way, I would do it for you, but after everything we've talked about, you should trust by now that this paradox you are in is the truth. You must have sensed it from the letter Ben wrote to you?" asked Henry.

"Who, Ben?" replied Ethan.

"Ben Franklin," said Henry. "Where's the letter from Franklin?" Ethan had no answer to give and shrugged his shoulders. "You haven't seen it?" Henry looked all around the room. "Where's the crate?" he asked.

"It's in the dining room."

Henry bounced off his seat and walked out of the room. "I'll be right back," he said. In a few seconds, Henry returned with the crate in hand. He popped off the top and noticed that all the insulation was still inside. Henry grabbed his cup of coffee off the floor and handed it to Ethan. With both hands, he reached into the crate. Just before he pulled the straw out, he looked back up at Ethan. "Do you mind?" he asked. Ethan shrugged and gave his approval. Henry pulled out all the straw and lining in the crate and tossed it behind him onto the floor. After all of it was removed, he tilted the box toward Ethan, so he could see an envelope taped inside.

"Take it," Henry said.

Ethan reached in and pulled out an envelope with a red waxed seal. He flipped it over to view the writing on the cover. It read *Ethan Thaddeus Pope, My Friend*. Ethan placed the envelope on the desk counter and popped the seal so he could remove the contents. He then carefully unfolded the letter and started to read.

My Dearest Ethan,

As dusk approaches on my partaking in this glorious world and this young country of which I am blessed to now live in, I am reflective on how bright the sunset of my life has been since your line crossed with mine. On that note, I found myself gazing up to the Moon reminiscing on your tale of how you found your way to "Colonial Philadelphia" as you put it. When I first met you, your enthusiasm for such menial things made me consider the questionable level of your sanity, but as you insisted on holding conversation with me, I saw something within you I never experienced with any other being I have encountered. It is what has compelled me to pen this letter for you before I insert it into this holding bin for your first journal. This letter will take more than two hundred and twenty-five years to find you. When it does, I hope you take great pride in recognizing the magnitude of your decision to come to this time and at a great sacrifice that can never be fully be compensated.

While I write this, forgive me for being presumptuous. As you have assured me that the world will remember me favorably, Lord willing, I would have done enough good for my character for it to carry through the years, so that when you read this letter you may recognize my forename. Yet, with the unpleasant possibility that you do not know who I am; rest assured that I know who you are and who you will be. My name is Benjamin Franklin, and I am reaching out to you from a time gone passed, to ensure you that the journey you have been informed of is indeed forthcoming. I know you will have to take a passage during what will be the most troubling and emotional period of your life. A loved one, such as a spouse, going through an ailment, as you have advised me, is enough to bring any loving soul to their knees in a desperate desire to absorb the illness so that the other may live out of harm's way. Such desires are devoid of realism. All that can be done is to do your part to ensure their comfort, their longevity, and their prosperity endures.

To be separated by great distances when a beloved departs from the Earth is a practicality experienced by so many of my friends and family. I too have found myself grief-stricken with great loss during my residence in London. My affectionate friend Deborah suffered without my company during her final days in December 1774 before my return from London. Perhaps your unique separation from your loved one and your unique benefit of not having to navigate through the depths of despair when her day is reached is what has helped you keep your affection for her as vibrant as it has appeared.

Over these past fourteen years when we have spoken, I have been overwhelmed with the emotion and the density of your bond to your love, of whom you found the strength to depart from so that she may live in a better place and fonder world. During these fifteen years, you always surprised me with a new story from your time shared with Lauren. You would have me believe your companionship lasted fifty years, not five.

In this reflection of our time, you have made this old man's life prosperous and fulfilled beyond expectation. Upon my return to Philadelphia in seventy-five, I desired to enlighten the young men of Congress regarding the mistakes I made in my youth when I was a representative in Albany. I wanted to provide them with my settled discretion on trans-Atlantic affairs, avoid the whirlwind of engagement for prosperity's sake, and live out my days peacefully with my grandchildren. Gratefully, I have seven grandchildren now to adore. Nevertheless, that was going to be my retreat from public life. Then you intervened and tried to convince me to amend my views with tales of British retribution against my fellow delegates and a lifetime house arrest for myself. Regardless of my stubbornness, and immediate rejection of your warnings, you persisted and I am forever grateful that you did.

I have missed your company greatly these past few weeks as you tend to our first president's inauguration in New York. I miss the conversations we shared on various topics, current and soon-to-be, during our games of chess. What you shared with me has given me a great hope in where we are going in the centuries ahead. I was born too soon, for I have no shame in admitting that I am angered that I will miss these milestones. Yet, to know that I have contributed in some manner to their existence does bring me immense joy.

Before I end this note, I wanted to remind you that even though you will know all about me when we meet for the first time, I will have no recollection of you. Do not be disarmed by an old man's obstinacy when you make your introduction and I turn you away. A true friendship attracts over time, so that they may find that spark that will forever connect them.

I know you may be conflicted with the task ahead, but I urge you to seek trust. Trust in yourself, and trust in the Almighty, and do not be afraid, my Ethan. Do not be afraid of your destiny. Your life is meant to serve a great purpose. Embrace it. Do not be afraid of the challenge. The world you played a part in creating is better off. Find pride in that precious opportunity. And finally, do not be afraid for your wife. Lauren will be tended to in your absences. She will have a long and glorious life. These are truths and 'these truths are sacred and undeniable.' Permit me to borrow that phrase for my own self-purpose today.

Unfortunately, I am failing to find the proper valediction to end my letter, so I shall simply say, thank you. Your timeless friend

Benjamin Franklin

Henry sat quietly on the sofa after returning all the insulation to the crate. Sipping the remainder of the coffee, Henry studied Ethan's reactions as he read the letter. The trembling of Ethan's hand and the shaking of his leg gave an impression that reality was settling in and could no longer be rejected as folly.

Ethan sat with his right hand resting on top of the letter. His eyes started to close, and he slowly began to hunch over. Henry leaned to look at Ethan's face and saw his head was dropping lower and lower until he was asleep. Henry was unsure whether he should wake him, but he did not want to sit in the office while Ethan was sleeping. Henry attempted to reach out his arm to poke Ethan's shoulder, but before his hand could make contact, the phone rang, which made Ethan spring upright.

A picture of Lauren appeared, with the sound of Darth Vader's breathing as the selected ring tone for his beloved. Ethan looked over to see Henry quietly laughing to himself. Ethan matched Henry's reaction with a smile of his own. "Yes babe," Ethan said. Henry remained silent and listened to Ethan's responses.

"Yes."

"Really? Wait, she just called and what did she say?"

"Therapy is not needed right now?"

"Likely needed in a couple of years."

"That's great."

"Yes, I know."

"Yes."

"Yes, I was looking today, I applied to two."

By piecing together Ethan's end of the conversation, it wasn't hard for Henry to conclude that Lauren was asking about employment. Ethan had the letter from Benjamin Franklin on top of the offer of employment. Henry saw Ethan take the letter from Franklin and move it to the side to view the contract.

"Babe, I just got another offer from the Post Office."

"Yes, wait."

"Yes, it is a great opportunity but . . ."

"But," Ethan closed his eyes and took a deep breath. "I want to make you aware that this job is going to send me away."

"I mean I'm going to have to travel to, to execute the role."

"Okay."

"How much? Oh, uh two-hundred and fifty thousand."

Ethan turned to Henry. "Can you hear her screaming on the phone?" he said.

"Yes, we'll celebrate tonight."

"I love you, too."

Ethan ended the call and placed the phone on the desk, leaned back in his chair, closed his eyes again, and reflected in the quiet of the room.

Henry waited for a minute to pass until he walked next to Ethan and said, "I know how difficult this is, but if it helps at all, by doing this, you are saving Lauren. It is not *in a way* you are saving Lauren, it is in a very *real* way."

"How's that?"

"Well, if you fail to go back to 1775," said Henry, "or you fail to persuade Franklin, then this reality will cease to exist and there stands a real chance that Lauren will cease to exist. By fulfilling your destiny, not only are you ensuring her prolonged health, you are also ensuring her life."

Ethan stood up and reached out to shake Henry's hand. "Then, for Lauren's sake, I will not fail," he said.

"I will not allow it," said Henry

"So now what?" Ethan asked.

"Now we will begin preparation," said Henry. "We are down to seventeen months before the lunar eclipse, so we have some work to do. Take this weekend for yourself, but on Monday we will travel to where this all began, so pack an overnight bag."

"Where are we going?"

With a smile, Henry said, "Philadelphia."

Chapter Fifteen

May 1, 1775: Leaving for Philly

After weeks of joint pain and nightly muscle cramps, I'm happy to say I slept through the entire night without waking up once from a spasm in some part of my body. I am hoping the same blessing is bestowed upon me this evening. The tension in my lower back remains, but I think that has more to do with my lack of mobility or the lack of firmness in my mattress rather than with the lingering consequences of traveling through a worm hole in an electromagnetic beam.

At the start of the day, I rely on the cane to counter-balance my, always weaker, left leg. My dominant right side is fine, by all accounts, but by mid-morning I can move about without assistance. I am still astonished and ashamed when I was told that Philip took only a week to return to his form. I think that was an exaggeration. For weeks now whenever I would attempt to move a leg, an arm, my fingers, my toes, or any joint that was interconnected to my skeleton, it would pop with every move.

Maybe he ate more bananas and sweet potatoes which accelerated his recovery? Which would be a miracle given bananas can't grow around here and when he *landed* this was an empty field. It had to be the sweet potatoes. Mary told me it took three weeks for her to fully recover when she arrived a year ago. Maybe it was my lack of training? I don't know. For those weeks when my joints were popping with the slightest move, Mary said it was arthritis, a side effect from the event. After every muscle stiffened at once, it created muscle fatigue that would be equivalent to a week of nonstop exercising at the gym for eight hours a day. She force-fed me milk, with this powder, and bananas, lots of bananas, for seven straight days. In the evening, I was only given tea and sweet potatoes, which I've never been a fan of, except on Thanksgiving. By the seventh day, I refused to eat any more bananas or sweet potatoes, which I now think prolonged my recovery when compared with my associates.

In any event, my return to mobility could not have transpired at a better time, for we leave at dawn tomorrow. We are to head down Swamp Creek in three river boats loaded with timber. The creek will take us to the Perkiomen, which meets the Schuylkill River. On our route to Philadelphia, the river flows through Valley Forge. There we will disembark to store some logs. After we spend the night, we will travel the twenty miles along the Schuylkill into the heart of the city. I am to ride with Philip and Mary, while the crew is designated to the other two boats, including the hand manager Andrew. Thankfully, earlier tonight, I made amends with Andrew before our departure in the morning and apologized for being so blunt ten days ago, when I asked him about his life as a slave during our introduction.

After the last boat was loaded, I approached Andrew, and I tried to tell him it was not my intention to offend. I explained how nervous I was when I came into his presence that evening because I had never met anyone in my life that lived under such subjugation, and I let my curiosity overcome my sense of decency. I also offered some rum as token of good will, with the hope that a little drink would help calm my nerves, let alone his.

Andrew stepped toward me until his huge chest was three inches from my face. He was a foot or more over my head with shoulders the width of a door. He then placed his hand on my shoulder and said in deep bellowing voice, "Best you learn how to speak to a man quick if you plan on speaking to Dr. Franklin." I almost relieved myself. My knees began to buckle, but I was not going to run away, which was all my mind was telling me to do. I then focused on what he said. At first I did not know what to make of that statement. Did he know why we were going to Philadelphia in the morning? Or did he know more? Philip and Mary alluded to what Andrew knew about me, but I wasn't sure if he knew everything. He knows I'm to meet Franklin but does he know "where" I'm from? I never asked them.

Trying to show he was not intimidating me, I nonchalantly asked, "Oh you know about Dr. Franklin?" I was hoping that he would take the question and divulge the depths of his familiarity with our actions.

Instead, his eyes opened, his brow knitted, and he lowered his head saying, "Of course, I know who Benjamin Franklin is. You think I'm stupid because I'm darker than you?"

I thought I was going to die. I tried to explain by saying, "No, I… I meant you know… who… I mean why… I mean who it is that we… that is, who I am… going to meet . . ." and then he started shaking me and laughing. It was a deep laugh.

"Do not be afraid, 'youngin.' I forgive you. I'm not going to hurt you, but it's fun to scare you white folk when I can." He then grabbed the rum out of my hand and tossed it into the water. "Don't ever take that stuff, you hear me? It makes men do the Devil's work. The man who used to be beat, had the wipe in one hand and the bottle in other. I never want to see you drinking this." I stood like a stone and didn't know what to do. Andrew asked again, "Are you hearing me?" I had no choice but affirm his instructions by nodding awkwardly. We left the dock and made our way back up the hill to the house.

On our way to grab dinner, up at the grill, Andrew told me that he knew everything about me, Mary, and Philip. About what we were setting out to really do and that he was not going to let any harm come to me. When I asked how he knew, Andrew went into such a long story that it took all of supper to complete. He enjoys a good laugh and sometimes he can go off topic but he always finds his way back. For my hand's sake as I write this, I'll summarize.

He told me that he was on the run one September night when a huge lightning bolt, bigger than anything he ever saw, hit the ground not far from him. It shook the Earth and the trees. Wanting to know whether anything fell from the heavens, he walked to where the bolt came down. He came upon a field near the river, and in the distance, he saw a man lying in the grass. He saw smoke coming off his clothes, and there were holes scorched on them, as if he just jumped out of a burning home. Andrew said he tried talking to him, but the man's whole body was shaking, and his jaw was clamped together. Andrew helped him any way he could that first night. He built a small shelter out of fallen limbs, a fire to keep Philip warm, and retrieved water from the river, but he was not responding. The next morning Philip finally awoke to find Andrew sitting near him, and they have been together for the past ten years.

Being a runaway, residing here at the mill, and working for Philip has given Andrew the security and income that he would be unlikely to find elsewhere. He said with the "storm" on its way, he would rather live here with Philip to see him through it. The storm, I imagine, is the Revolution. Philip told me at times Andrew plays the role of his slave to avoid any suspicion and any "inspections." A black man walking alone could be asked to identify himself. I believe not having the right identification could put Andrew back into the "system." Living in Pennsylvania, a more pro-abolition colony, Andrew was more protected while working with Philip, but neither wanted to take such risks. As perverted as it is for me to write this, that is the world I am living in right now.

Philip has succeeded in his mandate in establishing a successful timber mill and is known in many parts of Philly. While I am in town looking for Franklin, he will run his operation as cover. Delivering his supply, seeking more contracts, and speaking to the bankers or whatever he does. Mary will continue to act as his wife, Andrew will stay in town as the "live-in," and I will be the out-of-town nephew touring Philadelphia. When I asked why I couldn't be someone important visiting from New York, I was told that could pose great risk. Being from out of town, my unfamiliarity with the customs of eighteenth-century colonial lifestyles alone, could attract unwanted attention. I don't think they have anything to fear. Henry and I reviewed the dos and don'ts of colonial wisdom. And while I was recovering here with Mary, while getting acquainted, we reviewed what I should expect when we reach town and how I should act. We did this as we also discussed Benjamin Franklin, George Washington, and all other important figures I will encounter.

I am going to say I shall miss this place while I'm away. It was the log home I always wanted, minus the enormous windows and modern twenty-first century amenities, which I still seek out during my days here. *Where's the bathroom*, oh yeah, it's in the yard! This place was beautifully crafted. It may be the only colonial home with an open floor plan. The view of the river from my window is therapeutic when feelings of isolation creep in. The flow of the water reminds me that we are always moving, always in motion. And tomorrow we are moving, moving to cross paths with a person I am terrified to meet. I am praying for strength and courage.

Hopefully, the prayer will be answered in the next five days.

Chapter Sixteen

A Break in the Covenant Chain

than was resting peacefully in his hotel room near Independence Hall. The heavy blankets were wrapped around him like a cocoon while the air conditioner was set to a cool sixty degrees. Without a sliver of the outside world leaking through the carefully overlapping drapery, Ethan was resting in perfect comfort, ready to sleep the morning away. Without warning, there was someone pounding at the door, making a thunderous sound which made Ethan jump out of bed in the darkness of his room.

"Who's there?" Ethan shouted.

"It's me," the voice said.

Walking toward the door, Ethan flipped the light switch on. "Henry?"

"Yes, are you ready?"

"Henry, it's five-thirty in the morning! Are you out of your mind?" Ethan opened the door to see Henry wearing brown khakis and an ocean blue polo shirt. He gave a grin, "Nice look."

"Never mind that, let's go," Henry said. "I texted you twenty minutes ago. We're late already. Forget that we're a month behind, we have a scheduled meeting at six. We have a long day ahead of us and a lot to cover. Now get dressed, and meet me downstairs, they have the continental breakfast setup if you want to grab a coffee."

"All right," said Ethan. "Just give me a minute."

Down in the lobby, Ethan found Henry sitting in a chair by the fireplace, holding up local newspaper paper that covered his face. He cautiously stepped towards Henry with the plan to startle him by slapping the paper out of his hands in retaliation to how he was woken up. Just as Ethan was about to grab the crease, he heard his name called from the front desk. Holding his stance, he turned his head and saw Henry standing with a puzzled look on his face.

Henry then mouthed, "What are you doing?"

The newspaper was snatched back to show an elderly man, whose only resemblance to Henry was the brown khakis. The gentleman wore clean, well-polished, brown shoes, a blue button downed shirt with a white collar, and a yellow and blue striped tie. Embarrassed for a moment, Ethan remained still, holding in pose.

"Can I help you?" he asked.

Ethan retracted from his crouching stance, stood straight up, and extended his hand, "Hi I'm Ethan."

"Hello, I'm David," the kind man said.

"Sorry to bother you, I thought you were him."

David looked over at Henry, who was at least twenty years his elder. David smiled, "Oh, I can see how you could get us mixed up." Ethan politely smiled and took a step back to depart. When he took a step towards Henry, David asked, "What brings you to Philadelphia?"

"Oh, I'm here to relive history," Ethan said.

"Oh really? You're a fan of history? So am I," said David. "I've researched many cherished moments of our nation's past, President Truman, The Wright Brothers, and President John Adams to name a few.

But, you should always appreciate the absolute fact that none of those great moments of our history would have occurred had our founders not take that important first step in this town, all those years ago. This is the perfect place to get proper insight into our nation's founding and the start of our history."

"Well, I thought I had enough insight, but that man over there has made me aware of a few things I've never known before."

David smirked and shook his head in disappointment. "That's the historic illiteracy of your generation." He then pointed to Henry, "You listen to everything he has to say and learn how this town is more than events to memorize. When you're reliving our history today, remember that this city was alive with men. Young men, about your age, taking extraordinary risks so that you can do what you wish with your life."

"If you only knew," Ethan said.

"I do know," said David with a smile. "Now go live it." David extended his hand and winked, which made Ethan smile back.

Heading toward the door, Ethan turned to Henry, "Is he?"

Henry quickly answered, "Not one of ours."

Henry and Ethan exited the hotel on Chestnut Street and walked two blocks east without saying a word to each other. The sun had yet to rise, making the morning sky a hopeful cascade of night and dawn colors. It was a cool morning, but like many autumn days, the temperature was expected to climb to high 70's. Henry was wearing a wind-breaker, while Ethan walked out with just a button down, long-sleeved, shirt. The early morning chill forced Ethan to rub his arms as they approached the corner of Chestnut and 2nd Street, he abruptly asked, "Okay, why did we have to come out here so early and where are you taking me?"

"If you're going to retrace the footsteps of our forefathers, you should wake up when they did."

As they were about to reach Walnut, Henry pointed to the structure to their right. "You see this building?" Ethan gave it a look over. The design was simple, it had an early colonial American look, it stood three stories, and there were steps leading to restaurant on the first floor. "That's the *City Tavern*," said Henry. "During our founding, it was considered one of the finest taverns in the colony. Adams, Washington, Jefferson, and others, could be found dining in there, almost daily, during the years of the Continental Congress and Philadelphia Convention." As they continued to walk by it, Henry pointed back, "I'll have to take you there for the founder's meal later tonight." Standing on the corner, Henry directed Ethan west. "Let's go this way," he said.

Walking on Walnut Street, the red brick sidewalks and thick trees offered a scenic view as they made their way through the city. "Were these sidewalks here in 1775?" Ethan asked.

"Some of these walkways were."

At ten to six, the streets were quiet with only the sounds of nature surrounding them. Occasionally a car passed by, but it was not enough to distract Ethan's enthusiasm as he started to ponder the possibility he was stepping on the footpaths Franklin strolled upon. Henry was letting Ethan walk at his own pace, to give him time to observe the other 18th century buildings. When they made it to the first corner of South 3rd and Walnut, Ethan turned to Henry, "Can I ask you something?"

"Sure."

"Why Philadelphia?" Ethan asked. "Why did they meet here?"

Henry responded, "Well there were a few good reasons. The simplest is location. If you look at a map of all the colonies the British occupied in 1774, Pennsylvania was right in the middle and Philadelphia was the more accommodating to their approach of compromise. There was more risk of that objective failing should the Congress have met in the rowdy New York City or patriot-motivating Williamsburg, Virginia. Philadelphia was one of the most liberal governments in the British colonies, so it was felt to be the safest location."

When they reached the corner of South 3rd and Walnut, Ethan stopped Henry. "Why would it matter where they met? Weren't all colonies under British control?"

"Yes, but each was not equally as strict in their governance," said Henry. "Some colonies were never given the title of a Royal Colony. There wasn't a clear, concise order for each one to follow, and each colony felt that it was its own country and not subordinate to any other." Henry then motioned with his head. "Let's keep going."

"That's where I get confused," Ethan said. "How were they British colonies but separate countries?"

"No. Before the Revolution, some thought of their colony as a unique country, with a unique identity, and that's how some wanted to identify themselves. They were 'Virginians' or 'Massachusetts' Men'. Some Loyalists classified themselves as Englishmen, but after the colonies were brought together to fight during the French and Indian War, a new identity was being shared—American." Henry said. "But, when the delegates arrived in Philadelphia in 1774, many amongst them had yet to make use of that national identifier." As they walked, Henry sensed Ethan was not following him. "Here, to make it easier, where are you from?"

"Yonkers," replied Ethan.

"No," said Henry. "Where are you originally from?"

"Oh, the Bronx."

"Exactly, you were born and raised in 'The Bronx', and because of that you are among a small percentage of people who can say that. Now go into a committee with the other boroughs of New York City. Although you are all 'New Yorkers', and you are all Americans, which borough would you care about the most?"

"The Bronx?"

"Exactly," Henry said. "And that, of course, is politics. The colonies were separate entities, struggling to find commonality amongst them and compromise for all people, during the Continental Congress. Try to think of it this way; each colony was founded on different principles. They had their own governments, laws, in some early cases, money, they had distinct customs, religious beliefs, and so on and so forth. Although they all fell under the umbrella of the British Empire, many were not ready to sacrifice their authority and wealth with other colonies. Of the few things they agreed on, was they shared English blood. That, however, began to depreciate by the time the First Continental Congress was called."

"Depreciate?" asked Ethan.

"Yes," said Henry. "National pride, but think back when the Roman Empire was in existence. If a person said, *Civis Romanus Sum*, 'I am a Roman Citizen,' they were treated as such throughout the world. If one citizen of Rome was harmed, it would be considered an attack against all Romans. In 1774, if someone from the American colonies said, 'I am an Englishman,' to representatives of the English government, it was as valuable as mud. It meant nothing and carried no advantages. That's what I mean." As they continued to walk on top of the red brick sidewalks, they passed a building clearly from the Colonial Era. It had a quaint garden and white painted fence. Reaching the corner of Walnut Street and Fourth, Henry leaned his head over to Ethan, "Did I answer your question?"

Ethan hesitated. "Sure," he said with a shrug of his shoulders.

Ahead of them on Fourth Street was a large park. In the distance, some large red brick buildings could be seen through the shroud of trees. When they reached a small black gate, Henry pointed to Ethan to enter first. Walking along the narrow path, towards the structure, Henry said, "I want you to keep in mind through all of this, that I am not trying to convert you into a zealot. I just want to make you aware of the world that existed before July 4, 1776. This will help you understand the mindset of almost everyone you encounter. Not only is it essential for you to know all that will happen after July 4, 1775, it's important to appreciate the events which led the call for a congress to come to Philadelphia and meet here."

Henry pointed to the large building in front of them. It was a tall two level structure and had an old-style colonial design with large windows shutters on each one. As they made their way to the front of the building, Ethan noticed how it was not a clean square design. It almost looked like two buildings were forced together and only one side was given character, so people would know it was the main entrance with its double doors and windows on the second floor appearing to be twice the size of the windows on the first.

"I saw this building from the hotel," Ethan said.

"This is Carpenters' Hall," said Henry. "When 'The Carpenters' Company of the City and County of Philadelphia' completed its construction in 1770, it stood on the outskirt of the main city. Now it's surrounded by it. And, because the State House was being used for local government, the hall became a gathering place for patriots. Either on the lawn or in the interior, Carpenters' Hall served as a contributor to the voices of liberty. Unfortunately, it has since been overshadowed in popularity to the events that took place two blocks away, but I do stop by every time I visit the city and reflect on its importance."

The Georgian-style construct captivated Ethan's attention while Henry spoke. "Well, it still looks amazing," Ethan said.

Henry turned to stand between Ethan and Carpenters' Hall. "This is where the First Continental Congress took place," Henry said. "In here, men from several colonies effectively were committing treason for an illegal assembly and for conspiring against the King. Now, even though what happened in 1776 is more popular and justly celebrated, the events that preceded the gathering of these men in 1774 were just as extraordinary."

While observing the hall, behind Ethan a voice shouted, "Henry!" Ethan recognized the faint voice and awkwardly spun around, but before his feet could catch up, he stumbled a little on the bricks. Steadying himself he saw a familiar face. It was Audrey approaching them with a brown paper bag.

Henry leaned over and whispered, "You need any help over there?"

"Yes, I'm fine," Ethan said. "She startled me. That's all."

"Good morning, gentlemen," Audrey said. She gave the bag a little shake and said, "I have breakfast."

They walked over to two wooden benches along the left side of the building. From their seat within the park they were secluded from the rituals of the local Philadelphians as the morning rush started around them. As he grabbed a bagel and coffee from Audrey, Henry said, "I was just educating our friend on this building and the events that got us to the First Continental Congress."

"Did you cover the Albany Congress?" asked Audrey.

"No, I was waiting for our expert to arrive," said Henry.

"You're funny," Audrey said. "But if he's going to prevent Franklin from introducing the Albany Plan, he'll need to know what it was, why Franklin carried it with such pride, and why he was, or will be, so persistent on reintroducing it." Audrey took one more bite of her bagel before tossing the remainder back in the bag. "Okay, let's get started," she said, as she wiped her hands. Audrey then stepped in front of Ethan, and pressed both of her palms on each side of his cheeks. "Can you pay attention as I'm talking to you sweetie?" she said.

Ethan caught off guard, and unable to speak with food in his mouth, shook his head in the affirmative.

"Good, let's begin," said Audrey.

"When the delegates converged on Philadelphia in 1774 they were attempting to look for a course of action they could collectively agree upon, in response to the recent pressures placed on the colonies. Of course, we know how this played out, but what events drove them to take such drastic action? Some say it was the Boston Massacre, the Stamp Act, some like to go further and say it was the French and Indian War that started the downfall. For me, I have always viewed the establishment of America as a period in our evolution. The moment 'Natural Rights' was recognized and implemented as the core principle of its founding. It was not formed from one event. Many moments in history and natural elements were needed for the country to form. If you view the country's geography and its ethnology, it can give you a broader perspective and a deeper sense of gratitude that it ever came to exist.

"The Congress of 1774 was essential when we speak of actions leading toward the Declaration of Independence and the American Revolution, but twenty years earlier, a Congress was called on by members of Parliament to convene at a major trading post north of New York City, along the Hudson River. Its mandate was to settle a major dispute with the Natives who resided between the British colonies and their long-time adversary, France. This assembly is what led them down a path to lose America over the next two decades.

"To set the table, before 1754, the French were spreading across Montreal and Quebec. England established colonies along the Atlantic coast ending before Florida, which was a territory owned by Spain. The territory of the British–American colonies extended west to the Appalachian Mountains. On the other side of the mountains was a vast wall of wilderness and Native tribes. The Mohawk tribe, who were members of the powerful Iroquois Confederacy of North America, resided in the land west of Albany, New York.

"Since the founding of Albany by the Dutch in 1614, a 'Covenant Chain', a sacred bond, existed between the Natives and the Europeans of the trading post. The Mohawk's acted as brokers in the fur trade for many Native tribes west of the European settlements, and in return the Dutch agreed not to expand their trading company into their lands. As Britain overtook the territory along the eastern seaboard, including New York, it slowly eroded this bond. The influence of the Mohawk tribe began to weaken when Philadelphia was established as a major merchant city, but what really hurt them was when a trading post was created in Oswego, on Lake Ontario. This drastically reduced the leverage the Mohawk tribe possessed with the surrounding tribes, and the brokerage power they held with the British. Now the British felt they could expand west of Albany with little concern over the Mohawk tribe's protests. Then something happened in Europe in 1742, which sets in motion—everything.

"Being an ally to Austria, the British get pulled into a war. It was the War of Austrian Succession, but here in North America it was dubbed King George's War. The tension stretched across the Atlantic, but the kingdoms in Europe were not ready to engage in a war on two continents. With Britain distracted in Europe, French locals, on this side of the ocean, took the opportunity to attack some English fishing ports to protect their supply chain to Quebec. The French, who had a better relationship with the Natives of the Canadian region, allied themselves with rival tribes, Mi'kmaq, and Maliseet, and had them fight for their cause. With no military forces on the ready for war on North American territory, this engagement took some time to play itself out. Some forts were raided and some towns, such as Saratoga, New York, were abandoned. It was, however, a low priority because the real fighting was on the other side of the world.

"Because the French recruited the Natives, the British insisted that the Iroquois should fight alongside them to protect their land. The Mohawks and the entire Iroquois nation wanted to stay neutral and refused to engage in their battle. To entice them, members from as far south of Pennsylvania brought gifts to the Natives. The chiefs of some tribes attended conferences in Albany, Boston, and Montreal, acting as peacekeepers.

"At these conferences, the poor treatment of the Mohawks was discussed by Chief Hendrick Theyanoguin. The chief spoke about the abuse they had to endure from the men in Albany who treated them like children and slaves, and how they slowly had taken their freedoms. Unfortunately for the Natives, right when they were receiving just attention from the

European inhabitants, the war ended in 1748. Treaties were adhered to, France returned their captured fishing ports, and everything went back to normal for the Europeans. The chiefs, however, felt that they should have been at the table during the peace negotiations. The fact that they were ignored once again, only increased the resentment felt by many tribes, especially the Mohawks.

"As the years passed, the British tried to please the Mohawks out of fear that the entire Iroquois Confederacy would align with the French. Many people in the colonies and in London feared a French-Native alliance would obliterate any hope to expand west. Both Kingdoms knew that the rivers that connected the Ohio Country to the Gulf of Mexico was worth a lot of money, and Great Britain was not going to allow it to fall into the hands of the French.

"So, things stayed relatively quiet until 1753 when the new governor of Canada decided upon himself to expand south and claim the Ohio territory for themselves. He dispatched troops to set up forts along the terrain to create the trading route from Canada to the Gulf, thereby slicing the terrain of North America in half and confine the British to just the east coast.

"At that same time, Chief Hendrick of the Mohawks, fed up with the treatment from the English, traveled to New York City to speak to the Royal Governor George Clinton. Ever since the trading post in Oswego started, Europeans trekking between Albany and Lake Ontario were trading with members of the Mohawk tribe. Some of the trades included rum, which the Chief did not want his people drinking. With the decline of their control of the fur trade over the decades, the lack of inclusion when peace treaties were signed, the reduction of territory, and the negative influence the Europeans were having on his tribe, he finally had enough. On June 3, 1753, Chief Hendrick said to the Governor that if conditions are not altered, then 'the Covenant Chain is broken between the English and the Six Nations.' Clinton did nothing to appease the Mohawks, and when they returned home, they began to block any land expansion and any European merchant traveling between Albany and Oswego.

"Those acts alone were not enough for Parliament to intervene but when the scouting reports from a young major of the Virginia Regiment, George Washington, confirmed French forts were being built as far south as Pennsylvania, Parliament ordered additional forts to be built in response and reluctantly dispatched letters to all colonial governors demanding an assembly of representatives from each colony to address the concerns of the Six Nations Iroquois. This assembly was to void individual treaties each colony had with the various tribes and enter into a single new treaty as representatives of Great Britain."

"Wait a minute," said Ethan. "A break down in the fur trade with the Iroquois, out of Albany, forced England to call for a Congress?"

"Mostly," said Henry. "If the French formed an alliance with the largest Native confederation in the Northeast, to add to their partnerships with other tribes, and consider the existence of a strong Spanish colony in Florida, it would have squeezed British interests right off the continent."

"Think of it this way Ethan," said Audrey. "European Colonization was an inevitable part of exploration and evolution. Was it right? Was it just? Some argue it was not and it certainly was not from the perspective of the Iroquois and other tribes, but as long they retained leverage in the fur trade, the Mohawk's were the acting firewall to the Europeans gaining access to the Ohio frontier. However, the new ports in Philadelphia and Oswego had an adverse effect on the Mohawks, and as decades passed they were at a loss. Much like globalization today, there are net winners and losers. When the net losers reach a breaking point, and push back, there is a correction. Albany was called to be that correction."

Ethan paused to reflect. "Then what happened next?"

"Next?" replied Audrey. "Next Albany is visited by a politician with more world experience than any person in North America. Next comes, Benjamin Franklin."

Chapter Seventeen

May 7, 1775: Introduction

Before I record the events of the day, I want to state for posterity, should something terrible happen to me before I finish, that I had the great fortune of meeting Dr. Benjamin Franklin this afternoon. Although the encounter failed to exceed my expectations, the moment passed before I could control the anxiety dictating my behavior. I will state for the record that this was not entirely the result of nerves. Ever since Henry had disclosed the consequences of failure should I be unable to set Benjamin Franklin on the path of Independence, and from Dr. Franklin's one words of dismissing me during our introduction, I had always dreaded this first encounter.

In the late morning, Philip, Mary, and Andrew took me to the London Coffee House near the water's edge on Front Street. The plan was not to wait and meet Franklin outside of his home, but rather to cross paths with him in the street or at a tavern. He was likely to make an appearance in the City Tavern by Walnut Street, the Indian Queen on 4th and Market, or the Tun, down on Spruce. I asked why not wait here, at the coffee shop? This was his first day back in Philadelphia. It was expected for him to socialize throughout the city, and the London Coffee House was one of the most popular places to do so. Unsure where Dr. Franklin was going to make his appearance, they suggested that the City Tavern would be the better location. So, I left the fresh air at the water's edge to walk through the dirt and dust-filled streets.

I walked with Andrew, and we made our way on Market. We arrived at The City Tavern just when lunch began. The patrons around the entrance appeared to be of a more higher class than the people I left at the coffee house. When we approached the door, I walked as if I had been there before. The amusing thing was, I had been there before with Henry. When we entered, a man met us, and before he said anything, he looked at Andrew with an odd scowl. I glanced over and thought there was something improper with his attire, but there was nothing wrong with our appearances. In fact, Andrew filled out his suit better than I did. I turned back and firmly said, "My friend and I would like a table." Looking at the center staircase, the right dining hall was full of people, whereas the left was empty. He walked us to the empty hall and put a table against the wall. He then snapped his fingers, and another person brought over a movable wall over and placed it to block anyone from being able to see us.

Recognizing how the host disfavored Andrew's presence, we motioned to each other to remain quiet and eat in silence. When we were passively asked what we wanted, I ordered us both the scrapple and madeira. We sat patiently and looked around the dining room we were tucked away in. It was nice, of course I was more taken in with the fact that this place was only three years old, but last I was in here it was over 240 years old. When our food arrived, Andrew looked at his cup and said with annoyance, "Why did you order this?" I told him I needed it for my nerves. Thankfully Andrew nodded, accepted my reason for a little drink, and nothing else was to be uttered between us during our meal. However, while we were eating, I heard a new voice say he preferred to eat in solitude as he was nursing a terrible headache from celebrating too much last evening. Unfortunately, due to the portable obstruction I could not put a figure to the voice. I imagined if it was Benjamin Franklin, he would have been greeted by name, but if he entered annoyed, the staff would have respectively kept their distance.

The echo of each step excited my curiosity. I prepare myself to see Dr. Franklin but when the person walked into view, to my disappointment, he was a tall, slender, red head. He took his seat a few tables away, but kept his back to us. Several silent minutes had passed as we continued with our meal while the gentleman was drinking tea, reading *The Pennsylvania Gazette.* I continued to listen for the entry of Dr. Franklin but when the waiter walked over to place another drink on his table, I overheard him say, "Is there anything else I can get for you, Mr. Jefferson?" When I processed the name, I froze in my seat with excitement. I took such a deep breath in my astonishment that I started choking. The waiter and "Mr. Jefferson" looked over while Andrew patted me on the back. Unable to catch my breath, my eyes began to water, but I tried to lift my head up to wave that I was fine.

Andrew asked me what was wrong. After a minute, I finally caught my breath and told him the man sitting alone was Thomas Jefferson. Looking back, I shouldn't have looked amazed when Andrew asked who was Thomas Jefferson? I simply said, he was important. I could have said more but I knew giving the biography of a man who was only a few feet anyway, and more important had yet to live out half his life, would have been inappropriate. Unaware of how loud we were, I heard a voice echo, "Can I help you, gentlemen?" I turned to see that it was Thomas Jefferson looking directly at us and he did not appear to be amused. I immediately straightened up from my seat, at the same time I noticed the host stepped back into the dining hall and I was worried we were about to be asked to leave. Now that I have had a chance to reflect on the incident, I realized in that moment I was viewing him as President Jefferson, with all his accomplishments, and as the man who defined liberty by writing the Declaration. But at that moment, he had yet to claim any of those distinguished achievements. To the workers and patrons of The City Tavern, he was a revisiting delegate from Virginia. So, maybe I did not have to be so cautious with my interaction with Mr. Jefferson, but I still was polite, out of respect.

I said, "No sir, it's just I was telling my friend I'm a great admirer of yours. I read your work *A Summary View of the Rights of British America*. I thought it was amazing."

He smiled and said, "Thank you," then turned back around. Although he might have been agitated, my pulse was rising. I was so excited that I had the opportunity to speak to Thomas Jefferson.

I figured our conversation would end there, but just as I reclined back into my chair, Mr. Jefferson turned to both of us again. My posture straightened back up, he asked why we were dining alone in the hall. Though the reason was apparent to me, I politely provided cover for all parties. I said I too had a headache, which made him laugh under his breath. He then asked what brought us to Philadelphia. I questioned how he knew we were not from Philly, to which Mr. Jefferson replied, very confidently, that he could tell we were not locals for if we were, we would have "selected a livelier and more colorful place to dine." That account made Andrew laugh hard and loud, that echoed out into the hallway. Again, thinking our actions were going to have us removed, I slapped him on the shoulder so he would stop laughing. I told Mr. Jefferson that I was hoping to see Dr. Franklin here today since I heard he returned from London. Mr. Jefferson informed us that his friend Mr. Charles Thomas told him this morning, he had plans to meet the good doctor at Tun's Tavern. Upon hearing this news, I jumped out of my chair, thanked him, and excused myself. As I exited the room, I told Mr. Jefferson that I had something of great importance to share with Dr. Franklin, and it could not wait. Andrew paid and we walked out.

We made our way through the alleys and underneath the second-floor porches, which seemed to be everywhere in the city. In, out, and around crowds, Andrew and I zigzagged our way down to Water Street and Tun Alley. I remember Philip telling me to be careful if I went searching for Franklin in Tun's, for it was a known Masonic tavern. They protect their own, so I was not to let anyone know I was looking for Franklin, otherwise I would quickly have a lot of unwanted attention.

Heeding Philip's advice, my devised plan was to casually walk around the interior, and if I should spot Franklin, I would wait outside until he was finished. If I failed to recognize him, I would have to continue my mission, either waiting around Tun's or lurking about his city. The moment I stepped in, I saw someone look directly at me, I sensed that he knew I did not belong there. Being so used to seeing a host at every restaurant I ever entered, I figured he was there for a reason, so I told him I was just looking for someone. He didn't respond at all to what I said, when I stepped to my right, he remained quiet, so I just continued walking. I noticed a few faces were looking in my direction, but I did not let it bother me. I went into the back room and examined the people, but no one stood out.

I then made my way to the bar and glanced around all corners. To be honest, I could have overlooked him since I was searching for someone I had only ever seen in paintings, and to me, his face was a little different in each rendering. Had we arrived in the city two days ago, as planned, and not last night, we wouldn't have missed his celebrated return yesterday morning, and I would have already seen him with my own eyes. Of course, I couldn't blame anyone but myself for our tardiness. This morning I apologized again to Philip for grounding the boat and losing almost all the wood into the water. His response was amusing, he said, "I guess my old man couldn't teach you everything."

Regardless, I needed to find Dr. Franklin today, which left me to search for the man depicted in two-hundred-year-old paintings: old, bald on top, with a mullet, and those iconic spectacles. That description almost matched several men I saw in Tun's, but only two wore glasses. As I made my way to the final corner of the tavern, I did not find a face that I could identify as Franklin's with certainty. Feeling defeated, I stood still and leaned against the wall. Outside one of the windows, I heard the playful laugh of a female. I turned to look out the window and I saw two young women engaged in conversation with an older gentleman. The old man was wearing a gray tricorn cap, so I couldn't tell if he was bald. He did have hair coming down behind his cap. I bent over at the waist and tilted my head, as I tried to get a clear view of this man through the opened window.

He was wearing a plum-colored three-piece suit. The full coat came down to his knee, which met his bright white socks. The sun reflected off the buckle on his black polished shoes. Both of his hands met over the top of his cane as he swayed and bounced during his light-hearted exchange with the two women, who giggled with every word he said. As I stared at this encounter from the dining room, another elderly gentleman approached me and looked out the window to see what was holding my attention.

"You can always tell when Ben's around," he said to me. The sound of his name made the hairs on my neck stand up, and I was overcome with excitement. Holding my composure, I turned to him and asked how he could tell. He said, "There are more women walking about." I gave him a polite laugh and excused myself as I hurried my way to the exit. I had to force myself not to run.

I told Andrew to stay by the door as I slowly stepped in the direction of Benjamin Franklin. I could hear people greeting him as they passed: *Hello, Ben. Good day, Dr. Franklin. Welcome back, Mr. Franklin.* With every salutation, Franklin would raise his head and give a nod of acknowledgment. With one nod, his eyes passed in my direction, and he gave me a second glance before attending to his two acquaintances. My knees were shaking, my palms were sweating, my mouth was dry, and my chest was pounding. I was a complete wreck, but I balled my fingers and pushed my nails into my palms to help me stay focus. I was now several feet behind the women, who were still giddy as they bantered with the good doctor. I was about to speak when Franklin said, "You can stop staring young man. I understand how you must feel seeing a person of my stature before you. But I assure you, I am not a street act looking for an audience. If you have something to say, for God sakes spit it out."

I nearly stumbled, as I double stepped the few feet between us. I reached down to grab his hand and began to shake it, while never taking my eyes off his face. I told him my name was Ethan Pope and that I traveled a long way to see him.

"I'm sure it was a great distance," he responded. "I arrived home from London yesterday after a rough six-week trip across the Atlantic, so I know a thing or two about long trips. By chance, where did you come from?" When I told him I came from New York, he sighed in disappointment. I wasted little time and told him that I was in dire need of his audience to speak about something private.

Without batting an eye Franklin said to me, "Good lad. I have been in contact with the highest and the most influential Americans who have asked for my audience. Members of the local British government have asked for my audience. Relatives, friends, and neighbors of whom I have no need of, have asked for my audience. The Pennsylvania Council has asked for my audience, which will be the first request I tend to after I finish my conversation with these two charming women, I can assure you. And after I have met with all those decent people, if they should dare deserve such a profile, I will then tender my precious time to you. Until then, please do not be offended if I decline your request. At the present moment, my interests are with these pleasant creatures."

He turned to speak to the two girls again, but I impolitely interrupted. I could tell he was not pleased. I knew I had to make an impact. Otherwise, he was going to be angry with my presence now and any future encounters. I said, "Dr. Franklin, I wish to corroborate with you on your intention to resurrect a plan you composed once in Albany." He stared at me with a befuddled look. I thought for a moment that I had come on too strong and would have to retreat for the day.

But then he said, "To hell with my interests, you have me at a loss for words. Who are you?" I told him my name again, and then I assured him that I was not from the Pennsylvania Council, and that I represented no man going to the Congress. Neither was I affiliated in anyway with the Royal government. I said to him, "All I want is a chance to discuss the negative aspects of your approach."

He took a step back to look me over and then checked to see whether anyone was listening to our conversation. After surveying the area Dr. Franklin, stepped right up to me, and said, "I will arrive at Tun's at 2:00 p.m. You will arrive at 2:25 and not a minute before to interrupt my meal. I plan to leave the tavern at precisely 2:30. If you can hold my attention for those five minutes, think of it as a triumph for your charm. If at any moment, I miss one word you utter, either by your lack of proper command and annunciation of our language, or out of sheer boredom, I will abruptly interrupt you and conclude our meeting. Do we have an understanding?" Feeling victorious by his offer, I accepted.

I paced around the east side for hours, admiring the life being lived out in front of me. While I observed the movements and exchanges from the citizens, I reflected on how I was witnessing this will-be-great-municipality in its youth. It appeared to be more aggressive and chaotic when compared with the city Henry and I walked around in. There were a few areas you wanted to avoid and taverns you did not want to enter. People walked, almost wherever they wanted to. There was no order to the movement, it was sporadic how people crossed paths. However, there was a beautiful arrangement to it all.

When 2:20 arrived, I was waiting outside Tun's with Andrew. Against Andrew's warning, I entered a couple of minutes early but I couldn't find Dr. Franklin. While making my rounds, there was some commotion at the entrance, and a few people were getting out of their seats to gather. I walked over to see what it was about. The crowd parted at the entry to reveal Dr. Franklin making a grand entrance.

When he saw me standing in front of him, he said, "Oh darn, I was hoping you were unable to tell time. All right, well, you're here and I promised you five minutes, so sit down and please do not give me an upset stomach before I have their roast."

I opened with what I thought was going to be received as a compliment. I said, "Dr. Franklin you once said, "*Our Opinions are not in our own power. They are formed and governed much by circumstances.*" Dr. Franklin quickly noted that he never said that before. I then realized the passage I quoted was from a letter he wrote to his son. The only issue was the letter of reference will not to be written until 1784. Before I was given the opportunity to correct myself, a young woman stopped by the table and began talking to Franklin. He said a couple of things and told her to please return in a few minutes as he needed to appease the gentleman across from him, so he (me) would leave him to allow more pleasant company to join him. He then turned his attention back to me and said, "You're running out of time, young man." To which I noted that it was unfair for him to take time away from me when it was he who was speaking to other people. He responded with "You sound like a wash maid, and if a wash maid heard you just now, they would be offended that you were grouped with them."

I decided to dismiss his insult and proceed to my point. I told him that in a couple of days he was to be selected as a representative of Pennsylvania for the upcoming Congress. Franklin threw his hand in front of my face, to cover my mouth, and said, "I will assume you are a man of status where you come from. There you may speak your mind without concern for who may hear you. In this town, as a guest, I will instruct you to restrain your notion of philosophical assemblies. And there are those among us that hold their allegiance much stronger than you may at this moment."

I realized that I had made a terrible error of judgment. I wanted to show off my knowledge of his intentions, which was something Mary told me repeatedly not to do. I got caught up in the moment and said the word *Congress*. After Franklin's warning, I knew I had to show him that I was a person not easily intimidated. I told Franklin that I was not there to restrain myself. I was there to inform him that the *plan* from Albany would fail to meet the requirements of his other *philosophers* and that the only solution that would resonate with them was complete separation.

Franklin jumped out of his seat, grabbed me by the collar, and pulled me out of the booth. He then whispered in my ear, "I think it is time for your departure and should there ever be the misfortune of our lives crossing paths again, never make such a broad accusation using treasonous language while standing so close to me. Some people may believe that I, too, was seeking a swift end to my life with the help of a rope." He did try to push me away when he reached the word rope, and although I did not move much from his action, it did grab the attention of some tavern patrons. Without turning back to allow any onlooker to make eye contact with me, I abruptly made my exit. Andrew and I walked back to the London Coffee Shop where Philip and Mary were waiting to hear how my first encounter went.

Reviewing the day now, I can say with certainty, it did not go well.

Chapter Eighteen

From Albany to Philadelphia

In the park surrounding Carpenters' Hall, various people walked about. Some were obvious tourists, visiting the historic landmark with a map or camera in hand. Some were locals, either taking in the beautiful afternoon weather or hustling their way through it all. When noon approached, the lunch crowd slowly added to the ruckus. Workers from nearby offices started to take to the streets and flood the local eateries. As forecasted the temperature increased to 78 degrees. With the sun on top of him, Ethan rolled-up his sleeves, while Henry sat quietly, with his jacket draped over the back of the bench, under the shade of the tree. "Keep talking, Audrey," Henry said, "I'm going to make a call for cheesesteaks."

Ethan twisted in his seat and motioned to Henry, "Make sure you get it with cheese whiz," he said.

Appalled by the notion, Henry said, "What else would I get on it? American?"

As Henry called Pat's to place their lunch order, Audrey moved over to Ethan and sat next to him. "How's your wife?"

"She's good."

"I'm very sorry to hear what happened."

"But, you knew it was going to happen."

"True," replied Audrey. "But that doesn't mean I don't feel any different. It's terrible when you hear someone has to go through it."

"Well, she's doing what she can," Ethan said. "She's working and keeping herself busy as she takes blood tests and marrow tests, and bone scans, and PET scans, and CAT scans. It's trying on her patience. But, she's very positive, and when it gets hard, she has me to yell at," he said with a grin. "It's fine. There's no way to ever go back to the way it was before, you know? The best thing to do is what is necessary to ensure that she is cared for."

"I don't think I would be able to handle all of this, the way you are," said Audrey. "I mean there is a part of me that is jealous that I can't go back and see these moments in history. But, going to that time with no means of returning would be too much to emotionally process. You are very brave."

"Well," said Ethan. "Truth be told, I'm not doing that great today. I did not sleep well and was up for half the night after seeing Independence Hall. It gave me a knot in the pit of my stomach. I think just the sight of the building made this whole endeavor become more *real*. I was awake for hours envisioning an 18th century Philadelphia and imagining how I was going to live within it. Of course, that made me think of Lauren and having to leave her behind, which is something I still haven't been able to come to terms with. I really don't want to leave her."

Audrey stood in front of Ethan, "Lauren will be in great care after you leave. Trust me," she said. "Focus on the task before you. That might help you get through this."

"So," he muttered, "From everything you told me earlier, I have a few questions."

"Like what?"

"This Albany Plan Franklin wanted to bring back to the Second Continental Congress," said Ethan. "When does that come up? Or are we not there yet?"

"I'm glad you asked," Audrey said. "On May 9, 1754, Benjamin Franklin published, in *The Pennsylvania Gazette*, an article about the Virginia militia building forts near the Ohio River to counter the emergence of the French. His article noted how the French were operating in one direction, with one council, and by one purse, which was in sharp contrast on how the English colonies were approaching this recent advancement. Underneath this story was a cartoon of a snake cut into eight pieces. Each piece of the serpent had the abbreviation of a colony stamped on it. Underneath was a caption that read 'Join or Die.' For three months that cartoon and caption spread throughout the colonies. It planted the seed for the call to unite. This wasn't a call for rebellion against Great Britain, this was a call for all colonies to come together and create a central form of government for the British Empire.

"Franklin received praise from officials who were in favor of establishing a single body government, including the Massachusetts Governor William Shirley. When Parliament called for the Congress in Albany to resolve the Iroquois problem, Franklin and others saw an opportunity. When the Albany Congress assembled on June 19, 1754, all colonies dispatched representatives, except Virginia and both Carolinas. They deemed the issue a local problem and one that did not require their efforts. In all, twenty-one representatives and two hundred Native representatives attended the conference. Now you may think that's a lot, but you'll be surprised to know that several Covenant Chain meetings were held before this Albany Congress. Those meetings had only a few representatives from New York with roughly five hundred Natives in attendance. The small number represented the Natives' discontent with the English.

"The resolution with the Natives was resolved within a week, but the Congress lasted for almost thirty days. What exactly happened has been pieced together from stories told and written over the years after the event. In a journal held by New Hampshire Commissioner Theodore Atkinson, Chief Hendrick called the British 'women' when compared to the French, who he labeled as 'the men,' because they were building forts and surrounding them, and all the English did was talk.

"When both sides were able to form an agreement. The British rum trade ended, there would be no settlements without consultation, and all important trade routes would only be opened with the Six Nation's council. As for the remaining three weeks in Albany, that's where Benjamin Franklin and some other delegates drafted a proposal on an intercolonial government, which we know as the Albany Plan.

"Franklin noted in his autobiography that his original draft was put together on route to the congress. When he arrived in Albany, he was surprised to find several commissioners with similar plans. Once the matter with the Six Nations Iroquois was rectified, a vote was taken, and by unanimous count the congress affirmed a union should be formed. A committee reviewed each plan submitted and, of course, Franklins' was the preferred draft.

"The final proposal consisted of a complete government outline. A president general was to be selected by the Crown to dispel the impression that the government being proposed would not ultimately be controlled by Great Britain. A Grand Council would be made up of forty-eight members who were to be selected by the House of Representatives or General Assemblies of each colony. The plan also outlined many other things. Philadelphia would be the meeting place in three-year election cycles. The plan provided for the designation of a 'Speaker of the Grand Council' and for the number of Grand Council members each colony could elect.

"Finally, the plan outlined the role the president would have. He would have the power of Indian purchases, the designation of new land settlements, and the selection of a treasurer. The plan also stipulated that should the president die in office; the Speaker of the Grand Council would take on the interim role of president. To explain the reasoning behind every amendment, Franklin wrote an essay titled, *Reasons for a Union.*

"At the conclusion of the Albany Congress, news of Colonel George Washington's failed raid on French forts in the Ohio Valley reached the delegates. Although it was unfortunate that another engagement with the French was on the horizon, the delegates were relieved that they solidified the union with the Mohawks and the Iroquois. They had little fear that the Iroquois would turn against the British. As the delegates departed from Albany, some felt, including Franklin, with war officially being engaged on this side of the Atlantic, the call for a colonial union would have unanimous support.

"Unfortunately, when the Albany delegates returned to their local assemblies with the proposal, they encountered outrage and fear that this new form of central government would infringe upon their local powers to operate under the charter given to them by Great Britain. In a letter to Benjamin Franklin, William Clark wrote that he and the other commissioners at Albany were 'blockheads' and that they had devised a plan to destroy the liberties and privileges of every subject on the continent. In August 1754 in Pennsylvania, Franklin's own assembly rejected the plan, after the Governor praised the document. Franklin recorded in his autobiography that he was 'mortified' when the House decided to vote on his plan the day he was absent.

"Other colonies rejected the plan as well. South Carolina and Virginia, ignored it altogether, which was odd because it was the royal governor of Virginia who wanted a colonial union. New York reviewed it, but rejected it in the end, because they felt they were going to lose their strong power of negotiations with the Natives in Albany. The other colonies rejected it as well. Only Massachusetts and Connecticut attempted to create counterproposals, but nothing ever materialized. Each colony wanted to hold on to the supposed powers each possessed.

"In London, the ministry reviewed the Albany Plan, but the proposal never made it to Parliament for discussion. Parliament had talks in the past but no one ever wanted the colonists to form a principal body of government that could diminish British authority in America. By allowing each colony to function with its own laws, governing bodies, and economies, each colony was kept insignificant when it concerned representation in London. *Why give these people any power?* was the approach of the Lords. But, Parliament did do one thing in response to the plan. They allowed governors to form a council, which permitted them to order the raising of troops, the building of forts, and the access to the London treasury for expenses.

"Having more urgent matters at hand, Great Britain focused its efforts on the French invasion into the Ohio Country. It was seen as a blatant act of defiance to their treaty, and the engagement with Colonel Washington was an act of war. Some would think the rising tide of war would be a bad thing, but all of this was perfect timing for the English.

"After the War of Austrian Succession, Great Britain had become an ally with Prussia, one of the largest and strongest military forces in Europe. While the French and Indian War was in its early stages in North America, war had not yet been declared by either kingdom. Inland, the French with their Native allies stopped almost every British engagement, but the ships in the British Navy were destroying French docks and establishing blockades. Then, in 1755, the Prime Minister of England, William Pitt, saw an opportunity to crush the French. Not just in North America, but also in India and every place across the globe. He approached the House of Commons and said Britain needed a grand naval fleet. Borrowing a Dutch process, the British built a fleet of one hundred and five ships, with fifty-five thousand naval officers, by selling bonds. They paid Prussia and financed the American colonies to raise a military force. War was officially declared in 1756, roughly two years after Washington's first encounter with the French.

"With Britain's alliance with Prussia and Portugal. Russia, Austria, Sweden, and Spain joined France in their battle. It was the start of the Seven Years' War, and it was fought in North America, Europe, the Caribbean, Africa, and India. It was our first true World War and it all started because the French wanted the river we now call the Mississippi."

"That's incredible," Ethan said.

Just then a voice shouted from the distance, "Who ordered cheesesteaks?"

Henry threw up his hand and yelled, "Yooo!" He handed the young man two twenties' and told him to keep the change. Ethan unwrapped a beautifully constructed Philadelphia cheesesteak. The meat was burned just enough on the edges. It had caramelized onions, and a perfect helping of a cheese by-product, that was running down the middle, on the sides, and every place in between. Ethan never put the sandwich down, and it was gone before he realized it. After disposing the wrappers, Ethan leaned back on the bench. "That was amazing," he said.

"Glad you liked it," Henry said, as his sandwich was down to the last couple of bites.

Audrey ate half of her sandwich, wrapped the rest back up, and put it in her carry bag. "Where were we?" she asked.

Ethan was quietly meditating under the tree. With a sigh, he said, "War is declared."

"Oh, that's right," Audrey said. Seeing that Ethan was becoming too relaxed on the park bench, she kicked his feet. "Pay attention," she shouted. "This is important."

"Now even though the *Seven Years' War* was the name for the global war, the *French and Indian War* was in its second year in North America by 1756. The Native style of engagement differed from the European style. It involved guerrilla warfare, ambushing the enemy, and fighting down from treetops, spreading out within the wilderness, rather than confrontations in open ground with battalion formations. As much as it was unconventional and created a slight disadvantage at the start of the war, the unforeseen advantage was this style of fighting was training many men who would later be soldiers of the Continental Army, twenty years later.

"With the British concentrating their strength in New England and the Ohio Country, the French and Natives made some attacks outside of Pennsylvania. When General Braddock lost a battle near the Monongahela River in July 1756, the Natives moved closer to Philadelphia over the summer and fall season. By January they advanced along a seventy-mile front that was pressing the English against the ocean. Commander Franklin, yes, our Franklin, was called on to lead a militia of cavalry and infantry to rebuild the forts near Gnadenhutten, north of the city. Franklin was the senior officer due to his age, but he possessed no military experience. Fortunately, Franklin used the experience his son William gained during King George's War in 1744. As they maneuvered through the wilderness, Commander Franklin had his militia spread out wide, rather than have them march in the traditional rank and file. Should they be attacked, all men would be ready to react, instead of having to get into formation, and then engage.

"Because of Franklin's leadership and knack for visualizing improvements in almost anything he ever set his mind too, the militia successfully repaired the abandoned fort and established two more forts, fifteen miles apart, to establish a stronger front to protect Pennsylvania. Franklin improved the settlements in the area, routed out any local hostiles, and improved the morale of the militia simply by bribing them to attend religious service so that they could have rum. Otherwise, it was forbidden.

"Governor Thomas Penn of Pennsylvania considered Franklin a Caesar-like threat because of his popularity and political skills. Penn ended up calling an assembly, which forced Franklin to renounce his command, so he could attend. Shortly after Benjamin Franklin is asked to go to London as a representative of the colonies, ending his military career.

Overall, Franklin's experience as a commander was considered another hallmark of his ability to rise to the occasion.

"With a population in the colonies of roughly one and half million compared with France's seventy-five thousand in Canada, one would think the French did not stand a chance. But because of the alliances with the Native Americans, the French held back and ambushed many British forces. Just as Franklin wrote in his 'Join or Die' article, the French were one voice, one body, and the British were in pieces. This truth was revealed in the early stages of the war, with governors not supporting campaigns, changing major generals, and, of course, politicians acting as if they knew more than the soldiers. It did take some time to get everything in line, but once aligned, and with the strength of the much larger, newly reinforced, British Navy, the tide of war was turning in Britain's favor in North America.

"As in past wars, the French had a viable plan. They would invade some land here and there, fight until both sides made a truce, and then repeat the process. Sometimes, they would gain or lose land, and sometimes they would surrender one area to gain another. But the French never tried to annihilate their opponent. However, in 1759, the weaker French fleet sailed inland and tried to attack the heart of England. It was a disaster and most of the French naval fleet was lost. That move set in motion the domino effect of defeat around the globe.

"When the war ended in 1763, the Treaty of Paris was signed. Britain received Quebec, Canada, and Florida. Their strength in India was solidified as France was all but ruined in Asia. France also had to give Louisiana to Spain, yielding Spain's control of New Orleans in exchange for Britain as an ally. Which left everything east of the Mississippi to be owned by the British, and the French influence from North America disappeared with a signature.

"Great Britain now possessed the largest and most powerful naval fleet ever created. With territory on every continent, English companies controlled the major trade routes throughout the world. Without an equal anywhere on the globe, Britain, with King George the III now on the throne, was the largest empire man had ever created.

"With France out of North America, England would take advantage of their dominion and expand west when they saw fit. As part of the treaty, King George forbade subjects from trading beyond the Appalachians. Of course, by taking a position like this, a backlash was expected. The tribes that were a part of the 'Council of Three Fires', the Ojibwe, the Ottawa, and the Potawatomi, started burning forts and tormenting some locals in New England. To counter this growing rise of attacks, the King's military began to make its presence in North America. The red coats were put in place to provide protection, throughout the colonies. In Boston alone, ten thousand troops were deployed to defend against all foreign threats. Little did the King know, that by ordering this protection, he accelerated the unraveling of his Empire.

"Do you see the connection, Ethan?" Henry asked.

Ethan replied, "No, what am I missing?"

"Before the war, England was trying to hold the line in North America," said Henry. "But the French forced their hand by pushing south along the Ohio. They go to war, which included Native tribes, and in the end, England is compelled to spread their newly fashioned army with their red coats throughout the colonies for *protection*. As time went on, the red coats of the Royal Army became the symbol of tyranny to Americans."

"I see what you are saying," said Ethan. "Had France not caused a war, England would not have increased the size of its military and then have the army patrol the east coast."

"He's got it," said Audrey. "After the Seven Years' War, England was facing one major problem within their new Empire. Because of the expenditures of this new global warfare, they were in debt by more than one hundred and twenty million pounds. This debt turns out to be the catalyst for the transgressions that caused the colonists to protest and eventually revolt against their mother country.

"England invoked the Stamp Act to help pay the debt. It taxed anything imported and purchased. Franklin, now residing in England, voiced his opposition to these taxes. The Stamp Act was not a tax exclusive to the colonies, it was enacted throughout the empire, but the colonies protested it the most. Although it was repealed, other taxes and sanctions ended up being imposed in its place. This irritated many merchants, especially in Boston. The Royal Army that was there to protect the citizens, now needed to keep the citizens in line. The Boston Massacre was a prelude, and it thawed the façade of English uniformity within the colonies. Next came the protest against the Tea Act in Boston harbor. For their intolerable disobedience, came the Intolerable Act, which eliminated the self-governing powers from Massachusetts as punishment. From the frontline of Boston came a call for a new course of action.

"The voices against this suppression formed their argument at the start of the 1770s with the circulation of the *Committees of Correspondence*. The first to be represented as a patriotic figure was Samuel Adams of Massachusetts. His passion for liberty and his desire to perfect the art of being an antagonist willed Samuel, or Sam, Adams to create the *Sons of Liberty Party*. When other colonial figures started echoing the sentiments of Sam Adams, like Roger Sherman of Connecticut, and Patrick Henry of Virginia, it became clear that the hardships being experienced because of the British decrees were not just felt in the northeast, but throughout all the colonies. Inspired by this correspondence, enigmatic unofficial governing bodies were formed within each colony. As it became clear that the rising tide of British domination would create a serious rift between the colonies and Britain, these governing boards elected representatives from each colony to meet as a united Congress and to seek a resolution with a single voice."

"And they all met, here," Audrey said while pointing to Carpenters' Hall. "Sam Adams, his cousin John Adams, Richard Henry Lee, Patrick Henry, George Washington, and many more met inside this building on September 5, 1774."

"Wow!" said Ethan. "How many came?"

"Fifty-six delegates," Henry said, "but it was anything but harmonious." Henry got up from the bench and stood beside Audrey. "This was the first known time representatives from the different colonies came together on their own to discuss legislative affairs. On the first day, September 5, they met at the City Tavern and walked here much like we did earlier today."

"Can you tell me what they did inside?" asked Ethan.

"Sure," replied Henry. "Allow me."

Henry explained, "None of them were on the same page. Some wanted to reform the constitutional rights of Massachusetts and affirm the same for all British–America colonies. Some wanted to remain connected with the Empire but wanted to demand local congressional rights and natural liberties to be observed by Parliament. Then there were a few who advocated for complete separation, such as the representative from South Carolina, Christopher Gadsden. George Washington noted that 'no reflecting mind looked forward to such a thing.'

"Once inside they voted that Peyton Randolph would preside over the meetings, and Charles Thomas would be Secretary of the Congress. After that, they couldn't find common ground on how to pursue the *process*. How to vote? Who should vote? How should that vote count? Should the larger colony's vote carry more weight than the smaller ones? And how many representatives should the smaller colonies have compared with the larger? It was chaotic, and on the second day, it appeared with so many first-day issues still unresolved that this call for a Colonial Congress may have been a mistake. It wasn't until the room quieted that Patrick Henry of Virginia stood. He said, 'This is the first Congress, no former can be a precedent.' He also stated that government was dissolved, and that all boundary lines were erased. America was but one land, and he was not a Virginian—but an American.

"Slowly, they were able to make progress on how to proceed until they hit another snag. Who, and from which religion, was to start the day with prayer? Once again Patrick Henry addressed the Congress by saying that he was not a bigot and could hear a man of any piety and virtue, who was a friend to this country. On the third day, news reached Philadelphia that the British had bombarded Boston. With their agreed prayer to start their day, all men felt deep sorrow for the people of Boston. George Washington went to his knees during the prayer, and all were reminded of why they were called to meet.

"Benjamin Franklin wrote from London to Congressional Secretary Charles Thomson and stated, 'The sun of liberty is set, you must light up the candles of industry and economy.'

"Thomas responded, 'We shall light up torches.' That torch may not have been lit when the first Congress is compared with the events that followed, but it was a monumental first step that brought unity and established the idea that government is something for the people to participate in rather than be subjected to. After three months of discussion, the Congress ended. All colonies agreed to cease the importation of English goods and to establish stronger resistance to the Crown, so that Massachusetts would not have to stand alone against Britain.

"The so-called accomplishments of the First Continental Congress reached Benjamin Franklin, and he was not satisfied. He was disappointed that the delegates were unable to seize the opportunity using their collective power as he did in Albany, twenty years earlier. Leading up to the First Congress, Benjamin Franklin and his son William argued on the merits of the assembly so much that started the divide in their own relationship. To hear the Congress ended without strong resolutions added insult to injury.

"Franklin was also disappointed in Pennsylvania delegate Joseph Galloway. Who, with Franklin's encouragement, haphazardly introduced the outline of the Albany Plan as his own, calling it the *Galloway Plan of the Union*. It went nowhere with the other delegates, which made Franklin realize he had to attend the Congress when it reconvened in the summer. He must show them why his Albany Plan was the only way to avoid war.

"And this is where, and when, you step in, Ethan. When you first cross paths with Franklin in Philadelphia, he will have just returned from London. The Second Continental Congress is set to start in a few days, and Franklin has yet to campaign his plan to any delegate. You must let him know immediately that his intention of implementing the Albany Plan will fail. Franklin will very likely not want to hear this but due to your interaction he will immediately become less ambitious to discuss the topic with other delegates when the congress starts. This will buy you time to convince him to be for independence.

"However, the irony is, should you be successful, it will not be the end of the Albany Plan. After Franklin writes the letter to William Strahan calling him his 'enemy', he then uses parts of the Albany Plan to draft a new structure of government which he called the *Articles of Confederation and Perpetual Union*.

"Benjamin Franklin passed around this 'new' document in mid-July and a few delegates recognized the structure of government. Only in this outline the connection to Parliament was removed. But, in Franklin's diplomatic style, it left the possibility of reconciliation with the Empire. Also, echoing the sentiments of his Albany Plan, Franklin put in provisions to protect trade and engagement with Native Americans. Something that Franklin felt was vital to the prosperity of America. The problem was, he was too early. In the summer of 1775, only a few delegates were of the mind to separate from Britain, but the Congress formed a committee to review the proposal. It never came to the floor for a vote, but once the Declaration was passed, the Congress now needed to outline their *new* government, should they prevail in their revolt. Guess which document they used?"

Ethan let out a laugh, "This is crazy," he said. "Although, I really am enjoying this history lesson. You should become a professor."

Henry laughed, "I don't have the calling to be a teacher. That profession is for the strong minded and the tolerant spirit. I don't find myself possessing those qualities, but thank you for the compliment. Maybe I'll just tutor."

"Well, you're good at it anyway," said Ethan. "So, after preventing Franklin from using the plan as a tool of compromise, he uses it anyway to outline a structure of government? That is eventually needed the day after The Declaration is passed?"

"That's correct," said Henry. "That document had a strong twenty-year run in it. I'm not 100 percent sure but I believe it was also used as an outline when it came time to draft the Constitution. Which gave it a thirty-year run, when you think about it."

Henry then walked over to Ethan. "After the United States was formed, Franklin looked back at one of the original Albany Plan drafts and put a remark at the end of the plan on February 9, 1789. He wrote, 'On reflection, it now seems probable, that if the foregoing plan had been adopted and carried into execution, the subsequent separation of the colonies from the mother country might not so soon have happened.' Franklin also went on to give the sequence of events that occurred after the Albany Plan was rejected." Henry then sat beside Ethan, "I wonder where Dr. Franklin picked up that method of post analysis?" he said as he tapped Ethan's knee. "Regrettably, today, the weight of that document has all been forgotten."

"What time is it?" Audrey asked.

Ethan reached into his pocket to view the face of his phone. "Oh great!" he said.

"What?" asked Audrey.

"Lauren has been trying to get a hold of me," Ethan said. "Oh, and it is quarter to four."

"Okay, well I'm done," said Audrey. "I have some prep work to do at the office, and then I have a date to get ready for. Have a good evening, gentlemen."

"Have a good one," Ethan said.

"Oh, Ethan," Audrey said. "Tomorrow we review Ben."

"Thanks, Audrey. See you tomorrow," Henry said as Audrey walked away. He turned to Ethan who was busy with his phone. "Let's head back and get a few drinks before dinner," he said.

Ethan spoke to Henry without lifting his head, "Sounds good." He was too busy reading the text messages received from Lauren throughout the day.

> (8:05 a.m.) **Lauren: Good morning, my love. Good luck on your first day.**
>
> (9:07 a.m.) **Lauren: Heading to the Dr.'s**
>
> (10:40 a.m.) **Lauren: Hey babe, how is everything is going? I am at the doctor's office. They want to take another sample of spinal fluid. Not looking forward to this. On the bright side, I gave them your insurance info! So happy you're working again!**
>
> (1:12 p.m.) **Lauren: Babe? Is everything okay? I know you're busy, just let me know. I'm heading home now. I love you.(2:04 p.m.) Lauren: Babe???**
>
> (3:34 p.m.) **Lauren: Hello???**
>
> **Ethan: Hey! Sorry, had my phone on mute while I was in today's class. I had no idea it was going to be that long. I'm really sorry I'm not there with you for these tests. I'll be back in the hotel in about an hour. I'll give you call. Philadelphia is nice. We should come and visit it together some time soon.**

Chapter Nineteen

May 10, 1775: A Walk with Ben

After Benjamin Franklin tossed me out of Tun's for being so blunt, we decided the best course of action would be to avoid confronting the doctor for a couple of days and give any damaging sentiments a chance to recede. Being that today was the first meeting of the Second Continental Congress, I needed to seek his audience before he entered the State House. Last evening, I discussed with Mary and Philip the approach of avoiding discussion of the plan and just engage in general subjects of conversation to disarm Franklin, and retain any hope of achieving our objective. They both agreed, and at sunrise, Andrew and I headed over to Market Street to wait for Dr. Franklin, outside of his home. Upon his exit, I walked to the end of his pathway. When he turned, and saw me standing in his way, he groaned loud enough for me to hear and said, "I was hoping you left town."

I did not hesitate to apologize for my actions from the day before and told Dr. Franklin that I was inconsiderate last we spoke. As he walked towards me, I then asked if he would permit me to accompany him during his walk this morning. "On one condition," he said to me, "that you do not utter a word that could endanger my life." I agreed of course, and then he added, "Although you may have lived a fulfilled life, I am still too young to end mine."

"Aren't you sixty-nine?" I asked. For a reply, I received a tilted head, with two eyes glaring over spectacles. Before another second passed, I threw a single hand up and, again, apologized. From this exchange, I found his mood to be tepid, and none combative, which lowered my apprehensions to act aggressive in my need to be accepted by Dr. Franklin. It wasn't a reset, or a second chance. We stood in the presences of each other without the cordial façade, which normally takes multiple encounters between strangers to fade. Both of our intentions were already exposed, and we were now, familiar with one and other.

For the first few minutes, as we walked down Market Street, Dr. Franklin held a very slow and steady pace. He was not speaking directly to me or acknowledging that I was at his side. My initial impression was that perhaps he was slightly irritated with my re-emergence, but reflecting on the encounter, these actions were intentional. The slow pace was to give people a chance to notice him and shout out a salutation. People came from all directions, some crossed the street, just to shake his hand. We must have started and stopped our walk five times, maybe eight. All of this took place within the first fifty yards from his home. After witnessing this exercise unfold for twenty-five minutes, I was losing my patience and thought I could interject an ironic observation to get his attention away from his admirers. I said, "they must know you here." He gave me no response in return, but continued to acknowledge everyone else around us. When the small crowd dispersed, we continued on our way. For each and almost every woman we passed, Dr. Franklin would smile, tip his cap, and add a playful "good-day", which always received some flirtations laugh in return. I knew I couldn't let this go on, I had to break the growing silence between us, if this was going to work.

The night before, Mary told me to be patient, not to force a conversation if it doesn't present itself, and to speak only about our common interest. As Henry told me over and over, I would know I was having a conversation with Benjamin Franklin when the questions were coming from him. When it was finally just Dr. Franklin, myself, and Andrew again, a single passerby said, "Welcome back, Dr. Franklin," which made me think about his return from Europe. Fixated on that subject, I felt I found an opening and said, "You know the other day when we met, you reminded me of your multiple trips across the Atlantic."

The sound of cane touching stone filled in the silence that walked between us. As the brief moments passed, another feeling of despair crept in until Franklin replied, "What about them?"

I quickly answered, "I'll have you know that my wife and I were able to sail around Europe last year and we saw some beautiful places." I figured he would ask, where I've been to, and then take it from there. All he said was, "Good for you." The disinterest told me I was getting nowhere fast. I continued on that topic and started to name landmarks. I mentioned how I channeled through the canals of Venice, walked the streets of Rome, and entered St. Peter's Basilica.

Dr. Franklin then asked me, "What did you think of the Sistine Chapel?" But his monotone voice exhibited no enthusiasm in the question or care of a response. I didn't let it concern me. I told him that we were not able to enter because the line was too long. Not realizing the error of what I just said, Dr. Franklin asked, "What line?" I thought I may have exposed a discrepancy in comparison to an eighteenth-century visit to the Vatican. I was referencing my visit to Rome through an excursion package from a cruise we took last winter. Being uncertain of the present-day crowds in Vatican City, I had to cover. I said, "There was an event being held by the Pope and I couldn't get in on that day, but we walked around and enjoyed the ruins."

"Really," Dr. Franklin said to me, "why is that?"

The energy in his voice was now rising and I was beginning to feel good, but I was in immediate trouble because I didn't have a readied answer and I feared I was about to lose the rhythm of the conversation and his interest. As the State House steeple came into view I knew I was running out of time and had to slightly nudge him. I said, "The ruins reminded me that as our species continues to progress on this planet, there is an entity beyond comprehension that does not want one organized order presiding over all. The Romans, much like the Egyptian's, Byzantine's, and Ming Dynasties, were governing bodies who sought too much power, and eventually lost it."

Dr. Franklin stopped mid-step and began to laugh a little, which made me nervous. I thought I may have referenced the wrong empire, and he was about to mock me. He then started walking again and said, "Well the Egyptians were conquered; the Ottomans stepped into Constantinople, which got us out of the Middle Ages; but I guess your 'everything ends' theory can be applied to Ming. Oh, and I applaud you for trying to persuade me to think of the British Empire in succession to the empires and dynasties that preceded it, and that its time will eventually end. It was clever of you, Mr. Pope."

I tried to tell him that was not my intention, but he interrupted saying, "I believe it's absurd for a man to presume that his course setting on civilization is the most profound and, therefore, should be implemented without merit."

I responded by saying, "But sir, isn't that what this Congress is forming to discuss? To say that the course the King has set us on is unwarranted, unwanted, and needs to be changed?"

Dr. Franklin stopped again. "I don't like to walk with you, do you know that? Usually people just let me think aloud on my own." He then poked me with his cane, "And I told you not to reference anything that would bring harm to my being."

Once again, I had to apologize. And, once again, silence returned between us. As we stood facing one another, his cane hit the stone six or seven times. He looked hard into my eyes, and I began to debate the idea of just running from his presence, but then Dr. Franklin asked a question that surprised me. He asked which delegate or colony I was working for? I tried to assure him by saying, "Dr. Franklin I promise you there is not one person in the State House that knows me. Nor is there one colony that has sent me here on their behalf. I have no affiliation to anyone other than myself and my own self-interests."

He did not waste anytime asking me, "And they are?"

My mind was blank. The very realization of who I was speaking to was overwhelming and making it difficult for me to concentrate on the task at hand. I was desperate to save my dignity in that moment by revealing everything. I was ready to tell him I was from the future and the objective I was here to accomplish. But I knew, if I did that, in that moment. He would never believe me and he would avoid me forever. So, I reacted. I affirmed my stance and straightened my back. I stopped being in awe of him and encouraged myself to stop being intimated by him. I recalled a Franklin saying about peace and liberty so I thought I would use it. I said, "Damn it sir, I want what you want. Peace and security. I just want to make sure we don't surrender our liberties for them. Otherwise what good are they?"

Franklin smiled and gave me a polite head nod. He turned to continue his walk, at a faster pace now. I thought I was going to walk with him to the State House, or at least have a few more minutes to talk, but Franklin held his cane out across my waist and told me, "Now, I must ask you to leave, because I would hate for anyone to think you and I associate."

I gave him a casual laugh, but pleaded that I needed to continue this discussion at his convenience. I asked if we could meet after today's session. Dr. Franklin did not seem too pleased with my persistence, but he did say, "It appears to me that you have some insight on matters that you shouldn't. For I have yet to reveal my intentions to anyone, not even my kin. And although you may have surprised me the day before in the tavern, you have failed to persuade me. If anything, you helped me revisit my work from twenty years ago. You made me dust the cobwebs off the structure of a domestic government of which this country is in dire need. I will say this, if you traveled all the way to Philadelphia to warn me not to pursue the introduction of the Albany Plan to this Congress, you have failed. But consider yourself lucky. I have yet to find you repulsive, so if you would like to buy me a drink, meet me at Tun's at four."

Although I was relieved with the open invite, I was reluctant to continue our conversation in the pro-Franklin, Mason-supported Tun's. "I am abstaining from alcohol today. Could I instead buy you a drink at the London Coffee Shop?" Thankfully he agreed to the relocation. Seeing Dr. Franklin walk away from me, I felt like a parent who walks their child to school, only to be asked to leave them at the corner so they are not seen together, sparing the child's embarrassment. Only in this instance the child is a grown man and the school is a council that is about to change the world.

Andrew and I walked the streets for a while, not saying much to each other. Andrew knew the anticipation of seeing Franklin again was weighing on my mind. As we walked, I would feel a nudge on my shoulder every now and then, so I would not bump into things, run into people, or step in horse droppings in the street. Then, sometime in the afternoon, I heard church bells ringing, followed by guns firing. It was coming from the northeast, but where I was headed was in the opposite direction. When I saw the number of people walking towards the noise, I felt the need to join them. On Market Street, huge crowds began to form on both sides. In the distance, there was a large formation approaching. The whole scene looked as if a parade was about to come through. When the group got closer, I noticed there were military formations marching, with a good number of flag bearers, a lot of men on horseback, and a couple of horse-drawn carriages. Nearly fifteen thousand people cheered them as they made their way through the town.

It was hard to get a good look as they passed by, but I noticed one man on horseback acknowledging the people with a slight tip of his tricorn. He appeared shorter than his surrounding riders and he was dressed better than the militia men. As I analyzed him, his features were beginning to look familiar. I slowly walked alongside the procession, moving around people standing by, trying to get a better look. At one point, he looked over and noticed I was following him and that's when it dawned on me, who this man was and what the commotion was all about. I mouthed "Mr. Adams?" He nodded and tipped his cap to me. I grinned like a child and waved with enthusiasm at John Adams as he and the other delegates were being welcomed into town. There were hundreds of men on horseback so, of course, not all of them were representatives. I would imagine Sam Adams was in one of the carriages, but I never saw him. I stopped walking after my curiosity was satisfied and left the mass of people.

I arrived at the London Coffee Shop at the instructed time and sat at one of the tables near the street corner so I could see when Dr. Franklin approached. I patiently waited for more than an hour before he walked by with two other men, whose faces looked familiar, but at that moment I was too nervous to recognize. He saw me, I know he saw me, because he made eye contact but he purposely walked passed me. I jumped out of my seat, and I yelled, "Dr. Franklin!" This made the two men turn their heads in my direction, along with some people in the street. Dr. Franklin was aghast. He leaned into his two confidantes, said something and they went on their way. He then approached me with a quick pace. When he arrived at my table, he said, "You are persistent, Mr. Pope. I'll say that about you, but you do lack proper manners, which may explain why you sit alone."

Trying once again to prove the good doctor wrong, I made it clear that I was not alone and that my friend Andrew was a few tables over. That my aunt and uncle, who were going to join me shortly, were tending to their own affairs in the city. He then asked why Andrew was sitting alone and alluded to the idea that I was I embarrassed to be seen sitting with a black man. When I explained that Andrew was my associate and not my slave, he did not seem to believe me. Dr. Franklin proceeded to ask what profession I held. I told him I presently did not hold one and that I was in Pennsylvania working with my uncle at his mill. Franklin responded by asking how many slaves my uncle owned. I firmly refuted his accusation and told him there was not one slave on my uncle's land. I believe this gained his consent, but I needed to changed topics.

I asked how the first day went. He said, "It was promising and one of introductions." I knew that on the first day of Congress, they voted on Payton Randolph of Virginia to be president and for Charles Thomson to be secretary. Of course, he wasn't going to tell me, and I could not tell him what I knew. So, I continued to pry, but to throw off the presumption I was affiliated with anyone in the congress, I asked if he saw George Washington of Virginia. Dr. Franklin said, "he's the tallest man in the room, a blind man would certainly notice him."

Dr. Franklin then asked, "Mr. Pope, you have already made your intentions known to me, and I have expressed my desire to not consider or concede to your premonition of the congressional member's repudiation of my proposal." I tried to respond but he cut me off and continued, "Furthermore, I am insulted by your insinuation that I lack the political prowess to introduce a proposal of such magnitude." I told him that at no time was I intentionally undermining his abilities of persuasion. Again, he interrupted me saying, "To help my plan, tomorrow a letter from the fifth of February, signed by myself, William Bollen, and Arthur Lee, will be presented to all attending. It will validate how there are allies within both houses of Parliament on the other side of the Atlantic, led by Lord Chatham, all of whom I had an audience with before I left London. They assured me a central government in the colonies would receive strong consideration this time, as difficult as that may be for some to comprehend. Those allies, however, will not stand with us too much longer if the aggressions progress from here. After the Congress is made aware of this intent, I will be able to approach members in the coming weeks with the proposal of a national legislative body. Understand Mr. Pope that I am not going to consider withdrawing my solution for reconciliation. I certainly am not going to ponder the notion that such a common-sense solution would not be met with emphatic support, just because a stranger approached me and told me so. Having said that, Mr. Pope, why did you want to meet me here?"

I was frozen. He was so calm and sure of himself. Meanwhile I was a wreck trying to match wits with this brilliant man. I told him that I believed that the notion was valid, the principal was simplistic and profound. And then, I stalled. I did not know what to say next.

Dr. Franklin was shaking his head, "but?" he asked.

I said, "But I don't see you getting a majority. You know that some delegates are not seeking what you are offering. The internal engine that drives the body of Parliament is obedience. They think what is happening in Massachusetts warrants death to every person actively involved. And when more English loyalists hear that Fort Ticonderoga fell, it will only increase the divide. Even if you could get your proposal through, it would be used to wipe the mud off the boot of the King, if he would ever step on it."

Franklin pondered for a moment. With his silence came a small victory for myself. I thought for a minute I had him on the ropes. But then he said to me, "Mr. Pope, men never know what they want. That I have learned from experience. Some may think they know what they want, but illuminate them on the alternatives and they'll change. Take the people here in this great city. In 1712, they were the first legislative group to pass an act trying to prohibit the importation of slaves as a first step to abolishing slavery. Even though they failed at their first attempt, the people of this province continued to pursue it. They acted on their convictions, and not too long ago, stopped the act of importation, and this colony has benefited ever since. Why, just a couple of months ago, some dear friends of mine started a group called the 'Pennsylvania Society for Promoting the Abolition of Slavery and for the Relief of Free Negroes Unlawfully Held in Bondage'. The title is a bit wordy but its purpose is pure. It's the first of its kind in any colony and I hope after I resolve these present day matters I may be able to join them in their fight."

I knew what he was talking about, but I did not understand what he trying to tell me. I asked Dr. Franklin to clarify.

"Resolve, Mr. Pope; that is the point. Even though you may believe the task is unpopular, you never give up." I gestured to him that I understood the analogy and he continued. "The people did not give up wanting to rid this city of that savage practice, and in turn, I shall use their example to achieve a unified government. And after we accomplish that first step, we can then tend to broader, national matters. Including slavery. To this day, it perplexes me that we could not inherit the ruling from Lord Henley, a few years ago, that stated a slave who sets foot on English soil immediately becomes free. Are we not standing on English soil?" He then rose out of his seat and looked down at me and said, "It is in remedying those quagmires I want the men I associate with to recognize as the epitome of their congressional capabilities. Only together will we get what we want."

I asked, "And that is?"

"Deliverance," he said. His eyes grew very big when he said it, and he held his stare for just a few seconds, then in an instant, seemed to snap out of his trance and smiled. Before he left me, he said, "Now if you'll excuse me for departing so abruptly, I promised my son-in-law Richard and his associate that I would allow them to buy me dinner at the tavern."

After a long day, I conceded the argument for the evening and wished him well. Dr. Franklin took one step, then looked back to say, "I have an uneasy notion this will not be the last time our paths cross and you grace me with your company." He then walked off down the road.

Andrew made his way to my table and shortly after Philip and Mary arrived. We sat and reviewed everything that happened today. Andrew noted how Dr. Franklin impressed him because he never saw someone receive so much attention by just being outside.

Chapter Twenty

Can I Stop Slavery?

For Ethan, the brutal cold air that lingered in the northeast from December to February, made the time unpleasant. The density of the air only added to the feeling caused by nature's harsh temperature. Like an unwanted guest, the air that passed through in early December seemed to swirl around in one place for a couple of months. Ethan cringed at every entry into the unapologetic climate from any warm sanctuary. His discontent with travel during the frigid months of the calendar prolonged his sessions with Henry at The Roasting Plant. With three months before the lunar eclipse, it was common for there to be long stretches of silence between them after very long days dedicated to the final preparations of Ethan's upcoming journey.

Henry was taking a break and catching up on local news. Although the written news may not have provided the instant indulgence cable news provided, his mind was not at ease until he was educated on the stories of the day with the well-researched articles by the journalist of his newspaper. Ethan sat across from Henry thumbing through headlines on his Twitter feed that glowed from his Galaxy S7 Edge. Between the two of them was a chess game in which black was dominating. The white side had only the king, rook, knight, and two pawns, but the black side had those pieces as well as five more, including the queen. "It's still your move," Henry said, "whenever you are ready to resume."

"I'm still thinking," Ethan replied, as he continued to scroll through the world in real time. Several minutes passed without Ethan making a move. When his third peppermint mocha arrived, Ethan broke the silence and asked, "I'm going to ask again. Can I stop slavery?"

Caught slightly off guard, Henry flipped his newspaper down and looked to see who was around them. After ensuring they were alone in the shop, Henry plainly said, "No," and then he flipped his newspaper back up to continue reading.

"Wait," replied Ethan, "you need to explain this again to me. Why can't I stop some of this nation's greatest tragedies?"

From behind his newspaper, Henry let out a sigh, and gave the papers a quick flick of the wrists to stiffen the pages before he said, "I thought we discussed the other paradoxes you would create if you attempted such a feat." After a minute passed without a response, Henry felt bad for being short and wanted to know what Ethan was thinking. "Why do you ask?"

"I find that hard to accept. Why can't I stop slavery? Why can't I inform people of future horrific moments in our history and prevent them from happening? Why can't I inform Franklin of, let's say, President Lincoln's assassination?"

"We already spoke of this," said Henry. "It's hard enough that one moment in time needs alteration and that several require assurances. The last thing we need you to do is altering the line anymore."

"Okay, but what if, just hear me out, what if I don't abolish slavery in 1776. Instead, I say there's a guy named John Wilkes Booth who shoots Lincoln in Ford's Theater in 1865 after the Civil War. Why can't I say that?"

Henry responded, "Because you can't. It could have consequences beyond your understanding." He then brought back up his barrier of newsprint and returned to his article.

Another several minutes passed, while Ethan continued to read his Facebook and Twitter bulletins. Then his head popped up when another idea came to him. "Oh wait! I could just stop the Civil War!" Ethan exclaimed. "That would save President Lincoln's life."

Hoping that Ethan would give up his quest for approval, Henry avoided making eye contact. "Yep, that's what we want you to do, stop the Civil War." After another minute passed, Henry flipped a corner of his paper down again, and asked, "With no Civil War, how is slavery abolished?"

Ethan's demeanor assumed a slight air of defeat. "Oh, yeah," he sighed.

"OH, YEAH," Henry mockingly replied.

"Then that takes me back to my first question. I could help Franklin abolish the slave trade when the Declaration is created. Then with slavery abolished, I would have stopped the Civil War," Ethan said.

Henry gripped the pages a little tighter. As he began to think Ethan was neglecting the most crucial element of his upcoming journey, asked, "Haven't we been through this?"

Ethan sat back in his seat and responded, "Right, no slavery no adoption of the Declaration, no Revolution, no internal conflict, no civil war, no Lincoln. Sorry. I'm just uneasy with it. The journal has not updated in a few months, and you told me not to worry so much because in the end, I'm going to live through it. But with Franklin's hints on his distaste for slavery, I thought I could help matters and put him on the path to Independence and help him abolish the industry."

Henry dropped his newspaper again, "Okay, one more time," he said. "Let's go over this. Benjamin Franklin cools the tempers between the North and South during the debate on Independence. That was achieved because

Franklin understood the abolition of slavery and keeping the colonies united would require a few steps. The first step was the establishment of a new independent country, America."

"So how do I get him to be for that?"

"You'll need to guide him, not tell him," responded Henry. "Franklin's style of debate was to lead the person. Regarding slavery, Franklin started this debate in 1751 by attacking the slaveholder, not on the moral arguments but the monetary aspects of the institution. He did this by stating if you consider all the expenses of owning one slave compared with paying one person a day's wage, the slaveholder would save a lot of money paying the wage. Also, he tried to demonstrate how keeping a person against their will lowered their output. If a plantation owner paid for labor, their output would double because of the desire to work and the incentive to do a good job."

"I agree with that," said Ethan. "Why didn't others?"

"I don't know," said Henry. "There was a lot of money in the selling and trading of slaves. Much like today, people who are against something may not possess the money to sway public opinion. Not comparing anything to the ownership of a human being, but in today's political arena, similar monetary conflicts occur."

As a few minutes passed, the generous sound of silence returned and Henry thought Ethan had abandoned his endeavor to save the world, from everything. His grip on the newspaper began to loosen, the tension in his neck released, and he returned to reading the articles of the day. But then Ethan disrupted the peace as he asked, "So you're telling me there is no event in our nation's history I could prevent with the hope of avoiding traumatic tragedy and promoting a more harmonious life for millions of Americans?"

"Harmonious?" Henry asked.

"Yes!" Ethan replied enthusiastically.

"You have concluded that the prevention of one event prevents any other event?"

"That's not what I'm implying."

"Okay," said Henry, "Then let me ask you this. Will whatever you do stop something like Columbine?"

"Stop it without directing anyone to prevent it? No, because I don't know all the significant events that led up to it," replied Ethan. "But I could stop it on the day. I mean, I could even stop the Challenger explosion on the day of the tragedy."

Henry thought about it for a moment, then said with a smirk, "No," as he pictured the scene of Ethan explaining to someone in the eighteenth century the engineering marvel which was the space shuttle. "Forget the Challenger, how about something more profound and consequential on a broader perspective, like Pearl Harbor? Will you be able to stop that by stopping the Civil War?"

"I don't know. Would there be a World War II if there was no American Civil War?" Ethan replied, "I mean, you said how the American Revolution played its part in the French Revolution, so I don't know how to answer that." Ethan was beginning to become irritated but Henry's rebuff had yet to break his spirit. Ethan was perplexed that his desire to try and avoid the heartache and tragedy for not only Americans but for all humanity was not encouraged. Ethan continued to press on, seeking either approval or a better explanation.

Henry knew it was natural for anyone to ponder if they were already altering history in a positive way by having Franklin vote for the Declaration, what other events could be altered for the world's "good." He was not annoyed with Ethan for revisiting this topic but as Ethan's passion continued to manifest itself in their rapid-fire discussion, Henry figured he was going to have to paint a gruesome picture, and go more deeply into the rules of time alteration to smolder his ambitions.

"Here," said Ethan. "John Kennedy? Robert Kennedy? John and Robert Kennedy? I can stop that." Then Ethan leaned into the table and with an inquisitive look, asked Henry, "Or can't I? Hmmm?" he said sarcastically with his eyebrows raised. "Conspiracy?"

Henry laughed at Ethan's insinuation. "Shut up," he said, "And no, you are not allowed to stop the assassination. However, if you did try to stop the assassination by intercepting Lee Harvey Oswald, you most likely would stop the assassination. Okay?"

Ethan, having referenced enough of events that have occurred throughout history felt the next one would certainly attain Henry's approval. "9-11?"

Henry again paused with Ethan's latest query, and then he waved Ethan to come closer. Ethan moved his seat to the left side of the table thinking to himself, "I got him. He's going to tell me that *they* want me to stop 9-11."

"It's a very noble thought," Henry said. "But ask yourself *What are you preventing?*"

Ethan thought the question was patronizing, "What am I preventing!" he said to himself. "What an insensitive bastard!" Ethan looked perplexed at Henry and said, "I'm preventing some of our history's worst or greatest tragedies."

"All right," replied Henry. "How?"

Ethan threw his hands up. "By informing!"

"Who?" replied Henry.

"I'll tell Franklin."

"What?"

"I'll tell Franklin that on these dates the nation would go through some of the worst heartaches. People who had great promise and who could have done more for us as a nation, as a society, were murdered before their time."

"And by doing that, you will have prevented some of our nation's greatest tragedies?"

"Yes!" Ethan shouted.

"You're sure about that?"

Ethan gave himself a minute to ensure that he truly comprehended the matter and that such actions would be justified and necessary. Ethan confidently said, "Yes."

"By telling Franklin that on April 14, 1865, an American president would be assassinated in Ford's theater, would in turn prevent Abraham Lincoln from being murdered by John Wilkes Booth?"

"Why wouldn't it?" Ethan said.

Henry, not satisfied, physically signaled that his previous question to Ethan was still open by tilting his head slightly to the left while turning up his palm, and giving a twitch of his fingers to indicate that Ethan should *keep going.*

Ethan wanted another minute to think about it, "Wait," he said. The sounds in the coffee shop slowly faded and his concentration on the matter deepened further. Having been a master of time altering for only several months, Ethan required a few more minutes. The silence between them was beginning to reveal Ethan's lack of confidence in his argument. "Okay," he said. "Just telling Franklin that Lincoln should not go to Ford's theater on April 14, 1865, would serve no purpose because the assassin would still be alive. And if John Booth was alive, he would continue to act as the variable in Lincoln's death."

Henry started to nod his head, impressed by Ethan's theory.

Ethan was becoming more confident. "What if I say, John Wilkes Booth will assassinate an American president on April 14, 1865, and I instruct the removal of the perpetrator from the equation, at an early age? This would prevent the plot and the assassination in Ford Theater, thereby saving the life of Abraham Lincoln." Ethan felt as if he won and proved Henry wrong.

"How does the country reform after the Civil War concludes?"

"What?"

"The country," Henry replied. "How does the country reform at the end of the Civil War?"

"I don't understand," said Ethan. "The Civil War was over by the time Lincoln was killed. What does it matter?"

"Oh, it matters a great deal," said Henry. "Don't you recall? It was a year ago. We were in this room and I told you the death of President Lincoln was terrible and blood curdling, yet necessary to help achieve a new union with millions of our former Confederate citizens who had just lost hundreds of thousands in the defense of their perceived state's rights. The murder of Lincoln moved our nation passed the Civil War and into the next and most important stage of our existence. Lincoln's sacrifice was a requirement of progression and removing that or attempting to remove that will create anomalies that neither you nor I, nor anyone else, possibly can comprehend. And by introducing those anomalies to the timeline, through Franklin, God only knows where it would lead. How it would affect the nation's progression. How it would or would not lead to influx of Irish and Italian immigrants at the turn of the century. And how that would trickle through your linage with the exact moments of time and place to continue through generations to inevitably complete with the union of your parents and your creation."

Now recognizing how saving Lincoln could be an alteration that could rule out his own existence, Ethan appeared to be dumbfounded and could only respond with a moaning, "Oh."

"Would you like to take that risk?" Henry asked. "Would you like to risk a greater change in the timeline than you already have?"

"No," said Ethan.

"Exactly," said Henry. "Now I applaud you, I really do. The desire to right wrongs. To prevent such transgressions that have and will forever be marks on the profound impact the establishment of this nation otherwise had on humanity, and the global benefit the existence of this country has had over time, is commendable. I don't blame you for wanting to do more. You are a good person, so naturally you want to do good things. But again, neither you nor I, nor anyone who has been a part of this campaign can say for certainty what the ramifications of this reality would be if you strongly alter it anymore."

"I see," said Ethan.

"I'll say this, should you, for humanity's sake, attempt to abolish slavery? Absolutely," said Henry, "However, and it does twist my stomach to have to ingrain this in your mind. Trying to abolish slavery in that atmosphere you are entering, and knowing what we know, would never prevail with the need of all colonies supporting Independence. It doesn't matter if it's you or anyone else from this generation, some men in that congress would never have gone along. For instance, take Robert Morris, a delegate from Pennsylvania, who shipped slaves to ports around the colonies since importation of slaves into Philadelphia was prohibited at the time. He invested his wealth to fund the Continental Army. He created the first successful bank, called The Bank of North America, to finance the war. His investment would be equivalent of twenty-six million dollars today. This doesn't make him a saint? Absolutely not, but his investment, along with many others like him, were dire to the fiscal longevity of the cause. Rebellion's require financing, and many pro-slavery representatives possessed it. Doesn't make it right, it doesn't absolve Morris' sin, but it's worth noting that after everything was over, and we were a nation, Morris ended up dying in poverty. Did all pro-slavery representatives have similar downturns after the war? No, because two became president.

"The first step must be achieving Independence. The work of the Founders, will create a new nationality, defined with unprecedented moral perspectives. The work of the Framers will create a new national government, with ingenious structure. Both will depend on Franklin to adopt the mandate into the lexicon of humanity. Both documents will then beseech Lincoln to revitalize their expressions, and forever provide permanent context to the phrase 'all men are created equal.'

"I wish I could tell you not to worry or think about it. It's going to be difficult when you are there and even more difficult when you tell Franklin it can only be Independence with slavery. Franklin needs to have the year from July 4, 1775, to July 4, 1776, to quell the animosity from John Adams towards the southern colonists or it won't matter what you do. The Declaration will not pass. When we spoke about the original timeline, and Franklin voting against Independence, I told you that John Adams relied on Patrick Henry to work the delegates of the south. But in the end, those alliances were so weak that the moment Benjamin Franklin voted no, half the colonies changed their vote. With Adams working through Franklin, the bonds are much stronger, and inevitably benefit us all."

"So, it's more about the difficulty on the political end, rather than the, I don't know," said Ethan, "the 'space-time continuum'?"

Henry said with a smile, "Sure, that thing. And remember, Franklin is associated with the Pennsylvania Abolition Society during your time with him. After the Constitution is passed, in February of 1790, he will write the first petition to our newly constructed Congress, urging them to abolish slavery. He will declare that 'the blessings of liberty to the people of the United States should be done without distinction of color.' Yes, his petition failed but it will set things in motion."

"Then he dies two months later," said Ethan.

"Yes," Henry said. "You must let this course of action be as it is and let Franklin go down in history as a failed abolitionist." Henry then looked down and moved Ethan's rook to capture his queen, then moved his bishop, which put Ethan's king in check. Henry took Ethan's knight and blocked the bishop's check. "You must sacrifice in this game to win," said Henry. He then looked up at Ethan, "Do you know what move is next?"

"Yes."

"Oh, that reminds me. Don't forget, next week we are in Europe for research so you know where to go when you bring Franklin back for the Constitutional Convention. We're not site seeing, but after that you'll have two weeks to travel with Lauren."

"Yes, I know," Ethan said. He then held up his smartphone, turned the screen to face Henry, and with a grin he pressed the button that turned on his BMW i8, parked ten yards away.

Henry turned in his seat to see the car as it warmed up, he looked back at Ethan, "nice car," he said. "Christmas gift?"

"Oh yes," said Ethan. "I always wanted to drive it and I figured, what the hell, I only have three more months left to have fun."

"Are you sure you don't want me with you when you reveal to Lauren what's going on?" Henry asked, "I think it will make things easier."

"No, I'm going to do it on the cruise," Ethan said. "You got me that huge suite on the cruise ship, I'd like to enjoy it for a few days before I tell my wife I'm leaving her. Which I'm not looking forward to. You gave me the green light at Christmas but I couldn't have our exchange attached to that memory. It was our first Christmas in the new home and our last Christmas together. I figured in the middle of the Atlantic Ocean, on the transatlantic part of the cruise, I'll explain everything to her." Ethan then grabbed Henry's rook and cornered his king for checkmate. Ethan let out a sigh and looked out the windows to see white snowflakes falling from the sky. "All right, let me go home before the roads get bad," he said. Ethan zipped up his fleece, then put his scarf on, followed by his coat, and gloves. Thinking about the cold air Ethan said, "This is not going to be easy!"

"Isn't your fancy car right outside the door?"

"Good night, Henry."

Chapter Twenty-One

June 24, 1775: Revealed

Today was the sendoff for General George Washington. It has been two weeks since John Adams first proposed the idea of a congressional funded Continental Army to be commanded by the Virginian, and it's been nine days since the General accepted the post of commander-in-chief. A post that will unknowingly propel him into the annals of interminable history. His celebrated departure could not have come at a more crucial time for the people here in Philadelphia, as the weight of the reality of Britain's hold in Boston was felt even stronger after the news of the recent defeat at Bunker Hill was heard. It has no doubt united the Americans in a way no other act could have. I stood near the State House, on the edge of the crowd, ready to cheer and wish the General well on his journey to Boston to join the ragtag army.

While I waited, I noticed Dr. Franklin was walking away from the crowd. He was moving very fast for his pace. I ran up beside him and asked why he appeared to be so standoffish considering the tremendous celebration taking place before us. He said, "Those men humiliated me today and rejected my draft. I've never thought Dickinson would do this to me."

"Yes, I know," I said under my breath.

He then ranted a bit, saying, "They asked me to compose a petition to the King. Thanks to your nonsensical insight on political affairs, I composed my letter with apprehension to present an alternative formation of government to the Congress. I did suggest for his majesty, a reduced outline of government that was proposed once before, which may benefit the sovereignty of our bloodlines should his royal jackass find the once-sought-after unification, a just means to end the hostilities presently raging over here. I worked with Thomas Jefferson to preface it with some grievances shared by all Americans. I hesitated to ridicule or antagonize the leadership in London. In the end, they wouldn't even consider the draft and concluded that the commission would have to be postponed until a date they deemed appropriate."

Just then some canons were fired off in celebration and I jumped out of my shoes, dropped to the ground, and almost fell into Dr. Franklin. He looked at me like I was crazy for reacting that way. I stood up and straightened my clothes, and while I patted the dirt from my pants, out-of-nowhere he held his cane out across my chest.

While holding me back with his cane, he said, "Wait a minute, what did you mean 'you know'? How do you know? I'm the first person to leave the building. Everyone is still inside with the General. How would you have known any of this?"

I didn't think he could hear me over the noise of cheering, random gun fire, and ground shaking salutes. I tried to say that I meant it as a figure of speech.

Dr. Franklin said, "No, sir, you said it with absolute certainty. While I was describing what occurred, you looked at me as I do when people attempt to speak about topics I already have total comprehension of." Suddenly his demeanor changed and became inquisitive. He said, "You were belittling me. So why are you leading me on now, Mr. Pope? You knew about Fort Ticonderoga the other day before I or anyone in the Congress heard of the encounter. I didn't think much of it at the time, but the way you just seem to *know things,* and you can say the canon fire just now reminded me of your disclosure of that engagement. What else do you know that I don't, Mr. Pope? Why have you been lingering around Philadelphia for two months now? It's not just because your relation lives on the outskirts. Why do I keep crossing your path?"

I stood there knowing it was time, but it was not the right time. I could not possibly reveal my purpose in the middle of the city street with Dr. Franklin's emotions at such a breaking point. I decided to tell him that I was just a concerned citizen with some insight into the politics of the Congress.

He refuted me by saying, "No you're not. You're working for someone, and you've been handling me since the day you arrived. You're a spy, that's what you are. Allow me to explain something to you Ethan. You may have been able to conceal your identity for the past several weeks, but you became careless. You wanted to impress me, that was your downfall, and I discovered your true intentions. If you are not working for someone inside, then it's for someone who doesn't want compromise. It's someone who wants war? Is it your uncle? There's a lot money in crafting stocks for muskets and caskets for fallen heroes."

I assured him that my uncle was not attempting to become a war profiteer, but he did not accept it, completely. He said, "Well, I'm sorry to say, and you can reiterate this to whoever your proprietor may be, I will not give in to these tactics. Tomorrow I am reintroducing the Albany Plan as my true petition to the King, and if I should ever see you in my sight again, I shall ensure that you are removed and banned from my city forever."

And he walked away, leaving me standing alone in the streets. I returned to Mary and Philip to discuss what had just occurred. I retreated to my room to record these thoughts. As I reflect I'm looking out my window to a beautiful sunset covering Philadelphia this evening. The sunlight is making the Liberty Bell shine from the tower of State House. I hope this sunset is not a sign of failure. After what happened today I don't know how

I can get through to him. How I gained his trust from what I recall reading, is not working this time around.

Additional entry for June 24

I just returned from Franklin's home and I must write the events that unfolded while they are still fresh in my mind.

After Dr. Franklin left me, I sought out the council of Philip and Mary. We spoke about the current situation late into the evening. Philip felt that Franklin was bluffing with his threat to present the Albany Plan to the Congress. Mary, on the other hand, concluded that my presence must have accelerated the process within Franklin to come to a now-or-never decision. The best course of action to take would be to intercept Franklin on his way to the State House to inform him that I was not a spy for any delegate or any dignitary in existence. Mary suggested that I tell Franklin I was acting on my own and inject the tale that it was Thomas Jefferson who informed me on the proposed draft not going to table, when he and I spoke at the Indian King, a tavern Jefferson visits daily. We agreed that may be the most sensible argument and that would buy us more time. Given the fact that he alluded his government proposal in the first Olive Branch draft, and being that it was rejected, only implied that should he attempt a proposal tomorrow, it would fail to gain support. We adjourned for the evening, I wrote my entry above, and went to bed.

However, I stayed awake for hours consumed with the fear that I was not going to be able to have Dr. Franklin hold off his proposal and achieve my goal in the next ten days. I felt that the past fifty days had yet to show any strong indication that I was gaining leverage and that my time was up with the charade. If I was to convince Franklin by July 4, I needed leverage. The only way that was going to happen was if I revealed my origin. I jumped out of bed and yelled for Philip and Mary. I dressed quickly and explained to them that I was no longer putting off the inevitable. Consequences be damned, Franklin was being told tonight.

I ran in the dim lit streets of Philadelphia for blocks. The anticipation drove my emotions to their limit. My legs were weak beneath me with barely the strength to propel my body forward. My arms and hands were numb as if they had left my sides. My heart was pounding so heavy with the anxiety mixed with the adrenaline. It was like nothing I had felt since the day I proposed to Lauren.

Mary urged to not let Dr. Franklin know until he was in a state of mind to abandon the reintroduction of his plan, but I was running out of time. I could also tell from his departure this afternoon that he did not want to be in my company any longer. Add the probability that because of my pestering, his draft of the Olive Branch was dismissed. He likely was going to avoid me for a while. Whatever the reason was, I had no viable option but to inform Dr. Franklin why I was for being so persistent in seeking his counsel for the past month and a half.

When I finally arrived at Chestnut and 4th, I could see a small yellow glow from a still-burning candle coming from the second floor of his home. I took a moment to catch my breath and then walked to the front door and began calling for him as I discreetly knocked. After a few minutes, I heard rumbling coming from behind the door and something incoherent was spoken before Dr. Franklin appeared. When he realized it was me, I could tell from the scornful look on his face I might have disturbed him. The doctor wore a dark-colored dressing robe over a single white gown, tied at the neck. Not a tight-fitting piece of material, but it appeared to suit him nicely. Standing before me, he leaned on one of his walking canes. I was petrified, because I could tell he was very upset with my intrusion. Trying to introduce some levity, I smiled when I asked, "Catch you at a bad time?"

He stiffened upright a little, let out a grunt, and said to me, "Young Ethan, I have encountered some of the most bothersome and insensible creatures God has ever created, and I say to you with much confidence, you have out-shined them all."

I gave Dr. Franklin a courtesy laugh to break the tension for a moment, but I did not allow it to linger. I looked as sternly as I ever could to this great man before me and said in a demanding tone, "Ben, I must speak to you at this moment concerning something of the highest priority." I may have insulted Dr. Franklin by using his first name like that, but I was desperate.

He then lifted his walking cane and pushed the tip against my chest. I must admit I was getting tired of this antic. Part of me wanted to tug on the end of the cane and see him stumble, but that would not do me any good. In any event, with the cane in my center mass, Dr. Franklin said, "Anything you have to say can and will be said in the light of day if it is predicated with any bit of urgency." I swatted the cane away from my chest and had no option but to eyeball Dr. Franklin. I stepped up to his level and said, "No, Ben, what I have to divulge to you cannot wait for daylight. It is a subject that must stay between us. It must not risk falling on deaf ears, and it must be heard now."

Dr. Franklin gave me an inquisitive glance up and down. I feared he was going to close the door in my face. He stepped back and held out his left arm to grant me access into his home. As I passed in front of him, he told me I had "five minutes."

"What is it with you and only giving me five minutes?" I asked.

He told me, "When you are my age, there is no need to listen to people ramble on incessantly about nothing of interest, unless it is in the presence of a beautiful woman or a well-endowed widow. For their company, you will sacrifice wit and wisdom for the visual and possible physical satisfaction the fair sex will grant you. You, Ethan, may have youth, but there is nothing satisfying about your company, so you will get five minutes of my precious time."

He took a seat at his dining table. While he made his way over, I could not help but look around because I was standing in the home of Benjamin Franklin! It was too dark to truly appreciate it, but knowing this structure does not exist in the future gave me pause to appreciate where I was at this moment in time.

Dr. Franklin shouted, "Well," with a shrug of his shoulders, "you're losing precision time."

Not wasting another second, I jumped right into my revelation. "Yes time. Well, Dr. Franklin, you and I have talked on various topics, but I understand how you would perceive that my being here the past couple of months and seeking your audience is centered on the avoidance of introducing the revised version of your plan."

"Yes, which is something you keep failing to achieve, but please go on," he told me. I walked toward him to take the seat next to his. I gestured, asking if I could sit. He obliged with a lift of his nose and a grunt of some sort.

I leaned in and said, "Forget the Albany Plan. I'm not here to talk about that directly. Dr. Franklin, I ran over here tonight to disclose something about my life that you should find intriguing."

Franklin then rolled his eyes and said, "Are you sure want to hedge your wager on such an absolute? I have been intrigued by many dignitaries in my life and, so far, Mr. Ethan, you have yet to say anything of great substance to hold my interest."

My adrenaline was racing, my hands trembled, and my fingers were cold. This was it. I said, "Well, this just might peak your interest. Your lightening discoveries and experiments, along with the research of other scientists around the globe will help spark new discoveries and studies in the world of math and physics. Quantum and theoretical physics will grow exponentially over the coming centuries. Important men and women will apply those advancements to the creation of a mechanism that will be strong enough to generate an electromagnetic beam of light that could create a tiny black hole during a full lunar eclipse and send a subject through time. Now, I do come from New York, but I come from New York State. It is one of fifty that make up the United States of America, which has been a free and independent country for almost two and a half centuries. So you see, Doctor, I don't give a damn about your feelings on the Albany Plan. I don't need you to avoid presenting the Albany Plan. I need you to do something greater than that. That is why I came to Philadelphia last month. It was not to prevent you from offering a proposal for a unionized British-colonist centric government. It was to convince you to fight for the conception of a new one."

He just looked at me with no expression. I could not tell for certain if he was contemplating the legitimacy of what I had explained to him or was waiting for me to continue. I leaned in and reached out to touch his forearm. I looked up at him and reiterated by saying, "Dr. Franklin, I know you believe in reconciliation, in keeping unity, but I am here because that was tried once, and it had drastic ramifications. Trust me when I tell you, I'm not here because I want to be. I made a tremendous sacrifice to come back here to meet you; to have you vote for American Independence."

I did not say another word. I leaned back in my seat and waited for his response. After what seemed like an eternity, Dr. Franklin said, "When I first met you, I knew you were not from around here. I knew there was something odd about you. I just couldn't say what it was. Now, my disposition is that you are insane and probably need to be locked up for your own protection, let alone mine. Yet, and I can't believe you accomplished this, I am intrigued. Tell me, Mr. Pope from New York State, what else do you have to say?"

I was relieved with his response. It gave me an opening, and I decided that I would retell the stories Henry shared with me that first night, many months ago. I said to Dr. Franklin, "I am going to tell you two versions of history that stem from one event in time. For you to absorb what I say, I need you to release the governor in your reasoning to allow what I tell you to be properly absorbed. You will find this incredible, and it may be difficult to comprehend all aspects, but whatever questions you have, I will answer when I am through." Franklin gestured for me to proceed.

We spoke for hours about the parallel possibilities and it reminded me of how Henry and I went back and forth in the coffee shop. Only now I was in Henry's position, trying to get someone to accept the truth. At one point, I could see Dr. Franklin was getting tired, so I tried to stop for the day and told him that we could continue after we both got some sleep. I did not get the sense that he believed me but he did say something worth noting. As I got up to leave he said to me, "Ethan, you said after the Revolution we fight in a Civil War. Why?"

I told him, "It was to hold the union together after the election of the president that year, because the president campaigned on stopping the expansion of slavery to the new frontier and was known for being in favor of abolition for the whole country. So, after he was elected, some of the states immediately seceded. Antislavery became a national movement, and we went to war to preserve the Union. In the end, the president made it about freeing the slaves."

"Why didn't we abolish slavery after the Revolution?" he asked me.

"It wasn't the right time," I told him.

To which he sprung out of his chair, "Not the right time? Some of our colonies have tried for years to end the importation of slaves only to have England repeal the law each time for being contrary to an Act of Parliament. Now you're telling me when we have the opportunity to create a system of government on a blank sheet of paper, we need to *include* the practice of this institution because it's—not the right time?"

I tried to explain that we could review this later after we both got some rest. I tried to tell him to not to let it consume his thoughts and that we would reconvene from this point. Before he closed the door, he said, "Ethan, if I was for a moment to believe your whimsical anecdote, people would put me in an asylum for the rest of my days. So, I shall not repeat this to anyone. That I can assure you. And I press that you do the same, not because I believe you. It's just that you come across as a kind-hearted fellow with a propensity to fabricate the truth. I would hate to see anything happen to you because of your deception. I did enjoy the story you just shared and the depths of your creativity is boundless, but I leave you with this to understand. If I ever was for a new country, I would have tremendous reservations if the institution of slavery was not eradicated at its adoption."

Dr. Franklin then closed the door on me, and I made my way home.

I do not think I'm going to get much sleep today and I doubt he will either.

Chapter Twenty-Two

Sunset

Evening approached at the site, in Schwenksville, Pennsylvania, forty miles outside of Philadelphia. Towards the west, the horizon was illuminated with a fireball, bending, and stretching as its emanating light bounced off all objects in its path. The sky was a pallet of nature's purest colors. From yellow, to orange, to violet, to blue, the array of light spread across the atmosphere. The dark purple of night started to slowly rise in the east. Above the silo's line of site, some small cloud formations were scattered, but the night-sky was forecasted to be clear in time for the eclipse and *the event*.

Ethan sat alone on the rooftop of the observatory, taking small sips from a bottle of water. He reclined in a large padded chair which allowed him to rest his head to the side. His eyes were fixated on the beautiful illustration the world was showing at the very moment. Knowing that the hour was drawing near as the sun continued to lower beyond the worlds edge, Ethan's eyes began to tear. He then closed them both to allow his ears to fully concentrate on the sounds of nature. The gentle rustling of the trees and the harmonious chirping of the birds, began to calm his fears.

"Wow, that's nice," said Henry as he walked over and took the seat next to Ethan. After taking in the beauty of the sunset, Henry turned to see a tear running down Ethan's cheek. He reached out his hand and gave a couple of pats on Ethan's wrist. He then held it and said, "We're all set."

Ethan slowly opened his eyes and with his thumb and pointer he gave them both a swipe. When both fingers reached his nose he playfully snapped both to the floor as if he had just run his hands under a faucet and was air drying them. He looked at Henry and took a deep breath to gather himself. "All right," Ethan said, "nothing else to do but wait."

"Did you speak to Lauren?"

"I did. I wanted to hear her one more time."

"How is she holding up?"

"Well, she's doing very well, considering."

"How many rounds of chemo are left?"

"Just a couple. It's still amazing to me the week after returning from the cruise, she was told the cancer was becoming aggressive, and she needed to begin chemotherapy. If she didn't develop that cough, they wouldn't have done the CAT scan that revealed the bones were giving in. It's been difficult for her to process that everything is happening at once. I cannot tell you how annoyed I am that I will not be there for the remaining sessions, but we knew the timetable. And, that's the thing about cancer, it never cooperates. It always comes out of nowhere." Ethan continued to gaze out to the horizon. "Anyway, I spoke to her a few minutes ago, she's going to bed, and will not look for the lightning bolt. Then I just sat here and started to think."

"What were you thinking about?" asked Henry.

"Well, earlier I was thinking about how come the journal never updated after the July 3 entry from 1775," said Ethan. "It never divulged to me how I convince Franklin, or if I fail to convince him. It just stopped after

Franklin was annoyed with me for broaching the subject of Independence when he was talking to John Adams."

"I don't really know," said Henry. "The journal updates when you are educated on moments of history with which you will be involved. By those standards, the connection you make with Franklin is not rooted in anything tangible. It's intangible and therefore unique to the moment you experience. So, it's safe to conclude that everything we have discussed over the past eighteen months is predicated on this one showdown with Franklin on July 4. Your association with him will be solidified on what you say on the 4th."

"All right," said Ethan, "No pressure then."

"Well, I think we've covered enough for you not to feel any pressure. There's nothing more to cover. But when I saw you just now, your face didn't look like someone who was calculating. You were relaxed and in deep thought. What were you thinking about?"

"Oh," replied Ethan, "I was gazing at the sunset, and it made me reflect about a few things. I guess I got caught up in this being my *last* sunset here. Then I started thinking about what I am not taking with me. What I'm losing, or missing. What I will never have again in my life, and it made me wonder: *is this worth it?*"

"What will you miss?"

Ethan gazed out to the horizon in front of him, "Many things," he said.

"Like what?"

"Well Lauren, of course. She takes the first slot on the list. It may be a little melancholy to look forward to my life without her because she came into my life when it was needed. Things were slightly out of balance for me, and then she came along and, well, liked *me*."

"Love at first sight," Henry said. "How poetic."

Ethan laughed, "No, not really. We disliked each other in the beginning. She thought I was arrogant, and I thought she was a rude. Then one summer my roommate at the time was moving out, so I needed to move out as well. I decided it would be better to reset my world, so I moved back to my parents' house. The day I moved, I had five cousins help me. The first stop was in the Bronx, I arranged the moving truck to have all the essentials I would need placed in the rear. I would then take the rest to a storage unit I found in Yonkers at a low monthly fee. Now, if everything went to plan, Lauren and I would have never married.

"After we arrived at the Bronx and dropped everything off, we had lunch and relaxed a little. In the middle of the afternoon, we set out for what was going to be nothing more than a fifteen-minute drive to the storage unit. Only, not five blocks from my parents' house we were stuck in gridlock. We weren't even on the highway. We were on side streets. Every street, every road, I-95, and the Hutchinson River Parkway were jammed with cars. It was like a movie scene when a town is evacuating. For almost two hours, we were unable to get to the corner light. We were stuck! My cousins, who were in the car behind me, called to say they had to bail because their plan was to unload the truck and drive the three hours back home. When we reached the light, we could finally drive away from the traffic. They headed home by going in the opposite direction toward the George Washington Bridge and I went back to my parents' house.

"This was before GPS was reasonably affordable, so I needed help taking the back roads to Yonkers. Luckily, my sister knew how to get there so I followed her. Only she didn't know exactly where the storage place was, but a friend of hers who lived nearby could help us find it. When we got up to Yonkers, we stopped at a Dunkin Donuts to meet this friend. Lo and behold, it was the person who bugged me the most, Lauren. When she got out of her car something was different and I started staring from inside the truck. She was simply dressed jeans and a red shirt, but it was something else. She was now, well, perfect and beautiful. She was all those things in an instant to me. She guided us in her car to the storage facility, which was practically five blocks away, then she and my sister planned to leave. Being the little schemer I could be at times I asked, very politely, if she could help me push one of the carts to my storage unit to the fifth floor. I would move all the boxes and so on, so she didn't have to hurt herself. Keeping her company was all I wanted at that moment. She agreed, and she helped, and after that encounter it led to a more discreet passing the next time, more playful banter, and so on."

Ethan looked over at Henry and grinned like a schoolboy. Henry shared the moment with a grin of his own. "What caused the traffic?" Henry asked.

"A promoter put out a misleading ad in the paper," said Ethan. "The ad let people believe Jennifer Lopez was returning to the Bronx and was going to perform for free at Orchard Beach in Pelham Bay Park."

"Are you serious?"

Ethan's head popped up. "Wait?" he said as he turned to Henry.

Henry put both hands up. "No, no. Ethan," he said with a laugh. "We had nothing to do with that one."

Ethan smiled and looked back out to the horizon. "That's a true story," he said. "What's incredible is that I never considered all the small intricate events that had to precede it for the moment to occur. I guess these past eighteen months have rewired my take on how to observe moments in history."

"How so?" asked Henry.

"Well, an easy one to point out," said Ethan. "If the promoter did not put out that ad, then the roads would not have been packed with people. I never would have gone back to my parents' house, my sister never would have joined me, and thus she never would have called Lauren for help with directions. The other side to that is, if Lauren wasn't so terrible with directions, she would have just told my sister where to go instead of meeting us and leading the way. All of those little things added up to that moment in which I did a one-eighty with my attraction to her, and although she may deny it, she saw something too in all of *this*!" Ethan mockingly waved his hand in front of him, as a model does when they present a prize on a game show.

Henry laughed, "Okay, okay, slow down," he said. "So, have you thought about anything else that you might miss?"

The sunset was reaching its final stages, the bottom of the sun now touched the worlds edge and everything in the sky appeared to be in a blaze. The simplistic wonder and beauty amazed Ethan. "I shall miss little things, like movies," Ethan said. "I enjoy getting lost in a good movie."

"What's your favorite movie?"

"You know I don't know," said Ethan. "I mean I've watched *Amadeus, Star Wars, Back to the Future, The Wrath of Kahn, Goodfellas,* and *The Godfather* too many times to count. Does that make any of them my favorite?" Ethan took another sip from his water bottle, "But, *Amadeus* and *Fantasia* introduced me to another aspect of the industry I will miss. That's my appreciation for theatrical scores."

"Really? I never knew that."

"Well, it's not that popular to be a fan of scores. And I know, both were soundtracks of classical music but still, many movie scores are modern day classics. Everyone will recognize a mainstream theme like the *JAWS* theme, the *Superman March*, or the theme to *Star Wars*. I mean orchestral music is embedded in the scenes and sometimes is heard at the end of the film."

"When the credits hit, I hit the exit," said Henry.

"Most people do. What I find fascinating about some pieces is how it perfectly captures the emotion of the scene you are watching. Then when you hear the piece on its own, it can remind you of that scene and pull out that same emotion."

"Like what?" asked Henry. "Give me an example of your favorite piece from a movie score."

"All right, in the movie *Field of Dreams*, there is a track called 'The Place Where Dreams Come True' and in that arrangement, it covers two important scenes from the movie. One is where the James Earl Jones character walks into the cornfield and disappears or passes over. At least that's how I interpreted the scene. The second is where Costner stops the young version of his father and asks him if he wants to have a catch. The melody of the music holds for an extra second and that's when Costner receives the ball the first time from his father, culminating the reality of the moment being shared or relived between father and son. It's a well-done scene, and the music, the strings that are playing, pull at your heart strings. I must take that melody with me."

"Hmm, I'll have to listen to that," Henry said. "Are there other movie tracks I should revisit?"

"Oh, sure, 'Time' from the *Inception* score, 'The Love Theme' from *Superman*, and 'Princess Leia's Theme', 'Anakin's Betrayal', 'The Asteroid Field', and 'Yoda's Theme' from *Star Wars*."

"So, everything *Star Wars*?" Henry light-heartedly asked.

"Noooo," Ethan sarcastically replied. "You know what, I take it back. Yes, listen to anything Hans Zimmer and John Williams to make it easier. *Inception, Dark Knight, Star Wars, Indiana Jones, Lincoln*, to name a few. Add *Rudy* and *Apollo 13* too. But, you should know, once you go down the path of the movie score, *forever will it dominate your destiny*."

"Thanks, Yoda," said Henry. "You do know the classics were written during the time you are about go to? Mozart composed *Don Giovanni* in 1787."

"Yes, but I'll have to go across the ocean to the various performance centers to hear them," said Ethan. "I'm not entirely sure which composers, besides Mozart, were alive during that period or which part of Europe I would have to go to. We didn't have a chance to cover that. Also, I doubt they did tours of America during a bloody Revolution. 'And now, Ladies and

Gentlemen, for your listening pleasure, here is Mozart and the Sloatsburg orchestra performing Don Giovanni. Please watch for canon fire!'"

Henry burst out in laughter and said, "I'll shall miss you, Ethan. I truly will, but Mozart died in 1791 in Vienna. So now you have your place and composer to witness while you are living in the eighteenth century." Henry knew it was good to keep Ethan's mind off the upcoming event and keep him calm. But, after about a minute of silence passed, he asked, "So, what else is on your list?"

"You know, I thought about New York City," said Ethan. "Which made me think of the Yankees and the Knicks games I will not witness. Every October, ever since elementary school, when the NBA season started, I would hope with all my might that *this year* was going to be when the Knicks made their championship run. Of course, it never happened but, I never stopped supporting the dream.

"I'll miss watching big sporting events, like the NBA Finals or the World Series, or the PGA majors, like the Masters and the U.S. Open. The greater the event, the more people tend to gravitate to it. They take time to witness it, absorb it. Sports bring people together in ways nothing else can. Small towns close shops, so everyone can enjoy and support the local team. Cities rival each other when their teams compete. Countries unite when global sporting events are taking place. The moment is witnessed, rejoiced, and shared. Or, the event is painstakingly observed and is grieved for generations. And, no matter how dim the chances are, we all watch for the improbable or the impossible to occur. To bear witness to greatness, so that we can say, 'I was there' or 'I saw it.' Fans will hold their breath, pray, or turn their hats inside out for the chance of an improbable comeback. When the game ends, and there is a champion being celebrated, strangers will embrace each other in jubilation."

Ethan then looked towards Henry with a smile, "Much like the battlefield of the Revolution. Two teams. One underdog. One outcome." Ethan looked out and saw the sun was now gone beyond the worlds edge, and the horizon had a pinkish hue as the navy-blue darkness moved to submerge it. The cloud system that was present earlier, moved out of the region, revealing a clear night sky. Ethan looked up and saw the Moon, awaiting to participate in his journey. His heart trembled at the sight of it. Ethan turned back to Henry and said, "All of those things, I will miss greatly but don't get me wrong, I'm also excited. I mean this sky, will be the same sky above me when I'm there. The river flowing along the edge, will be the same river I will travel down with Philip and Mary. I am going to see great people and do great thing, but I feel sad that my time here is almost at an end."

Henry saw fear in Ethan's face, and how he was trying to hold it back. He reached out and touched the backside of Ethan's hand. Smiling, he said, "I thought you were going to have Disney World on your list."

"Well, sure, I'll miss going to Disney," said Ethan. "That place holds a lot of fond memories for me, and I've had a couple of life experiences there as well. My parents brought me there when I was just a tiny infant and I proposed to Lauren at the restaurant in the castle. They put her ring in a glass slipper with our names on it. It was an amazing experience for us both, but it only happened because of the incident that occurred at the golf course the day before. She came with me, just to ride around in the cart, and I ended up being paired with two people who said they worked at Disney. At one point, I accelerated the golf cart right when she was about to drink a red PowerAde, it spilled out, and ruined her favorite white tank top.

"Had that not happened, I would not have known the person I was paired with was a manager at one of the restaurants in the *Magic Kingdom*. When I told him, Lauren would forget about the mishap the next day after she received her ring, he informed me about the proposal service at the restaurant. So, thanks to him, the manager called me and we arranged it all, with only several hours to work with. After the main course ended, they brought out a white plate with a white dome. The dome was then removed to reveal the ring in a glass slipper with rose peddles sprinkled around. The slipper was engraved with our names and the date of our engagement.

It was perfect. The worker was so excited that she was unable to take one clear photo of the moment, they were all blurry. But still, I'll carry that moment with me forever." Ethan then dropped his head in anguish. He closed his eyes and let out a sigh.

"What's wrong?" Henry said.

"Hmm?" said Ethan, as he continued to keep his eyes closed. "Oh, nothing. I was just remembering something Lauren said last night before I left."

"What was that?" asked Henry.

Ethan got up from his seat and walked towards the railing. "Lauren tried to convince me to stay by telling me if I skipped *this* eclipse, we could go to Disney and stay in the bungalows at one of their resorts." Ethan then turned back to Henry. "But I mean I can list a dozen things I will reminisce about when I am back there. But it will not matter, because above all, I'll miss her, my family and all the moments I'm not going to be a part of. All the holidays, and birthdays, and reunions." Ethan began to fight back his emotions. He wiped his eyes, "I need to be careful, thinking too much about these things might make me reconsider Lauren's offer."

"Well, I've never been there," said Henry. "Maybe I should consider going after tonight."

"Where?" asked Ethan. "Oh, Disney?"

"Yes," said Henry.

"Well, I meant to ask you, what are you going to do after this is all over? What will tomorrow hold for you?"

"Me? I'm going on a very long vacation, maybe to Bora Bora since you mentioned bungalows earlier. Then when I get back, I shall have a light work schedule as a consultant, for I am semi-retiring. Since I don't have to watch you anymore, my days will be a whole lot easier."

"But Kronos is going to continue to monitor?"

"Yes," said Henry, "that's the role we are going to subject ourselves to. It will drop the budget and make a few people happy."

"Well, I hope after all of this, it was worth it."

Henry was taken aback. "You said that twice now. Is it worth it? Of course, it is. Everything that Franklin and Kronos, and all who assisted us along the way, to culminate at this moment, was worth it. And, everything you are about to do, and will do, is worth it.

"You have an opportunity to go back in time and change an event that will have a profound impact on the world. People, all the time, contemplate about altering a moment in their past. Before you learned about all of this, didn't you think about changing something in your past? How many times have you heard someone say, they wish they could tell their younger self not to do this or that? Or the ever so common, 'I would give myself the winning lottery numbers.' There's no creativity there! Or, 'I would become a computer programmer and develop Apple and Microsoft.' Both entities? At the same time, really? How about a regret from a relationship? I have heard too many people say, 'if only I didn't get into that argument' or 'if only I didn't purchase that ring.'

"Clever people who want money think about moments in time when they should have taken a risk, started a company, or invested in one, like Apple for instance. However, they never contemplate for a second what occurs after point B is crossed. Point A is the investment. Point B is what comes next. So then, what would come next? We know it would not be as easy as a person, living in a one bedroom apartment, sitting in their living room, thinking about, 'if I could go back in time, I would tell myself to buy stock in Apple Computers and hold it until it hits $500 dollars.' Then suddenly, with a snap of the fingers, they have billions of dollars in their account, while still residing in the same apartment. That's not how the laws of time operate.

"We know *if* that person had the ability to meet their younger self, and *if* they were able to make that investment in the 1980s, or even after the tech bubble burst, that person who had the original thought in their living room would cease to exist. Their life, from the time of the investment, would go down a completely different path. The question is, on this new path, what will happen to all of us? Now, it's highly improbable that all lives would drastically change, but it is certain that when that person became a billionaire, they would be more influential in the world, which will alter the lives of various people within that spectrum. Also, that billionaire would experience the life everyone with money goes down.

"Franklin said, 'having been poor is no shame, being ashamed of it is.' The people who wish for more money tend to have money issues to begin with. We know it can purchase the tangible and the high-priced bits of joy and superficial happiness others may never be able to indulge in. But is that true happiness? Franklin also said, 'Money never made a man happy yet, nor will it. There is nothing in its nature to produce happiness. The more a man has, the more he wants. Instead of its filling a vacuum, it makes one. If it satisfies one want, it doubles and trebles that want another way.'

"People who come into money also come into a whole heap of problems they never imagined. The new money brings with it new friends with hands and lots of them. And those hands are never satisfied. 'Who is rich? He that rejoices in his portion,' said Franklin. You give this person ten thousand, you give that person fifteen, and the other person will ask, 'how come I can't get fifteen?' People who loved you when you were just 'you' might abandon you or at least step back. Those new people who came when the money arrived will only stay if the money is available. Should anything happen, they'll be gone before the party is officially over. In the end, that person who sat in their living room, without that fortune, were they better off than living a life with it? Once again, just like Franklin noted, 'Happiness consists more in small conveniences of pleasures that occur every day, than the great pieces of good fortune that happen but seldom to a man in the course of his life.'"

"Wait," said Ethan. "Are you trying to remind me, again, not to setup investments for myself?"

Henry nodded with a smile. "I'm having a little fun with you in these last few hours."

"I see," said Ethan. "Before you said something about regretting relationships. Why did you say that?"

"I did?" said Henry. "I guess over the past few decades, seeing and hearing people go through the trials and tribulations of relationships, I've become jaded in my counseling. However, I'm not one to really speak on what is required to form strong bonds. When someone reflects on love lost, there's a multitude of reasons why it ended. Sometimes they reflect that if they stopped themselves from getting into that last argument, then the relationship would still exist. The truth is, if the relationship was so fragile that one argument broke the bond, then in all probability the relationship would have ended on the next dispute. 'If you would be loved, love and be lovable' was Franklin's saying. Sometimes, relationships ending, can be the right choice.

"A divorced woman may never consider how different her life would have been had she not found love, and now lives in Westchester with her new husband and their two children. Would she have found the same happiness if she stayed? Would she have been able to overcome and cope with the presumed death of her son. Would she have been able to fill the void in the silence of her house as you devoted your life to your work, and never gave her the companionship she desperately needed in her time of solitude and depression? All the while you told yourself, it was for the best.

"You have a wonderful opportunity, Ethan. Many before you made sacrifices for this moment to arrive. After you go, what happens here, how people choose to live their lives will be an amazing gift. They will go about never knowing who gave them that gift. But those who came before you, to get us to this night, they understood what was at stake. I think every person who contributed to The Franklin Project, knew the key principle is that—living in this country is a life worth living. Good or bad, perfect or not, it is worth everything to ensure it remains."

"Henry?" Ethan asked inquisitively, "Are you okay?"

Henry looked up to Ethan who was staring back, perplexed. "Don't worry about it, Ethan. It was for the best. My ex-wife never knew about this, and she wasn't one to give her being to it. I knew it when we met, but I also knew why we met. The excitement of our new relationship quickly faded for both of us. I knew I could never bring her in, so I had to keep everything from her, and so did Philip once he learned about his destiny. After our son left, it seemed only fair to let her go on her own." Henry took in a deep breath, he looked around the sky above as the stars began to appear. "That was a long time ago anyway," he said. "I'm focused on today. And tomorrow, I'm going to focus on me."

"Good," said Ethan.

"Ethan, if there is one last thing I can tell you, it is to carry tremendous pride in what you are about to do with your life."

"I will Henry, thank you.".

Henry looked up again, and turned his head toward the Moon. "Clear night," he said. Henry then noticed the half-finished bottle of water on the table. "You need to drink all of that liquid. There's another one downstairs waiting for you."

"I can't," Ethan said. "It tastes awful."

"You must," said Henry. "It's a concentrated potassium-based liquid. The electroshock is going to do a number on your muscles."

"Will this improve my recovery time? I don't want it to take three-plus weeks, like it was recorded in the journal."

Henry laughed, "No," he said. "This is much stronger, it's what Philip was given before he left. The only thing to keep in mind is that your bladder will fill up much faster, so when you arrive and are paralyzed, do not be annoyed at me when you relieve yourself while you wait for Philip and Mary to rescue you. Okay?"

"Okay," Ethan said as he reached down to pick up the bottle. He winced and drank the rest of the contents. "Oh God, that's nasty!"

"Good," Henry said. He then rested his hand on Ethan's shoulder. "Are you ready to live history?"

"Really?" Ethan said with a grin.

Henry laughed and said, "Sorry. It sounded better in my head. Okay, let's head down."

Chapter Twenty-Three

The Day After

The day turned into tomorrow, and for those select few on the inside, the day was unlike any other before it. The apprehension of ensuring that there was a tomorrow vanished, and what took its place was affirmation. After two hundred and forty years, tomorrow, with its great sense of ambiguity, returned. While the noon sun shined bright in a clear blue sky, Henry made his way through the neighborhood of Bronxville, to make one final delivery before he left for his six-week vacation. Having been removed from the role of postman for some time, Henry was pleased to perform this last assignment.

After the event concluded, and was by all accounts, successful, a deep sense of pride came over him. He was proud of being the one who completed a mission that was started nearly two and a half centuries ago. He reflected on all the men and women who came before him. Who were just as dedicated to accomplishing the objective, which Henry viewed as tethered to the Declaration of Independence. Without the Declaration, much would not exist. Without sending Ethan, it would not exist.

It was not all jubilation for Henry, as he was carried a sense of loss. This was not an unfamiliar feeling, by all accounts it was the third time he witnessed someone leave for this mission. The first person to go was Mary. Although Henry was younger than her, he was infatuated with his mentor, and her leaving left an emptiness, similar to what one feels after their first break-up. The departure of his son was more intimate and caused tremendous pain, but Ethan's presence helped Henry cope with that loss. Now with Ethan gone, he was alone, and for the first time, had no one to fill the void of his solitude.

Henry stopped a few houses down from his destination. He was justly intimidated to park in front or approach the door. It had been a while since he had last seen her, and knew he was the last person she would want to see, today or any other day. Henry calmed his nerves by telling himself that the visit was much-needed closure, so both could start the next chapter in their lives and move on.

Walking in the cool spring air, Henry cautiously approached the foot path that led to the front door. Glancing into every window he checked to see if anyone inside might have spotted him. Half way along the path, he heard a noise coming from within the house. With each step he took, the faint sound was becoming more audible. Henry paused and felt a weight drop to the pit of his stomach. The sound resonated down his spine. For a moment, he was frozen still as he listened to the muffled sound of sobbing. Henry was now an arm's length away from the door. He balled his fist, took a deep breath, and knocked.

The sobbing suddenly stopped, and the sounds of nature filled the silence. The chirping was louder, the wind grew stronger, and the trees rustled with their new small spring leaves. He closed his eyes and took one more deep breath, as he heard footsteps approaching from the other side. The lock was unhinged and the weather seal gave a slight pop as the door was pulled away. Henry opened his eyes and as the door opened, he swallowed and said, "Hello, Mrs. Pope."

Lauren wearing a salmon-colored dress, with a matching head wrap to cover her head, remained still in the entry way. Her skin was slightly pale but the makeup she applied balanced her complexion. She was radiant, even with the painful side effects of chemotherapy. The cool air on her bare skin made small goosebumps appear along her forearms. The wind would pick up at times which made Henry adjust his stance but nothing, not the wind or the cold air, made Lauren move as she glared down at the person, she felt, took away her husband.

Henry could see she was not going to respond to his greeting, so he decided not to let another second pass without speaking. "I know you have zero desire to see me today or any day, but I figured this was best. Not enough time has passed for either of us to have worked through the grief. Maybe speaking to each other now could be therapeutic and help you avoid feeling bitterness as you undoubtedly will as the days and years progress." Henry paused for a moment to see whether Lauren was ready to respond. The only movement she made was involuntary, with her eyelids and lungs, so he continued. "I have every confidence that you understand the magnitude of our lives in the outcome of Ethan's sacrifice. His life served a purpose greater than anyone living could ever imagine. He is the reason we are here today. He is the reason there is a today, and because I know this, I'm fine with you aiming your anger toward me."

"I am not angry at you," Lauren said. "I'm aware of what could have happened should Ethan have stayed. I'm aware of his actions, his patriotism, and his devotion to this *cause*." I'm also aware that he did not have to go *yesterday*."

Upon hearing this, Henry's back stiffened. Lauren could pick from any number of subjects to establish an argument, but he did not think she would start with this one. He was now visualizing his response, but he needed to be careful not to insult her intelligence. "I won't patronize you, Lauren. There were other days, future eclipses, where we could have sent him back," Henry said.

"Then, why didn't you?" she replied. "Why did you take him from me now, when I needed him the most?" Lauren was visually exhausted, she leaned right shoulder against the side of the door to help her stand. Lauren wiped the tears from underneath her eyes as she continued, "I researched it myself and found three full eclipses within the next fifteen years."

Henry responded, "You need to consider how Ethan would have lived once he arrived in the eighteenth century. As his age increased, it would have posed many risks. One risk was how the founders would have treated him. Being younger than all of them, and from what we learned from their writings, they all treated and protected Ethan like a son. Also, we needed him to live a long life so he could accomplish all his tasks. Finally, we wanted assurances that he would survive the trip itself. Ethan gave us a description of the effects it took on him when he arrived."

"I know, I read what he wrote about his recovery," said Lauren.

"Well," said Henry, "you'll be pleased to know that we gave him a stronger dose last night which might have reduced his recovery time to under two weeks. We'll need to check the journal again."

Standing above Henry gave Lauren a sense of authority and seeing how he remained reserved made her feel that she was in control of the conversation. "You know, when I awoke this morning, the rest of the pages were filled in," Lauren said. "A part of me always hoped it was Ethan writing the stories at night. Making everything up and just having a little fun at my expense. When he first told me, I thought he was saying everything because he wanted to leave me but didn't have the nerve to say it." As her emotions rose, her voice started to crack, "So he fabricated this whole scenario, just so he could run off to God knows where.

"Then when he had me read the journal, and Franklin's letter, it scared me that there was a chance he was telling the truth. When I saw the faint lightning bolt last night and saw the rest of the pages filled in this morning, you can say it put those dreams to rest. I realized I was never going to see him again in my lifetime." Lauren rested her fingers on her forehead as the tension was building. "Oh God," she said as tears began to fall from her face again, "I'm never going to see him again."

Henry began to step toward Lauren. When he was beside her, he extended his arms out to embrace her. She rested her head in his chest, as she continued to grieve. While holding her, Henry thought of something that might help matters. "When my son Philip was sent, I was mentally and emotionally prepared for the sense of loss his departure would bring, but last night, I had a feeling of loss that kept me awake all night. Ethan was my project, from the day he was born. So, Lauren, I can understand what you are going through. That's why I came by," he said. When the wind picked up, Henry asked, "May I come in?"

Lauren, gathering herself and feeling less resentful said, "Sure, come in."

"Thank you," Henry then paused and turned back to the street. "You know, let me get a package I have for you in my car." Henry took one step on to the road bed, but turned to Lauren and shouted, "Go inside, I'll be right back."

Awaiting Henry's return, Lauren quickly cleaned up the living room. She arranged the throw pillows, folded the blanket on the sofa, and organized all papers scattered on the coffee table.

When Henry returned, he was towing a large wooden crate on a handcart. He carefully lifted the handcart into the home, through the entryway, to place it in the living room where Lauren was standing. "Delivery, ma'am," Henry jokingly said.

"What is this?" Lauren asked.

"This is . . .," Henry started to say, as he tilted the box off the cart to put the long side on the floor. He then lifted his arm, reached his hand out toward the box to present Lauren with her delivery, and said, "for you!" Henry then rolled the handcart back to the entryway and closed the front door. As he wiped both hands, Henry continued, "This is something for you to go through when you're alone."

Lauren looked over the size of the box and immediately recognized that it was the same type of box Ethan brought home when he won the contest. She looked up at Henry and asked, "Do you know what's in it?"

Henry paused and observed Lauren's face. He could see she looked worried, as if what he just brought in was going to have a negative effect on her life. "I assure you that the items within this box will bring you no harm," he said.

"Do you *know* what's in it?" Lauren repeated.

Henry responded, "Yes, I do."

"If it's all the same, I would prefer not to have this in my possession. Can you please take it from my house?"

"May I ask why?"

"My husband is gone, apparently because he was sent back in time to speak to Benjamin Franklin. Why was that his job? Why someone else couldn't go back and say, 'Hey, if you vote against the Declaration this is what will happen, so don't do it', is beyond me." Speaking in a restrained matter, Lauren's voice began to rise as she continued, "But, because a scientist, from another time, had a chat with Franklin. Which, mind you, I think that whole thing was fabricated just to patronize him. That event then caused my husband to win a post-office contest, receive a journal, and then eighteen months' later leave, forever!"

Lowering her voice, she concluded, "That is why I don't want this box from you, Henry. The last crate that was brought into our home ended someone's life, as far as I'm concerned. I would prefer not to be involved in anything else regarding this matter. I don't want anyone to know I have something in connection to this operation, if that's what you call it. I don't want anyone from the government or the United States Postal Service's *secret* programs to bother me ever again. Just bring me my mail and let me live in peace."

Henry, not wanting to battle Lauren's emotions, gave her a minute to grieve. When her breathing returned to a calm rhythm, he said, "I loved your husband like a son. I watched him grow up. I knew with him, as I knew with my own son, the tremendous sacrifice they both were going to make when the time came." Henry moving his way to the love seat said to Lauren, "Let's sit."

Lauren walked adjacent to the coffee table to sit on the sofa. Before she sat she asked, "Would you like something to drink?"

"No, thank you," replied Henry. "First, like I said, you are in no harm. Few know of its contents, and we no longer have a need to detain them, so there it is." Henry adjusted his position and leaned forward a little. "Second, I would suggest that you not reflect on your husband's life having ended yesterday just because he is not present with you now. I promise you that he lived a marvelous life, one to be envious of. His contribution has flowed through generations and will be present every day from now until the end of time. So, he is very much alive." Henry leaned back again and said with a smirk, "At least, that is how I choose to look at it. There is one other thing. You said the 'original time' story was not possible."

"No, I said it was fabricated. I believe you made that whole story up," Lauren stated.

Henry laughed, "Yes, I remember. Look, I'm not aware of how much Ethan told you during this whole process, but about this 'loop' Ethan was caught in, the origin of that event did occur. That is an absolute. We just don't know how many times we have gone through this act since that original event, with the scientist, took place. I told Ethan that when he goes back in time, we, you, and I, are going to continue this timeline. Whereas he is going back two hundred plus years, and the timeline will start again from that moment. To make it easier to understand, Ethan goes back in time and speaks to Franklin. A Revolution occurs, America is created, then comes the Civil War, World War I, and World War II. Then Ethan is born, Ethan grows up, and Ethan is sent back in time, and that timeline starts all over again." Henry put both palms up and said, "How many times has this happened? We have no idea."

"So then how do you know how this started?" Lauren asked.

"Because Ethan tells us," said Henry. "Ethan relays the story to Franklin every time his life starts in 1775. That story is carried through two centuries, and when Ethan is born and lives his life during our time, it's told again. But when our Ethan, your Ethan, heard the story eighteen months ago, he was hearing it for the first time. Then he goes back in time and the process starts over. That is why it's called a *causality loop*. If it was a causality straight, I suspect Ethan would still be here with us."

"Why aren't multiple Ethan's running around in the past? Why is there only one if you keep sending him back repeatedly?" asked Lauren.

"That I can't fully explain," said Henry. "Einstein's theory suggested that each person in the timeline is unique, and each unique world-line cannot overlap. It's a law of time travel, I guess." Henry then smiled as he said, "It's too bad we can't share that knowledge with the world. But that explains why everything was wiped clean on the day of his birth, and then the day after he was sent back, everything returned . . . sort of."

Lauren reached for a tissue from the box on the coffee table and wiped her tears. "I'm sorry. I know you came here to try and comfort me and to stop me from feeling sorry for myself or feeling anger toward Ethan for being so selfish and leaving me to fight and walk through this life without him. Without his warmth! Without his care! Without his love! How am I supposed to move on with my life in twenty-four hours?"

Lauren's crying was heavier now, and she was not able to control her emotions any longer. She was sobbing even more strongly than when Henry first approached the house. He knew that the feelings Lauren was experiencing were as powerful as if Ethan had just passed away. Henry knew this feeling and knew no words were going to help. Henry rose from his seat and told Lauren, "Stay seated. I'll get you a glass of water."

Lauren relaxed in the living room while she heard Henry opening and closing her kitchen cabinets. Henry then shouted, "Where are the cups?" After the sound of another cabinet door opening she heard him say, "Ah, here they are."

Henry yelled out, "Ice?"

"No, thank you."

The calming sound of water rushing from the faucet into the glass already was soothing to Lauren. After a few moments of solitude passed, Henry returned.

Lauren reached out to grab the glass from Henry. "Thank you," she said with a small smile.

He knelt beside her, looked into her red, teary eyes, and said, "Lauren, today you have yet to grasp the magnitude of Ethan's love for you. When I told Ethan the ramifications on our world should he not go through with this plan, his only concern was your safety and longevity. I told him that the Lauren he knows would not exist, and that I could not guarantee that a 'Lauren' existed in the original timeline. The only thing that remained constant in both timelines was that we could guarantee the existence of an Ethan. You said that Ethan was selfish. You must believe me when I say Ethan did not care about time travel. Seeing Benjamin Franklin, John Adams, and the other figures of our history did not influence his decision. The assurance that *you*, the one he loved, would live on was the primary factor in his decision."

Lauren looked bewildered. It was as if she had been enlightened instantaneously, but her heart was contradicting what Henry had just said.

"Do you understand now? He would rather sacrifice his life, so you can live yours." Henry emphasized.

"I know he loved me," Lauren said. "I know I should feel a tremendous sense of pride. My husband has done something extraordinary. He is having or has had one of the most amazing experiences—one that a lot of people only dream of. I wish I could have experienced this with him. I just miss him so much right now." Lauren reached out for Henry's hand, tapped it, and said, "Thank you for coming by. I'll be okay. I just need some time to grieve right now. I'm entitled to."

Both stood, and as they came face to face, Henry said, "Well, that's why he wrote the journals. So you could share his experiences and I suggest you do. I would definitely read the next entry."

"What's the next entry?" Lauren asked, as she made her way to the front door to let Henry out.

"If I'm right," Henry said, "because this journal stopped updating at July 3, 1775, it should tell you how Ethan was able to convince Dr. Franklin to be for American Independence."

"Wait, journals?" Lauren asked. "I thought this journal was written by Ethan for himself."

As he stepped though the entryway, Henry, now standing outside, looked towards Lauren, and replied, "No, we used the first journal to connect Ethan to the event. To nudge him toward his true destiny and to inform him of his purpose. From the day he came in for his quote, unquote *awards*, we were able to establish the connection between Ethan and the journal."

"What do you mean?"

"The journal pages updated in connection to what Ethan was exposed to during the past year and a half," said Henry, "which is why it has always been planned, between Franklin and Ethan at the time, that he should receive only the first journal. If he possessed the others when we reviewed all the moments of our history from Franklin to yesterday's event, it may have compromised his interpretation of what was needed from him." Henry took a small step toward Lauren and leaned in to whisper, "Ethan, in the beginning, thought his only purpose was to connect with Franklin. But you see, because we spent months training Ethan on how to see our American history unfold, with the assistance of Mary, Philip, and having Andrew at his side, Ethan will engage appropriately, and his actions will appear more genuine, less artificial. Which will help him operate when working with Franklin, Washington, Adams, and so on."

"Why didn't you just tell him?" asked Lauren.

"Those were the original instructions from Franklin and then echoed by nineteenth-century Ethan," Henry said with a grin. "Who am I to disobey orders from those two?" He then extended his hand, and as they shook, he said, "I want to leave you with some advice Lauren, pace yourself. This is not a suggestion for your grief, that is something for your friends and family to help you through. It's for everything you will find in this box. If you take in each day, as Ethan did, I think you'll get the shared experience you hoped for."

"All right."

"Wait," Henry said as he held up one finger. "Don't do that exactly. I just realized it would take you over thirty years to complete! Regardless, I recommend you pace yourself, and I suggest you read the next entry in Ethan's first journal before you open the crate."

"Why?"

"It will give context to, well, everything."

"I will. Thank you, Henry. Thank you for coming by today to check on me, and for bringing over this crate."

Henry smiled with relief, as he could see his decision to engage Lauren today was, by all accounts, the correct one. He playfully lifted his right hand to the side of his forehead, and with a salute said, "It's what a postman does, ma'am."

"What are you going to do now?" Lauren asked.

Henry turned away from Lauren and viewed the road ahead. "You know, for the first time, I have no notion as to what the next move should be." He then looked back at Lauren, and said, "The pieces have been rest, and I am seeing the world with a new perspective. It is an odd feeling when that sense of purpose you carried all your life is gone, and you now find yourself gazing upon a new sunrise, not knowing what awaits. But, as it was said, I will not be anxious for tomorrow. I will let today's own troubles be sufficient for today." Henry walked halfway down the foot path before turning around one last time. He gave Lauren a big smile and said, "Starting tomorrow, hopefully those troubles will be what room service I want rowed out to my hut in Bora Bora."

Lauren let out a deep, healing laugh, "Good-bye, Henry," she said.

"Good-bye, Mrs. Pope."

Chapter Twenty-Four

July 4, 1775: Checkmate

Today was such an emotional experience that should I not record it with the respect and attention it deserves, I will have done a grave disservice to its rightful place in unspoken history.

When the morning arrived, I met Dr. Franklin at his residence, and asked for his company in the afternoon after today's session with Congress completed. He agreed, and I spent the day revising my arguments. On the way to the tavern, I contemplated the reasons behind Dr. Franklin's constant recoil from being for Independence. It was obvious from the start that this was not a man who was going to follow my instructions based solely on my origin. Of course, looking back, had I just engaged him politically without revealing my birthdate, and things of that nature, I may have been able to succeed, but that would have required more time.

It was clear to me that slavery, although a resurfacing argument, was not his principle deterrent to accepting the idea of separation. There was something else, but he wasn't telling me. Over the past few weeks, while I could see his counterpoints weakening, he would always pull back the moment I felt certain he was going to concede. A clear indicator Dr. Franklin was leaning towards ceasing to seek reconciliation with the King, was when he told me last week he was not keeping the one-thousand-pound salary from the Postmaster General assignment, but instead was going to donate it all to help wounded soldiers. Given his state of nonconformity, he may have thought of his selfless act as a short-term contribution while still trying to stem the tide of war.

Before his arrival to the tavern I was trying to imagine how stressful it must be, to be "Benjamin Franklin." Given his popularity in the world, the admiration many people in America carry for him, the respect every delegate holds for him, the powerful influence he possesses, and how beloved he is in this state, he clearly is sobered knowing the gravity of his decision and how, at the stage, it's the acting arbiter for every person living in North America. So, trying to be the individual that orchestrates the proper run of words that resonates with his global-formed consciousness, to lure him to act upon what is requested of him, was never going to be an easy task.

Since my arrival, I have always remained cognizant of my place within his social circles and been clear-sighted that I was never the only person trying to persuade the good Doctor these past two months. Thanks to the lectures from Henry, and now Mary, I anticipated his confidant Joseph Galloway was going to urge him to secure a compromise with their plan, as Joseph himself attempted during the first Congress. I was also aware that Joseph was to hold a meeting with Dr. Franklin at his estate which was to be more than just a discussion about reconciliation. Henry and Mary instructed me to never ask what transpired there, just to be aware of the change in his demeanor.

They were both right, for ever since his return from Galloway's estate in Trevose, New Jersey, a few weeks prior, Dr. Franklin appeared to be less irritated when we spoke about various topics surrounding separation. It did dawn on me earlier, while I waited in the tavern, and confirmed now by reviewing my past entries, that after his dinner at Trevose he started to use the word "Americans" every time he referred to the people. Which was a good sign, but today, I needed him to start using another word—America.

When Franklin arrived, he was intrigued to find me sitting in the booth waiting for him. I was not the object of his interest, it was the chessboard I set up. He took his seat and with a cautious grin asked me, "What is this?" I told him let us not debate for now. Let us pretend to enjoy each other's company, without apprehension, and play. He was white, and I was black. My early movements pushed four pawns two spaces and moved both knights in front, to give me a four-row cushion. To engage, I sacrificed my bishops and two pawns, to the Doctor sacrifice of two pawns and one knight.

As we played, I made a series of physical motions and light-hearted comments. At one point, the doctor was contemplating his next move. In boredom, I began tapping my fingers on the table to which Dr. Franklin asked, "Would you please cease doing that? It is vibrating the table." I threw up my hands in mercy and yelled for a couple of drinks. When the barmaid brought them over, I told her to hand me both pints because the good doctor was deep in thought and the impact of setting the glass on the table could cause great disturbance. For my lack of courtesy toward his concentration, I received a glaring looking from Dr. Franklin.

I set myself up for the attack. Nine pieces remained on the board. His king protected by the queen and a rook on the right side, with a single pawn on the opposite side. I had my king, two rooks and the queen, with my own pawn blocking his. I had the win in a few moves, but I was not playing for the win. While Dr. Franklin considered what to do, I started humming *Let's Go Fly a Kite* from Mary Poppins. When I reached the refrain, I started to softly sing the words, "Let's go fly a kite, up to the highest," then I stopped, and when I said "kite", his head sprang up.

When he asked me what I was singing, I could see he was disarmed. I dismissed his question and responded by asking, "This game is perfect, don't you think?"

Dr. Franklin said, "This is not a game of amusement. This game teaches you many things. It teaches you about human life."

"How so?" I asked him.

Dr. Franklin explained, "The game teaches a person how to consider the consequences of one's actions. With each move, there is a risk of loss and the hope of favorable change for redemption and victory."

I replied, "What about sacrifice for something greater?"

He nodded and said, "Of course, if the sacrifice is wise." I then took my queen and moved it diagonally to set it right next to his, which put it in line to be captured. I kept my finger on top of the piece and looked at Dr. Franklin. Being that he is a prolific chess player, I could tell from his expression that he questioned my move for less than a second before he envisioned how the rest of the game was about to play out. By moving my queen to that spot on the board, it forced him to move his queen one space to capture mine. His queen then would be right in line for my rook, leaving my second rook to corner his king for checkmate, and that would be the game. I'm confident that my chess playing had nothing to do with getting the best of him. I'm certain the disruptiveness of the tavern and my distractions played a larger role.

"Dr. Franklin, sometimes you have to sacrifice to win," I said.

We sat quietly in the booth for a couple of minutes. He was looking at me but he was not annoyed; in fact, he was calm. He said, "Ethan, I cannot in good judgment send young men to die on my behalf when I know I have been entrusted with the faculties to save them and avoid an all-out war with our fellow brethren." My hands were trembling under the table. I felt a piece of me was about to die. I was failing, and it was the evening of the fourth.

Dr. Franklin continued, "I'm sorry Ethan, while you have attempted to convince me that my actions will have drastic ramifications to some people you hold dear, you haven't considered the evidence that those people you love, I shall never meet. Why should I save those who will not be walking the Earth for another two hundred years, when I can look outside this window and know there are Americans I can save today? Moreover, you tell me that if I follow suit and join the Congress in passing this Declaration, I should look the other way on the argument of slavery? That I am not permitted to improve this nation, yet I am supposed to create a new one? How will the world remember me?

"I'm not perfect, I never pretend to be. I know my hypocrisy in this arena, as I owned slaves and promoted their availability in my newspaper. But I came to my senses and have tried for the past twenty years to have people see that slavery is an abomination, I've tried even more so over the last five years, and I will continue to try for as long as the Lord allows."

I thought he finished, and just when I was about to speak he abruptly cut me off and said, "I have made great contributions for my country and traveled the world on its behalf. I have met kings, queens, and other folk of the highest stature. You tell me if I do nothing except oppose the Declaration in the final hour, I will be despised for all time? You have still yet to convince me that reintroducing the Albany Plan is not the responsible act for establishing a secure nation. That adopting it will in all likelihood, amend our relationship with England, protect us under the cloak of the British Empire, and avoid further bloodshed from the young men in New England. Ethan what can you possibly tell me to make me disregard my assessment?"

Before I replied, I asked the barkeep for a serving of rum to calm my nerves. When it was delivered, I took a quick shot and handed the glass back. The alcohol was so strong that it felt as if it had burned a hole in my throat. I forced myself not to cough, but that may not have been the best course of action to take before I went into my speech. Having rehearsed it several times over the past two days, I was ready but my voice wasn't. Just when I was about to speak Franklin re-asked a question that I thought was rhetorical.

He asked, "How will the world remember me?"

In that moment, Dr. Franklin revealed his true reservations on the matter and, much like his chess pieces in front of him, I had him in check. I knew what to say, and in my mind, I was ready, but I held my tongue due to the burning alcohol in my throat. The dramatic effect of silence assisted me greatly as it helped calm the tension between us. After a couple of minutes passed, I was ready to answer. This is what I said:

"Dr. Franklin, we have explored the sociological and the practical. Neither has completely resonated with your mind and heart. Let us take a moment to examine the spiritual. For although you never conceived that your life would contribute to a legislative body that held the commanding power of a king by sending men to war on its behalf, let us celebrate that, with the grace of the Almighty, the life you have experienced has brought you here. Your wisdom, your enterprise, and your influence could be observed as an instrument of the Lord.

"The birth of a nation called 'America' may not have been the plan of our Father but the inevitable reduction of regal pedigree overseeing and controlling fellow human beings is the next step in our social evolution as a species. After this milestone is achieved, other nations will follow suit, and as identities unify, nations will form global unions based on social and economic benefits, not imperial. Then, unexpectedly, after joining its allies, and working with an Englishman named Churchill to extinguish evil during a world war, America will become a global power. And will share that responsibility until the day after Christmas, two hundred and sixteen years from now, when, without a military engagement, the second world power monetarily collapses on itself, leaving America as the reluctant unipolar hegemony. All because the structure of its government will be for the people and by the people and that foundation will solidify itself as the gold standard of civilization across the globe.

"Will we make mistakes? Of course, and as we continue to evolve from this moment in time, we will strive to correct those mistakes along the way. This moment is not about correcting them all. That is not practical. Would it be triumphant if all transgressions could be overcome in a single event? There is no denying that it would. I'm telling you as someone who has lived in the commonwealth two and a half centuries from today, it would have been, it could have been, a different country. But it is not to be. The blood and the lives that will be sacrificed to win the war for liberty while generations remain shackled and enslaved, will be a scar on the establishment of this new country. A country that will be made for people to be free.

"However, it will not start as a country in which all people were free. It will take ninety years for the hypocrisy within the decree to be reconciled. Then it will take another hundred years for the chauvinism to be exposed and addressed in the courts. After that, it will take generations to mend. But it is only from the foundation, worded in the documents waiting to be transcribed, and conjoined to the spirit sprouting in the Americans across the land, that we can achieve these milestones.

"There will be individuals on both sides of the argument who will prey on the misguided and weak minded. Their actions, their words will stifle progress, but in the end, they will fail. Evil will always fail no matter how just the origin makes itself out to be. Those who are witnesses, but are not followers, will not allow this evil to saturate humanity. This country will be a wonderful demonstration of the human spirit. It will be imperfect, but I can tell you with God as my only witness, it will be glorious. It will be admired. Others will try to make a facsimile. Others will try to adopt certain laws. However, none of these reproductions will succeed as well as what you and your contemporaries construct over the next ten years because they are all missing the single, most relative, and most important element. That is, the residing spirit within each participant of this country, which either equals or exceeds the perception the framers equate at inception.

"You will design a country that is operated by its citizens, not by royal appointment. You will design a country that encourages and celebrates individual achievement. You will design a country in which everyone, at times, operates via philanthropy. Profits will guide us. They will consume a small percentage, but they will not impede the American spirit that is alive today and that will ripple throughout the generations. It will follow a code. This is your country. Love it. Protect it. Live for it. And pass it on.

"What occurs over the next decade will shine a light of hope for millions as history unfolds. It will take time. It will not be without sin, without shame, without remorse, and without forbearance. But the ideal of America will be magnanimous. With the grace of God and the resilience of all benevolent souls that participate in this idea, it will inspire hundreds of millions of people throughout the world. When I left, the country was over two hundred and thirty years old. But should America's existence on this plant be measured in a day, when I left, the sunrise had yet to breach the horizon.

"And as far as your personal achievement in this, it's important to know that the inevitable conclusion of your life shall shine beyond its sunset. Your actions alone, which are still to be taken, will be remembered by the clear majority to be brave, humane, patriotic, and unprejudiced. Others will have their own crosses to bear and the stigma of their actions will be their epithets. You will present an alternative opinion for equality, and although you may fail, your voice will echo beyond the chamber walls and carry weight through time. Your representation of the unrepresented slave will call out the shameful acts of our nation as more join your call.

"You are in your twilight. No one is expecting you to raise the sword against your brother and save us from all our present and future indiscretions. That will come, eventually, and no one will ever say it was exclusively your responsibility. Your soul can be at peace for the events that will come over the next two hundred years. This step you are about to take will be perceived as inhuman, since you are going against the largest military the world has ever witnessed, but what is failed to be achieved, will be absolved.

"Although never equated to scripture, what your heart desires will be fulfilled by a man from Kentucky named Abraham, if you can believe it. He endures tremendous hardships as the country kills itself trying to preserve what you created and will obliterate the institution of slavery in the process. The perfect souls, those with hindsight, will always remind us that Abraham's true motives did not include the abolition of slavery on the first day of cannon fire. Only, they will always overlook his sentiments that were boldly articulated in a town called Peoria, several years before the conflict, where he breathed new life in the words inscribed on the Declaration to be composed sometime from now. And then used those words to pay homage to fifty-thousand fallen men, at a battlefield, one hundred and twenty-five miles west from here. The self-evident law that 'all men are created equal.'

"I know I am providing supplementary information, but it's crucial to comprehend that in the end they killed him for succeeding. Those that opposed him politically or the many who saw him as the oppressor of Southern 'values' during the war did not wish for his assassination. Abraham was not a martyr in the end, but his legacy was secured the moment his life was taken from him. It's as though he was sent to save us, but in the end, he unknowingly sacrificed himself to ensure that his contribution to this country, and this world, was forever preserved. Which is why, when we speak of 'American values', Lincoln is included with the names of Washington, Adams, Jefferson, and Franklin. What you will start, he will finish.

"But you need to achieve the first stage. I promise you that the failure to absolve the mortal sins of your fellow countrymen will be rectified. But this resolution will not be seen in your lifetime. That man from Kentucky, leading us in the very bloody affair, will direct the nation on the right path. That is the second stage. As we struggled and stumbled with our humanity, roughly two hundred and thirty years from today, the nation will elect a man of black descent to the role of president. This will not be the final stage, it will not extinguish racial divides, as some ironically perceived it would. Regardless of the decisions that stem from the election of Barack Obama, the moment will be enlightening to millions of Americans, it will be redeeming for a multitude of generations, and it will be celebrated worldwide. But none of this will happen if you do not take the first step."

After I finished, Dr. Franklin did not say a word. He turned to gaze out the window. During that period of silence, I feared for the worst. He showed no signs to indicate that what I just said had moved him in anyway. I had my fingers interlocked on the table, but as each second passed, my anxiety grew. I let out deep breath and brought my hands up in front of my mouth. I began to rub my thumbs together when Franklin finally spoke. I did not hear what he said, so I leaned over and asked him to repeat it. He said, "Inhuman? No one says achieving Independence was inhuman. You made that up."

To be honest, I never heard anyone except Henry say it was "inhuman" for winning the Revolution. At this point, there was nothing to do except tell him the truth. I explained that my postman told me, to which Franklin let out a belly laugh that alerted the whole tavern. I thought he was attracting too much attention, but he laughed so hard and long it disarmed me and anyone else in the place. I had to remind myself that I was the fish, or the guest, and Dr. Franklin was the celebrity. After he finished laughing, he grabbed his drink and held it up toward me. I held my drink up beside his and said, "God is with you Ben, be not afraid," to which he touched my glass and in a toast said, "To America."

I did it.

Chapter Twenty-Five

For Lauren

L auren struggled to balance between succumbing to the anguish brought on by her husband's departure and the desperate need to yield to Henry's heartening anecdotes. Refusing to give into remorse, Lauren placed her hands on the arms of the accent chairs and forced herself to move to release her grievances. Standing in the silence of her once-cherished home that was now vacant of the companion she envisioned growing old and gray with, Lauren closed her eyes and took three deep breaths.

Her eyes were red and burning from all the tears she had shed. With the base of her palms, she rubbed both eyes then used the pressure to rub her forehead, down to her temples, to her cheeks, to her chin, and back to her ears. With one final deep breath, Lauren turned around and made her way to the crate. It was an aged piece, made of wood, but it was not an antique when compared to what Ethan received when he won the contest. It measured about four feet wide by three feet high. Examining how the crate was sealed, Lauren saw she would need to get Ethan's tools from the basement.

With a hammer and screwdriver, she attempted to pry it open at the corners. With every swing, Lauren's curiosity swelled, which made the speed of her motions increase. After several minutes passed, the cover became loose. She tried to have the clumsy piece of wood slide down the edge, to gently place it on the floor. But the disproportionate weight was too much to handle, and with a thud, the corner hit the floor. Lauren winced, hoping the damage was unnoticeable. When she walked over to examine the impact, there was a small mark left. "Way to go," she said with a sigh, as she lightly kicked the piece.

At first glance, all Lauren could see was brown straw and a large envelope placed in the center. She reached for the envelope and examined the cover, which read "Mrs. Pope, Westchester, New York." Lauren then turned it over to see a wax seal in its center. Not wanting to damage the seal, Lauren carefully opened the seam on the edge of the envelope. Inside were two pieces of paper. The first one was addressed to Lauren, the second was titled, *On the Morals of Chess by Benjamin Franklin.* Curious to know the contents of the personal letter first, Lauren sat and read.

To the fair Mrs. Lauren Pope,

It is with great pleasure I write to you on this day. I have heard so much about you, that it saddens me deeply to know our lives shall never cross paths. However, our lives are connected through your beloved. He has shared with me some of the most delightful anecdotes, which he tells with such care and attention that I almost feel at times I too experienced the event and that the memory is my own. The story of his proposal to you in Disney's World is such a wonderful tale of one man benefiting from his clumsiness.

I am presently without his company, as I attend to matters in France while he travels under the care of General Washington. Surprisingly, for someone I have known for a short period of time,

I miss his wit and his unabashed attempt to educate this old man with his youthful and sometimes naive life lessons. I know you must have a feeling of loneliness on this day, as I do now, but it is amusing that we are both grieving the same being even though centuries separate us. You and I are the beneficiaries of one person's selfless act. His sacrifice is yours, and your sorrow is witnessed in his eyes when he permits regret to overtake his memories. Memories, I believe, are his only motivation to continue on this journey he has found himself a part of, a journey which began in Philadelphia a few years ago.

The purpose of this letter is to not only express the affection I hold for your husband, I also wanted to express my appreciation for your sacrifice and kindly share with you a draft of an essay I composed. It was inspired by your husband's lack of self-control when we played a game of chess on the night he persuaded me to be for American Independence. I hope you find it amusing and perhaps some of my descriptions will be familiar to you.

I wish to end by saying Ethan's early successes have been achieved only through the grace of his character, which was created through his life experiences, but most of all from the deep affection he holds for you. That was accomplished only by allowing Ethan to freely live his life with you before bringing him back here. I know that does not ease your sorrow for his departure from your side, but please find solace in knowing that he could not have done any of this without being a part of your life, as short as that may have been.

May health, happiness, and countless blessings be presented upon you.

B. Franklin, 1779

P.S. It is my intention for you to receive this letter the day after Ethan left. Should my instructions fail to be followed, notify the authorities.

Lauren was touched by the idea that Benjamin Franklin cared enough to take the time to write her a letter. His words were endearing and she could sense Franklin was honest in his affection towards her husband. Lauren then read Franklin's rules on chess and found them all amusing. She was already aware of this essay. It was one of thousands Ethan familiarized himself with, back when she assumed all the research on Dr. Franklin was due to some newly found interest he gained after his first trip to Philadelphia. Since she could now see how they were about Ethan, it made the words more personal.

The essay described the benefits of playing chess daily. It noted that playing chess can help train someone with the traits of foresight and sacrifice as well as when to be cautious. Of the rules Franklin listed, number seven was Lauren's favorite. It read, *"If your adversary is long in playing, you ought not to hurry him, or express any uneasiness at his delay. You should not sing, nor whistle, nor look at your watch, nor take up a book to read, nor make a tapping with your feet on the floor, or with your fingers on the table, nor do anything that may disturb his attention. For all these things displease. And they do not show your skill in playing, but your craftiness or your rudeness."*

As flattering as it was to see a Benjamin Franklin essay inspired from the chess match Ethan recorded on July 4, 1775, Lauren's curiosity for knowing the rest of the contents inside the crate took precedent. Carefully, Lauren returned the letters back inside the envelope and set it aside. Standing over the crate Lauren noticed three inches in from the right side was a single slate of wood acting as a divider. Inside the gap, Lauren gripped the top layer of insulation and pulled. With all the straw stuck together Lauren lifted the narrow, yet long, strip and moved it over the edge. The thin strip of protection flopped over to the floor with no concern.

Within the exposed wedge was a long, paper wrapped, item. With her right hand, Lauren gently pressed on the paper with her fingers. On the crates edge, the paper bowed with the slightest touch. As she brought her fingers in toward the divider, the paper started to stiffen and when she was an inch away, Lauren was touching something solid. Running her fingers away from her, there was no change in the density of the package. The paper was stiff along the left and hollow on the right. "This may be a picture frame," Lauren thought. She attempted to lift it out from the string in the center but with just a couple of cautious tugs, there was no movement to get it out. She would need to relieve the stress from the divider.

On the other side of the divider and having the greater amount of volume was still a mystery to Lauren for all she saw was straw and paper. Lauren reached in and twisted her hand through the thin streams to feel how deep this protection went. Halfway up her forearm, her fingertips contacted a solid object. By the handful, Lauren lifted the protective insulation and threw it behind her on to the floor making a mess wherever it landed. After removing the top layer, the contents started to show themselves. Lauren took another envelope out of the box to examine it. The writing on the envelope was in Ethan's hand writing, it read "For Lauren, please read this first." Lauren turned it over to see a wax seal in its center that was similar to the envelope from Benjamin Franklin. Lauren used her right thumb to push against the side of the wax, but it was not moving. Then with her thumb and forefinger, she slowly ripped the paper from the wax and broke the seal. Lauren gently slid the paper from its protective pouch so as not to tear it, and once it was safely out, she let the envelope fall to the floor.

To My Only Love, who has given my life a purpose that has eclipsed any vision I may have started in my youth.

This letter will not be the first I compose to you after the night our hands last touched, but I wanted it to be the first you received from me. Dr. Franklin was insistent that his letter reach your person before mine.

When you read this, only a day would have passed since you and I gazed into each other's eyes, and I left your embrace. For me thirty-three years shall have passed since I saw your beauty, touched your skin, kissed your lips, and heard your voice. And there has not been a day since I left you that I have not retrieved the memories that reside in my heart and soul to find much needed comfort. Those imprinted memories of you have allotted me the strength to move about my days.

First, let me assure you there has been no other woman to capture my affection during my time here. As I write this, I cannot help but find the humor in the fact that I may be the only man God has ever created who can honestly tell the woman he adores that his love is timeless and will be forever. Second, not a day has passed where I haven't reflected on my decision to take on this honorable task at a time when my presence would have provided great comfort to you.

In all, I hope you can find some comfort in knowing that my arrival was a success and that being present for these momentous milestones in our nation's conception has filled my life's meaning and purpose for being sent here. I have met some of our most cherished figures of the past and created friendships that I carry with me to this day, although there have been some I have lost along the way.

Andrew's death in Yorktown was so painful, because I told him not to fight before I left for Europe to retrieve Dr. Franklin. I still regret that I didn't take him with me. After Andrew, I was fortunate to not have to face death until Dr. Franklin passed in 1790 and then President Washington nine years later. I can honestly say of all the famous individuals I have engaged with, they were the two I was most fond of. President Adams and Jefferson are wonderful company, but they are men who live in the moment, and I found myself at times in the way. It just so happens that President Adams sent me an invite up to Quincy a few weeks ago, and I am on my way up there now. I am without Mary and Philip on this trip, as a dear friend of ours has recently become very sick and they wanted to stay at the mill to tend to his needs.

I was determined to revisit Yonkers when I reached New York on my journey, since I did not have a chance to walk through my memories when I was in the region with, then, General Washington. But today, looking at the Palisades on the Hudson River from Philipse Manor, it brought back a flood of emotions. It made me want to run to where our lives started in that apartment on the hilltop and find you waiting for my embrace. Being overcome with such feelings is what has inspired me to write this letter today.

In the crate, this letter destined for, you should find four additional journals that cover in some detail the consequential endeavors I undertook, so that you may find a deeper sense of purpose for my departure. There are some encounters I do wish you were present to witness. I hope my accounts properly convey the magnitude of some of them. Of course, when I read the first journal before I left, I thought it was incumbent on me to record every moment of my life in this time. But after thirty plus years of writing daily, sometimes multiple times a day, I am done, madam. All actions for our country and for Dr. Franklin's Project within his postal service, are complete and in God's hands. I am fortunate to know where it will end up and how it will all begin, again. But do not worry, my love, for I will never stop writing letters to you, letters of my love and of anecdotes from my future travels.

Along with the entire story of my venture from my initial encounter with Dr. Franklin to the great moments that followed with all the figures of our past, are gifts for you, thanks to Dr. Franklin and some of our early Presidents.

I do not know how each day will go from here on out, but I do know I must make it another twenty-five years, for I have a letter in my possession from the first postmaster general for the future postmaster in New Salem, Illinois.

I know you are reading this the day after but luckily for me, I have had some time to choose my words. If I had only one opportunity to share my true feelings for you it would be, Thank you. Thank you for loving me when you did. Thank you for caring for me. Thank you for being there for me when I needed you the most. I wanted to be loved by someone who took me for all I was, good or bad. You did that.

I know I'm not present to hear your response, but I need you to assure me that my sacrifice will have a purpose and that you will live your life. That you will seek, give, and accept love again. I pray that you will.

I love you,

Ethan

Yonkers, 1808

Lauren dropped her hands, and the letter rested on her lap. Her tears streamed down each cheek and one droplet landed on the paper causing a small water mark. She gathered her emotions to fold the paper and inserted it back into its envelope for its protection. Lauren placed the letter atop of a small stack of magazines and discarded mail. In the quiet of her living room, she closed her eyes, and rested to regain her composure. When she was ready, Lauren walked across the room and tried once again to remove the large item.

Lauren began removing all the contents within the box. The items included a walking stick, a compass, and several other small wrapped items. In the corner were books wrapped in the same suede Ethan's journal was wrapped in. There was a single tag on each one with a short description. One book read *Riding with Washington,* another was titled *Franklin, Europe, and the Convention*, another just had *1790* as the title, and the last read *Mr. President(s)*. After removing most of the items toward the base of the box, Lauren could finally slide out the single slate that was holding in the largest item.

In her hands, Lauren affirmed the protected item was a picture frame. She put the base on the seat of the sofa and leaned it back to rest. She then grabbed a pair of scissors to cut the string that was tied around it. With a surgeon's touch, Lauren sliced through the paper creating a hole so she could use her fingers to tear it apart. Gently, Lauren discarded the protective shell and revealed the framed work of art. She observed the painting with marvelous pride, for looking back at her was a seated Benjamin Franklin and standing behind him, with his hand resting on Franklin's shoulder, was her beloved.

ℐcknowledgement

I wish to take a moment to express my appreciation to those who helped me along the way. *The Franklin Project* is one of my greatest achievements and I am very grateful to have been able to share it with you, the reader.

It started in 2004, when I began to ride the 6 train from the Bronx to Lower Manhattan. I worked near the World Financial Center and during my first week I walked around the area to familiarize myself with local shops. I stopped at a Borders on Broadway, near Trinity Church, and picked up Walter Isaacson's biography on Benjamin Franklin, part of a "3 for 2" sale. Mr. Isaacson's book hooked me into the world of colonial America, a subject my father exposed his three children to at a time when going to Disney World was more interesting than visiting Fort Ticonderoga and Williamsburg. But, the biography on Benjamin Franklin raised sentiments that were unknowingly embedded during my youth. After I finished that book, I couldn't stop. I purchased David McCullough's biography on John Adams and then Joseph Ellis' work on George Washington. A couple of years later, six months before I was to be married, I was laid off and found employment in mid-town; it might have made the ride on the 6 train shorter, but I still carried a book with me. It is only fitting to thank those authors, and all the authors, whose books helped me reach the final page.

As I was finding my way to what The Franklin Project would eventually become, I heard an elected official say, during the debate on the Affordable Care Act, "No one knows what the founding fathers meant." In that clip, I found my angle; have someone with today's perspectives and morals be forced to live in the colonial America and record their eyewitness accounts during the founding of the country. That revelation led me down a path of research and writing which took, on and off, eight years to complete. I should thank that elected official for the inspiration unfortunately I do not remember their name!

My first manuscript weighed in at 130,000 words. After I brought that down to a reasonable number, my cousin David Vincenti, an accomplished poet and a trusted source, was generous enough to give his time and this story a read through. My uncle-in-law Alfred Cardone, a writer himself, also gave his time to read my first draft, and there is nothing I can do to show my gratitude for their advice and encouragement during the last two years of this project.

I would like to thank the people at BookBaby for providing the services and the means for this book to make it out into the ether. And John Milligan at JMilligan Design, for reeling me in from my original ideas of cover art, to show me that less is more.

Next to thank, and appropriately so, is my wife Laura. She has been very patient with me during this process. When I told her shortly after our engagement that I wanted to write a book, I don't think she expected it to take 12 years. Also, I don't believe Laura was prepared for the library I was going to build in our office. It seemed like every week, two or three books would arrive to help with my research. And, while I read up on many topics to make my story as factual as possible, I also relied on life experiences to help shape the story and the main character.

When we married, the life we dreamed about evaporated in just a couple of months. Two months after we said, "I do", without a care in the world, Laura started down the road of cancer survivor, as a Multiple Myeloma patient. Her determination and perseverance has been inspiring and I am grateful that she has these qualities as she confronts this illness.

At one point in the process, I stopped writing for almost a year, I was stuck. It wasn't that I did not know what to write about. I was stuck trying to find a new and different means of sending someone through time. It was during this time Laura started chemotherapy. When the treatment completed and we were told this would need to be done again in the future, I was determined to finish this book, and it was at that time I pieced together my time travel scenario. Once I accomplished that, the flood gates of creativity opened and everything else seemed easier.

I also would like to thank my parents for always allowing their son to ramble on about the story he was writing. They and my in-laws have been great supporters of this project, and have been tremendous supporters to Laura and myself as we have gone along our road together. Last summer, while I was on my tenth revision, my mother, who is the cornerstone of my optimism and modesty, was diagnosed with stomach cancer. She, too, with the great support of my father, is confronting this battle with the same bravery and determination as Laura.

Their road ahead is the reason this book is complete. The bravery they've shown for their journey that is before them, inspired me to finish the tale of Ethan's journey, and continues to inspire me today.

Bibliography and References

Brands, H.W. (2000). *The First American: The Life and Times of Benjamin Franklin*. New York, NY. Doubleday

Ferguson, Niall. (2003). *Empire: The Rise and Demise of the British World Order and the Lessons for Global Power*. New York, NY. Basic Books. (Original work published 2002)

Frandin, Dennis Brindell. (2002). *The Signers: The 56 Stories Behind the Declaration of Independence*. New York, NY. Walker & Company.

Franklin, Benjamin. (2004) *The Autobiography of Benjamin Franklin/with an introduction by Lewis Leary*. New York, NY. Touchstone.

Houston, Alan Craig. (2008). *Benjamin Franklin and the Politics of Improvement*. Yale University.

Isaacson, Walter. (2000) *Benjamin Franklin: An American Life*. New York, NY. Simon & Schuster.

Isaacson, Walter. (2003) *Benjamin Franklin Reader*. New York, NY. Simon & Schuster.

Jefferson, Thomas. (2005). *Autobiography of Thomas Jefferson*. Mineola, NY. Dover Publications. (Original work published 1821)

Kashatus III, William C. (1992). *Historic Philadelphia: The City, Symbols & Patriots, 1681-1800*. Lanham, MA. University Press of America, Inc.

Kelly, Joseph J. (1973). *Life and Times in Colonial Philadelphia*. Harrisburg, PA. The Stackpole Company.

Lanning, Lt. Colonel Michael Lee (2000). *African Americans in the Revolutionary War.* Citadel Press.

Lemay, J. A. Leo. (1987). *Benjamin Franklin: Silence Dogood, The Busy-Body, and Early Writings.* The Library of America.

Lemay, J. A. Leo. (1987). *Benjamin Franklin: Autobiography, Poor Richard, and Later Writings.* The Library of America.

Middlekauf, Robert. (2005). *The Glorious Cause: The American Revolution 1763-1789.* New York, NY. Oxford University Press, Inc.

McCullough, David. (2001). *John Adams.* New York, NY. Simon & Schuster.

Moore, Frank. (2013). *Diary of the American Revolution: From Newspapers and Original Documents Vol I.* Windam Press. (Original work published 1860)

Shannon, Timothy J. (2002). *Indians and Colonists at the Crossroads of Empire: The Albany Congress of 1754.* Ithaca, New York. Cornell Paperbacks.

Thompson, Peter. (1999). *Rum Punch and Revolution: Taverngoing and Public Life in Eighteenth Century Philadelphia.* Philadelphia, PA. University of Pennsylvania Press.

Taylor, Alan. (2002). *American Colonies.* New York. NY. Penguin Group.

Thomas, Hugh (1997). *The Slave Trade: The Story of the Atlantic Slave Trade, 1440-1870.* New York, NY. Simon & Schuster.

Yetman, Norman R. (2002). *When I was a Slave: Memoirs from the Slave Narrative Collection.* New York, NY. Dover.

Zimmerman, Larry J. (1996). *Native North America.* London. Duncan Baird Publishers.

Highlighted References

Franklin, Benjamin

- (1754, May 9). Join or Die. *The Pennsylvania Gazette.*
- (1754, July 10). The Albany Plan of Union.
- (1775, July 5). Letter to William Strahan
- (1779). Morals of Chess.
- (1789, Nov 9). An Address to the Public. Pennsylvania Society for Promoting the Abolition of Slavery, and the Relief of Free Negroes Unlawfully Held in Bondage.
- (1789). Plan for Improving the Condition of the Free Blacks.
- (1789, March 25). Sidi Mehemet Ibrahim on the Slave Trade. *The Federal Gazette*

Website References

Bellis, Mary (updated 2016, Aug 20). *History of the United States Postal Service.* Retrieved from About.com website: http://inventors.about.com/od/todayinhistory/fl/History-of-the-United-States-Postal-Service.htm

Franklin, Benjamin (1775, July 5) Image of letter to William Strahan. Retrieved from Library of Congress website: http://www.loc.gov/exhibits/treasures/images/bf0010.jpg

Iaccarino, Anthony. (updated 2016, July 28). *The Founding Fathers and Slavery.* Retrieved from Encyclopedia Britannica website: https://www.britannica.com/topic/The-Founding-Fathers-and-Slavery-1269536

Jefferson, Thomas (1950) *Jefferson's "original Rough draught" of the Declaration of Independence.* Retrieved from The Papers of Thomas Jefferson, Princeton University Press website: https://jeffersonpapers.princeton.edu/

Kline, Pamela (unknown date). *The Olive Branch Petition.* Retrieved from Revolutionary-War.net website: http://www.revolutionary-war.net/olive-branch-petition.html

Lehrman, Lewis (unknown date). *Mr. Lincoln and the Declaration.* Retrieved from Lehrman Institute website: http://www.mrlincolnandthefounders.org/commentary/

Teller, A. & Park C. (unknown date). *Women in the U.S. Postal System.* Retrieved from Smithsonian National Postal Museum website: https://postalmuseum.si.edu/WomenHistory/index.html

United States Postal Service. (2012). *Mail Service and the Civil War.* Retrieved from the USPS website: http://about.usps.com/news/national-releases/2012/pr12_civil-war-mail-history.pdf

Unknown. (2010, Jan 8). *Benjamin Franklin's Articles of Confederation.* Retrieved from usconsitution.net website: http://www.usconstitution.net/franklinart.html

Unknown. (1995, July 4). *Signers of the Declaration of Independence.* Retrieved from ushistory.org website: http://www.ushistory.org/declaration/signers/

Unknown. (unknown date). *Sunrise Mill History.* Retrieved from Montgomery County website: http://www.montcopa.org/DocumentCenter/View/3510

Unknown. (unknown date). *A Brief History: The Nation Calls, 1908-1923.* Retrieved from FBI.gov website: https://www.fbi.gov/history/brief-history

Unknown. (unknown date). *The Deleted Passage of the Declaration of Independence (1776).* Retrieved from BlackPast.org website: http://www.blackpast.org/primary/declaration-independence-and-debate-over-slavery

Unknown. (unknown date). *The Evolution of the U.S. Intelligence Community-An Historical Overview.* Retrieved from Federation of American Scientists website: https://fas.org/irp/offdocs/int022.html

Proceeds from the purchase of this book will go to the following charities and institutions:

Memorial Sloan Kettering

Memorial Sloan Kettering Cancer Center — the world's oldest and largest private cancer center — has devoted more than 130 years to exceptional patient care, innovative research, and outstanding educational programs.

For more information visit: https://www.mskcc.org/

Leukemia & Lymphoma Society

The Leukemia & Lymphoma Society (LLS) is the largest voluntary health organization dedicated to funding research, finding cures, and ensuring access to treatments for blood cancer patients.

For more information visit: http://www.lls.org/

No Stomach for Cancer

No Stomach for Cancer (NSFC) is a worldwide leader in raising awareness, advancing stomach cancer education, and supporting individuals and families affected by all forms of stomach cancer.

For more information visit: https://www.nostomachforcancer.org/